I0613919

LEARNING TO LOVE IT

A Novel

By

Bill Leubrie

The
Samain Press
2011

Published by

The Samain Press
Seattle, Washington

First Edition, 2011

All rights reserved. No part of this book may be
reproduced in any form or by any means without prior
written consent of the Publisher, except for brief
quotes used in reviews.

ISBN-13: 978-0-61546-846-4

© 2003 by Bill Leubrie. All rights reserved.
Chapter Nine © 2011 by Bill Leubrie. All rights reserved.

For DRS

"Feeling is the universal solvent."

MEPHISTOPHELES

*My art will fascinate you. I will show
You things no mortal eye has yet beheld.*

FAUST

*What, poor thing, have you to show me? When did
Your sort ever comprehend the mortal
Mind and all its high endeavor? Still,
Perhaps you've food which sates one never;
Ruddy gold that flows like mercury
Away; a game which none who play can win;
A girl who from my very breast with ogling
Eyes a neighbor snares; high ambition's
Joy divine that once achieved dissolves
In air like meteors. Show me fruit that
Rots as soon as picked, and trees whose leaves
are daily shed and daily grown anew!*

MEPHISTOPHELES

*A job like that won't frighten me.
Tricks like that? My specialty!*

Faust, Part I Scene 4

Henry Irving as Mephistopheles

A NOTE...

...for those readers (probably about everyone) who will be puzzled by the familiar technology herein referred to by funny names in contexts just a trifle off. This book was drafted in the 1980s, before any of that stuff was thought of, and set in a future reasonably far off from then. Yes, I invented the flash drive, the iphone, and the tablet computer, at least conceptually. I simply didn't have Microsoft's and Apple's Marketing Departments' genius to know what to call them. I only wish I had the royalties! (Note to Legal: I make no claim.) It all still seemed to fit into the story well enough, so I decided to leave it as was (okay, I'm lazy) in hopes some people will be interested to see where a forward-looking fantasist thought we might be in a future advanced even a bit from today. Only Chapter Nine seemed to require updating. You'll spot the added paragraph.

Chapter One
HAVE A COOKIE, LITTLE BOY?

ne of the world's central ironies is that most of the people in it can't be happy unless they're at least a bit miserable as well.

You know the type. When things are going well, they're bored, that is, when not engaged in a variety of nervous pursuits. With secret wistfulness they keep a lookout over their shoulders for the reversal they know is only a matter of time. *Losing keeps you sharp*, they say. When the inevitable setback hits, they breathe a sigh of relief and immediately start working themselves toward success again.

Though you might wonder why. In itself, no success is ever enough. It always has a fatal flaw to spoil its perfection. Solve a scientific problem and more open up before you. Write poetry the critics love, but don't quit your day job. Write a commercial blockbuster, but avoid the literary supplement to your Sunday paper. Become a financial success and someone will sue you every time. Besides, how rich is rich enough? No level of success can satisfy the eternal "More." The striving after happiness never ends.

The reverse is also true. There are very few misfortunes in life so grim some irritatingly irrepressible person won't find a gleam of satisfaction despite them, even if only from ignorance of any better condition of life. For every Cassandra radiating gloom amidst plenty and privilege, an irrepressibly determined and optimistic Mr. Macawber beams good cheer from the depths of poverty and misery.

The context changes, but people never do. So, if people will make themselves unhappy when they should be happy and vice versa,

1

perhaps the quantity of happiness is pretty much a constant. Perhaps, despite the ever-evolving state of civilization, increased leisure time, labor-saving devices, life-prolonging discoveries and the invention of the electric charcoal grill starter, people are, on balance, about as happy or as unhappy as ever. For example, ancient people were as blissfully accepting of the limits of their knowledge as we are of ours, and spent no more or less time worrying about what couldn't be changed than we do; though ignorant of microbiology, they went on having the very best time possible right up until the gods inflicted a plague, just as people in earthquake zones today spend little time worrying about The Big One until it collapses their cities on top of them.

Perhaps, although we live longer than people did when there were more perils in daily life, the absence of these perils means we live each day less intensely. Certainly, while we understand more about the world than did the ancients, we search for personal satisfaction as restlessly and heedlessly as ever, even to our own destruction. Just as Agamemnon ignored Cassandra, modern people may pay lip service to overpopulation, pollution and the sorry state of the biosphere, but, for themselves, intend to keep right on making babies, overusing the earth and strewing cheap plastic trash hither and yon until the food runs out.

With these propositions Herbie Manning depressed himself on a gorgeous afternoon in early April. As in the macrocosm, so in the microcosm.

He supposed that, if how happy you were had nothing to do with the state of the world and your place therein, it must have to do with your internal layout, with who you were. Either you were a happy sort of person or you weren't, and that was that. What was the point of all that worrying and striving, then, except for its own sake? To be happy, why make more than the minimal effort to change what you could, and accept or ignore the things you couldn't?

He stretched out his long spindly legs, crossed at his size-15 sneakers and exposed to the sun by cutoff jeans, and stared across the water from under the bill of his baseball cap. Whence he sat on the terrace cantilevered out over Lake Michigan from Olive Park,

Have a Cookie, Little Boy?

Chicago's skyline shimmered in unusual spring heat. Across the water, ranks of towering spires stretched off to either side and receded into the distance, shimmering gently as cubic miles of concrete heated up. The city seemed to grow as Herbie watched, to thrust itself upwards into the sunlight in harmony with the universal response to spring manifested all around him in the park bursting with fresh green shoots.

> *Come, love, it is the first of May.*
> *Outdoor fucking begins today.*

Herbie frowned as the inane little verse ran through his head. That it wasn't May yet was not the problem. In common with the rest of humanity, he was pretty dissatisfied, though he wasn't really all that sure why. At 34, he wasn't doing badly. He was self-employed. The one-man accountancy business he ran out of his apartment in a nice old section of the city was going well. His clients liked him and kept coming back for more. He did not miss getting up at 7AM to half choke himself with a tie and spend thirty minutes standing up on a jolting swaying El-train while gum-popping secretaries treaded his over-large feet. His self-employment freed him from bullying superiors and sneaky subordinates, the office politics he'd never been much good at anyway. It paid the bills and allowed an occasional extra such as the shiny new titanium 18-speed leaning up against his park bench he used on nice days to get back and forth to his clients downtown, just as he had today. A substantial new job, at least a week's worth of number crunching and analysis, nestled inside his backpack on the bench beside him.

Footsteps and loud voices approached on the promenade behind him.

"You're shitting me. She let you *what*?"

"Yeah man, and she was cherry too. Fuck, she really wanted it bad. See? She even wrote her name on me, right here—Hey! Watch it, jerk!"

Herbie turned. Two teenaged boys were strutting by, shoving and joking each other along. They wore tight jeans and tank tops, and, despite the heat, carried black leather jackets. Their long hair, one's black, the other's blond, waved in the lake breeze. The sight of them inspired Herbie with wistful longing. They caught him looking, which meant no escape.

"Hey man, spare a cigarette?"

Herbie fished one out. The blond had a red bandanna around his leg an inch below his crotch, across from it in ballpoint pen, "Debra was here." Good for Debra.

"Thanks man, gotta light?"

Herbie lit it for him.

As the boy puffed it, he stuck a hand into a back pocket and tensed up to show the muscles of his arm and torso. His buddy casually hooked his jacket over his shoulder and bulged his crotch at Herbie. They looked at him expectantly. The kind of pause ensued during which many things might happen.

None of them did. The boys shrugged and sauntered off down the promenade. *Hustlers*, Herbie thought, *straight ones. Don't give much for the money. Young too. Jailbait!* He watched them recede, hair waving, asses wagging in the tight jeans, and felt a hot stirring between his legs. *The blond walks like he's got something big up his butt.*

Their talk floated back on the breeze. "Fag." "Yeah, and ugly too, man."

The stirring between Herbie's legs died a swift death. He turned back and stared at the city without seeing it. True, he thought, he was no beauty. When he looked at himself in the mirror, he saw a body that, at 6'5", was much too tall for its 140 pounds. High-waisted, he seemed to be all arms and legs held together by an undersized, band-aid torso. Herbie reminded himself of a kid's stick drawing. Even more hopeless, he thought, was his face, his features all too close together in the middle of it. *A circus clown, that's what I should have been,* he thought. *Could've done the stilts act without props. Or makeup.*

When he'd been younger, he thought, youth had added a certain freshness to his appearance that had made him marginally attractive, especially in baggy clothes and dim light, but now, a few wrinkles around the eyes, a receding hairline and a dime-sized bald patch at the back of his scraggly brown hair were early warning signs of old age and death. A decade before, hustlers had written him off on sight, and there'd been a chance that other sorts of hot young guys he met casually in parks and at the shore might stick around, find something to talk about, maybe smoke a joint and/or go off with him to listen to some music, and other, more nebulous maybes. It had happened, once or twice. Now, hot young guys always had something else to do, and every hustler in town had a radar screen that registered him in high relief. He'd become a mark.

Not that he was unwilling to go with the flow. In the several years since his personal path of least resistance had led to patronizing hustlers regularly, they'd come to fascinate him as a class. He liked their fearless, macho masculinity, their dirty talk, their youthful bodies and their practiced professional skill. He was touched by their vulnerability. Fearless? Youthful? They were too young to know what fear was. He envied the natural, almost unconscious way they turned sex appeal into power, as measured by money. Still, he found these encounters ultimately unsatisfactory. He could not shake the longing to be desired by a beautiful boy for himself, rather than merely because he could pay. That this had never happened seemed to reflect unfavorably on... well, on who he was. With every passing year, he became more successful at the material aspects of life, and his self-worth diminished.

The encounter with the two boys seemed to typify and sum up the situation. Slowly, the pain of it faded. Herbie got up and went to the rail. The sun shone on the water as brightly as before. Birds still sang. The park and the city went about their business. Sailboats out on the lake dotted the horizon, oblivious.

Herbie's eye caught out in the middle distance, where something small bobbed in the water. Among the greens and grays of the lake, a speck of deep vivid blue rose and fell on the four-inch swell, maybe 150 feet out from the terrace. As he watched, the waves pushed it closer. A box of some kind, bright colors winked on its sides. It washed directly toward him, eventually running aground among the rocks beside the terrace. Little waves banged it back and forth against the embankment, making small noises of metal against stone. Its paint gleamed gaily up at Herbie.

Huh, thought Herbie, *maybe something lost off a sailboat.* He went around the railing and scrambled down the rocks to the water's edge. He lifted the box from the lapping wavelets. The eight-inch cube weighed almost nothing. Empty. Against the deep blue of its top and sides, a colorful antique illustration showed a woman in 19th-century costume offering a small boy in knickers and suspenders a cookie out of a box just like the one in Herbie's hands; an infinite regression of small boys on tiptoes reached for cookies, greed writ ever smaller upon their faces. "McCandless' Fancy Selection" wound around the illustration in spidery, Spenserian script, the single word "Chicago" at the bottom in smaller type. An antique cookie box in form, but in superb, mint condition, its paint as fresh and unmarked as the day it had been made: no rust, nor even any scratches from banging against the rocks. *Probably a reproduction*, Herbie guessed, though he didn't find any modern manufacturer's name or copyright claim anywhere. Nor was anything stamped on the painted metal of the bottom. The gauge of the tin was unusually heavy. The edges where the sides joined the bottom, instead of being beaded together with a separate strip of metal in the way of modern cans, were turned flat and pressed together with occasional small oozings of frozen metal from between. *Huh. Maybe it's genuine, after all. Looks brand new!* He tried the lid, which proved stuck fast.

Herbie climbed back up to the promenade. He dried the box as best he could on the grass and stuffed it into his backpack for later examination. Finders keepers. Maybe, if it were genuine, it might be worth something.

The sun in his eyes reminded him it was getting on toward late afternoon. Time to go. He wheeled the bicycle out onto the promenade and, with a one-legged mount, started slowly back around the curve of Olive Park toward the skyline.

Bicycle riding was one of Herbie's few purely unalloyed pleasures. His long legs gave him a tremendous advantage. All up and down the miles of lakefront promenades and bicycle paths, few other riders would bother racing him more than once. Humiliating them in his dust, scattering beachside bathers and terrified small children in his reckless advance, was one of Herbie's favorite things, about the most fun you could have with your clothes on, in his opinion.

Today, no one wanted to race, so he kept a leisurely pace. On a bench by Oak Street Beach, Herbie saw the two boys, their legs sprawled forwards, one on either side of a bald elderly man with a cigar, a potbelly and a brief bikini. The man had his arms on the bench, one behind each boy. The boys looked bored, but hungry and vaguely vulpine. Herbie turned his head resolutely to the water and increased the pace.

Three miles later, he arrived home dripping sweat. He hoisted the bicycle to his shoulder and carried it up the 63 steps to his apartment. He parked it in the spare room, stopped into the living room to drop the backpack on his desktop, then headed kitchenwards thinking thoughts of dinner.

As Herbie inventoried leftovers at the back of the refrigerator, the wallphone burst into jangling racket a foot from his ear. He straightened abruptly and banged his head on the freezer compartment. *Damn!* Savagely, he reached for the phone. "What!"

"I'm taking a survey. Is your refrigerator running?" A barely post-pubic voice croaked out the question. In the background, others like it giggled with muffled malice, waiting for the punchline: *Why yes, it is. —Then you better go catch it!*

Herbie soothed his bumped head. His mouth crooked into an ugly smile. He'd been waiting years for this. "NO! IT ISN'T! I'VE BEEN CALLING AND CALLING YOU PIGFUCKERS FOR DAYS, AND I WANT TO KNOW WHEN YOU ASSHOLE MORONS ARE COMING TO FIX IT!"

Stunned silence on the line. Click.

That's got it, Herbie thought. He'd just returned his attention to the refrigerator when the phone rang again. *Not had enough, eh?* He swiped the receiver off its hook. "AND ANOTHER THING!..."

This time, however, banging music and a gabble of voices issued forth at blast volume. "Hi hon, it's *meee!*" Herbie's so-called boyfriend, Jorge. Jorge spoke in exclamation points most of the time, a tendency exaggerated by screaming over the noise. Herbie wondered what bar he was in—probably The Bird in Hand. That one was usually good for a little teatime cruising.

"Sorry kiddo, I'm being pestered by some kids."

"Hey, me too!" Jorge giggled. The noise on the other end of the line flattened. Through fingers muffling the mouthpiece, Herbie heard: "Ooh, wait a sec 'til I get off the phone!" Obviously not the same kids. The noise returned. "I'm at my mother's!"

Sure. "She got a new stereo?"

"What was that? The music's too loud! Anyway! I only called to say I can't make it tonight! My cousin wants me to come look at his new dog!"

It just kept getting better. "What was that? Doggy fashion?"

"Cute! Cute! I'll say this for you, lover, you have a truly filthy mind! No! Dog! Hey, I'm on a tight schedule! Gotta run!"

"Look kiddo, there's not much about you that is tight, which is why you've got the runs. Try a dose of the pink stuff."

A sigh came down the wire. "*Very* cute! I'm hanging up now! Are you going to say good-bye?"

"No."

The click came, cutting off the music. Herbie hung up the phone. Cute, indeed. Jorge was Latino, in Herbie's estimation, the kind of kinky Spanish boy who had to try to get himself fucked to death before he turned 25, got fat, and had to grow a mustache in order to pretend to the other Latinos he was what they'd call a man. Mr. Reliable, baldfaced excuse and all. *I Wonder Who's Screwing Him Now.*

Boyfriend in name, maybe, but Herbie didn't seem to see very much of him except when he wanted something, a new pair of Italian shoes maybe, a dime of grass, or some new trinket of junk jewelry, of which he already wore far too much.

He's just using me, was Herbie's glum thought. *When everybody else is busy, he comes over here and thinks up something he wants to compensate himself for paying attention to me. I wish my taste in sex objects was a little less good. What does it get me?*

What it had gotten him this time was the unanticipated prospect of killing the evening by himself as best he could. All in all, it had been a fairly depressing afternoon.

He found the remnants of last week's lasagna in the refrigerator. Afterwards, when the dishes were stacked in the dishwasher and the pot set to soak in the sink, Herbie cast around for something to do. Idly, he checked his marijuana garden under lights in the pantry. He collected some dried leaves and rolled a joint.

Firing it up, he strolled out to the living room. He flopped in his easy chair and flipped through *TV Guide*. Made-for-TV movies. Lame sitcoms. Family-oriented drek. Cop shows, cop shows, cop shows: police propaganda in assorted flavors.

Pledge month on PBS. Shark month on The Discovery Channel. *Not entirely dissimilar*, he decided.

So much for TV.

His current book was at his elbow, but right at the moment he was rushing from the grass and wouldn't be able to concentrate. Later.

He took another hit on the joint and held it until his head swam. He picked up a remote. His stereo lit up, tuned more-or-less permanently to the town's preeminent classical music station.

> "...your station for classical music
> 24 hours a day. That's a lot of
> B e e t h o v e n ,   M o z a r t   a n d
> Tchaikovsky..."

...and not a helluva lot else, Herbie thought. Christ, how he despised Top 40 classical music programming. Had they no shame? To play the same damn stuff over and over and over again?

> "...We turn now to another item in
> our complete traversal of the 600

works of Johann Strauss, Jr. Here
now is *The...*"

He silenced it in disgust. *Enough alrightalready!*

Herbie finished the joint and dropped the roach into a stash
box. He lit up a cigarette, an Export Special. Getting stoned always
turned him into a chainsmoker for half an hour. He liked Export
Specials. Although they were more expensive and less generally
available than regular production cigarettes, they were also smoother
and more flavorful. You could smoke them endlessly without ripping
your throat out.

Herbie was very thoroughly bored, and irritated by a nagging
sense of something he'd forgotten, something he wanted to do, a
sense almost of something calling him, right at the edge of memory.
He wandered his dark and silent apartment. He shrugged off the
feeling. If it were important, it would come to him. He was
considering going for a walk when the knapsack caught his eye, there
in the middle of his desk.

The atmosphere in the apartment turned vaguely surreal.
Maybe it was only because he was so high in a darkened room, but his
surroundings seemed suddenly squished flat, two-dimensional and
colorless, from which the knapsack bulged itself forwards in high, 3D
relief. He stared at it through a long second of silence. Was it only
the blood pounding in his ears, or was that actually a *heartbeat*
pulsing faintly from inside the nylon? *Come hither, come hither,* sang
a small wordless voice in his mind. The knapsack was calling him,
somehow expectant and waiting—insistently, bulgingly pregnant.
Before he knew it, he'd been pulled toward it a step.

What?

He shook his head to clear it. The room returned to normal.
In any case, he'd remembered what it was he wanted to do: the old
tin, "McCandless' Fancy Selection," from the shore that afternoon.
He wanted another look at it. He fished it out of the knapsack, which
looked oddly deflated and dead without it. He put Martinu's First
Symphony on the stereo and took the box back out to the kitchen
table.

Have a Cookie, Little Boy?

The first surprise was its weight. At the lake, it had seemed empty, almost weightless. It had sat on top of the water like a balloon. Now, it was surprisingly heavy, four or five pounds at least!

Was he just stoned, or was it getting slightly heavier all the time? Huh! He bumped it down on the table and pulled up a chair for a detailed examination. The woman in the antique dress offered the little boy a cookie as gracefully as ever. The little boy as greedily reached for it. Then it happened.

Herbie jerked back in his chair and gave a yelp that ended in a startled screech. In the silence that followed, his neighbor across the alley turned to stare at him through the open windows, then banged hers down hard.

He winked at me! The little boy turned his head and winked at me! Get a grip, Herbie, be cool. He can't have! He's a fucking picture on a piece of tin! Maybe it's the grass. That's it, it must be the grass. Boy, good shit! Gave me a real turn.

Somehow, this explanation did not quite satisfy. Visual hallucinations on grass weren't normal at all, certainly not on one joint, and decent though it may have been, the shit was only his homegrown. As far as explanations went, though, it was the best he had.

Rather shakily, Herbie lit another Export Special and took a deep drag. He felt himself calming down a little. *I guess I'm okay,* he thought. *When things start saying "Eat me," I'll know I've gone down the rabbit hole for good!*

He picked up the box again, with both hands. Ten pounds. He shook it gingerly. There was definitely something inside, after all. It made a sound. Like sand, maybe. Or no, like the ocean in a seashell, or maybe like the swish of ballgowns on polished parquet. Tara, Versailles, the Hermitage, Schönbrunn Palace. Whatever it was, it was soft, tantalizing, otherworldly. It called to him from far away across time in the same small wordless voice he'd heard from the knapsack. *Come hither, come hither!*

He bumped the box down. He pretty much had to. It weighed at least twenty pounds. He examined it warily. The pictures did not move this time, yet somehow ached with desire. He dragged

11

on his Export Special. He tried the lid, but try as he might, he couldn't budge it.

He laid his cigarette on the lip of the ashtray, got a screwdriver from the table drawer and began to pry off the lid, carefully so as not to mar the paint. The sea whisper from inside grew to a rumble and then a roar as he worked, combining with the complex harmonies of the Martinu symphony floating from the other room in unearthly swell. The lights browned. Herbie realized he was bent over the box, working furiously and focused in on it so that it occupied virtually his entire attention. He tried to look up, and couldn't! He panicked. He tried to throw down the screwdriver and get the hell away. Instead, he found himself working more maniacally than before, if that were possible, no longer concerned with preserving the paint, slashing at the box with the screwdriver. He felt trapped in a dream like a roach in a gluetrap. He commanded himself to wake up, but didn't.

Suddenly the screwdriver found just the right purchase between box and lid, and twisted with all Herbie's muscle behind it. The lid moved slowly at first, then flew up and away. An intense flash of light and a violent upward agitation in the air above the box snapped Herbie back in his chair so hard it went over backwards. The fall spreadeagled him helplessly on the floor with the chair between his legs. He covered his face. The roaring crescendoed into a sweeping climax in the music from the other room. Both died away together.

Silence.

Absolute silence, such as one never hears in the city.

Not only the music, which was not nearly over, but traffic noise, sirens, ventilators, El-trains rumbling—the ubiquitous whitenoise background of city life one normally never notices—all had vanished. Gone too was the breeze from the open window. Only the ticktick of the kitchen clock broke the silence, exactly in time with the beating of his heart.

In this unearthliness, Herbie opened his eyes and cautiously lowered his arms from his face. He gaped in the absolute shock of his life.

Have a Cookie, Little Boy?

His Export Special was still on the lip of the ashtray. In the windless air its smoke rose straight up and curled... and curled into the semi-transparent form of the most beautiful boy Herbie had ever seen. The vision had long thick gold hair curling into the smoke halfway down its back. Big-boned hands and arms depended from broad shoulders. A long precisely muscled torso converged on lean hips and dancer's legs, one of which was cocked coquettishly, exposing a thick bulge under the skimpy loincloth that was its only garment. The face was seraphic. Large green eyes looked out beatifically above stripes of Indian warpaint. The vision opened its wide mouth, flared its straight nostrils and took a deep breath that sent zephyrs of exquisite perfume circling through the room, shaking the figure itself on its pencil line of cigarette smoke and rippling the beautiful muscles from top to bottom.

The vision sent the gaze of those hypnotic eyes around the room and rested it finally on Herbie. Herbie felt blessed, inspired with numinous and powerful erotic feelings, as if choirs of god's own angels were beating off in front of him.

The vision did another, longer, slower take around the room and peered out the window up at the sky, emanating a whole range of emotions which washed over, around and through Herbie one after another: relief, exultation, wistfulness, and, as its eyes settled once again on Herbie, wariness and calculation. "So okay," it murmured. "Here we go again."

I'm dreaming, Herbie thought. Only in dreams did you know what other people were feeling in this palpable way. Then there was the voice. Did it come through the air in the usual way, or directly into his head in some fashion or other? Herbie wasn't sure. All he knew was that it seemed to be all around him, indissolubly bound up in the intricacies of that subtle perfume. He inhaled in great lung-filling gasps.

The vision looked Herbie over, sprawled staring on the floor. Herbie was unable to tear his eyes from this perfected embodiment of his innermost erotic fantasies. The vision's every glance and movement sent flashes of hot energy zinging through his body.

13

Evidently, the feeling might be somewhat less than mutual. The vision planted its wrists on its hips and glared at him. "You know, honey, nobody with eyes bulging out of their sockets that way can ever be anything like attractive, and goodness, Muriel, didn't your mother tell you to keep your mouth closed when you weren't eating, talking, or sucking cock? Where were you brought up, a Gallo bottle?"

"W-what? Oh." Herbie closed his mouth with a snap that hurt his jaws. He tried to blink. "Wh...where did you come from?"

"That's right. The mortal always begins by asking a stupid question. What *is* the matter, were we playing peekaboo?" The vision sighed. "You have uncorked the proverbial genie in a bottle. Lucky for you. Union rules say I have to be *very* grateful."

"Really." That might be something. Herbie disentangled himself from the chair and got to his feet. He ran his eyes up and down the lovely body, and felt desire quickening once again, despite the vision's unattractively swishy manner. He wondered exactly how grateful *very* grateful meant. He was owed a favor? He definitely knew what he wanted. Even if, as seemed likely, the being wouldn't give much of a damn about sex with him, he'd learned from all those hustlers not to mind guys who didn't, especially if they'd put a little effort into faking it. "Any chance you could become a bit more, ah, substantial?" He approached the vision and gingerly reached out a hand.

"Cut that out! It's not nice to grope Mother Nature!" The vision leaned forwards and slapped Herbie's wrist.

Herbie felt only a light brush of breeze. He retracted the hand. "Oh, okay. No offense." *Proverbial pricktease, more like.*

The vision looked Herbie up and down. "Let me be very upfront with you, Maud. I do not want you to get the wrong impression. You are not my type." It waggled a smoky hand and smirked. "You should have *seen* the expression on your face!"

This is definitely a dream, Herbie sighed. So rejection followed him even there. However, rejection was familiar. He could handle it. Maybe it was even a good thing. With sex out of the bargain, he could relax and deal with this the same way he dealt with salesmen at the door, or at least try—but then, this wasn't really happening, was it?

He righted the chair and sat. "Uh huh. So you're a genie? In a cookie tin? Humbug!" His eyes gleamed. "I know what you are: an undigested bit of beef, a blot of mustard, a crumb of cheese..." His memory of Dickens ran dry. "Sorry, but I don't believe any of this. One way or another, I am definitely dreaming." He meant it.

"Well, pinch yourself, Myrtle. I am very serious. Do it!"

Herbie did. It felt just like a pinch.

"Are you awake?"

"I reserve judgment."

"As long as you pay attention! We need to talk business." The vision stared at him steadily. "Actually, I am rather more than a genie. I am a djinn. Do you know what that is?"

Herbie shrugged. "Sure. You mean like in the *1001 Nights*."

"That's good, very good. Exactly like in the *1001 Nights*, with one important exception. This is not a fairy tale! This is real! What we are doing here is serious, girlfriend. It can be as wonderful for you as you can imagine, literally! It can also be a colossal bummer. If you treat this as if it were a fairy tale or a dream, there will be big trouble. Do you understand?"

"Sure," Herbie smiled. This was truly a very strange dream. His glance strayed to that fat bulge beneath the vision's loincloth. Sex out of the bargain or not, it was hard to ignore what clearly was very impressive equipment. He caressed it with his eyes, and felt his own crotch respond. "Aladdin got to rub the lamp. For me, though, 'as wonderful as I can imagine' definitely involves rubbing something else."

"Hello? Earth calling, Maxine. Listen up!"

Herbie allowed his gaze to wander slowly back up the lovely torso toward the face. When it got there, there was a long pause, during which the vision was very patently unamused.

"Your predecessor died," it said.

Herbie's smile went flaccid at this clinker in a chord of beautiful music. He took it as a clue he was about to wake up. In fact, he tried. Nothing happened. "I've heard of dick of death," he

15

said, disconcerted and playing for time by trying to keep things light, "but isn't that stretching the point a bit?"

The vision rolled its eyes in disgust. *"Mortals!"* it breathed feelingly, and twisted uncomfortably on the pencil line of cigarette smoke, which was getting a bit thin as the cigarette burned out. "Light another, will you? Until I get my strength back, I need the smoke so I can be substantial, unless you would rather talk to a whirlwind or a burning bush, either of which might be a bit hard on the fixtures."

Herbie lit two, one for himself and one to place on the lip of the ashtray besides the first. The smoke curled up. Once again, the vision stretched, and once again, Herbie found his eyes irresistibly drawn to that big bulge between its legs.

"That's better. Now where were we."

Herbie collected himself. "My predecessor died," he said, and raised an eyebrow.

"That's right. He did. There are rules here, procedures, a lot you have to understand. If you do not..."

The djinn drew himself up. "In a probably futile attempt to avoid this possibility, which in my experience has been a completely lost cause with you mortals, I will now deliver the standard introductory lecture on the metaphysical nature of the universe, short version. Please stop me whenever you do not understand something, which I am assuming will be frequently."

The djinn leaned forwards on his thin column of smoke, obviously in deadly earnest. "Here goes. In this universe, there are *two* kinds of lifeforce, the physical, possessed by mortal creatures such as yourself, and the metaphysical, which belongs to immortal kind, such as *moi*."

With difficulty, Herbie shifted into lecture mode. The sheer absurdity of this whole situation threatened to interfere with concentration. "You're... immortal."

"Oh good. *Something* is getting through. There is hope. Yes, well, immortal with certain reservations. I will get to that. These life forces, yours and ours, exist in completely interdependent symbiosis. We create each other. You create us, and without us, you do not create anything at all. Are you following me?"

"Hold it hold it. One thing at a time. You say *we* create you? How?"

"A question! You are paying attention. I am encouraged. Yes, you create us. For simplicity's sake, let us say we are the sum total of your hopes and dreams, your aspirations and desires, your innermost wishes, humankind's eternal striving concentrated, purified and translated to another plane." The djinn aimed an ethereal finger at the heavens.

"What?" This was all very interesting, and he had to admit the special effects were impressive, but Herbie wasn't willing to have his intelligence insulted at the best of times, let alone by an hallucination from a cookie box. "What are you talking about? Collective consciousness? Sounds like bullshit to me. And hopes and dreams? What kind of sugary crap is that? You sound like a cross between *Pilgrim's Progress* and *Peter Pan*! I'm not buying it." Food poisoning, that's what this was. Maybe Dickens wasn't so far off, after all. He had wondered whether that lasagna might be a day or two over the limit.

"Very well." The djinn's voice was level. "It is a metaphor, I admit it. I am doing my best to explain this in words of one syllable so we can get to the essential business here as quickly as possible. So why don't you pretend for a second it is literally true and see what it gets you?"

Herbie closed his mouth and decided he'd play along a little farther.

"Thank you. These forces, yours and ours, the mortal and the immortal, the physical and the metaphysical, exist in precise balance—and here comes a Concept: that balance is called, in technical terms, The Balance. Simple. Easy to remember, no? Keeping The Balance is very important. The health and well-oiled functioning of both worlds depends on it. Normally, this is not a problem. The Balance is always kept from your end. You mortals are mostly ignorant we exist, and even if you were not, there would still be nothing you could do to stop the flow of power to us. Hoping, dreaming and aspiring are eternal human traits. As they are eternal, so are we. But the same is not true in reverse. We can destroy you, if we like."

"Excuse me? Hopes, dreams and desires can destroy people?"

"Surely, when they take on a life of their own. As I said, a metaphor. Besides, there are far fewer beings in the metaphysical world, but together, we are as powerful as you. That means each of our individuals is immensely more powerful than one of yours—and remember, we are *not* physical beings. We're made up of the pure stuff of power itself. We *are* it, and we employ it directly."

This was ridiculous. Herbie's already considerable sense of this conversation's absurdity increased, amidst which a sobering thought struck him. *I'm in the hospital. I must have fallen off the bike this afternoon and hit my head. I'm in a coma. Any minute now, there'll be a tunnel and a bright light...*

The djinn was continuing. "This *could* make any one of us deadly."

"But doesn't."

"That's right. If we kill a mortal being, the mortal power that individual possessed transforms. It changes from your currency to ours and passes to us, and believe me, Mabel, we are often very tempted to augment ourselves. Like in your world, we have politics you would not believe. A little extra power comes in handy for all kinds of things—but then, The Balance has been tipped. Suddenly, there is more immortal power than mortal, because the total amount of mortal power has been diminished and ours increased—and when one side becomes topheavy, the results can be majorly disastrous."

Herbie was following this with difficulty. "But how can one side become 'topheavy'? If you are some kind of metaphorical manifestation of us, wouldn't diminishing us diminish you, too?"

"An *intelligent* question!" The djinn's eyes widened in surprise. "And so it would, though not immediately. We can coast for a while, and just as no living being gives up its existence without a struggle, we have strategies for increasing the effect—and, naturally, each of us thinks the problem ought to be somebody else's.

Politics, as I said. Because in the long run, you are right; we are supported by the hopes, dreams, etc., of the mortal world in general, so ultimately there would no longer be enough of that to go around. Somebody will have to pay."

"So what happens when mortals kill one another? Doesn't that reduce the 'mortal power,' whatever that is, too?"

"No. He who does the killing gets the benefit, that's the principle. So, when mortals kill one another, the power remains in the mortal world. Somewhere, the survivors reap the benefit, even if only in the most unfocused way, if only because there is now one fewer person around to screw up the planet. But the benefit can also be focused and used much more directly. Your ancestors grasped this quite clearly. That is why living sacrifices of all kinds were so very popular for such a long long time.

"Accordingly, when *we* do the killing, mortals obtain no benefit of any kind, one fewer person or not. The power adheres to us and conflict develops. Ours is a strictly hierarchical society, and our hierarchies exist in a jealously guarded state of detente. But now, somebody is more powerful than he should be. Others may have to dip into the mortal world for power to force him back into place. More mortal things die, and the disequilibrium deepens. Things can get out of hand. The existence of both worlds can be threatened. It has happened. Because with disequilibrium comes instability. Ultimately, of course, the metaphysical world will sag into balance, but before then, the longer the power hangs around out of balance, the greater becomes the likelihood of an automatic correction of completely unpredictable nature."

"A what?"

The djinn shrugged. "When the metaphysical world draws power at a rate the mortal world can not sustain, it creates a sort of vacuum. Just as physical nature abhors a vacuum, so does power, which sometimes blasts itself back into the mortal world by whatever is the easiest way for it to go. Like I said, unpredictable. And usually disastrous. These events are often indiscriminately explosive, involving loss of mortal life. When this happens, because nobody is directly responsible, the freed-up mortal power adheres noplace. It

19

dissipates, producing a new disequilibrium. The ultimate nightmare is a cascade of automatic corrections as one disequilibrium leads to the next. Stopping that can be really expensive. We definitely do not wish to risk it."

"So you don't kill anybody."

"Hardly ever."

"That's very reassuring."

"Sometimes, it is unavoidable. Long ago, we came up with a compromise, agreed solemnly among us all around, and very strictly enforced—and here comes another Concept: this compromise is called The Bargain. It says we can take the mortal power only when to do so is necessary to preserve our own existence and thereby preserve The Balance from our side. The catch is that whatever power we take must be returned to the mortal world as soon as possible, and then, it must be employed by mortals for mortal purposes only, rather than deviously employed by the one who took it using a mortal creature as an agent. In the words of The Bargain, the power has to be given back *to the first mortal creature we see when the emergency is past, and in whatever form that creature desires.* Do you begin to see where you fit in here, darling?"

"Oh yes, my predecessor who died, I suppose." Herbie smiled. "The first thing you see? Even if it isn't human? Suppose I'd opened you there in the park and the first thing you saw out of the box was a squirrel?"

"That squirrel right now would have the biggest damn nuts you ever saw, and we would not be having this conversation, which for me would be a definite plus!"

"Hey! Let me get this straight. You guys, whoever you are, get to help yourselves to us whenever it's convenient, and now you tell me I'm the beneficiary of some such deal? That I now get Three Wishes? Man, I still think you're food poisoning."

"What?"

"Forget it."

The djinn spoke through clenched teeth. "I will have you know I am doing you a favor. The first thing I really saw out of the box was a cockroach climbing up your kitchen wall, and its desire was company—lots and lots and *lots* of company. Still think I'm food poisoning?"

Herbie lifted his arms in mock surrender. "Okay okay! Three Wishes!"

"THIS IS NOT A FAIRY TALE!" the djinn exploded. The diaphanous form of the beautiful boy disappeared. The lights went out completely. The smoke from Herbie's Export Special billowed and glowed a loathsome puce. Inside it, Herbie caught a glimpse of something scaly and foul with coldly irradiative eyes. A noxious, rotten odor replaced the subtle perfume. A long snaky arm tipped with jagged claws shot from the cloud and grabbed Herbie by the wrist in a painfully material grasp. A voice like the exhalation of a tomb sounded softly, very close to Herbie's ear. "In a moment, I will reach inside your mind and choose, myself, from among your desires, something to please only me."

In a flash, the apparition passed. The lights were normal. The vision of the beautiful boy was back on its pencil of cigarette smoke, giving Herbie a grim stare. "But I would rather have your cooperation," it said. "That's closer to the spirit of The Bargain."

"Hey, no need to overreact," Herbie said weakly. He was shaking. He still felt the clammy, disgusting touch of those claws on his wrist and the numbing strength of their grasp. Just perhaps, he thought, he should start taking this seriously.

"When at last I have your attention," the djinn continued, "I am going to tell you a very short story with a very sharp point." He stared at Herbie, an elementary school teacher waiting for unruly children to settle down and concentrate their focus. The silence lengthened.

"Yeah fine, I'm listening." Speaking of which, he noticed that the djinn's voice now very definitely came at him from the being's mouth in vibrations through the air. When, exactly, had the change taken place?

"The last time I was found was in 1871. I was in a very different and altogether more luxurious container. A self-styled gentleman aptly named Nathaniel Bummer bought me in a curio shop. He thought that, once I was cleaned up a little, I would look

21

very handsome on his mantlepiece. But after he opened the bottle, he thought, much as you do, that I would look even handsomer someplace else. Mr. Bummer was very rich. Besides a lot of money, he had contemptible desires, abominable taste, very little imagination, and vile breath. Typical mortal. His command was the creation of a fantasy land in which I would reside and wherein he could visit me any time he liked to play out a racist and predatory little sex fantasy called The Cowboy and the Captured Indian Brave, thus the loincloth and the warpaint. I know you noticed. But not six months after he found me, one of these nasty little scenes ended in disaster. He had just got me all trussed up and was warming up the branding iron when I noticed the scenery turning brown and starting to curl up around the edges. A fast peek out at the real world showed me, to my horror, that the whole fucking city was on fire!"

The djinn made a dramatic pause. "Usually, fire is one of the easiest physical manifestations for us to control. We use it all the time, and for all kinds of things, but nothing exceeds like excess. One thing no metaphysical being can survive is a firestorm, and we were right in the middle of one! The house was going up all around us. Escape was impossible. I cancelled the fantasy and decanted us straight into the nearest available container. Among Mr. Bummer's many antisocial tendencies, he liked to eat cookies in bed. Unfortunately for him, the protective sealing spell is so strong I can not break it again on my own, and that takes more power than I have. So, before the fire got him, I did. I took his mortal power away from him to seal myself in, and I have to tell you, zapping him gave me the greatest possible pleasure."

The djinn opened his hand. A thin stream of fine dust trickled down and formed a neat conical mound in the ashtray. "Meet the late and most vigorously unlamented Mr. Bummer. Bad taste is its own reward, I always say."

Herbie was inclined to agree.

The djinn continued. "So there I was. Surely, I thought, there would be someone sifting through the rubble. I would sing my little siren song and hope for better luck next time, but no. They steam-shovelled the whole mess into Lake Michigan, and me with it.

22

Me! Landfill! There I have been all this time, watching the world change and go by, powerless and in prison as usual, stuck among the lakebottom rocks out by Navy Pier. Until last night, when the storm washed me loose at last."

The green eyes blazed emerald fire. "Now get this! *I am sick and tired of prison!*—and through the stupidity, horniness, and cupidity of one damned mortal after another, I have spent centuries there! This, of course, is half the reason The Bargain says we have to return the power by fulfilling a mortal desire. The College of Archons, who are very definitely the powers that be where I come from, feels it discourages taking the mortal lifeforce except when absolutely necessary. Mortals by and large have such stupid and greedy desires that granting them almost always lands us in more trouble than before!"

The djinn leaned forward and aimed a finger. "But you, Millicent, are going to be different. If you are not, so help me, I swear by my Secret Name that, just as for Nate Bummer and his sick little snuff fantasies, the punishment will definitely fit the crime! So choose now, to the meager limit of the pissant's worthless life! And choose wisely!"

Herbie's mouth flapped open and shut soundlessly. If this were genuine, the stakes were enormous. What was safe and what wasn't? How much did a human life buy in the djinn's currency, anyway? "Advise me," he muttered at last.

"Since you ask," the djinn said coldly, "I advise you pick something that leaves both of us in the real world to observe results. I also advise you to choose something that transfers all the power at once, instead of risking the kind of unpredictable automatic correction that led to Mr. Bummer's untimely though well deserved demise. Further than that, I can not advise you and remain within the letter of The Bargain. Even this is stretching it."

"Hold it hold it!" Herbie's mind worked furiously. "Are you telling me the Great Chicago Fire was one of these automatic corrections?"

"To be honest, I can not say for sure. At the moment it happened, I was preoccupied, and since then, I have been out of

23

touch, but bringing together the supposed preconditions for the Fire—one cow, one lantern, one dose of kerosene illegally mixed with gasoline, one strong, dry southwest wind and the necessary large degree of unlucky synchronicity—easily could have been paid for with the power in Bummer's account. Those things were probably hanging around the neighborhood already, just waiting to be put together. The other essential ingredient, considerable human ineptitude and stupidity, was, as always, free for the asking. —And then, when we came out of the fantasy, I wanted to use that power to make the seal even more secure, but it was gone. *Something* emptied the account that night. So, the answer to your question is a very definite *probably*, and if it led to the kind of cascade failure I was talking about, that would definitely account for it." He thought about that, and muttered, "I wonder what They had to do to stop it. I may not be very popular when I get back. But what is new about that?" He scowled, then shrugged. "Look, this talk wastes time and tempts fate. Now that the power and I are back in the world, every second counts. So get on with it." The djinn sighed a bleak sigh. "Let me see what I am in for this time."

Herbie spread his hands in confusion. "I can't! If it's as important as all that, I need to think!"

The djinn's face showed exasperation melting rapidly into grim resignation. "Very well, Martha, I will buy that. It's your funeral, and that might not be merely a figure of speech. So take your time, do it right. Twenty-four hours, and not a minute longer."

Herbie relaxed, reprieved. Once again, he felt free to admire the djinn's mesmerizing face and body. Wistful longing swept over him. "Uh, you don't suppose," he said humbly, "after this is over, if I make a good choice and it all works out okay, you might throw me a little boff? Just once? Kind of a friendly gesture to seal the deal, maybe? I'm not into weird games."

There was a pause. *Maybe I could have phrased that better.* Too much dealing with hustlers had warped his sense of the amenities, Herbie thought ruefully.

Have a Cookie, Little Boy?

The djinn expressed contempt in every line of his being. His beautiful hand twitched the loincloth aside. The sound of a thick gurgle of liquid filled the air.

He's pissing in my ashtray, and with a dick like a firehose, too. Herbie guessed he had his answer.

The djinn finished his whizz and stretched languidly. Out of the rapidly dissipating smoke from the drowned Export Special shapely and very solid-seeming ankles and feet stepped onto Herbie's kitchen table . *"Goodness* me! Will you *look* at the *time!* I am *decades* late for a date with a *very* horny man! So un*like* me! Where *are* my props?" As he spoke, a small whirlywind developed about him there atop the kitchen table. His figure blurred, and then, for a moment before disappearing completely, seemed to transmogrify into that of a drooping young man with a soulful expression, a chest stuck full of arrows, and a foot-long hardon. The whirlywind itself diminished in size. Within seconds, it dissipated completely, leaving only a hint of the words, *Coming, Your Holiness!* echoing insanely through Herbie's brain. The kitchen clock chimed 9:30.

City noises blew in through the open window. Fresh spring air moved the curtains. Martinu floated down the hall once again. Herbie blinked, and shook his head to clear it of these phantasms' last vestiges. *Good night! What a weird hallucin...* The word died two-fifths unthought as his gaze lit on his kitchen table, whence neon yellow-green fairy piss dripped and puddled on the floor.

His calling card! With each drip, icy coils of realization wound him about. He obviously wasn't dead or in a coma, and he'd never heard of an hallucination you had to clean up with a mop and a bucket. This was no dream, either. It had been unreal, all right, but not at all like a dream. Frantically, he struggled to recall the details and what the djinn had said. He found it all burned in his memory, preternaturally clear and unambiguous. The renewed breeze stirred the air and brought a last, faint hint of the djinn's marvelous perfume to Herbie's nostrils. *This happened!* He fought down a tendency to panic.

It seemed he was to be given a gift whether he wanted it or not, a particularly wonderful and/or dangerous gift, depending on

25

how he chose. He gulped. Very well, he would accept the challenge. He would ask for his heart's desire, whatever that was... He smiled. If, as seemed apparent, he was fated never to enjoy the djinn's luscious body in his bed, he knew what he wanted instead. Maybe he wanted it more.

Later, in bed, turning the whole thing over in his mind, several things struck him sharply. The first was that absurd business about the metaphysical world being created from people's hopes, dreams, desires, aspirations, and innermost wishes. How the djinn had hurried through that! He sure hadn't seemed like the apotheosis of anybody's hopes, dreams or aspirations, except maybe the Marquis de Sade's. Then there was that bit about the two worlds being symbiotic. How, precisely? In what way did the mortal world draw on the metaphysical? The djinn hadn't said much about that at all, and he, Herbie, hadn't gotten around to following it up. While he was at it, it also occurred to him to wonder how it was that only humanity's hopes, dreams, desires, etc. in this world seemed to equal the sum total of its lifeforce in the other. Those things were important, sure, but that wasn't *all* humanity was about, was it? And if the metaphysical world were truly sustained by these things, how come overdrawing their account seemed to result in megadeath among mortals? He had a hard time making that work out to equivalence in compensation.

There seemed to be some essential information missing. True, the djinn had said it was all a metaphor—but for what, exactly, Herbie wondered. *But for what?*

* * * * *

The next day he wasted no time worrying about it. He spent the morning and a good part of the afternoon at his bank and his broker turning every cent he could cajole, leverage or otherwise acquire into cash. At the bank, this meant swallowing several hefty early withdrawal penalties, and some of his assets weren't convertible to cash at all on such short notice. He gritted his teeth and endured it for the sake of what was to come. On the way home, he stopped and bought some new jeans and a pair of athletic shoes in the latest fashion. He had to guess the sizes, but then, years of buying little surprise gifts for hustlers had given him a pretty good eye.

Back home, he pulled down a suitcase. First into it went things like socks and the shirts he figured might fit. When that was done, he wandered the rooms looking for other things to pack.

One by one as his eye lit on them, he turned his treasures over in his mind. To his surprise, he found a reason not to take them every time. Books? Too heavy, and replaceable besides, mostly. Musical recordings, ditto. Clocks? Pictures? Vases? Candelabra? Knickknacks? No. Why weigh himself down? Into the suitcase finally went the slim files of his creative writing hobby—stuff he didn't particularly care to have picked through by strangers, but didn't want to destroy, either—a few photographs, a treasured paperweight or two from his desk, and the douche kit from his bedside table.

Herbie was vaguely disquieted. *Is that all my life 'til now comes to? Some odds and ends and a few file folders?* Suddenly angry, he walked across the room, picked up his favorite ashtray and his current book, slung them into the suitcase and slammed it shut.

Next, he sat down at his desk and pulled pen and paper forward.

> Dear Mom and Dad,
>   By the time this reaches you, I shall be gone, probably forever...

He looked a long hard look at what he'd written, then tore it up and threw the pieces away. His sense of disquiet increased. He reached for a new piece of notepaper and stared at it, furrowing his brow. After a time, he pushed it away again and slumped in his chair, defeated. *Maybe I'll send them a postcard or something now and again, if I can, just to let them know I'm alive,* he thought.

He got up. Hands in pockets, he wandered the darkening rooms. Slowly, thoughtfully, he paused to stare at everything again.

There was such a lot of stuff, all redolent with the love and attention he'd lavished upon it. He suffered a pang at the thought of abandoning it. There was his comprehensive collection of kitchen utensils and gadgets, painstakingly gathered one piece at a time, and at such great expense. There was the spice rack he'd had custom-built to hold sixty jars. Examining his spice rack was like examining his life. *Christ, what did I ever make with turmeric?* He supposed there must have been something—the jar was definitely a tablespoon or two low; then he remembered his experiments years ago with Indian cooking. That really had been a lot of fun. Why had he stopped doing that?

He shrugged and moved on, past the plants he'd nursed tenderly and never forgotten to water, past his furniture and other belongings lovingly scrounged from a hundred antique shops, each piece of which had appealed to him so strongly he'd simply had to have it, past his books and music, his friends when he'd had no others, his prized collection of antique clocks, at least one in every room, possibly the most valuable things he owned, an investment for the future and the product of certain accounts he thought it best by far should remain forever unaccountable. His things were a summation, all he had to show for his years of living thus far, the fruit of grinding work, the witnesses of his joys and frustrations. What reserve of his soul did it represent? Why was it all so hard to renounce?

Answers not forthcoming from the silent walls, he sank into his favorite chair in the living room. Outside, twilight deepened to dusk. The room swirled with memories: good times, bad times, friends he'd known, a few he'd loved—pain and loss, past and present.

Was it worth it? A new beginning?

Almost, he decided to change his request. A million dollars. Ten million. A hundred million. With that kind of money, much would be possible, and these wrenching difficulties would not arise.

No! This was an unique chance, a chance to escape the inexorable constant of human happiness, the perpetual struggle to make the most of things one couldn't change that had depressed him so at the lake yesterday. Well, now he could change them—and he would. The choices were limitless. He had only to choose among them.

The enormity of it awed him. Beyond all hope and reason, the threshold was there, it seemed, suddenly and tantalizingly real. He had only to step over, into his heart's desire. Yet he was reluctant. Why? He frowned in the gathering gloom. His very reluctance irritated him. Why should he not reach for what he had always wanted? Why was he hanging back?

As he always did when a feeling bothered him, he attempted to analyze it into insignificance.

It seemed to him then that perhaps this reluctance was a very human thing. This was a Choice, a big one, and most people feared choices. Why was obvious: because most people were so bad at them. They looked back at their youth when life had been all choice, and saw the ones they regretted, the possibilities foreclosed, and were unnerved.

Herbie saw how, as youth passed, matters gradually arranged themselves so as to relieve people of the burden of choice, how all choices, successful and unsuccessful, tended to reduce the future choices available. For instance, if your career choice worked out well, it might never be necessary to choose another, while an unrewarding career might leave you without the resources to deal with the dislocation and economic hardship of starting over—and the longer your resume got in one field, the more reluctant prospective employers might be to give you a chance in any other. Either way, you could end up stuck with your earliest choice for good or ill.

The longer you lived with your choices, successful or not, the greater your investment in them became, and, not unnaturally, as your investment in your choices grew, so did your perception of their value. You might be bored sick of the town where you lived, but the longer you stayed there, the harder it was to leave. Moving meant giving up your house, your friends, your job, your roots that went ever deeper as time went by, not to mention the ever-increasing amounts of sheer stuff you accumulated and what they were going to cost to move or replace!

The clock kept ticking too. As you grew older, your reserves of the stamina to endure risk and its consequences decreased, as did the time you had left to rebuild what you'd given up, or to start over yet again if the choice went wrong. As time went by, people learned to live with their choices because they had to. They made the best of the consequences, until in the end, at last in old age, for better or for worse, there were no more choices left.

Herbie saw his own place in the pattern clearly. While his life may not have been particularly satisfactory, he'd made it reasonably comfortable; while limitless possibilities now opened before him, taking them meant renouncing the years of vital struggle it had cost him to make it so. Equally disturbing was the thought that changing his circumstances meant the experience and expertise he'd gained dealing with his old life now would be worthless, leaving him once again as he'd been in his youth, adrift without guidance to face life alone. Who knew what he'd be up against now? It sounded good; it was what he'd always wanted, but...

This time, understanding his reluctance had not made it go away. Rather the reverse. In the now complete darkness of his living room, his plan ceased to look like a grand adventure and began to seem instead like terrifying folly. He wished the djinn really had chosen to fulfill the heart's desire of a squirrel, or even, with important reservations, of that cockroach on his kitchen wall. No, that was impossible, wasn't it? Surely the djinn, given the admittedly unenviable experience with human choices he seemed to have had, would have chosen some such option had it been available. By the peculiar logic of the metaphysical world as the djinn had explained it to him, he supposed the power had to be returned to the same sort of entity whence it came. Only the same sort of creature could have desires of the size and complexity necessary to use the power completely and appropriately. The grand adventure was on, whether he liked it or not. Then he remembered the preparations he'd made for it downtown today, and thought, *it'd better be.*

His courage returned. The reward was his heart's desire, the lack of which had, in his opinion, crippled his life. Now, against all reason, it was very tantalizingly on offer. Of course he would take it! He'd be crazy not to, wouldn't he?

As the promised hour approached, he amused himself creating an appropriately magical atmosphere. He remembered how the djinn had needed smoke to be substantial at first, though he'd turned solid enough later on. Herbie was eager to be of service if it would help. He lit a pile of sandalwood incense in a brazier and placed it on the corner of his desk, whence the smoke rolled up in a thick pillar. Aesthetic curiosity stirred to see the soft and sensuous play of natural light across the djinn's lovely body. He lit oil lamps and candles everywhere in the apartment, and built a big fire in the fireplace.

Settling down in his desk chair, he waited.

At last, 9:30 struck. Clocks everywhere in the apartment chimed and dinged out the half. The final vibrations of the chime from the kitchen clock, perpetually offset thirty seconds behind all the others, floated down the hall and died away.

Nothing happened.

For one sickeningly empty moment, Herbie considered the possibility he'd been the victim of a weird and sadistic hoax.

Then the air pressure changed; his ears popped. A breeze whistled through the rooms, extinguishing the candles and even the oil lamps. The brazier and the fire went out with simultaneous whooshes: the brazier billowing a final mushroom of smoke up into the air; the fire as if sucked straight up the chimney, leaving the room in darkness.

"Are you mad?" a voice said. "After everything I told you? *Things catch fire* that way."

The desk lamp went on. To Herbie's surprise, he was no longer in his desk chair. He was across the desk on one of his deliberately hard and uncomfortable client chairs. In his own chair was... the djinn? No longer a seductive siren, the figure in Herbie's chair was fiftyish, paunchy, gray-bearded and balding. Immaculately groomed, it wore a gray, pinstriped three-piece suit and gold-rimmed glasses. Before Herbie was, in fact, the very image of the humorless

31

intimidating rectal surgeon who'd long ago treated him for anal warts.

The apparition was using a gold-tipped ivory-inlaid Montblanc fountain pen thicker than a finger to write in what seemed to be a case file. At last, it removed the glasses and looked up at Herbie with startling, coal-black eyes, a tiny dot of fire in the center of each.

"Dr.... Dr. Thorsen?"

"Don't blither. You know who I am. Your 24 hours now have elapsed. I hope you've made up your mind."

Herbie relaxed a little bit. "Oh, it is you. I expected... That is, I liked your previous, ah, incarnation better." He managed a weak smile.

The djinn did not smile back. "Unfortunately, after a prolonged period of incarceration, I am usually so weak as to be unable to appear in any but my original form, the one in which I was created. This hideous fact has been responsible for much trouble. However, I assure you, if I have my way, this is the only form in which you will ever see me again. Consider it a token of my sincere hope we never see each other again at all. So put temptation out of your mind! This is a professional visit, young man. Familiarity will be completely out of place."

A raucous buzzing sounded, rather like the stereotypical quiz show's reward for a boob answer. Herbie started and looked around, but the noise seemed to come from noplace in particular.

"Oh yes," the djinn said grimly, "I am required to notify you that, to assure you receive proper service, one or more of my colleagues may listen in. My Archon was displeased at the amount of advice and information I gave you yesterday. In His *opinion*, I stepped rather too close to the line. Thus, we are monitored." He pursed his lips in distaste. "I am not to influence your choice. I may offer accurate, verified information and predict consequences, if from known fact. That is all. You will hear that sound again if, in my colleagues' opinion, I depart from this course of action in the slightest particular. Now what can I do for you." The djinn made this a demand, not a question. He fixed the glasses on the end of his nose and picked up the pen.

Herbie shrugged and attempted to match the professional manner that seemed to be required. "I believe we have the matter of my heart's desire to settle between us."

The djinn inclined his head a bare inch—as Herbie recalled, Dr. Thorsen's version of a nod of assent—and over the glasses, fixed Herbie in a clinical gaze as if examining some not altogether welcome efflorescence in a Petri dish. *Shit,* he thought, *he's even got the bastard's bedside manner, playing with his glasses and flashing his $800 pen and all the time making you feel like shit for having a problem only his specialty can fix. Homophobic bastard. If he wants $250 for the visit, too, I'll...* As he seemed to be getting somewhat off the track, he pulled himself together and forged ahead.

"Very well then. My heart's desire. I want a new body, and I want the one you appeared out of the cookie box in yesterday, blond hair, green eyes, muscles, big cock and all."

The djinn put down the pen with one hand, swiped off the glasses with the other, and stared. "*That* body? *My* body?" he asked with every appearance of a being choosing its words with extreme care. "You want my aspect?"

Herbie smelt a trick, and was not about to be deflected by fancy wording. "If by that you mean the body in which you appeared out of the can yesterday, the answer is yes."

The djinn frowned angrily. "What? Surely, what you mean is..." The buzzer cut him off.

The djinn jerked his head up to look at the corner of the ceiling behind Herbie. "He has a right to understand what he's asking for, doesn't he? What if..."

Herbie whipped around to look. Up in the corner of the room was... only the corner of the room.

The djinn did not wait for him to turn back. "Young man, *that* body is my original aspect, a one-off custom creation the Archons devised for their own amusement at certain little gatherings they used to have. It is exceedingly libidinous. It ejaculates six times a day minimum, whether or not this is convenient. It attracts greedy attention everywhere. Everybody wants something from it, and it

33

wants something from everybody and usually gets it. Are you sure this is what you want? Constant sexual urgency?"

Herbie smiled. "I wouldn't change a thing. I want to be able to make people feel the way I felt when you first popped out of the box at me, so turned on they can't stand it!"

The djinn held his eye a long second. "I see." He picked up the pen and made a note. "Will there be anything else?"

"There will. Also regarding the body, I want perfect functionality. I want perfect health. I want complete, total immunity to every disease, poison, syndrome, parasite and degenerative condition that ever was, is or could be—to anything that might conceivably impair appearance or functionality. I want, in fact, eternal youth."

The djinn looked up at him over the glasses. "The word 'eternal' bothers me. It suggests immortality. This would seriously overdraw your account. Choose again."

Herbie thought a minute. "Very well. I still want perfect health and functionality as before, and I still want never to age. I ask that my life should continue until I make the decision to die."

The djinn glowered in disgust. "What happens if you get run over by a bus and lose a limb?" He leaned forward with a particularly menacing stare. "*Accidents happen.*" He underscored the words by jabbing at Herbie with the fountain pen.

"Too true. I was going on to say that, as part of my perfect health, I want instant regeneration to original condition of any part of that body which should be damaged through accident or oversight on my part in specifying these requests. I want to live in that splendid body, and I want it kept perfect and splendid until I choose to die."

The djinn was contemptuous. "Regeneration? Humph. Were I you, I'd ask for head regeneration now and skip the rest of it, and that's my sincere advice!" He sat up and pointed the pen like a finger. "Let me tell you, young man, if I *can*..." He threw a vicious glance up at the corner. "...that when that aspect was the only thing I was, being it full time was a misery..." *Bzzzzzz* "...after a century or two, anyway—a very brief space of time!" The djinn scowled.

Herbie smiled. "So what happened?"

"You, I suspect, won't last nearly as long. When the Archons finally got tired of it hanging around constantly begging to party, they recreated me full djinn—an option which will *not* be available to you."

"Well, I expect to manage. I don't intend to limit my scope of operations to a small group of the clapped out power elite. By the way, I'm glad to hear your Archon things don't hold their group gropes anymore. Evidently, they won't miss it."

"You're right. They don't hold them anymore. They grew bored. You will too, IF I must go ahead with this... A moment. I must consult my colleagues again."

The djinn stared up at the corner. When he looked down at the file again, his face was expressionless. His lips formed the word, *Assholes!* To Herbie, "You're adamant? This is your desire?"

"Yes."

"Then I suppose you must have it." He made a note. "All this will still leave a minute plus balance in your account. Have you considered the effect on your family and friends when you appear in a new and completely dissimilar body? Your condominium association, for instance? Your parents? How will you convince anyone it's you, especially with a perpetually gummy pelvic region?"

"I thought that might require some continuing investment."

"Not necessarily. We could make rewriting their memories a one-shot operation, and it would close the account neatly." He poised the pen over the file.

Really? As simple as that? He was tempted. He'd opened his mouth to agree when, with a pang, he again remembered certain of the arrangements he'd made downtown that morning, arrangements predicated solely upon the proposition "Herbie Manning" would be disappearing quickly and forever. He consoled himself with the notion of a fresh, unused life in which to start over, in which he wouldn't have to deal with his own past mistakes. "Really, I believe I'd rather make a clean break. I'd like you to put whatever balance is left into... well, into good luck," he said softly.

"Good luck? That's really rather nebulous. I'm not sure how to prescribe that."

Herbie nodded. "Then let's leave it nebulous. Let's have it affect fate in such a way as to help me get things I want—no, that, but more than that, to help me get things that are good for me, just as the universe may decide."

"Good will from the universe. How to do that not as a continuing investment..." The djinn pursed his lips in thought. "Yes, I can see a way. Perhaps here's a note of sense in the business, at last. Pity it's so small." He made a final note and closed the file. From his inside breast pocket he produced a prescription pad and scribbled on it briefly. "Well, that's that." He tore the top sheet from the pad, folded it once and pushed it over the desk. "Follow these instructions promptly, the minute I'm gone. I wish you much joy of your requests. I defy *anyone*," he said, glancing upwards, "to say I've not done my best to make this come out well all around."

He screwed the top onto his fountain pen and placed it carefully in his pocket. "I suspect you've been very unwise, and will regret your decision quite soon. The one bright spot is that I do not expect to be without my aspect for long."

The djinn stood up and scowled at him. "But no matter. You've asked, and your wishes will be granted." He walked purposefully to the fireplace. "Good luck to you, young man. Obviously, I'll be seeing you again after all—to collect, if not," he scowled again, "before." And laying a finger aside of his nose, up the chimney he rose.

Herbie smiled to himself as he looked down at the prescription:

J. THORSEN, MD, FACS
Asshole Professional

Eat me

Herbie took off all his clothes. Naked, he went to the kitchen and poured himself a glass of Chateauneuf du Pape. He balled up the

36

prescription note and washed it down. It left an incredibly bitter aftertaste.

The effect took him almost immediately. A sensation of tingling warmth at the center of his being mushroomed outwards and escalated into all-encompassing burning pain. Every cell in his body shrieked agony. He lost his balance. Writhing on the floor, he endured a sensation as if some integral and familiar part of himself was being precisely excised by a white hot knife—with infinite, painstaking care, but without the benefit of anesthetic.

After a few endless-seeming minutes, the pain reduced itself to the warm tingling with which it had begun, then subsided altogether. Rather unsteadily, he got to his feet, rather unsteadily because his body didn't seem to handle the same way at all. Out of habit, he ducked at the doorway although it was now comfortably above his head, and lost his balance again.

Unnoticed, the dark something left behind on the floor dissolved into myriad twinkling stars and disappeared.

Carefully, he stood up again and made his way to the bedroom, where the mirror revealed the realization of his wish. The djinn's body was his. He whooped for joy, and promptly lost his balance again. He toppled over backwards onto the bed. One thing, he noticed, his new body wouldn't need to be taught. A compelling, awesome fire arose in his crotch as his new cock, enormous and shapely, arose with it. He jacked it off fast, gasping as spurt after spurt after spurt after spurt of incredible ecstasy hit the ceiling.

"Fanfuckingfantastic," he sighed. As he struggled to his feet, the realization hit him that his new cock could even now be made every bit as erect as before. He had only to command. *Astounding! Delightful!* He smiled broadly.

In the next half hour, he practiced walking, sitting, standing. With practice came assurance. He was astonished at how graceful and powerful he felt. At last, for the sheer, amazing joy of it, he practiced masturbation again too.

When he had his breath back, he put on a shirt and wriggled into his new jeans. Picking up his suitcase and the briefcase with his money, he made a last, goodbye tour of the apartment, then left it forever, closing the door softly behind him.

Also behind him, the image of Herbie Manning's despised, cast-off body lingered in the bedroom mirror, which sang softly.

Under the spreading chestnut tree,
I sold you and you sold me.

The mirror considered this. "Not original, but on point," it murmured. Seconds later, it held only a darkened room.

Chapter Two
SOME VERY STRANGE BIRDS

well-known fact is that history is written by the victors. A lesser-known fact—possibly because it embarrasses the victors and undermines the rhetoric of their victories—is that no society can change its system of government overnight, no matter how passionately it may desire to do so. Old habits and expectations linger on and on and on.

Thus, after short and sharply unsatisfactory interregna, Napoleon and Hitler succeeded Louis XVI and Wilhelm II. Thus, Lenin and Stalin were tsars more capable than some and no more paranoid than some others. Thus, corrupt democracies supplant corrupt dictatorships, and vice versa. Thus, tribal societies dress up like democracies, but continue their time-honored tribal wars in their time-honored ways, and respectfully invite the world please to mind its own business (unless, of course, it would care to enrich the tribe currently ascendant). Thus, totalitarian one-party states ruled by strongmen are succeeded by democracies which express dissent by insurrection and crush it with emergency rule—and when they do vote, choose for their leader the strongest strongman around. Thus, some countries rely on coup d'etat, death squads and mob action for political process no matter who runs the place.

This is not to suggest that the deathless human struggle to change and evolve is futile. Change does take place of course, but only slowly, in response to enormous pressure, and not always in the direction visionaries might consider most useful. Thus, after decades of Marxist indoctrination, was Russia's struggle to better itself by reintroducing capitalism hampered by the people's repugnance at the thought that, under capitalism, one man might become wealthier than another.

Although there's been no particular reason to mention it before now, our story takes place well into the 21st century—in fact, in only the third year of the Great Revision. In the Great Revision, the process took one of its less dramatic forms. The Great Revision was not an advance, a step forwards with which society would have to catch up as best it might. Instead, it institutionalized changes long in the works and made them not only the facts they largely were already, but law as well.

Since then, the victors have been busy with their histories as always. Children are taught all about it in grade school civics: how the President and the Congress beseeched the world financial establishment to shoulder the burden; how the financial establishment held back out of respect for the historic Old Constitution; but how, at last, the heroic Charter Institutions made the heroic self-sacrifice, accepted the necessity for the good of all and with a single stroke of the pen prevented the total breakdown of society and kept the richest nation on earth from becoming the poorest overnight while sewing the seeds of world governance the benefits of which are now obvious to all, etc. etc. etc.

Well.

As even a civics teacher would admit, the enormous budget deficits of the late 20th and early 21st century were the root cause of the Great Revision. —To the vast surprise of the new millennium's citizens, who (a) thought the whole thing firmly under control, and (b) were sick of hearing about it, anyway.

In the 1980's the cost of the massive savings and loan debacle (who remembers that now!) and the large enrichment of defense contractors in the name of pushing the tottering Soviet Evil Empire finally over the brink quadrupled the national debt. In the early '90's, in response to public pressure, senators, congressmen and presidents talked about deficit reduction a good deal, but did no more about it than cut the rate of increase. Even then, tax cuts for the wealthy, deliberate myopia about future obligations, overly optimistic revenue projections and flat-out phony bookkeeping rendered this no more than a sop for public opinion. In the late '90's, to everyone's surprise and relief, a booming economy produced the first budget surpluses in decades, but, instead of paying down the deficit, these were used up in even more tax cuts, and in new defense spending despite the absence of any national enemy worthy of the name.

The more complicated systems become, the more unexpected ways to fail they contain. Inevitably the economy went sour. The surplusses disappeared. The deficit did not. Under pressure from all those tax cuts, the enormous pool of Baby Boomers reaching retirement age and demanding the benefits they'd paid for all their working lives, relentless pork barrel spending and image-building military adventures, the total obligation inched ever upwards with no end in sight.

Meanwhile, poorer countries sold off the last of their natural resources, the mainstays of their economies, and the American economy absorbed one third world default after another. The Oil Wars further damaged it, and when world oil reserves began to run out altogether, the worst blow of all fell, one of those good news/bad news things. A process for producing electricity from nuclear fusion proved practical at last, but utility companies naturally wished the public sector to pick up the massive tab for building the new plants rather than risk their bond ratings by borrowing that much money, and the timing of the discovery allowed them to carry their point.

Government obligations increased, but revenues faltered. While the population grew, American business continued to maximize profits by downsizing, outsourcing and decruiting its workforce, who then no longer had an income from which to pay taxes, but who certainly felt themselves entitled to retraining and basic support underwritten by tax money no one able to wanted to pay. Under job pressure from this permanent pool of people now superfluous to the economy, those who did find jobs had no choice but to accept a lower standard of living—which also meant less taxable income for the government.

Clearly, this could not continue. The day drew nearer when the government would be unable to meet its obligations and conduct public affairs at the same time.

The alternatives were debated endlessly.

Raise taxes? Impossible. Upon whom? For some time, the middle-class had been sliding down the ever more slippery slope 'twixt rich and poor into the ranks of the latter, who could pay no more. The rich, who controlled the taxing process though lobbying, political contributions and propaganda, not only would pay no more, but applied continual pressure to pay even less.

Reduce expenditures? Surely, but only to a point. Agribusiness unlimbered its wallet at the threat price supports for produce no one wanted might disappear. Defense contractors suffered agonizing withdrawal pains at the slightest suggestion of separation from the public teat, and mobilized their remaining workers, unemployed persons hopeful of jobs, fast food workers seeking better ones, and local military base communities to their cause. Elderly voters rebelled at the threats of eating catfood and going without health care. The poor threatened riot when ever more of them seemed to be raising their children in dumpsters.

Increase the money supply? The enormous inflation thus produced would ruin everybody anyway, and destroy the dollar as a world currency besides.

Renege on the national debt? Unthinkable! By this time, virtually everyone owned a piece of the national debt in one form or another, either in government securities, as pensioners or shareholders in trust companies and investment funds loaded with government paper, or as employees and shareholders of businesses dependent on banks for operating and development capital, banks themselves dependent on their government investments. Reneging was identical to the Great Default itself. The shadowy figure of ruin for all gibbered and pointed a bony finger everywhere you looked.

Still the day drew closer. Eventually, the very date when default must occur could be determined by the innermost Treasury circles. Efforts to shroud the dread date in secrecy were unavailing as government officials scurried frantically in search of some, any solution to the problem. Rumor rampaged. On the rare days it was allowed to open at all, the stock market plunged and surged hundreds of points, flushing wealth from the system at an astonishing rate. Ordinary citizens quit their jobs and went on binges spending every cent they had. The price of gold and collectibles skyrocketed as wiser persons bought valuables, only to be robbed of them by those who'd spent their money. The police no longer could cope, and in some places participated in the sacking. Vigilance committees sprang up everywhere. Preachers proclaimed it God's curse for tolerating abortion, homosexuality, socialism and rock 'n roll, and many believed. The foundations of America's financial industry, already in recession, cracked and rumbled, dangling the nation over the abyss of depression. The price of government paper wobbled and wavered but did not fall. Wiser bankers realized there was, in effect, no longer enough of anything but other government paper for which to trade the vast quantities of it they possessed. Allowing its price to fall would produce the very cataclysm all sought to avoid.

Now, if you or I overextend ourselves to the point we are unable to pay our bills, we declare bankruptcy. We then may be absolved of our transgression with the stern admonition to go forth and sin no more, or, if our debts are more substantial, our creditors may band together either to dissolve us and split our assets, or set us up to run again under their watchful supervision. If a major institution threatens failure, one on which the wealth of the ruling elite depends, the government steps in as lender of last resort to save it "for the good of all." But when the richest government on earth fails, who can save it?

Foreign lenders were appalled, and not merely at the large quantities of U.S. government paper they possessed. They had weathered the default of the third world, and might very well weather the default of America as well. But with America bankrupt, their largest, best and easiest export market would be gone, and with themselves in weakened condition from the losses they had sustained in all these defaults, could worldwide financial implosion be far behind?

A truly imaginative solution was needed, and one which would not affect workers, small investors, retirees, shopkeepers and pension plan participants, in short, the ordinary people without whose toleration no government can survive for long.

Historians disagree. Some say the banks waited until the world teetered upon the brink because it took them that long to agree on their plans. Others maintain that they waited solely because, from the first, they intended their control to be total. Their fiat had to be non-negotiable; there must be no time for argument. In any case, less than 24 hours before the Great Default must be declared, Harrison Keeler Frogmorton III, Chairman of the nation's third largest bank, appeared in the Oval Office before the President, Cabinet, Chief Justice and Congressional leaders assembled to proclaim the Consortium Council.

It was quite simple, really: in secret, "so as not to alarm the public," a Consortium had been formed of all the world's largest banks. Together, he said, while American taxpayers concentrated on paying off their obligation, the Consortium would guarantee the nation's most essential expenses. The Secretary of the Treasury broke into nervous sobs of relief. Excited babble upwelled in the room.

Frogmorton lifted a cautionary finger. Naturally, he said, there were a few, ah, conditions. The babble ceased as if cut off with a switch. If the banks were to place their own credit and future stability on the line, it was only fair they should have control over how their credit was used. Therefore, the Consortium Council, of which he, Frogmorton, had been made president so that an American still should be visibly in control, would henceforth rule by decree over all fiscal concerns of the United States government, including (but not limited to) taxation, budget, purchasing, currency, reserve bank lending—the works. There would be no appeal from these decrees. Naturally, the Consortium also would need absolutely unlimited powers of investigation and enforcement to root out every trace of waste, fraud and corruption. Naturally.

In the ensuing silence, Frogmorton produced the Agreement. He placed it on the President's desk and extended his own gold fountain pen, uncapped.

It's outrageous! roared the President, *Ah won't touch it!*

It's flagrantly unconstitutional! opined the Chief Justice.

That's right! said the Speaker, *There'd have to be a Constitutional Amendment! An Act of Congress!*

An Act of God! said the Secretary of the Interior, who had been a preacher and knew Him personally.

Frogmorton shrugged, put the Agreement away and turned to go.

Uh, hold on thar, young feller, said the President.

Fifteen minutes later, Frogmorton did leave—with the signed Agreement in his pocket. He gave the President his pen as a souvenir. Congress passed the requisite Amendment in short order, becoming the first politicians since the Roman Senate to legislate themselves into obsolescence voluntarily, and with relief, at that. God's comments went unrecorded. Nobody paid any attention to the Chief Justice's.

As for the people, they barely noticed the change. Although the Consortium's new powers of investigation and enforcement eliminated the last of their judicial protections, decades of struggle to combat the moving, often invisible and sometimes illusory targets of crime and terrorism, and of holy war against drugs, sex criminals and pornography already had increased police power and reduced the people's rights to privacy and due process to the point they had not many left to lose.

During those same decades, increasingly poor education and the unrelenting barrage of television sound bites had accustomed the people to making electoral decisions on the basis of loyalty to the flag, crime in the streets and abortion. In these things, they were quite sincerely assured, the Consortium Council had no interest. The people's elected representatives would continue to exercise 100% of the authority they always had.

Oh yes, taxes. The Consortium made its most solemn promise *never* to raise taxes on the poor and middle-class, a promise it actually kept, for a while.

The Consortium Council became the fourth and by far the most powerful branch of government. The United States of America ceased to be a republic and became what it secretly had hankered to be since the very days of its founding: a plutocracy. What the hell, it was better than going broke.

The Consortium Council did not fool around. They were businessmen, as they would tell you if you were so unfortunate as to be buttonholed by them at lunch. As such, they were uncomfortable with any concern, large or small, running at a loss. There was no reason, they would tell you, why the United States couldn't be run according to sound, proven business principles. Not only should it not run at a loss, but eventually—and here their voices would lower and their flinty eyes gleam—it might be made to show a profit for its investors, that is, themselves. Want to buy some bank stock?

Immediately upon taking power, the Consortium addressed its concerns about waste and fraud. As virtually its first official action, the Consortium Council established a vast security apparatus, the Commission to Reduce Accounting Problems, to deal with those attempting to interfere with profit. Hastily formed as an interlocking web of Treasury agencies, bank security departments and private consulting firms, its agents answered only to the Council, which answered to no one.

After a short but highly embarrassed interval, the Council's second official action outlawed any reference to their new Commission by its acronym, an injunction ignored by high and low, at least at first.

During the early period in which our story takes place, when the roles of all governmental bodies were shifting in doubt, CRAP was all powerful, and somewhat secretive about its personnel and their powers too, lest people be alarmed at the sudden elimination of the last of their personal rights. The full extent of its control was largely a mystery to those not directly concerned. CRAP was actually a sort of evil joke for a while. An employer might gently warn an erring employee to shape up, "before you become an accounting problem." Later, of course, "to become an accounting problem" held much more sinister implications. Nobody joked about it then. In the end, the United States was only briefly a plutocracy. It turned itself into a police state with almost indecent haste.

In years to come, the bureaucracy and the army together obtained some control over CRAP. Eventually, the three of them—the bureaucracy, the army and CRAP—ruled America together, just as the party, the army and the KGB ruled the USSR at the height of America's anti-communist hysteria, which is an irony.

On the day our story resumes, a morning not quite three months after Herbie Manning walked out of his own life forever, the most fearsome of these eventualities were still comfortably in the future. In the lingering joy and relief at society's recent salvation by the Consortium Council, speculations about them were the sole province of gloomy left-wing cranks, who were themselves distinctly out of countenance these days. There was no taint in the air to spoil the joy a young man might feel hurrying through Chicago's canyons to a job he loved.

On this, another brilliant day, the sun dazzled off thousands of gold-, blue- and mirror-tinted panes. Clean-lined stone spires yearned upwards as if toward financial security, as if aspiring to touch that great clearinghouse which surely must lie just beyond the soft blue dome of the sky. The city hissed its usual workaday tune of telephones, computers and electric cars.

Flocks of pigeons wheeled among the towers as Greg Whitbread turned into AmalCon Plaza, starting bunches of the small gray neurotics into the air. *Awwk! How dare you interrupt our breakfast of this delicious trash! Awwk! Go away, or we'll shit on your briefcase!*

Greg smiled as the pigeons settled back down behind him, rather crossly, he thought. *Silly birds.* As he approached The Amalgamated Consolidated Confederated International Bank Building, he craned skywards, an eager victim of vertigo as his mind tried automatically to resolve the tower's parabolic upward curve with the vertical pull of gravity. The multi-level plaza, all steps, terraces and fountains, contributed to the effect. *Probably deliberate,* he thought. *Keeps the depositors' minds off counting their less-cash-returned.* His smile grew wider.

He strode along the great glass windows of the main floor lobby, checking himself out sideways in the glass while trying hard not to be too obviously narcissistic. His hand reached automatically to straighten a tie that didn't need it. *Perfect,* he thought.

He definitely approved what he saw: pearl gray slacks above black loafers with gold doodads echoing navy blue blazer's gold buttons echoing short sandy hair. Was the burgundy tie a little too blatant? No, with the blue blazer and white shirt, a patriotic touch! The grin on his peaches-and-cream face threatened to become idiotic. He rejected it in favor of his well-practiced expression of sober competence, the expression usually worn only by IRS auditors and sufferers from chronic irregularity. Altogether, the impression was of a trim, athletically set up and conventional young man hurrying to a meeting with superiors for which he was about to be precisely on time. Just right.

The glass wall ended abruptly. Greg tumbled out into Dearborn Street foot traffic, and almost collided with a uniformed security man munching a McSoyburger. Sorry!

Inside, the gray granite elevator lobby echoed emptily. Most of them upstairs already, he thought, hard at work making, losing, trading numbers. An elevator stood open, its stainless steel interior clinical, antiseptic. In his imagination, he broke a strip of paper whenever he entered an elevator at AmalCon: "Sanitized for Your Protection." The doors hissed shut. He pushed 70 and was lifted.

This very self-satisfied young man, the rising star in the offices of Catchem, Billem & Stickem, Accountants, Investigators & Collectors, approached his first solo meeting with his firm's biggest client eagerly. He'd been told only that they would discuss a new assignment. Who knew what it might be or where it would take him? Although the drudging number crunching and poring over computer records might, and probably would come later, this was the best part: learning the new story.

Some Very Strange Birds

The doors whished open on a long dark narrow empty hallway. At its distant terminus, like the tunnel's end in a Freudian dream, beckoned the well-lit outer office of Morgan Jaye, AmalCon's Senior Executive Corporate Vice-President for Customer Security. Less commonly known as the appointment was really quite recent, Mr. Jaye was also Central Regional Director of CRAP.

The building's general gray granite theme repeated itself in Mr. Jaye's anteroom. Four rough-hewn gray granite walls kept the corrugated stainless steel ceiling and the discreet gray rug from sandwiching the only spot of color in the place: Morgan Jaye's receptionist at her gray granite table. This lady seemed chosen particularly to accent the room—neon orange-red hair, very pale complexion, brilliant scarlet dress, even red nail polish. Greg wondered idly whether Jaye had a fit if she wore a different color. Or maybe the bank bought her clothes. This seemed unlikely, but on Mr. Jaye's ionospherically executive level, who knew? She had a magazine open on her gray granite. Stylishly togged jocks played tennis, caught in mid-lob. *Sports Illustrated? Better Bra & Jockstrap?* "Good morning, Mr. Whitbread. He's expecting you." As she repeated his name into her viewscreen, she eyed him approvingly, up and down. For an instant, they made a neat tableau, she watching him, he caught by the tennis players. Ultimately, the jocks rather spoiled the effect, having eyes only for each other.

"You can go in now." He looked up and nodded brightly. Her eyes followed him as double doors to her right glided apart, silhouetting him in a blinding beam of sunlight. As he advanced to be swallowed into its golden depths, his hand raised itself once again to straighten the tie that didn't need it.

Mr. Jaye's corner office contrasted sharply with the gray granite building core. His 800 square feet of floor seemed to float between glass walls. The room swept up a full two stories in height and contained a thick jungle of plants, some of which nearly touched the ceiling. Gaps in their foliage offered dazzling glimpses of the city below. The calls of exotic birds played from concealed speakers.

Although banking was Mr. Jaye's business, birds were his passion. Greg had heard he was well respected in ornithological circles as a sometime sponsor of study expeditions to the planet's remoter places. He also had a fine collection of birds himself, though rigid import restrictions meant this collection could be of no particularly arcane interest, rather sadly for Mr. Jaye, perhaps.

"I had live birds here once," Jaye had remarked to Greg and his boss, Wiley Catchem, on a previous occasion, "but the Housekeeping Department complained they messed the carpet. Cretins."

"What happened to them?" Greg had asked, as Catchem nudged his ribs with a sharp little elbow.

Jaye's brows contracted. "The Housekeeping Department?" he asked blandly. "They got their wish."

"The birds, sir." Catchem poked him again, harder.

"My wife didn't want them, either," Jaye said, while Catchem inspected the ceiling for cracks. "Cockateel stew is dreadful. So is divorce."

This time, Greg resolved to concentrate only on the business at hand. He strode up the beam of sunlight toward the clearing at jungle's end. Behind the desk, a two-inch slab of plate glass set across gray granite supports, Mr. Jaye looked a little like a bird himself, that is, if birds could weigh 300-plus pounds and rattle glass coffee cups on their glass saucers with deep bass calls.

Jaye waved him at a chair. "It'll be just a second while I copy the file for you." He spoke a command at his viewscreen, an angled slab of otherwise clear glass loaded with LCD circuitry, and kept his attention there.

Greg sank into a chrome and rubber mesh chair, and waited. For a man who wielded such awing power, Jaye was normal enough looking, if very imposing. Several thousand dollars' worth of dark gray broadcloth three-piece suit, silk shirt and English shoes encased his vast bulk. His large face was florid. A strip of gray hair encircled a bald pate and ran down the sides of his face to meet at the bottom in a beard. Normal? Rather like a crafty Burl Ives. A hooked nose and bushy tufted eyebrows above sharp little gray eyes made the birdlike impression so startling in a man of his bulk.

The credenza behind Jaye's desk whirred softly and emitted sheets of paper. Except for the tray that received them, the glass viewscreen on its stand and the usual small equipment, the desk and credenza were bare. Greg noted with approval that the immense litter of papers and files he had seen here on previous visits was nowhere in evidence. AmalCon was a conservative institution rather behind the curve on office automation; paper had largely disappeared from internal operations in many businesses some time since, being reserved for when law or courtesy required a hard-copy signature, or for occasions, presumably such as the present, when material must leave the building it might be desirable to protect from the uncertain security of the information superhighway.

This evidence Jaye's operation was coming up to date impressed Greg a good deal. As, to his certain knowledge, the rest of the bank still buried itself in paper, the upgrade here could only be CRAP's doing. They really seemed to have their act together. Greg looked forward eagerly to impressing Mr. Jaye in return. This could be the best chance to show his stuff he'd had in a while.

Jaye swivelled for the file. "I have something here which will interest you."

"Another absconder, sir?"

"Well, yes and no. This one didn't work for AmalCon—or at least, hadn't in some time. Free-lance accountant. Had been for..." he checked the file "...some four years now. Small clients, mostly, not one over a million dollars in yearly gross." Jaye fixed him in a direct unblinking stare that made Greg squirm. "Odd-looking bird, tall, gangly, beady eyes—like a stork." He made a face as if he rather liked storks and wasn't happy insulting them with the comparison. "But then, you know him, don't you? Here he is." Jaye passed a page bearing a single large graphic over the desk to a surprised and suddenly alarmed Greg.

Herbie Manning! Greg's eyes rolled heavenwards. Conscious that Jaye was gauging his reaction, he controlled his face and studied the picture. In fact, he remembered it. Manning had won the bike race at AmalCon's annual picnic one year. When had it been? Oh, a long time ago, while they'd both still worked here. The event had been commemorated in the bank's house organ. There he was, all pipestem arms and legs draped over a 10-speed bike. Tight racing shorts showed knobby knees and big feet. Above the arms and legs was the typical baseball cap and foolish grin. Greg's stomach churned in revulsion at the sight. At the bottom was the picture caption: "Analyst Herbert Manning (Securities) won the mile sprint and showed us all how to give customers a run for their money."

Greg chose his words with care. "Yes, sir. We worked together in the Securities Department when I first got out of college." He shifted uncomfortably.

"Well, the staff wonders if there weren't a bit more between you than that. The records show Manning made a massive effort to get you hired in the first place."

"Yes, sir, as he never ceased to remind me." *Damn Herbie Manning to hell,* he thought furiously. Would the trouble he caused never cease? How unfair!

He forced himself back to the immediate problem, this line of questioning, which was going alarmingly. "I didn't know him before I came here. I had one interview with him, and others with other people. Then I was hired, and everybody was looking at me funny. He never ceased to pester me. He was... very personal, sir. He never let up! Everybody seemed to think we were... And when he left..." How could he describe *that* to Morgan Jaye? He probably didn't have to. Greg wilted. His hand strayed from his lap toward his tie. "...well, I've never seen him again."

Jaye's hard stare softened, but not a lot. "The file does indicate Manning's, ah, homosexual proclivities. That must have been very disturbing in a co-worker." His tone was neutral, an interrogator's on a fishing expedition.

"Very, sir." Greg looked at the floor.

Jaye nodded. "Yes. The unanimous opinion of your co-workers from the time is that you probably bear him some animosity. Do you? Would you like to be the one to bring him to justice?"

No! No! Just keep him away from me! was Greg's instantaneous panic reaction. *Anything but that!* But turn down business? For personal reasons? Wiley Catchem wouldn't like that at all. And then, Greg himself had spent many a morning shower fulminating to himself about just what he'd like to do to Herbie Manning if he ever got the chance—which, possibly, had just arrived.

He did his best to match Jaye's cold efficient tone. "I'll gladly do whatever I have to, sir. 110%. What's he done?"

Jaye nodded again, and seemed to make his decision. Looking down, he turned papers in the file. "Very well. The facts are these: investigation shows Manning to have been behaving in character until..." another glance at the papers "...April 2nd. He even took what was, for him, a fairly sizable job the day before. However, on the 2nd, he appeared in the business lobby downstairs and turned all his available assets into cash. Then he disappeared."

"Assets, sir?"

"Closed out his brokerage and checking accounts, and cashed in his securities and IRA—incurring several substantial pre-maturity penalties, I might add. When he was done, he had in excess of $70,000. He took this in cash, in $100 bills.

"On his way out of the building, he stopped to use the ATMs. He withdrew funds against his credit accounts up to the limit. What he did next is the problem area. He had account information on a number of individuals and small companies obtained through his business. He seems to have used his own cash card to raid these accounts, quite a number of them at different banks on the network. Inside half an hour, he exhausted the funds from all three machines, more than $100,000. Luckily, it was after the lunchtime rush, or it might have been more."

Greg was intrigued, his discomfort forgotten. "But how did he... I thought it was impossible to..."

"It *is* impossible!" Jaye roared, and Greg jumped. "I supervised the safeguards on that system personally, and I will assure you there is absolutely no way to access more accounts than actually are encoded on the card! But he did it, and I want to know how!"

"Oh. I think I'm beginning..."

"To understand why I'm personally involved in the theft of a mere $100,000? Yes. We replaced the amounts stolen from his clients, in most cases before they knew anything was wrong, and apologized for a 'clerical error' to the rest while rectifying their inconveniences. No one must ever know this is possible, at least before we find out how he did it and ensure it cannot be done again."

"No clues in system programming?"

"Obviously, I am investigating that. Our consultant, Garrison Griffin, who designed the system, confesses himself baffled, as I am myself. I have an entire roomful of people checking over every line of program code connected with the ATM system, the computers connected to the system, and as far back up the line as we can go. There is no clue yet, but that is not necessarily surprising when you consider the millions of code lines to be analyzed. It could be years before we find what we're looking for this way, and if it's cleverly done, we might never find it at all."

Griffin's name had struck a spark in Greg's mind. "You know, Manning and Griffin were really very chummy while I was here." Greg himself had once thought Griffin's friendship might be advantageous to his career, but had never managed to get close to the man.

Jaye gave him a piercing look. "Yes. Others have remembered that too. I have some of my brightest people on it, but so far, they haven't succeeded in linking Griffin to this. And may never. If he were involved, he would have had the opportunity to remove the computer evidence immediately after the theft, before any alarms were raised—but then there's this: Griffin was himself a client of Manning's. His account was raided and his money replaced by us along with the rest."

"Smokescreen."

"Possibly." Jaye scowled. "However, in the absence of actual evidence, suspicion regarding this institution's most trusted confidential consultant must remain on hold. We have him under minute covert observation—which is for your ears only, at present." Greg nodded. "Meanwhile, the investigation continues. The point here is that, if we could solve this business without Manning, I might be prepared to forget about him and bury the $100,000." Jaye waved a lordly hand. "I'd post it as consulting expenses paid him for pointing out a flaw in our system and refer him to the IRS-

Enforcement Division as a tax cheat. However, it looks as if we are, indeed, going to need him, and as long as we do, I'll have the $100,000 back too, out of his gangly pock-marked carcass, if necessary. I want him!"

"It's been three months! What do we have on his whereabouts?"

"Nothing firm, and were it not for a fluke, nothing at all. This Manning turned out a great deal cleverer than his personnel file would suggest." The big man frowned. "Later that same day, April 2nd, he said hello to one of his neighbors in the hall on the way to his apartment. It's all in here." He tapped the file. "Unfortunately, he was not there when my men showed up at 6:00 the following morning. No one saw him leave. Furthermore, if he packed at all, he didn't take much. No clothes, possibly. Most of his drawers and closets appeared fully loaded. He has not been seen since. No trace of him whatsoever has been found."

Greg looked up sharply. That was interesting. In these days of massive personal documentation, interlocking data nets and omnipresent video surveillance, getting lost and staying lost for any length of time was nearly impossible, and CRAP's first order of business had been to acquire all the best, most experienced trackers in the business. That they had found nothing was suggestive. "How sure are you..."

"That it wasn't foul play of some kind? Considering the nature of certain elements of his client list, we can't be. However, one piece of possibly relevant evidence was found in the apartment." Jaye produced a piece of paper, torn, and pieced back together in a clear plastic slip.

> Dear Mom and Dad,
> By the time this reaches you, I shall be gone, probably forever...

"This suggests his course of action to have been voluntary, but not conclusively. I have people checking into the foul play possibility, looking back into his personal and business relationships as far as we can go. Frankly, if he doesn't turn up soon, his will be one of the more fully documented lives on record anywhere, and it's all solid dead ends!" Jaye's roar broke into an unexpected squawk that startled them both. For an instant, the banker looked quite disconcertingly mad, his eyes gleaming and beady like a parrot's.

"Yes, sir." Greg cleared his throat. "You said something about a..."

"A fluke? Yes I did." The big man recovered himself. "That's why you're here. We had some luck tracing the money. Oh, not the cash from the ATMs. That's unrecorded, unfortunately. Luckily, it so happened that when the floor officer sent down for the $70,000 in $100 bills Manning withdrew from his own accounts, the staff were just unpacking a new shipment from the Federal Reserve Division, and made up his package off the top of that. Thus, by deduction, we know what serial numbers they gave him. Some of those bills were used that same evening at the Amtrak ticket desk at Union Station, though no ticket was sold in the name of Manning and none of the clerks on duty remember who might have given them those particular bills. Nor do they recognize his picture. Nor has he been seen in any of the general surveillance video taken that night at Union Station or at any other point of exit from the city. We would have expected him to stand out because of his height. However, just recently, a few more of the bills have turned up, in New York City. Again, Manning does not appear, but the money does."

"I see. You want our firm to go to New York, wait for more money to surface, and chase down who's passing it."

"In a nutshell, yes. We've made that money hot, just as if it were marked money involved in some crime or other. In fact, that's the story we used—not too far wrong, either. Your job will be to trace it."

"Cash." Greg made a professional grimace. "Always a problem."

"Indeed," said Jaye feelingly. "Expensive to produce and handle, liable to counterfeiting, difficult to trace. We've tried to eliminate it, and will just as soon as we can ease the public into paying a transaction fee to buy a stick of gum. Without cash, this would have been a simple matter."

Greg frowned. "As I understand it, the part we can trace is only $70,000 out of $170,000 or thereabouts, and it's in $100's while the unrecorded money is in $20's the way it came out of the ATMs. Why would he use $100's if he doesn't have to?"

"I acknowledge the problem. The search for those bills has been intense, but only six have turned up. Obviously, he's using the other money, mainly, if, in fact, it is even he who is using it. That, please note, has not been established. Damn it, it's the only clue we have of any sort, whatever! At least, the money must lead in his direction."

Greg nodded. "Okay. So, in case no more of it turns up right away, I assume you can give us other places to start looking. Manning's New York acquaintances? Hobbies? Lifestyle?" Greg winced at the word the instant it was out of his mouth.

"It's all in here. Although none of it is producing anything, it surely won't hurt for you, with your personal knowledge of the subject, to turn it over again while you're out there. I don't envy you. His taste in society seems, ah, unusually repugnant, in the main." Jaye made a delicate gesture, as if the very paper on which the facts were recorded shared in this repugnance by association. Recorded birdcalls broke through the stillness. A great modern sunlit city peeked through the jungle.

"The other teams are drones. If this can be solved by droning, they'll do it, but I rather think it will take more." Jaye's credenza beeped self-importantly and produced a small gold and white rectangle. Jaye reached for it and passed it over. "Naturally, you'll be given every assistance."

Greg caught his breath. A CRAP card, and it had his name and hologram on it! He would be omnipotent! He stared at Jaye, unbelieving.

Jaye nodded solemnly. "You, personally, are to head the New York investigation. Use your own people or any of ours. I've watched you working with Wiley, and with your personal connection to the subject... You show great promise, an aptitude for the work. You now have great power to match, temporarily. Use it in my interest, find me Manning and the money, and the reward will be equally great. I am prepared to take a strong interest in your future, to assign you to the Commission permanently and attach you to my personal staff."

Greg gulped, bugeyed. "I will not let you down, sir."

Jaye nodded. "I know you're young, but I have full confidence in you to use your intellect as enlightened by experience."

Greg spoke softly now. "And Manning? What will happen to him?"

"Don't you worry about him." Jaye smiled pleasantly. "Once I've finished with him, he'll be birdseed."

* * * * *

Quite unexpectedly, Greg realized that, while he'd thought his problem was knowing Herbie Manning too well, in reality, he hadn't known him nearly as well as he'd thought.

After the morning in Morgan Jaye's office, the first step had seemed to be spending the afternoon at Manning's apartment looking over the file Jaye had given him and refreshing his memory of Herbie's personality, however distasteful that might be. The apartment shocked him. It revealed irritating depths to the slovenly offensive insinuatingly familiar bore he'd come to know and loathe at AmalCon.

The books were the first thing. The place was stuffed with books, thousands of them. Shelving covered every available square foot of wall space, even in the kitchen and the bathroom! History, philosophy, current events and literature—especially literature. As best Greg could determine from his own distinctly perfunctory education in the subject, Herbie's library—there simply was no other word—encapsulated a pocket history of the novel from the seventeenth century to the present. While it amazed Greg to think anybody actually might have read all this stuff, much of it bore Herbie's personal touch: his name and a date on the flyleaf, notes penciled in the back. Herbie's books bespoke a sincere interest in literature and, in these days when tablet viewscreens and books in datacapsule form were making inroads into the publishing trade, possibly an antiquarian collector's interest, as well.

Greg himself wasn't much of a reader. His preference in entertainment ran to movies and TV, with only occasional light reading thrown in. This latter all came from the office: generally, beat up paperbacks and hypernovel datacapsules he read and passed along. Mysteries were big at the office, especially those with embezzling crimes in them. Reading these and sniggering at the stupidity of the detectives and the hopelessly implausible plots were essential to smalltalk around the coffee machine—which sometimes made getting through the things more like work than fun.

Herbie liked this sort of stuff too. Besides his serious books, popular paperbacks filled a wall in the bedroom, mostly mysteries and science fiction. Altogether, Herbie's apartment boasted a vast amount of the printed word to be found all in one place at one time, Greg thought.

Next came the music. The apartment contained more than six hundred CDs and datacapsules of music, nearly all of them classical. The only sort of music Greg knew much about was the popular kind the radio played over and over again. Classical music was an impenetrable wilderness: indistinguishable composers and periods, dark tuneless melodies and endless ways to embarrass oneself in party conversation. Oh, he knew the famous numbers everyone knew: Beethoven's Ninth, the 1812 Overture and William Tell, whom he identified dimly as the piece's composer. For the rest, he couldn't see the point of finding out anything about it, supposing he'd known how. Yet Herbie seemed to know it well.

The rest of the apartment also fit the impression of a cultured person with educated taste. The furniture was old and solid with plain lines, immaculately restored finishes and new upholstery. Top-quality appliances gleamed in a contemporary kitchen. A large oriental rug smiled up at the living room, its pattern an intricate array of bright blue, white, red and yellow birds going about their business in a flowering tree. A carefully tended collection of plants loaded a bay window.

Greg himself never had more than one plant at a time, received as the occasional gift. These invariably died of neglect. "The man who invents the self-watering plant will make his fortune," was Greg's stock comment about plants. Herbie's all bore little tags with the address and room number of Morgan Jaye's office, clearly awaiting only the end of the investigation to become part of the big man's jungle. Jaye's reputation as a discriminating collector spoke well for Herbie's taste in this area too. Greg wondered what would happen to the rest of Herbie's things, among them expensive knickknacks, antique clocks, an impressive sound system, the latest in entertainment-quality viewscreens, a marble-topped dining room table.

One interesting thing: the file said a cache of five marijuana plants also had been found, flourishing under lights in the pantry. Tsk tsk. He went to look. Only the lights themselves and a few crumbs of dirt scattered on the floor remained.

From the pantry, he carried his investigation out into the kitchen, where the largest spice rack he'd ever seen, including some he'd never heard of, dominated a wall. The well-stocked refrigerator reminded Greg, who relieved the monotony of burgers and pizza with frozen dinners, of his mother's, except he didn't recall eating this elaborately as a child. Greek olives, pesto, tandoori sauce—what on earth were capers? Looked nasty, whatever they were. Four bottles of beer with an unfamiliar label, some tiny microbrewery, caught his eye. He grimaced in disgust as the apartment's atmosphere of connoisseurship started to get to him. *How pretentious!*

Herbie's home impressed and intimidated Greg in spite of himself. This made him angry, that this thief, this *faggot* thief—that *HERBIE*, forchrissake—could have this effect on him.

Only the clothes made him feel better. Herbie had no taste in clothes whatsoever. He favored shapeless jeans and baggy sweaters. All the socks had holes. The apartment contained no underwear at all. Had he packed it? Perhaps he just never wore any. *Ick.* As Greg fingered this miserable collection—an act which made

60

him itch to wash his hands—his natural superiority returned. His hand strayed to his expertly chosen burgundy tie. He smiled at himself in the mirror and reflected that, after all, if you looked like Herbie, how much good could clothes do you, really?

He sat down at Herbie's desk and opened the file. Manning's work presented more puzzles. Greg was used to embezzlers. He knew what to expect in their ledgers: a tendency to sloppiness, a carelessness over nickels and dimes, questionable deductions, and small thefts gradually growing larger over time. Manning's work showed none of this. His accounting work was as precise, accurate and ethical as Greg's own. His corporate clients all claimed to have received excellent service. Many had demanded to know when he'd be back. They thought him indispensable! Why, Greg wondered, did a guy like this, respected and depended upon by his professional contacts, a careful planner, suddenly go berserk and rip everybody off? How could this happen?

True, there was an entirely different and rather surprising element on Manning's client list as well: a cabal of middle-management types discovered in the course of this investigation to be operating a multi-level marketing scheme in illicit substances, several antique dealers trafficking big-ticket items of possibly unstable provenance, and a well-known circle of professional gamblers. For this clientele, Manning appeared to have provided a cautious money-laundering service, advice on tax-free investments and, doubtless, on day-to-day recordkeeping and ways and means too.

He'd been both careful and resourceful. IRS-Enforcement had no file on his activities in these areas. Of course, Manning wouldn't have known that. Maybe he'd lost his nerve. This illegal activity was a relatively recent development in his business. He wouldn't have been accustomed to the pressures involved. Perhaps he'd developed paranoid delusions over routine delays in bank processing and strangers who happened to follow him in the street. Could this have caused his flight?

Greg shook his head. His flight would have shown more preparation: with only a little planning, he could have avoided taking the dousing he had on his securities. Besides, for someone capable of the careful, almost elegant balancing of risk and reward with which Manning managed his illegal trade, it was just too thin. The punishment nowadays for this kind of activity was a fine—a very stiff, punitive fine, but still only a fine. In fact, as the Consortium Council struggled to increase revenues and decrease prison costs, the punishment for virtually all crimes except those of wantonly depraved violence had become a fine. Grand larceny, however, was an exception. You still went to jail for that, and stealing $100,000 was definitely grand larceny. Thus, if any such thing had been Manning's motivation, his crime was a stupid one on its face—it risked a jail sentence atop the fine. Tracing people was one of CRAP's specialties. Manning, as an ex-AmalCon accountant with connections in many places, had to have known they'd find him no matter where he fled. Except they hadn't. Greg frowned.

Of course, a more likely possibility was that, somewhere along the line, Manning had turned one of his shady clients into an enemy, an enemy worth fleeing for his life. This was an attractive possibility, the one everybody thought most likely. By far the largest portion of the Manning field force was engaged on it at this very moment. The information on Manning's clients and their illegal activities became more interesting daily. Yet, not only could none of them be connected to past crimes of violence, being in the main dabblers just like himself, they had no obvious grounds for dissatisfaction. He appeared to have served them cleverly and well. Though his fees had been abnormally large to this clientele, he did seem to have acted strictly in their interests, just as in his legal trade. The investigation continued.

Altogether, examination of Manning's business had so far left unresolved the problem of why all of a sudden he needed $100,000 and why he was willing to risk so much to get it.

Neither did his personal life answer these questions. In fact, it raised others. Wouldn't a fellow like Manning—well-read, obviously discerning—know other people like himself? Wouldn't he want people with whom to listen to his music and talk about his books? Why, instead, would the greatest portion of his acquaintance be among the male prostitutes at the sleazebag Attaché Arms Hotel a few blocks away?

Greg sat at Herbie's desk, chin on his hands, as he considered this question. Manning's education and taste were genuine. The apartment brooked no denial of that, despite the equally incontrovertible testimony from the fun-loving crew down at the Attaché Arms. The consensus held that, for a john, he was okay. A guy could make $50 or $100 from him if he really needed it. He'd buy marijuana or hash if the price was fair. If a fellow got into real trouble and wound up on the street, Manning would let him crash at the apartment for a few days, if he'd behave. Manning was slippery about giving promises—he was still a john!—but always kept the ones he made.

Despite fond expectations, the team had not found the kind of trouble here they had expected. Manning had run through money steadily with hustlers, but not more than he could afford. Further, CRAP's investigation showed that none of the hard-core Attaché boys were connected to drug or crime business big enough to give Manning a $100,000 problem, a problem serious enough to make robbery and disappearance appear worthwhile. It seemed no one, including crime heavies, trusted male hustlers. A sleazy guy was a sleazy guy. Besides, the boys themselves seemed to have shielded Manning from serious involvement in such illegal trades as did exist at the Attaché Arms—other than their own, that is.

This was not because they liked him. In fact, they despised him! Despite his value, he was still only a john, there to give as greatly as needed for as little in return as possible. Yet, an honest, relatively dependable john being about as rare as an honest, relatively dependable hustler, they also valued him as a community resource. They even claimed to have disciplined the occasional jerk who'd behaved a bit too rapaciously, lest Manning be spoiled for everybody. Their thieves' honor burned hot and bright in the transcripts. Greg found it all moderately unbelievable.

There was more. Though sleeping with whores might be merely practical to anyone as homely as Manning, the level of social interaction suggested something deeper. The boys' only complaint was that he was around too much, always including himself in, even when he didn't seem to be in the market for anything particular. He seemed to want to be accepted, to be *friends*. This meant they had to be friendly and interested in him in return with no guarantee they'd get anything for it right then—a real hassle.

Greg shook his head. Here was a fellow, a seemingly acute and canny businessman who, in his spare time, played denmother to a gang of dirtballs. Could he really interpret their greedy regard as genuine respect? Such things were far from unheard of among normal, heterosexual people, obviously. Lots of solid citizens had blind spots where their sleazy itches were concerned. Why just last year that Rev. Whatsisname had been uncovered at the Peekaboo Motel on Cermak Road doing "missionary work" with an exotic dancer, or so he'd said—and sure enough, the lady had confirmed that, yes, he had spent an awful lot of their time together on his knees. The press remained deeply suspicious.

Maybe it was something like that, or maybe not. Rescuing the fallen didn't jive very well with Greg's own, personal experience of Manning's proclivities. He shrugged. Whatever the explanation, Greg now had a solid lead where in New York to go looking for Manning. If he was there to be found at all, hustlers might not be far away.

He felt himself going cold as the implications settled over him. Where did one start looking in New York for male prostitutes? How would he know?—and what would he do once he did? *He* wasn't queer, he told himself. Disturbed and angry, he rose from Herbie Manning's desk and stalked about the apartment, lost in increasingly muddled reflections of his own.

Not until he'd made the entire circuit and come back to the desk did he spot it: a brass letter opener peeked from beneath a pile of paper, evidently an antique, the broad blade held firmly, impossibly, between the jaws of a fox whose curving body served as the handle. It had about it an air of power and respectability—a hint of secrecy and sneakery too. He stared at it. It stared back. It seemed to sum up Manning for him in a way no other single object in the apartment could. On impulse, he picked it up and put it into his briefcase.

He froze. Had it, the fox, *winked* one hooded brass eye at him just as he'd closed the lid? Impossible. Too bizarre to contemplate. His head was beginning to be filled by troubles enough as it was. Once again, his hand strayed upwards to straighten his already impeccably adjusted tie before exposing it to the world again.

* * * * *

As he drove home up Halsted Street through the now late afternoon, the unease that had gripped him in Herbie Manning's living room turned to anger. He saw men and boys everywhere—sauntering in the sunlight or standing in lazy groups on streetcorners—ultra-fashionable in the latest shorts and sportswear, stereotypical in black leather and chains, or undetectably normal in jeans and T-shirts except that, to a well-practiced eye, the haircuts were a bit too irreproachably perfect, the jeans a bit too tight and the bodies a bit too trim, muscular and supple-looking. It drove Greg nuts. *It's a WEEKDAY,* he wanted to scream. *Don't any of you fags WORK?*

They were everywhere in this neighborhood, a constant reminder. How he hated them! Sometimes it seemed he had spent his entire life fending off the suspicion... well, that he was one too. The fact no one had ever actually accused him of this was confirmation the effort had been successful, but at such a cost in aggravation! He was *not* a faggot, forchrissake. He'd always made damned sure everybody knew it too.

By the time he entered his apartment tower's garage, he was enraged. He gunned his little electric car across the sidewalk a foot in front of an elderly woman with two shopping bags. She screamed at him and staggered back. Insulated from the world in air-conditioned quiet, Greg saw her face startlingly twisted with venom, the words lost as he swooped past into the calm darkness beyond.

The incident was a sure sign he needed to get himself under control. When at last he was out of the elevator on the 23rd floor and safely inside his small white condo, he allowed routine to pull at him. In the bedroom, he hung up and brushed his office clothes, exchanging them for soft old jeans and a college jersey. By the time he returned to the living room, some semblance of rationality had returned.

He considered his anger. Although society's homophobia did seem to be moderating a bit with the introduction from Paris a few years back of the Pasteur Institute's series of new, completely effective vaccines against HIV-1, -2 and now -3, there were still forces exerting tremendous pressure in backlash. These forces continued to blame the gay community for the enormous and ever more cataclysmic losses of life AIDS had inflicted, and to demand retribution, notwithstanding the facts that gay people these days were infected with HIV in no greater or lesser degree than the general population, that regardless of what degree of responsibility might have attached to gay people for having spread the epidemic unknowingly in its early years, almost all of those infected at that time were now dead, beyond blame and retribution both, and that homophobes themselves, through opposition to realistic sex education and attitudes, were at least equally responsible for what the epidemic had become, though naturally they pretended otherwise.

The illogic of homophobic argument had not failed to impress Greg, though he avoided admitting this. To him, the rights and wrongs of the matter were irrelevant. Homosexuality was controversial. As such, mainstream business shunned contact with it wherever possible. When such contact could not be avoided, most large businesses cultivated a neutral public posture tinged with cautious contempt. In private, they assured liberal politicians of their unshakable commitment not to discriminate in any way. In practice, they simply did not hire or promote openly gay people into managerial positions.

Greg wanted nothing whatever to do with it. That's why this assignment was so goddam perilous. Almost like some kind of test, it plunged him squarely into queerdom's deep end, whence he must retrieve the prize without getting wet.

So could he do that? *Why not?* was the instant and easy response. He'd bear down on Herbie Manning twice as hard as on a normal subject, just to make sure everyone saw how much he hated him and everything he was. What was to worry? No one could possibly connect him with such behavior. *Of course I'M not queer, am I.* As always before, the result of this comfortable rhetorical inquiry was fast, superficial self-satisfaction and reassurance.

Yet, his basic unease did not diminish. He explored it, and wondered whether this time the problem wasn't precisely his long-held and deeply-felt habit of open distaste for homosexuality and gay people. To fulfill his new responsibilities and win the promised place of power, he would have to deal directly with forces which never failed to produce kneejerk revulsion in him. Greg had sufficient training and experience as an investigator to know that facing those forces in this condition would reduce his efficiency considerably. So, just a little gingerly, he allowed himself to explore the sources of his revulsion. To his surprise and not a little to his discomfiture, the question reappeared, this time *as* a question: *I'm not queer, am I?*

Of course not, the quick and easy answer came.

A warning bell tripped somewhere in the back of his brain, one that, rather sickeningly, he suddenly knew had been there all along. *Am I?* An abyss of uncertainty dropped queasily before him, as, again, it seemed he'd known very well it would.

—Because this was not the first time he had glimpsed these uncertainties. At a certain level just below consciousness, he'd known as long as he could remember they were there lurking, waiting for the moment he'd lower his guard. Always before, the mere act of confronting them had been enough to make them cower. *This is bullshit,* he had told himself. *You can talk yourself into anything if you're paranoid enough, even nonsense like this.* Flee, however, they would not. So he had avoided them, shelved them. Excuses to take this line had been plentiful: societal intolerance, peer group pressure, career ambitions. Now, one of these same forces and a very important one, his ambition, seemed to impel him toward confrontation, not avoidance. How did the scales balance now?

LEARNING TO LOVE IT

The war raged silently in his mind, becoming ever more seriously disturbing. He tried to shut it down, to retreat into avoidance once more, to "save it for another time," but could not. Try as he might, he could not get the worms back into the coffin. More than the assignment, Morgan Jaye's offer and the chance of sticking it to Herbie Manning, all the varied unhappinesses of his life arose and gibbered at him. He had a new and disturbing sense that all the chains binding him led directly into this very abyss. Again, he had a sensation of always having known this on some level or other, simply of never before having made the conscious connection.

What was happening, here? *I'mnotqueer, I'mNOTqueer... Well, I'm not, am I?* The familiar revulsion, dread and contempt rushed full upon him, together with a not-so-familiar and altogether uncomfortable sensation of rising panic. Impatiently, he pushed back at these feelings, striving to replace them with some approximation of rational thought.

Just to be doing something, he opened his briefcase with the vague intention of unpacking his files. There on top was Herbie Manning's fox-headed brass letter opener. He picked it up. It felt cool, heavy, solid and substantial, somehow comforting. At last, silence reigned in his head.

He pulled himself onto the surface of his dining table and sat crosslegged, watching the late afternoon sun suffuse the city below in golden haze. Moodily, he turned the letter opener over and over in his hands. *Of course I'm not queer,* he thought. *How could I be? Being queer means having sex with your own kind, and I've never done that, no.* Again, the warning bell clanged. He frowned, searching back through all his memories, just to be positive. *But that,* he thought, *that doesn't count, does it?*

He was remembering his childhood, a completely conventional one in the suburbs of the city. He'd been seven or eight years old. There'd been a whole gang of them, little boys all. While the girls stayed in the yards skipping rope, playing house and having teaparties with their dolls, the boys roamed the neighborhood making pretend war on the kids from the next block, playing cops and robbers, or maybe aliens and space crusaders with their toy guns.

No matter what they called the game, it always involved everyone running and hiding, sneaking up on each other, firing off a bang and yelling, "You're dead!"—to which, of course, you had to make the correct reply: "No I'm not! *You're* dead!" BANG! Yelling and arguing followed, the end result being a thoroughly good time had by all.

The only interloper in this exclusively male elysium, he recalled, had been the tomboy, Nancy. Unsatisfied with the girls' daily round of dolls, jumprope and teaparties, her talents demanded wider scope. She'd done everything she could to prove herself worthy of inclusion. She'd climbed the tallest trees, done daredevil tricks on her bike, yelled louder and run faster than any of them. These abilities gained her a measure of grudging respect too, though not until the day of the Great Raid did her victory become complete.

Until then, the girls' daily teaparty had been sacrosanct. Perhaps it was merely that nobody'd thought of it before, or perhaps too many of the gang had older sisters. Whatever it was, when Nancy called them together to outline her plan, there was unmistakable reluctance. "What's the matter with you *boys*," she'd demanded, dripping scorn from every pore. "Are you *afraid*? Of *girls*? You guys are all a bunch of *sissies*! I *dare* you!" Resistance ended forthwith.

Nancy divided them into two teams, one to attack from the alley, one to come around the house from the front. There was to be no escape.

Greg was on the alley team. Excitement mounting, they took up their positions behind the rear fence.

The teaparty was well under way. This day the occasion was more elaborate than usual, somebody's going away or something. All the neighborhood's girls were in attendance. Adele Williams, who was twelve and thought herself too old for dolls, had, at the insistence of her mother, allowed her little sisters to persuade her to be grande dame for the occasion. Adele sat at the head table giving orders. "Janie, you have to sit next to Sharon 'cause you've got Barbie and she's got Ken and they're *engaged*. Annie, your rag baby has been *naughty*, so she has to sit in the *corner* and gets no cookies, and *you neither*!" Annie had just begun to wail when came the signal.

With a bloodfreezing warwhoop, Nancy led her band around the house and into the festivities fulltilt. Toy guns at top ratatattat, Greg and his gang hurtled through the gate and joined the fray.

Undoubtedly trite though it had been, Greg smiled to think of it even yet. He remembered it as a grand and glorious, vast confusion: flimsy cardtables overturning; everyone screaming full out; dogs barking; little girls in frilly dresses getting muddy immediately in the spotless yard and running about bumping into each other; a steady hail of dolls, dolldishes and paper partyfavors filling the air; nosy cross old Mrs. Blacklow next door calling the police. He remembered Adele Williams' mother, a smiling pitcher of Kool-Aid held uselessly above the battle, her mouth opened in a perfect "O" soundless through the ceaseless fusillade, and somewhere through all this, Adele herself, untouched (who would dare!), the waves parting before her (she knew how to scratch!), flouncing back into the house and slamming the door. The boys had never had a grander day.

Punishments followed of course. There were corners to be sat and licks to take—lightly given by fathers who once had been boys themselves, who saw the humor of it and could sympathize, especially when bridge night conflicted with the playoffs on TV. The glory remained, a triumph to treasure forever, and which they owed solely to Nancy.

When at length their penances were paid, she ruled them utterly. A born leader, she organized their games, judged their contests and planned their days. "Okay, this morning we'll have bike races on Zachary Street. After that, we'll tease Mrs. Blacklow's police dog, throw stones at the haunted house on Burr Avenue and go see if Mrs. Morgan has any cookies today." It was swell, like a perpetual summer camp minus adults with no sense of proportion about harmless childhood fun.

She also pioneered new territory. Their neighborhood lay in the suburbs, but only just. The city line was at the boulevard a block away. Across it lay Magellan Park. Designed in the early 20th century in the style of Frederick Law Olmsted, it once had been very elegant with groves and fields, a rock garden, a golf course, wooded walks and an ornamental lagoon overlooked by a romantically ruinous stone tower on a little hill.

These days the particular city neighborhood Magellan Park was meant to serve had seen better times. Most of its former, middle-class residents had followed their jobs out to Edge City. The rest scanned the real estate listings nervously as property values plunged. Many of its houses were empty and many more were looking distinctly run down. Its voting strength was off. Its alderman was in jail.

The park had suffered with the neighborhood. No one now mowed its lawns, which had run to prairie grass. Underbrush taller than a child filled the gardens and groves, through which wound a maze of rabbit runs and low passages no one but a child could penetrate. Weeds choked the ornamental lagoon. The ruined tower was dangerously ruinous, indeed. Only the golf course had been kept up, mainly through the patronage of suburbanites, who paid stiff fees to cross the border and play its nine short holes.

Naturally, this potential child's paradise was off-limits to Greg and the gang through universal agreement of the neighborhood moms. "We don't want you kids over there. You'll fall and hurt yourselves. You'll get dirty! There's too much traffic on the boulevard! We want to be able to find you when we want you!"

In the past, the gang had chafed at these restrictions and sneaked into the park when they dared, but to no avail. Sooner or later, one mom or another would notice the unusual absence of childish uproar and get up a posse. The offenders, if found, would suffer the embarrassment of being led by the hand back across the boulevard to neat, boring civilization. If not found, stiff punishments awaited when at last they reappeared, given out by exasperated moms who had searched in vain, likely as not watched from the underbrush by their errant offspring.

As with all forbidden things, these limitations only increased the park's attraction. The hopelessness of the situation threw a gloom over all the gang's proceedings—heaven visible, but out of reach. Some days, they just sat on the curb of the boulevard, idly counting cars and watching it longingly.

71

LEARNING TO LOVE IT

When Nancy took charge, she went from backdoor to backdoor. To each mom she explained how there really wasn't anything to worry about in the park. They'd be careful, stay together, cross the boulevard at the light, wear old clothes to get dirty in, stay out of the water, and not bother the golfers. She also told each mom every other had already given in.

Something surprisingly aggressive in Nancy's cogent presentation, articulate beyond her age, took the moms off guard. She behaved as if she expected no challenges, and received none of significance. The secret longing of all the moms for a little peace and quiet in the afternoons helped her too. At last, only one restriction remained: they could go, but only if *Nancy* went with them. The moms would hold her to her promises.

Immediately, the neighborhood was deserted while Magellan Park reverberated to toy guns and yelling. Joy ran unrestrained. Wild, unkempt trees dared climbers to poke their heads up through the surface of a rustling green sea. Fascinating bugs, frogs and even snakes lurked down by the water. The ruined tower, overgrown by vines, became their jungle gym. The underbrush provided an endlessly changing scenario for fantastic games. Hide and seek ceased to be boring and pointless. They climbed the fence at the park's edge and searched for arrowheads on the gravel shoulder of the expressway, and actually found one once.

Through all of this, Nancy did her best to keep her word to the moms, to keep her reputation intact and them all in good status thereby. She'd fight any boy who suggested skinnydipping in the lagoon. Tree climbers had to be wearing their oldest clothes. They had to ask her permission even to look out of the underbrush at the golf course. She kept them together as much as possible. Those who straggled out of bounds during hide and seek faced her wrath.

Disaffection stirred. If she started out as camp counselor, as first among equals, she ended up as policeman, as substitute parent. That her side always won their games and that she routinely outdid them at all their activities certainly didn't help, either. She had begun by begging admittance to their select circle and wound up supreme boss dealing by fiat and mandate, a sort of parental right monarch.

In even the most benevolent dictatorship, loss of freedom chafes. No one likes to feel they have no right to question orders, especially when restrictions are justified by "your own good" or "the good of all." Even the youngest people feel entitled to an opinion about such things. The gang began to long to be rid of their overlord, to recall wistfully the old, pre-Nancy days of carefree male anarchy. Grumbling began. Some of the older boys mounted small challenges which Nancy beat back with taunts and, when necessary, her fists.

Her taunts had changed. Before the park, her favorite had been, "Yeah, you always do what your Mommy tells you, don't you, you sissy!" Now, it was more like, "Hey you, your *mother* put *me* in charge. You'll do what *I* say or you're gonna get it." She had been completely co-opted. The gang felt it as a betrayal of sorts, without knowing how to put it into words.

External factors spurred further challenges to her authority. While many families in the city neighborhood outside the park had already packed up their minivans and headed down the expressway onramp never to return, some still remained. The gang occasionally encountered city children in the park.

Although these hotly resented the encroachment of the suburban children on their territory, there wasn't much they could do about it. The times had turned against them; their numbers were depleted. In the beginning, the gang encountered them singly or in small groups and easily beat them off, although usually not without taking a parting shot or two along the lines of, "Oh *yeah*? At least we don't take orders from a *girl*, ya buncha sissies!"

Eventually, a single sniper sat out of range, on the golf course or in a well-exposed tree where the gang dared not attack him, and day after day hurled these insults until he ran out of breath. "You chicken," Nancy would scream, "come here and say that to my face, you sissy!" The sniper only laughed the harder. Nancy learned to bear these taunts in glowering silence and lead the gang out of range. Still, the sniper had his effect. Resentment grew, revolution smoldered.

Nancy's reign, begun with the best intentions in the full triumph and glory of power, was doomed. Perhaps even she knew it. Looking back on it from the present time, from the vantage point of several years in corporate life, Greg was amazed she lasted as long as she did, enduring multiple threats any one of which might have sunk a lesser leader. That it took so much to depose her was a tribute, in a way, to her leadership skills and force of personality.

In the end, the littlest of them all finally faced her down. Little Tommy Mulligan may have been five years old. Never the less, he was three-foot-four of anarchy incarnate. For such a small boy, he was excellent at baseball: he could hit a window at fifty paces. He bit the heads off his little sister's dolls, he went fishing for goldfish with a kitchen strainer in the neighbor's ornamental pond, and although whatever he'd done to Adele Williams' kitten was unknown, the canny animal now dove for cover at any scent of his approach. In short, he did exactly as he pleased. He acted out each whim heedless of parental consequence. It became apparent he had a high tolerance for pain.

This day he pouted in deep disgrace. In the morning, his baby sister, aged three, had been discovered tied naked to a chair. Tommy explained they were playing "Hostage," a new game he'd learned about on TV. Although his captive seemed to be a willing participant and had not been hurt in any way, Tommy was dragged off to his room screaming something about ransom, where he was to go without lunch and stay until dinner.

Tommy was not the sort to take this with fatalistic grace. Jimmying a screen, he shinnied down a drainpipe that wouldn't have held him had he been five pounds heavier (and didn't when the time came), and ran for the park.

Nancy had already collected the gang at the traffic light and was long gone. Skipping among oncoming traffic, Tommy dodged across the boulevard and plunged headfirst into the underbrush of Magellan Park, where he headed for the rock garden.

This was a canyon carved some ten or twelve feet into the earth and lined with narrow limestone terracing. Originally, ferns had grown in the terrace beds and a small stream had whispered beside a footpath among the carefully arranged rocks of the canyon floor.

These days, the stream no longer flowed. The pipes that had fed it were dissolved into rust. Tall trees grew along the canyon rims. Large gnarled roots skewed the limestone terraces, which supported a variety of volunteer undergrowth. Saplings and big broadleaved bushes crowded the walls, sending up foliage to meet overhead and shower the canyon with squashy purple fruit. The trees and bushes blocked all sunlight from the canyon bottom, which was thus free of vegetation. This made a private place entirely screened from prying eyes. As footpath access had long since disappeared into a thicket of undergrowth laced with creepers, the rock garden was hard to find even by accident. This secret place was much favored by lovers, of whom much evidence remained. A tattered blanket, beer cans, candle ends, broken glass and the occasional spent condom littered the stones of the stream bed. Naturally, the gang loved it on sight. They'd come across it only after diligent exploration, and having found it, could only access it by a steep scramble along the canyon walls and terraces. As it was easily the coolest place in the park on a hot summer day, they'd taken it immediately for their clubhouse.

Tommy found them there, sprawled about and panting after a hot hour running and playing ball in the meadow above. He burst upon them from overhead, a shower of dirt, small sticks and berries preceding his actual presence. The gang sprang up at the first sign of an intruder, lest it be some of the detested city rabble. With anticipation up at the prospect of catching one and giving it a good pounding, they were a bit disappointed when only Tommy dropped among them.

He didn't exactly manage a graceful landing. Still, with the aid of his little rear, he made a pretty good two-then-three point landing in the dirt.

"Oh, it's only you. How did you get here?" Nancy demanded. "Did you cross at the light?"

"Yes." He got to his feet.

"Was it green?"

"Look what I found! Pretty!" He held up a small gravel stone which, even in the dim light of the rock garden, sparkled with flecks of mica.

Nancy swept it out of his hand to clatter among the stones of the stream bed. "You listen, you!" Tommy's head swivelled to follow the stone. The beginnings of a pout appeared on his face. "Hey, I'm talking to you! Your mother sees you out on that boulevard by yourself, you'll catch it good and the rest of us won't get to come here any more. Just look at you! You're filthy!"

This was true. His light blue shorts were caked with dirt. His shirt, more appropriate to spending the day in his room than to crawling around the park on his belly, hung open to the waist, all its buttons lost. There were green stains on it and a rip on one shoulder. "Look at that shirt," Nancy continued. "You're gonna catch it for sure."

"I don't care." Tommy stuck his chin out, defiant. He looked like a diminutive Winston Churchill, minus only the cigar.

"Lookit, brat. You've broken all the rules. You've got to go back home, and because you have to go, I have to take you, and because I have to take you, everybody else's got to go too! You've spoiled it for everybody!" At this, there was considerable grumbling, not much of it directed at Tommy, either.

"No! I won't go!" His face reddened. "I'm not a brat, neither! City kids are brats. Let's get 'em!"

Nancy was losing patience. "Hey! How many times do I have to tell you! Your mother put *me* in charge, and not only that, I'm bigger than you are, and everything you can do, I can do better! So when I tell you you're going home, you're going!"

"Oh yeah?"

"Yeah!" Nancy took a step forwards. Her hands became fists.

Tommy stared up at her, unfazed. "Betcha there's one thing I can do you can't!" A sly look crossed his face.

"Bull!"

"Betcha can!"

"Can't!"

"Can!"

"Can't!"

"CAN! And if you can't do it, you've got to let me stay! Betcha!"

"Crap! Rules are rules, brat. We're going!"

To this point, the rest of the gang had only looked on at this typical scene of their domination. But now it was looking like a fight and interest was piqued, if only to see it. More voices joined in, egging it on. "Hey, Nance, let's see what he can do!" "If he beats you, he stays!" "Yeah Nance, that's fair." "Yeah Nance." "Yeah."

Nancy's stance did not slacken. Nor did her murderous stare leave Tommy's face. "Okay brat, you got it, but after I beat *you*, I'm gonna beat your bratty butt all the way back to the light."

They waited to see what Tommy would do. What he did had the shock value of a cattle prod in a swimming pool. He stepped back and pulled down his dirty shorts. Underneath, he wore no underpants. Holding his elastic waistband down with one hand, he took his tiny thing in the other and sent a stream of golden pizzle onto the stones at his feet.

Except for Tommy's drizzling into the streambed, there was stunned, breathless silence. Toilet training suburban fashion rigidly precluded this sort of thing. Thou Shalt Not Pisseth Against the Wall, or anything else for that matter, was very definitely the rule.

The silence broke as they began to see how Tommy's challenge would apply to Nancy. A nervous giggle or two cut the air. Most of them confidently expected her to stunt the shrimp's growth permanently. Everyone held their breath in rapt anticipation. In Tom Lehrer's immortal phrase, there's nothing like death to enliven an otherwise dull afternoon. —Except for Greg, who had no sisters, and merely wondered in mute resignation why she didn't simply drop her pants, whip out her own thing and pee longer, harder and farther than Tommy, the way she did everything else.

Instead, anger crossed her face, swiftly replaced by disgust. She dropped her fighter's stance, and, without a word, tramped off around a curve in the canyon. They heard her climbing the wall out of the rock garden. Then she was gone.

It took them a minute to realize they were free. When they did, they hollered in delight and slapped Tommy's back. "All right!" "Way to go, man!" "Guess you showed her!" "Thought she was gonna kill you for sure, man." Someone at the back of the crowd explained it to Greg, to his amazement. "Really? You mean girls aren't just like us?" "Be cool, man. They'll hear you."

There were surprisingly few consequences of Nancy's abdication. She did go to all the backdoors and resign her commission to each mom in person, but when she made her recommendation that the gang be barred from the park thenceforth, the moms made no effort to hide their disappointment with her. Those who didn't already know it suspected permissions and freedoms were easier not to give in the first place than to rescind later.

At Tommy Mulligan's house, Nancy also suggested to Mrs. Mulligan that she consider reform school as the only viable option for Tommy. Just then, an adult male voice floated from the front of the house. "Edna! Gimme a beer willya? Fifth inning's just starting!" Mrs. Mulligan threw up her hands in resignation and closed the door.

Thus, the gang got to go skinnydipping in the lagoon after all, to the very great indignation of the elderly ladies and gentlemen sunning themselves on benches along its far side, many of whom repaired homewards in disgust, returning with their other spectacles (and sometimes binoculars), so as to fulminate their indignation all the more graphically and accurately. Once or twice, a lone, elderly and overweight policeman gave chase, though the gang lost him without difficulty in the underbrush.

In the early mornings when no one was around, they dove for golf balls in the ninth hole water hazard. These they sold back to golfers on the driving range until the park district, whose concession they undercut considerably, chased them off.

In this first flush of freedom, they weren't as strict about always staying together as they had been. Once or twice, small groups of city kids caught isolated individuals or pairs and pounded them most embarrassingly. Although they almost always managed to avenge these insults, they soon saw for themselves the wisdom of staying together, and resumed all activities as a group.

This included the ceremony of their liberation. Once a taboo is broken, it stays broken. More and more frequently, they gathered in the rock garden to micturate together into the stream bed. Without knowing precisely why, they were intensely interested in their bodies, and particularly in the portion of it concerned with this act. As their fascination progressed, they stripped progressively further and further, until at last they all got completely naked for the ritual act.

Nor did it stop there. As time went on, they explored one another's bodies, displaying and comparing their tiny hardons. By summer's end the gang was spending the best part of every afternoon in the rock garden engaged in their puerile orgy.

Greg squirmed uncomfortably at the memory, and as he remembered that he himself rapidly had become the chief instigator, always rounding up the others for a trip to the rock garden, this discomfort enlarged into burning shame. Quickly, he told himself that what they'd done was not in any way an erotic activity as adults think of it, that it was all terribly prepubic and innocent with no sexual titillation whatsoever attached. He could not remember that the exact attraction of the activity had been anything other than obscure to the participants. Although it had a large thrill of the illicit to be sure, if that had been all there was to it, the interest would have worn off after very few repetitions. As he analyzed it now, there also had been something deeper and far more compelling, something like an hitherto unnoticed instinctual itch stumbled upon by accident and scratched with equivocal yet intriguing results.

From atop his dining table, he frowned at the gathering glory of what looked like becoming an unusually spectacular sunset. He had a surprising revelation: despite the shame, he found a nostalgic longing for those days. It seemed to him as if those long ago intimacies with the guys were the last human relationships he had ever had unafflicted by guilt, inadequacy or power politics. This chilling, lonely thought filled him with sadness.

—The more so because they had been so brief. All elysia are transitory, and this one was no exception. It could not go unnoticed forever. One day a hated voice floated down from above, "Oh my god, will you look at the little queers all jacking off! You jerks must be really sick!" The sniper!

They didn't know what queers were or even what jacking off meant, but they knew it was an insult: that it was bad and therefore didn't apply to them. Naked as they were, they swarmed up the terraces and caught the sniper when, in his haste to escape, his T-shirt caught on a branch. He was smallish, about their own age, with very white skin, black hair and eyes. He screamed bloody murder about queers. One of the guys kicked him in the stomach to shut him up. They tumbled him down the slope, stripped him naked, and bound him hand and foot with vines.

They had him at last, the hated sniper, their chief tormentor. "Okay men, we got him. Now what do we do with him?" one of the older boys asked.

Their captive groaned on the ground. As they paused to consider the options, Tommy Mulligan resolved the question in by-now familiar fashion. He walked over and slowly, deliberately, urinated on the sniper's head. The gang froze, stunned. "Tommy, no," somebody said. "Oh shit."

The captive was speechless with rage and shame. A little shameful themselves, they decided to forego the usual pounding. When Tommy ran out of ammunition, they rolled the sniper through some mud and berries, then unbound him and made him walk naked whither the lagoon touched the grove. While he washed, shouting threats and reprisals, they put down his clothes and melted into the woods. At least, they knew he'd never dare tell.

They'd gone too far, and knew it. And they'd been called queers. They did not go to the park in the next few days. Then came Labor Day weekend: time for school and a whole different set of activities.

Perhaps some of the gang thought to ask elder brothers just exactly what "queer" meant, or perhaps they put two and two together on their own. However it happened, things were different when once again the park's bare branches fleshed out with concealing summer foliage. When someone—with another rush of shame, Greg recollected it had been himself—suggested a trip to the rock garden, the other boys replied, practically in chorus, "Naw, that's kid stuff. Let's go swimming!" Under the new scheme of things, when a boy had to relieve himself, he now announced the fact so others could stand guard while he scuttled off behind a tree for privacy. Modest decency ruled the day, with only one exception.

Little Tommy Mulligan took a special liking for Greg and attached himself permanently as Greg's best friend. Although Tommy was two or three years younger and smaller in stature, Greg didn't mind having him for a constant companion. Tommy was always coming up with new games to play and creative ways to get into trouble. Greg's contribution was in putting on the brakes when Tommy went too far. Tommy would accept correction from Greg he would take from no one else, and even drop a really bad idea entirely at Greg's insistence.

The two boys pulled each other in opposite directions, compromising in the middle. Each provided something of benefit to the other: excitement and leadership for Greg, safety and sanity for Tommy. Perhaps needless to say, while Greg's parents were less than enthusiastic about this arrangement, Tommy's were ecstatic, and cheerfully would have had Greg live in their house with them if they could have arranged it.

Tommy had a new game this year, and Greg loved it at once. Every once in a while, he would pull Greg aside and say, "Hey, let's go be bad boys." Greg knew what this meant. They would slip off into the underbrush to a private, secluded place, a pocket-sized clear space deep under the bushes they were sure nobody else had discovered. There, they took off their clothes and had what Tommy called "butt fights." These were wrestling matches, the object of which was to see who could plant his asshole immovably on the other's nose. Although smaller, Tommy was easily Greg's match at this. As often as otherwise, it ended with Greg on his back, Tommy kneeling on his arms, his head pinioned between Tommy's legs, and Tommy's little butthole planted firmly on his nose. "I gotcha! I

81

gotcha! You give in? Say 'Uncle'!" Greg would mumble "Uncfel," and that would be that.

This game might have gone even further, except that Greg was worried. A reasonably correct definition of "queer" had by this time filtered through the gang. "Queer is when one guy sucks another guy's dick," is what the other boys said. He made sure they never did that. It seemed a pointless idea, anyway. The unanimous opinion was that queer behavior was perverted, and that there was something about it which would render any boy caught at it liable to mocking jeering ostracism for life. While Greg didn't think what Tommy and he did qualified, it did seem awfully close. Still, when he won a butt fight, Tommy's nose wriggling around in his asshole did feel surprisingly interesting.

This pattern continued throughout that next year. Greg and Tommy pursued their private games in the park in summer, and alone at Greg's house in the winter when his parents were at work. Their situation was pretty much idyllic—until, inevitably, change ended this elysium too.

First, the gang lost the park. The laws of supply and demand ensured that no city neighborhood could remain half empty for long. This one was now in transition. New people were moving in at an ever increasing rate.

The new residents were unlike the old, and dramatically unlike the suburbanites across the park. New boys began to be encountered. They had olive skins and braided, elaborately patterned black hair. They wore strange-looking clothes, gold chains, and smoked cigarettes. The older boys knew what they were, and called them Ricans.

Their weaponry was scary. None of Greg's friends had ever been known to carry a knife, or to use one for more than play whittling on stray sticks. Yet, the very first of these new boys they cornered and surrounded pulled one, crouching low and twisting about as if to repel attack from any side. The gang considered this definitely unfair. If you were cornered, you were supposed to surrender, get pounded and driven off. That's what had always happened in the past. Threatening people with knives was not in the plan. They told him so and ordered him off.

More and more of the new boys appeared, usually now in small groups. The gang pulled together. Tommy and Greg ceased to wander off on their own. There were several scary near confrontations, made scarier because the new boys spoke incomprehensible Spanish at them, defiantly from across a neutral ground. The gang was made to feel nervous and inadequate, as if it was their fault they didn't understand.

The older boys were worried. The gang tended to stay more to the wooded areas when they moved and to post lookouts when they stayed in one place.

The end came. One day as they walked in silent single-file through the bushes, there was a sharp pop like a firecracker or a car backfiring on the boulevard. An odd, thin scream followed, suddenly choked off. Freezing instantly, each boy counted their number. No one was missing. Slowly, they pushed on down the narrow twisty track. About 100 yards ahead, signs of a struggle appeared; freshly broken twigs littered the trampled ground. The trail of damaged shrubbery led to a small pocket in the underbrush, the very place Greg and Tommy had used for their own, private games. A boy lay there on his back, hands bound behind him with vines. He had a small hole in his chest that bubbled and sucked air when he tried to breathe. His throat had been cut from ear to ear. Blood soaked him and slicked the ground, a lot of blood.

They knew him: the black-haired black-eyed sniper they'd once humiliated in the rock garden. He looked at them weakly and died, the last of his breath bubbling up through his blood. In the ensuing silence, Tommy crossed himself. So did several of the others.

The gang was just beginning to murmur among themselves when a cold voice cut at them, the speaker unseen in the undergrowth—a slightly older voice, a hoarse, just barely pubescent voice deepened with adult menace. "Yeah, you pray for him. No more you can do for him now. We all around you. You pray for his soul, then you get out of here and you never come back. We own this park. You come back and we kill the resta you too. And don't you never tell nobody what you seen here. Cops come after us, we come after you and kill you all."

Greg felt himself grow sick with fear. As in a nightmare, he grew weak-kneed. He thought he might throw up. Tommy's hand slipped into his. The gang slowly backed down the trail. When they heard bodies moving through the trees behind them, they lost all restraint and ran. Each knew how many side trails might allow pursuers to circle around in front of them and cut them off. They ran heedless through the brush, on trail and off, and plunged straight across the boulevard, scattering traffic in an agony of blatting car horns. Only when they reached the far curb did they stop, panting for breath, staring wide-eyed in horror at the park across the street.

They decided to take the newcomers at their word. There and then, they decided their story: they'd been swimming in the lagoon. This was in fact true. The old folks must have seen them, as usual. They hadn't been anywhere near the part of the park where the sniper lay.

A day or two later, a police detective called at Greg's house, just as they were returning from some evening function at Greg's school about which Greg no longer remembered anything. The detective proved to be a personable and very smartly dressed young woman. She spoke with Greg's parents in the dining room. Greg heard their voices. "Yes, he goes to the park." —Greg's father. "A gun? My son? Never! I wouldn't have one of the filthy things in the house!" —*Good ol' Mom,* thought Greg, his ear pressed to the door. Chairs scraped, and Greg fled. His father found him and brought him back for private inspection by the detective.

"My! You are a handsome little fellow, aren't you!" Her speech was slow and sugary, the tone kindergarten teachers use. For several years now it had grated on Greg when adults used it to him at school. It grated on him now. "I'll bet you're smart too! Are you smart, Gregory? Do you get good grades in school?"

Greg shrugged. His marks were excellent.

"Well, I hope so, because only a very smart person can help me. Would *you* like to help me, Gregory?"

This tugged at Greg in spite of himself. How many chances does a gradeschooler get to tell adults something they don't know? He shrugged again, but looked her in the eye for the first time.

He stuck to the prepared story. Swimming, yes. Murder, no. The detective looked at him quizzically, head cocked to one side. She moved her chair closer, almost touching him. "This is a serious business, Gregory. Little Jimmy Snyder has been murdered. He was shot with a gun and then badly cut with a knife, a horrible, pointless crime. Isn't that a sad and terrible thing to happen to a little boy like you? Imagine if it had *been* you. Wouldn't you want whoever'd done that caught and punished?"

Greg supposed he would.

She smiled sadly. "I'm really disappointed in you, Gregory. Your little playmates are all very smart children. They've all told what you saw that day. I'd be sorry to think you weren't as smart as they are."

They'd told? Just like that? Who'd told, and what? He asked.

"But Gregory, if I told you that, you wouldn't be able to tell me what happened that day in your own words and show me you're smart too. Wouldn't you like to do that?"

Well, if they'd told, Greg supposed he should prove he knew just as much about it as they did, and get this very irritating big person to stop treating him like a kindergartner. But wait a minute! The Ricans would be over here gunning them down and slicing them up in no time! He could picture it clearly! Were they all nuts? Just what had been said?

The detective watched his puzzlement closely to determine if her bluff would work or whether he really knew nothing as he pretended. In what may have been meant as a soothing gesture, she leaned closer and smoothed the lapels of the little blazer he'd worn at the school. She straightened his little tie, oozing control.

With the nightmare image of malice-filled demons cutting his throat clear in his mind, the pressure of her hands on the tie around his neck was constricting, claustrophobic! He jerked backwards in the chair and scrabbled at the tie, struggling to erase the memory of her touch. "I don't know anything! Nothing happened! Go ask the Ricans!" The moment he said it, he knew he was in trouble.

Her head tilted. "The Ricans?" she asked smoothly. "Tell me what Puerto Ricans have to do with this."

Greg knew he'd been tricked. If anybody had said anything about what they'd seen, she wouldn't have had to ask. He thought fast. "They've got knives," he mumbled, "I've seen them."

"Did you see any Puerto Ricans in the park that day? Any knives?"

Greg shook his head and wouldn't budge, though she kept at him until the stress got to him and he started to cry. Even now, Greg's face burned with the humiliation she'd made him feel. He was glad he'd told her nothing. *She didn't do a very professional job,* he sniffed, perhaps a bit unfairly.

She'd had to give up. He fled to his room, unable to keep his hands off his tie, straightening it over and over again until at last he tore it off and threw it into a corner.

When the detective had gone, his parents were almost worse. He stuck to his story stubbornly. In desperation, his father barred him from the park forever, and gave him a rare and completely unnecessary stroke with the belt to underscore the message. Greg didn't need to be told. He never intended to set foot in Magellan Park again.

In the next few days all the boys had tales of similar harassment. Miraculously, no one had told. The newcomers' threat had been entirely effective. The detective had tried the same trick on all of them, but plagued by nightmares of what they'd seen and by fears of olive-skinned assassins climbing in their bedroom windows or ambushing them on the way to school, they'd all figured, hey, if the other guys wanted to end up bubbling their lives away in a pool of blood, that was their lookout. All had stayed clammed.

They sat on the boulevard's curb and looked at the park—once again, a gloomy forbidden wilderness. Now, however, its old air of mystery and promise of adventure were replaced by real terrors and a sense of ultimate defeat. The park was lost, indeed.

Next, Greg lost Tommy.

The gang's reverses threw them back on the neighborhood for entertainment. Only now they were older and not as excusably cute. They could do more damage. Tolerance was not high. The neighborhood had gotten used to the peace and order provided by the boys' daily excursion to the park.

Cross old Mrs. Blacklow sat on her back porch, telephone in hand, and scanned the yards all day long, the number for every boy's parents in her speeddial. Not a movement escaped her. Tommy Mulligan was her pet target. She called Tommy's mother several times a day complaining about every move he made, harmless or not, in a pure, mindless vendetta, the restrictions of age avenging themselves on the careless freedoms of youth.

Worse, her vendetta was hatefully partial. Greg's father often did yardwork and odd jobs around her house, and although Greg was always with Tommy and usually equally responsible for whatever mischief they did, Mrs. Blacklow had never a word to say against him. She reserved her spleen for Tommy alone. She imputed everything they did to him, frequently embellishing when the truth sounded weak.

After several weeks of multiple daily phone calls, the Mulligans lost their patience. Tommy's father got on the line. He was a police sergeant, and used his best police sergeant's voice to call her a useless old bag. He threatened to complain to the phone company about nuisance calls if she ever phoned again. The phone calls stopped.

Shortly thereafter, an afternoon came when Greg's parents took him off to visit relatives. Tommy whiled away the day picking the lily-of-the-valley that grew as weeds alongside the Blacklow house. Mrs. Blacklow saw him and, in a move probably designed to embarrass the father as well as the son, called the police about a prowler stealing her flowers. Two patrolmen arrived, who did see an opportunity to play a joke on Sgt. Mulligan, assuage Mrs. Blacklow and teach Tommy a lesson all at the same time. With mock seriousness, they handcuffed him and took him off to the station house.

By the time they got there, Tommy's Winston Churchill imitation was in full scowl, though hauled up there in shackles before his father, he looked a lot more like a miniature Edward G. Robinson. "Stealin' flowers, Sarge," the patrolman said with a not entirely successful effort at a straight face.

A good laugh at the tiny glowering felon was had by all—by all, that is, except Sgt. Mulligan, who was not the slightest bit amused his son should be displayed as a junior juvenile delinquent, even a comic one, before the Captain and the men. When the shackles came off, he took Tommy into an interview room and gave him an ugly-edged talking to involving no TV for a month, indefinite delay on several new videogame datacapsules he'd been promised, and ominous warnings about what further was to happen when the sergeant got home.

Nor was Tommy amused at being laughed and yelled at in turns, and all for doing nothing wrong, for picking weeds! When he returned home, he was seething, and Greg was not there to restrain him. Tommy figured that, as long as he was going to get beat on anyway, he might as well earn it. He gathered a handful of stones and deliberately broke every window in the Blacklow house. He ignored the old woman's screams and the big dog's frenzied racket in its run, the while taking calm aim, coolly going about his work of retaliation.

This had to be the end. Sgt. Mulligan knew the vendetta between the two houses must cease at once for the peace of the neighborhood. Then too, as a police sergeant, he had to be seen as able to control his own family.

Even before paying for Mrs. Blacklow's new windows, he put Tommy in for a Knights of Columbus scholarship to St. Vitus, a military boarding academy famed for its tough love approach to Troubled Youth—and so it was done. Greg lost his best friend. Shortly afterwards the Mulligans moved away altogether. Greg had never seen him since.

With Tommy's departure and the termination of their private games ended Greg's only active experience of homosexuality. *Not even!* he thought. *Just a lot of silly kid stuff.* Little boys did that, and didn't necessarily grow up to be queers, either! Why, most of those guys, in fact all he knew about, were now married with kids of their own! *They* weren't queer! True, Nancy was a little strange: last he'd heard, she ran a motorcycle repair place somewhere near Seattle. But that was different. He wished he knew something about Tommy Mulligan. He had no idea where Tommy was or what he was doing, but he was dead sure Tommy wasn't one of these fruits prancing up and down Halsted Street or anywhere else! Mercenary soldier was probably more like it. Besides, Greg's life since had been completely blameless and untinged with homosexual sympathy. Rather the reverse!

Once Tommy was gone, Greg gradually forgot him. There was so much else to do. In high school, Greg had new friends.

He went out for track. He liked hanging around with the jocks. They sneaked cigarettes and beer when they could and sat around talking tough. He especially liked the easy camaraderie of the locker room and the showers. He finagled his locker between the two handsomest, best-built boys on the team and always made sure he got to the showers the same time they did.

Although there was lots of covert adolescent homoerotic play of the usual towel snapping sort—once even a wrestling match in the showers that had been broken up by the coach and earned the whole team a week's detention before school—that's all there'd been. The positive consequences of earning a queer label were nil. The negative consequences were obvious.

In the entire school, there were only two openly homosexual boys. One, with the ridiculous name of Lamont Alcock, which was quite a burden all by itself, lived in a small apartment by the railroad embankment with his mother, who was a cosmetician. Cosmetology was also Lamont's stated career objective. Although pudgy and uncoordinated, he had a certain flair. One day he came to school with his hair painted plaid.

The other, Willis Boothe, came from a wealthy family in an elite neighboring suburb. He was well-built and good looking. He was also a very nellie queen with a penchant for crushes on working class boys.

Both these unfortunates came in for merciless razzing. They were virtually the only students everybody in that large multi-suburb school knew by both sight and name. Their smallest doings made instant snickering gossip. Greg remembered lots of it.

Willis cherished a hopeless not-so-secret passion for the golden Apollo who quarterbacked the football team—a passion so strong and pure as to require no physical resolution, which was a good thing; his hero was completely disinterested. Yet, as his father happened to work for Willis' father, he treated Willis diplomatically. He smiled and nodded when they met. Sometimes he'd actually pass a few words of smalltalk when no one else was around. He invariably contrived to disappear when Willis was being tormented. These marks of unusual favor cemented Willis' devotion. To be near his beloved, Willis voluntarily spent three years as student manager of the junior varsity and later the varsity football teams.

This servile position entailed putting out and picking up equipment, and cleaning up after the team in the locker room. Even the homeliest team members whom Willis wouldn't look at once delighted in teasing him, then made up stories about how they'd summarily and humiliatingly rejected his advances. Although Willis' opportunities for retaliation were pathetically limited, he did the best he could. When it came to cleaning up after his chief tormentor in this regard, the 280-pound center known affectionately as "Hog," Willis held his nose with one hand and picked up Hog's equipment with the tips of the thumb and forefinger of the other, pinky daintily outstretched. This occasioned a small continuing laugh at Hog's expense. Hog retaliated by making up and putting around a story about how he'd come early to practice and found Willis sniffing his locker, a hungry look on his face. The team forgot Willis' gesture immediately. Hog's story seemed to banish it to the realm of unrequited love, which was a great deal funnier. His impersonation of Willis' hungry face was much in demand for weeks.

Of the torture of Lamont Alcock, Greg knew less. Lamont carved out a niche for himself in the Theater Department, where he did makeup and hair for virtually every show during his four years.

90

The theater being an essentially tolerant place, he was safer there, at least until he emerged.

No matter how inoffensive he might have been, his very presence was still an affront to real men everywhere, and they made sure he felt it. No boy would share a lavatory with him. They ran shrieking into the hall the minute he came through the door, his despairing wail cutting through their laughter, "Aw, c'mon guys, cut it out!" The most common taunt was, of course, a play on his name: "Alcock! All cock and no balls!" Lamont heard that several times a day for years.

Gym class was endless routine torment for both boys. The wrestling coach, who had a flair for sadism directed impartially at the world at large, always paired Willis with the best-looking boys in his weight class just to see their discomfiture and disgust, especially when Willis won, as happened not infrequently. To be beaten by Willis was a two-week disgrace. The coach, however, was not to be construed as doing Willis any favors. The worst happened during one such bout with an especially delectable opponent. Willis lost control of his excitement and arose with darkly dampened crotch—or so the story went, anyway. True or not, the entire school snickered of nothing else for months. Certainly, there came a day when the coach stood him up before the others and delivered a five-minute sermon on the basic lack of hygiene inherent in certain behavioral choices. Willis heard the last of that only when he graduated.

Neither Willis nor Lamont had any friends at all, and could not as much as speak to one another in public lest an instant rumor of immorality sweep the school and result in detention or expulsion for both of them. Girls tended to look at them, especially at Willis, shake their heads and say, "What a waste!" Boys ambushed them with jeers and physical intimidation on their separate lonely ways home from school. Each found the word AIDS scrawled on his locker several times a year as the concomitant rumor spread, though, as far as Greg knew, it had never been true of either of them.

These images of gay people and gay life had stayed with him ever since. They were the first gay images he had ever seen with his own eyes. Greg saw no reason, then or now, why he deserved to share the miserable life of picayune, trivial, petty, unimaginative torment they illustrated. From the safety of the track team he'd jeered and snickered with the rest. If this was what it was like to be queer, he wanted no part of it. Queers were disgusting and pitiful, eternal losers who were and deserved to be shat on by everybody, outcasts, the butts of every cruel joke. They were there to provide contrast, to show by negative example how good life was for real men. He knew he wasn't like that. He had the respect of his teammates. He was a man.

In college, he repeated this pattern. He joined a jock fraternity and engaged in its pursuits avidly. Panty raids, toilet papering the trees in front of bitch sororities, drinking and vomit parties—no act was too disgusting. If the guys did it, it was okay by him.

There was just one resident crocodile in this otherwise satisfactorily macho wallow.

Everyone seemed to be complaining about women. This bitch wouldn't put out. That slut was so stretched out she douched with the firehose. This cunt was a pricktease. That ballbreaker just had to be a lezzie, and on and on, anon. The bottom line? Although sex was the number one preoccupation and topic of discussion around the Pi Iota Gamma house, it didn't seem as if anybody was getting much.

Greg's problem was somewhat different. He truly liked women's company, sometimes. He was a little more soft spoken with them, at least when the guys weren't around. They made a pleasant change from the endless macho racket of the house. He liked to talk with them about more than just making it. When he made a date to study with a woman, he actually wanted to study and trade help and advice with her. These traits, combined with his fresh face and slim muscular build, made him a popular date.

He gained a reputation as the only real gentleman at the Pi Iota Gamma house and, without intending to, worked the trick exactly right. His study dates went from wondering if they'd have to fend him off with a sharpened No. 2 pencil to wondering whether he'd ever make any move at all. Some of them eventually decided that, if he wouldn't, they'd take the initiative themselves.

The truth was that Greg was really nervous about sex. Oh, he'd done his share of necking in high school—but making it? For real? That high school necking had been curious. He'd get hard for the first five minutes, after which it quickly had become like kissing his sister—or what he imagined kissing his sister would have been like if he'd had one—all gooey lips and octopus hands without much excitement attached. As for making it, he had pretended to high moral standards that were, by that time, long out of date. While he'd taken some ribbing about that from the guys, lots of the girls had liked and respected him for it and defended him to his friends, which made it all right. However, this tactic didn't work as well in college, where the general level of sophistication was much advanced and "high moral standards" only got you pegged as painfully strange.

When in his freshman year the first of his study dates to lose patience put her hand purposefully on his knee, it came as an unwelcome interruption to what he was doing. "Gosh, Cindy, I've really got to finish this math homework or Professor Pinkum will have me for lunch. Look here on page 126..." He developed a misinterpretation of Cindy's character and posted her phone number on the second floor bulletin board back at the house.

The next one to try it used better timing. They'd already closed the books and were having a friendly glass of wine in her room. By then he'd also developed a more accurate impression of the tenor of the place and what was expected. He gulped and tried to go along. Failure. "Gosh, Laurie, I'm sorry. I don't know what's wrong with me. You're so attractive, it makes me nervous."

Although he certainly was nervous, her attractiveness had nothing to do with it. He had merely followed what he knew to be the formula for successful lying: mix your lie with enough truth to make it sound sincere. This time, though, it added up to the wrong thing to say. Laurie knew that, with attraction in the mix, nervousness could be overcome by familiarity. When she challenged him to a rematch, he couldn't refuse without sacrificing his story. They tried again the next day, and again the day after that.

Greg became determined that, by god, he was gonna do this or know why not. He resolved to cease all masturbation and let his horniness build up until he'd accomplished his mission. On the fifth attempt, when it became apparent Laurie really was going to let him keep trying until he succeeded, the nervous pressure disappeared. Finally, he was able to relax and keep it up all the way to orgasm.

Afterwards, he was oddly disappointed. The experience simply hadn't lived up to all the hype. It had been curiously mechanical and uninvolving, a lot of sweaty effort and rolling around to accomplish what he could do for himself a lot more conveniently. Was that all there was to it? He just couldn't see what all the fuss was about.

He needed time to think. A week went by during which he made no move to call Laurie. When finally he passed her on the quadrangle, she made a furious face and refused to stop and exchange pleasantries.

Greg decided he didn't care. He'd made his point. He wasn't queer; he'd made it with a woman at last, thank god, though the experience seemed highly overrated. The condoms he wore in those days preceding the Pasteur Institute's AIDS vaccine didn't help matters, he decided. He'd have been very tempted to blame them, except that, while everybody bitched about condoms, nobody else seemed ready to give up on sex because of them. He concluded that his interest in sex seemed somewhat insufficient. So, was he heterosexual or not? He was, but only mildly, he thought. He decided he was more asexual (a convenient word he'd happened on somewhere) than anything else: not much turned on by anybody. If he really had to relieve his horny itches, and, like everybody else, he certainly did once in a while, he decided he much preferred masturbation, where there were no condoms, no pressure, and you could work at your own pace.

Yet, he still liked women friends, and needed them to keep up his reputation back at the house. Through a period of trial and error, he developed his policy. He put off the women who tried to make him as long as he could under cover of gentlemanliness. "Gosh, do we really know one another well enough for this?"

Generally, he could hold them off until they got bored or disgusted enough to find themselves another date.

When this tactic failed ("God, Greg, you've already heard my life story twice. What do you need? My birth certificate? My social security number? A letter from my mother? Let's do it!"), he would oblige. When he succeeded, he let the relationship go on only long enough to become public property. He pretended for the guys how much he preferred playing a wide-open field, and moved on to develop new female friendships.

When he failed, as happened with a certain irritatingly predictable regularity, he'd explain mournfully to his partner all about the childhood camping accident with the hatchet that, while not leaving a scar, had rendered him impotent in a way no treatment yet devised could help. He'd beg these women to keep his secret. As they'd generally gotten to know him and like him pretty well by the time they started making moves, they'd usually agree, provided he didn't try to cover by announcing from the belltower that he'd fucked them. He struck a number of bargains of this sort.

Naturally, not all of them could keep a secret. Some others were justly suspicious of his story. These were easily neutralized back at Pi Iota Gamma. "Oh, that bitch is pig city, man. She begged me, but the only box I wanted at her place was the one to keep the beer cold." He could say this and similar crude things with such a genuine air of aggrieved innocence that the house dissolved in laughter.

That these attempts at excusing himself didn't always sound right was immaterial. The house looked at the large number of women passing through Greg's life and thought it knew for a fact he was getting ten times as much as the rest of them combined. The faint suspicion his prowess occasionally might be something less than 100% only disarmed envy, made him likable and human. Ironically, failure at sex secured his reputation as a stud.

In this way, he got through college.

He looked forward eagerly to life in the city. He'd be living alone, so his private life would be his own business—at last, at last.

His new job at The Amalgamated Consolidated Confederated International Bank was just a super opportunity for a guy right out of college, so super, in fact, he'd rather wondered why they'd given it to him. There had to have been applicants with college courseloads more suitable to the position, and probably actual job experience as well. Fortunately, his supervisor, Herbie Manning, was just swell: helpful, friendly, understanding of the limitations with which he began the job. The outlook couldn't be better.

This cheerful view of his prospects lasted just 48 hours. The morning of his third day one of the women caught him at the coffee machine and asked him flat out if he was gay. He denied it in horror. Then, with a just-in-case-you-don't-already-know, she told him the awful truth: that Herbie Manning was an unapologetic known homosexual; that his own reputation was being questioned up and down the long rows of cubicles. He'd have to watch his step and act fast to keep it.

Greg was horrified! Damn faggots! What more would he have to endure to avoid that label? He returned to his cubicle to find Herbie in the aisle telling a small group what great buddies he and his new assistant were. The group turned to him and, it seemed to Greg, only just avoided snickering in his face by dint of massive effort.

In the following days he found out precisely why he'd been hired over what, indeed, had been a considerable list of more qualified candidates: namely, because Herbie Manning had fought for him and refused to take no for an answer. Not only was this no secret, everybody seemed to know! People he checked for confirmation seemed surprised he asked. They assumed he'd been in on it all along. Rumors of a relationship between them were rife on the floor. Greg saw people watching them every minute of the day, waiting for verification of what they believed they already knew.

Greg was truly torn at first. Not only had Herbie gotten him the job, but, on top of his own duties, Herbie had cheerfully assumed the large portion of Greg's job Greg did not yet understand, and was unstinting in helping him along. Greg *wanted* to be grateful, and more than that, desperately needed to keep this help and assistance coming. Herbie seemed hurt and uncomprehending Greg wasn't more reciprocal, more friendly in return. At last, he reproached Greg with it, and told him himself what he'd done to get him hired.

As per Herbie's usual practice with his personal business, he chose to have this scene right out in the aisle. Greg heard silence descend around them, saw heads poke up. He wanted to cry with shame, but wouldn't. That would finish him for sure. He managed to keep his voice low. "Uh, Herbie? I don't want you to think I'm ungrateful. I appreciate all you've done. And are doing. Really. But Herbie, could you take your hand off my shoulder? Please?" Greg wanted to sink straight down into the carpet and disappear. He saw the rumor born of a lovers' quarrel—neighbors signalled, knowing smiles—to all of which Herbie seemed oblivious.

This seeming unconsciousness of what people were thinking typified Herbie. He appeared to have no idea what impression he made. The dominant feature of his public style consisted of seizing the merest hint of conversational relevance to bray out iconoclasms such as, "Did you know the Roman Catholic Church was originally invented for a religion other than Christianity?" or "Most people think Latin is a dead language, but really, it's the most widely spoken language on the planet." Naturally, these things begged explanation, which Herbie gladly would provide, at length. He seemed to enjoy displaying his erudition at the center of attention. Yet no one was impressed. Nobody likes a know-it-all. People who bought into these lectures seemed to say, *Okay, I'll bite*, and walked away afterwards shaking their heads in unconvinced amusement. Greg felt humiliated for Herbie just watching. Herbie was an opinionated bore, and the enthusiasm with which he offended conventional wisdom and the values of his hearers to get the attention he sought lent his voice all the unique qualities of a car alarm on a sweltering afternoon. Homosexual implications aside (supposing that possible), the thought people might associate Greg with Herbie's behavior quickly had become insupportable.

So what could he do about it? Sexual harassment, that's exactly what Herbie was doing to him, he told himself, though Herbie had yet to venture a direct proposition—but saw no way he could file a grievance. Win or lose it, he'd look ridiculous, and forever mark himself as a complainer. Men were supposed to sort these things out among themselves, so he set about doing just that.

He redoubled his efforts to learn his job. At last, he was doing it all himself. Finally, he was able to put Herbie at a distance. He spoke to him only when spoken to, and only when that was business. He curried favor with Herbie's superiors so he wouldn't have to depend on Herbie to tell them how well he was doing. He never missed an opportunity to speak disrespectfully of Herbie when he wasn't around. He resurrected his college tactic and dated women now and then, making sure they came onto the floor to meet him at closing time.

Slowly, painfully, he made his point. The floor began to see it as a massive joke on Herbie—began to see that he'd tried to bribe Greg, but that Greg was incorruptibly normal, after all. Greg reinforced this in the tried and proven way he'd learned in high school, by acting out made-up stories of Herbie's seduction attempts that sent his hearers into hysterics. The floor believed these stories immediately, thank god.

Through it all, Herbie never let on he knew what Greg was doing. Maybe he didn't. Although people did think Herbie a character, he didn't have as many friends as he thought. At company social functions, where people usually were unwilling to volunteer for a lecture over white wine and canapés, he tended to end up spending a great deal of time by himself.

Greg didn't know how much he knew, and didn't really care. Herbie kept up a steady stream of inane chatter, dropped occasional insinuations about a mysterious something they might "have in common"—a concept Greg found more than a little offensive in and of itself—and still tried to touch him now and then. Greg did his best to ignore the whole of it, but at last told Herbie he'd hit him if he ever touched him again. Herbie seemed honestly surprised and hurt.

Greg gradually forgot the valuable things Herbie had done for him. He told himself Herbie's motives had been suspect—more than suspect, insulting!—that therefore, he owed Herbie nothing. Greg came inexorably to loathe him for the trouble he'd had to endure. He loathed Herbie's ugly slouchy lounging presence in the next cubicle disturbing Greg's concentration with his baloney-filled lectures. He hated his cheap suits, his unkempt hair and his serene defiance of petty procedural and conduct regulations, especially his chain smoking. Greg tried to complain about that, but failed, even though smoking was officially prohibited. Herbie demonstrated conclusively that all the smoke he produced disappeared into the intake duct above his cubicle. Because the bosses valued his contribution and nobody else was complaining, he got away with it. Greg swallowed his chagrin. After all, it was the spectacle of Herbie smoking, his defiance of the rules, that Greg disliked, not the smell of it. Especially, Greg hated the stupid leering grin Herbie was always hanging in his face like a spoiled pumpkin. It embarrassed Greg no end. He saw it in nightmares. He wanted to kick it.

At last, the bosses seemed to take pity, and promoted him. Although his new cubicle was on the other side of the room, Herbie dropped by to pester him there too. With an effort, Greg maintained normal civility. He felt instinctively how disastrous a scene would be.

Greg put everything he had into his new job, working extra hours to surpass his superiors' expectations. In fairly short order, he had his reward. He was promoted again. He was now supervising a large section of the floor, Herbie included! His new job came with his own little office off to the side. He took possession in the grim certainty he would now proceed to resolve the Manning situation in short strokes. He dropped all pretense of being nice to Herbie.

Unfortunately, firing Herbie turned out to be impossible. Now that he saw Herbie's work in comparison with others', how the guy got away with what he did was obvious. His work was easily the best on the floor. Grounds for dismissal that would hold up under AmalCon's review procedures were non-existent.

Greg's self-control wobbled dangerously. By this time, hatred had destroyed his judgment. He declared war. He issued regulations aimed directly at Herbie's uncouth unkempt unprofessional presence. He prohibited sloppy dressing and messy haircuts. He cracked down on excess visiting among the cubicles and, waving the firecode, on confabs that blocked the aisles. He demanded rigid compliance with all the petty procedural details Herbie had always ignored in lordly fashion.

Quit, sucker! Goddammit, quit! he screamed inwardly every time he took a new action of this kind. So that this vendetta should not be seen clearly for what it was, he enforced his new rules mercilessly against everyone. He withdrew Herbie's exemption from the smoking ban.

Then, when at last the cocksucker did quit... Greg dissolved into instant humiliation and fury at the memory, and banished it.

With Herbie gone, Greg tried to loosen up, relax, and enjoy—but too late. His relentless pettifoggery had alienated the sympathy and respect his coworkers had had for him when he began his reign. By this time, those who'd liked him and looked forward to having him as their supervisor unanimously felt betrayed, and with discontent rampant on the floor, his own superiors now had universally labelled him a poor manager. Infuriatingly, unbelievably, the loss of Herbie Manning was one of the chief items they held against him! They became unshakably convinced it had been a mistake to advance such a young man to a leadership role. His career was damaged in a way it would take years to repair. He blamed Herbie for that too.

It became apparent he'd have to change companies if he wanted to advance himself again anytime soon. He lunged at the first decent opportunity he heard of, which happened to be with Wiley Catchem.

Life at Catchem, Billem & Stickem in the years since had been easy by comparison. There were no faggots drooling at him all the time. Although several of the women appeared to think he was just dreamy, he pursued a public policy of keeping his business and personal lives strictly separate. This was acceptable, though it didn't make him wildly popular. What they didn't know was that he had no personal life. 100% of his energy went into his job and his career. With renewed intensity, he cultivated the image of an intelligent young man completely dedicated to doing good work and getting ahead, and backed it up with long hours of hard plugging—evenings, weekends, holidays, whatever it took. His superiors rewarded him with their admiration and interest in his career. In his current position as Wiley's personal assistant, if the respect of the office bordered on envy and fear, well, those were the breaks. At least it was respect, which was all he asked.

The sunset had faded. The lights of the city spread out in a vast luminous carpet to the horizon in all directions. His knees were killing him. He unkinked himself and slid gingerly off the table. Slowly, he stretched, and touched his toes. His body felt good: strong, supple, useful and desirable. He circled the darkened room, looking out at the view from every direction his corner apartment commanded, then flopped in his easy chair.

So why did his life feel so empty? What he was, he admitted at last, was *lonely*. He certainly wanted *someone*. But who, and what for? For sex? His supposed preference for masturbation was a myth. Masturbation was convenient, yes, but increasingly boring of late and fraught with difficulties... So what was his problem? Asexuality? His lack of sexual interest in women was no delusion. He'd wished this not to be true many times and striven to overcome it, failing as often as not.

What else was there? Animals?

He smiled sourly. He felt, as ever, the mental walls surrounding the answer. He knew now why he had always shied away from approaching the barrier to inspect what lay inside: it gave at a touch.

The evidence was irrefutable—his interest in other male bodies, repressed but never far below the surface: the huge fascination he'd had with that prepubescent exploration in the park and naked games with Tommy; how he'd timed it just right to be in the showers with his favorites on the track team, trying not to stare too openly; how he'd always chummed up to the best looking most masculine guys he could find; how after one of those stupendous frathouse drinking binges, drunk to mindlessness, he'd pulled the covers off his comatose roommate (how gorgeous *he'd* been!) just to watch the fellow as he himself fell asleep. He thought on how disturbingly phallic imagery had been creeping into his otherwise tightly controlled masturbatory fantasies lately, and how, when he'd given up masturbation as a consequence, horrifyingly vivid male-dominated wet dreams had been the ever more frequent result.

This had to stop. In desperation, he determined on an experiment. He discovered he was still holding Herbie Manning's brass fox-headed letter opener. He put it aside, pulled down his pants, took his cock in his hand, and let his mind wander freely, all barriers down. Instantly, unbidden images of the men and boys he'd seen on Halsted Street that afternoon filled his mind. He hardened. Gradually these resolved themselves into one image: Willis Boothe as last he'd seen him years ago, his pretty face and handsome body. Four strokes later, he orgasmed.

In the moment of clear-eyed calm that followed, he knew what he was and what he wanted.

Gay? Although that's what queers called themselves, he didn't feel particularly happy. He felt lonely, worried and deeply depressed.

How had this happened to him? The conventional wisdom, to which he'd always subscribed, was that homosexuality was a choice, a perverse choice made by those with nothing better to do than thumb their noses at society and all its hard-won values real men had died to defend. Part of the attraction of this notion, he now realized, was that it had always allowed him to believe that, if homosexuality was a choice, he could choose it *not*. Yet in the end, though he'd despised it and fought it to the limit of his strength, here it was! He felt trapped into something evil, something the world condemned and hated. Why did he deserve this? He didn't feel evil. He felt as if all his life he'd tried to do the right thing, to do what was demanded of him by society and his peers. Was it his fault he'd come to this?

No, he decided, it wasn't. He didn't know how or why this had happened to him. He wasn't a bad person; he was just himself, the same as he'd always been. Only now, he'd admitted something he'd never dared to before. He was unchanged: same person, same character, same inner self. The only difference was that this inner self was now revealed—to him, if no one else. He didn't feel he ought to be kicked, jeered and despised for this. He was still Greg!

Now that he knew what he was, he struggled not to hate it. Gay Pride? He had always dismissed that with a scoff. Did queers really feel there were things they had that normal people didn't? Beautiful, accomplished things worthy of some sort of pride?

What positive things had there been about Lamont and Willis, those whining laughingstocks he'd so despised? What things might they have had in which to feel pride? With a certain degree of shame, he realized it had never occurred to him to find out. Certainly, there had been unsuspected depths to Herbie, as he'd discovered this afternoon. And himself? What was to be admired there? Right now he wasn't too sure.

Could queers really feel and think themselves as good as everyone else and demand everybody else think so too? He certainly hoped so for his own sake, because right now he didn't feel the slightest bit gay. He felt queer as could be. Just how was he supposed to shuck his shame at that, let alone express any pride? Pride meant not caring if people knew. What would happen to his career if they found out at the office? What if Morgan Jaye found out? He cringed at the thought.

He quailed at facing the world's hatred and disapprobation. He thought again of Lamont and Willis, how their faces had set, jaws clamped, into wooden expressionlessness when they were taunted. He thought he understood. They had known what he knew now: that they were just ordinary people with no choice about what they were. They had borne their injustices as best they could. Had they really felt these to have been unfair? He'd supposed all along they knew as well as everybody else that what was happening to them was what they deserved. With increasing humility, he recalled now they had protested the injustice done them many times, and that the fact they'd done so had only incited more injustice against them. If the queers hadn't known their place, they must be taught it.

Another wave of shame swept him for the way they'd been treated. His face grew red. He literally writhed with the agony of it. He'd meted out a fair share of the world's injustice to them himself. He'd taunted them. He'd delighted in passing and exaggerating the

103

sniggering gossip, same as everybody else. "Alcock! All cock and no balls!" he had cried.

So what did he think of Lamont and Willis now? His instant reaction was that they'd brought their troubles on themselves by being so unnecessarily blatant. *Unnecessarily?* Perhaps they'd had no more control over their speech and mannerisms than over their sexuality itself. He frowned. What, exactly, had they done to earn their queer labels in the first place? Surely, it had to have been more than just a little fruity speech and flouncing around. With shock, he realized he didn't know. With all the made-up stories people had floated about them, telling truth from fiction was now impossible. Conceivably, it had been something as childish and innocent as what he'd done with Tommy in the park, the only difference being that they'd been discovered at it. He gulped. *There but for the grace of god...*

All at once, he felt a surprising affinity for them and was deeply ashamed. He'd done his bit and more to make theirs a cruel life, as much by omission as otherwise. Now that he was about to be in the same boat, he thought, he wished he'd done something to stand up and stop it, that, at the very least, he'd had the guts to offer pretty Willis some kind of friendship.

And Herbie? What did he now think of Herbie? He didn't know. Maybe he had treated him badly. When you really looked at it, Herbie's "sexual harassment" never had been anything like explicit. Maybe his persecution of the guy had been as much from terror as for cause—but then, lonely socially repulsive old Herbie really had thrust him into an impossible situation! Maybe there'd been so much pain on either side conflict had been inevitable. He didn't know. He'd been so angry at Herbie for so long, he wasn't ready to give it all up at once. He'd find the silly jerk, then see how he felt.

And himself? He'd paid a price too. In return for his respectability, he'd been lonely and isolated in the midst of the jeering laughing crowd. An awful lot of average adolescent life had passed him by and left him a spectator. He'd never gone steady or had a teenage crush. At times, the loneliness of it had been boneshaking. Being queer made life hard, no matter how you sliced it.

Or was it society that made it hard, not the thing itself? The view through the crack in the closet door is a narrow view, and he dismissed this thought as a whine. How could it be fair to demand the majority change its opinions just for him? As so lately a card carrying member of the majority himself, this seemed a breathtakingly impudent thing to ask. Yet, as long as he had no choice but to be what he was, wasn't he entitled to his fair share of what the world had going? Where did the majority's rights end and his begin? Confusion.

He felt as if all his life he'd been tumbled about blindly on the current of the world's expectations. He'd been led into Magellan Park and kicked out of it. He'd done his best to do what society said it wanted from him, taking his opinions and his conduct from the crowd. In high school and college, the crowd had taken him, hungry for membership and approbation, into all sorts of foolishness.

He was a born follower. He supposed that would never change. Even now, his interests, his taste in clothes and even his political opinions all came from the office, just as if he'd been issued them along with his desk and his viewscreen. In his desire to fit in and be an ordinary person, he'd allowed himself to be led by the nose every step of the way, every day of his life, and had ended up noplace, alone. Suddenly there was no one to follow. He must shed his old identity and try to find a new one.

He wandered to the windows again and looked wistfully at the neighboring tower's thousand dioramas of ordinary weekday evening life. People ate, watched television, read, talked, worked, entertained, and yes, the exhibitionists on the 18th floor were at it again. That he would ever have a life like that as a queer was hard to conceive. He tried. He pictured himself coming home, his male lover (face blank) in the kitchen wearing an apron, making dinner. *Hi honey, I'm home!* He shook his head. It seemed a faintly ridiculous picture. He supposed he'd get used to it, that is, if he was lucky.

At the moment, he wasn't quite sure just from where that lover would materialize. He knew there were gay bars right beneath his windows, down there on Halsted Street. But what if someone saw him? Worse, he had no idea how to behave in such places when you knew nobody. Was he supposed to go up to people and introduce himself? He, who fancied himself so calm, self-assured and skillful in dealing with ordinary, normal people, couldn't quite bring himself to face it. Worse yet, he knew the new guy in any scene always fell into the wrong crowd at first. He had no idea how he'd avoid that. He wouldn't know how to tell one crowd from another. He didn't know what crowds there were, how gay society was organized. He needed a friend to take him and show him the ropes. Why, with someone like that, knowledgeable, protective, sociable and popular, it might even be fun, a real adventure! But where would he find this friend if not in the bars, and how would he manage the bars without a friend? *Catch 69,* he thought gloomily. In a twist of gallows humor, it occurred to him that, with Herbie Manning, he certainly had missed the chance for an orientation lecture.

The New York trip seemed to offer a possible way out. New York did have one of the larger gay communities on the continent, he'd heard. It was comfortably far from home too. Making a fool of himself needn't haunt him forever. It seemed his business there inevitably would take him among gay people. Perhaps he'd pick up something useful. He might manage a good deal of personal exploration in his off-hours, if only he could keep his wits about him, watch his drinking and stay out of his colleagues' sight. Morgan Jaye's assignment was turning out to be convenient in all sorts of ways. Maybe. He would have to be very, very careful to arrange things so as not to reveal his secret.

His mind wandered onto the assignment itself. In this insecure, doubting mood, he fixed on a tiny reservation about it that had been nagging at the back of his mind all day. The career break was almost too good to be true. The last time that had happened, with Herbie Manning, something else had been going on.

If the mission was as crucial as Jaye said, Greg hardly felt qualified to be in charge. Of course, he was acquainted with the subject, but that only qualified him to advise the investigation, not lead it. True, he was a good accountant, and a good detective too, who had never failed an assignment, but then, he'd never had an assignment precisely like this one. It didn't seem to require his accounting skills at all. The crime's dollars and cents were thoroughly well understood already. Surely, any Treasury agent would be more qualified than he. Between CRAP's regular staff and Catchem, Billem & Stickem alone, there were dozens of grizzled law enforcement veterans for whom tracking down hot money had been a 30-year way of life. Wouldn't skills and experience such as that be infinitely preferable to his own youth and relative inexperience? What was going on here? While he couldn't figure it exactly, everybody knew Morgan Jaye, that fearsome old bird, was capable of surprising things. That's why he had his position.

Greg shook his head. He knew he was tired, emotionally drained, and no longer thinking clearly. There'd be as many of the grizzled veterans as he wanted in New York for advice. Perhaps Jaye merely felt the need for fresh eyes and youthful energy. Perhaps Jaye really did think he had talent, and really was offering to take him under his wing. Perhaps all that hard work was now paying off even bigger than he'd imagined it might.

He didn't want to think about it anymore. All sorts of currents ran contrariwise in his head. He was drained by the emotional conflicts of the evening. He felt a deep sense of guilt about his attitude toward Lamont and Willis, beautiful Willis. He felt anxious about the future, about the long and surely dangerous road to whatever happiness he might find. He felt peace too, the peace of a final resolution to the tension of lying to himself that had plagued him since puberty. He felt calm and relieved to know now who he was and be sure. Yet under it all was loneliness, the loneliness that gripped him when he was alone in bed at night, that penetrated and shook his very bones with the knowledge that never once in his life had he experienced a true emotional exchange with an equal—someone he loved and longed for, and who longed for him in return.

His head ran with questions. To his surprise, he found Herbie Manning's brass letter opener back in his hand, held in a tight grip. He must have picked it up again without noticing. He put it down abruptly, with a conscious air of finality. He was tired—hungry too. *Eat in the morning*, he thought dully, and trod off to bed, to sleep made restless with troubled dreams.

* * * * *

Morgan Jaye sat in the darkened great hall of his faux Gothic mansion. From the depths of a wing chair he stared into the fire, poker in hand. The flames leapt and sputtered beneath the gargoyles on his mantelpiece, and twisted themselves into the orange glowing image of a troubled Greg Whitbread undressing for bed. "*Eat in the morning...*" The words whispered in his head.

"Enough, enough," Jaye muttered. "Stop this. To tread this way through someone's innermost, most private thoughts... it's an obscenity."

Slowly, the image unraveled. The fire became an ordinary fire and burned low. A brass firedog in the shape of a griffin yawned and stretched its eagle's head and wings. Brass plumage rattled. "'What a piece of work is a man,' eh?" the firedog said. "Don't complain. You wanted to know, 'Why Whitbread?' and I'm doing my best to oblige by showing you the qualities that went into his selection. We want you to be happy."

"Humph. If you supposed this demonstration would bolster my confidence, it's gone awry. This boy, at any rate, seems more like merely a piece of work. He is completely wrong for this assignment. He is simply too young and inexperienced to find me Manning and that money. It's so obvious, even he wonders about it. Why on earth do you want me to use him?"

The firedog-griffin stretched its lion's hindquarters. "Goodness, I do seem to be spending all my time in brass implements lately. My joint aches. Pun."

The big man only glowered.

"Because he'll do, and that's that. He's innocent as they come in this day and age. We'll be able to lead him easily." The firedog preened itself, keeping one basilisk eye on Jaye the while. "Besides, he was handy."

"Well, I don't like it. On your say-so, I've placed him in a position crucial to the success of that undertaking, but a position far beyond his experience and maturity. Then there is this, ah, emotional instability, this newfound perversion of his, which he intends to combine with *my assignment*! That troubles me deeply."

"The Master thinks he's perfect. End of discussion."

Jaye rumbled dangerously, a volcano shifting in uneasy sleep. "I have grave misgivings! He's ambitious, and I've motivated him with ambition—what else can I do to get him to try his best?—but ambition makes men do foolish things."

The firedog sneered. "Your word, I'll take for that."

Jaye went white-lipped with fury. "*I've* done foolish things? Through *ambition*? How dare you! I've had to struggle all my life just to stay level, and the unending foolish situations in which I've found myself have all been the result of our bargains, every one!" Jaye struggled to control his bitterness. "And you taunt me with ambition. It's happened again and again when I've had a problem. You come to me and offer to help. You order me to do something with no apparent connection to my problem, and poof! The solution is apparent, but my trousers are down around my ankles and there's a surprised, foolish expression on my face. This time, it's the Manning investigation which has nothing to do with the problem I've come to you to solve. I've had enough! That investigation is the most crucial professional matter on my desk. This time, I want to know how all these things hook together and what to expect. I need to know whether or not I'm actually going to get Manning and solve the ATM thefts."

"Why? Wouldn't it be more fun to be surprised?" The firedog smirked.

The big man clenched his jaw. "I must know now! I demand it! Your meddling in my handling of that affair entitles me to know!"

"Does it? Better get your lawyer to check the fine print on your agreement with Master." The firedog grinned nastily. "Master *likes* lawyers. And who knows?—I don't: maybe you won't look so foolish this time, though you'd sure be a picture with your pants down around your ankles."

The firedog lifted one of its lion's legs to scratch, saw its wings were in the way, and thought better of it. "Look, this carping is pointless. You've got a deal with Master. As always, all you have to do is what you're told. If you didn't want this bargain, why did you make it?"

"You know very well! I'm being squeezed! Blackmailed! Destroyed inch by inch! Resurrecting our connection was absolutely my final option."

"Oh yes, the lovely little birdies, though in this case, the bird in your hand is only you diddling yourself."

Jaye roared with rage. With lightening speed and agility surprising for his bulk, the banker leaned forwards and struck the poker on the firedog with all his might. Metal clanged on metal. The poker spun from Jaye's hand and fell at his feet.

The firedog cocked its head. "That was pointless."

The big man sat back, rubbing his wrist. He glared. "Then there's the boy himself. In my experience, you destroy everything you touch. That boy is valuable, damn you. He might still have a real future in my operation, if his career is handled properly."

"Really." The firedog widened its eyes in mock amazement. "Despite his *perversion?*"

"If he'll stick to his resolution regarding absolute discretion in his personal life, I can use him, though I grant you, possibly not on my personal staff. He's just the kind of intelligent and dedicated hard worker good at taking orders that's unusually hard to come by. Then too, it's possible I'll need a good operative with entré to the homosexual community one day. Our personnel policies have always put us at something of a disadvantage in that area. Can you assure me I'm going to get him back?"

"I give up. This game is boring me. If I had the answers, I'd tell you, honest, but I don't. I'm as blind to the grand design as you are." The firedog shrugged its shoulders, discovered it hadn't any, and made a disgusted noise. "And so what? Look, your bargain isn't about Whitbread. At this point, if you want him back, all I can do is register your request, though from *my* experience, if you do get him back, I wouldn't guarantee you'll still want him. Good nightshade, what does it matter, one mortal more or less? There're billions of them. Why worry about him?"

Jaye glowered in dissatisfaction. "Whitbread or not, you assure me I'll get relief from the blackmail? That *is* what our bargain's about."

"Of course," the firedog snapped. "Master agreed, and that's that. Have we ever failed you?"

"No. But enough is enough. I like predictability, and I like to do business with principals, not least because they usually *do* have the answers. Lately, it's occurred to me I've never met this master of yours."

"Believe me, you'd rather not."

"Humph."

The firedog clacked its beak in exasperation. "Honestly, you mortals make me tired, all of you. No one can do you a favor without endless kvetching. All you've got to do is hold up your end—and, oh boy, you'd better." The firedog's tone became very sharp, indeed. "What I *do* know is that, at this point, you and your bargain have become *part* of the grand design. Back out now, and you will be *obliterated*."

Jaye smoldered. He reached for the poker and opened his mouth to speak.

The firedog cut him off. "Bah. Like you said, enough's enough. I'm killing the fire. Go to bed."

Jaye closed his mouth. The firedog was become mere brass. Jaye carefully replaced the poker in its rack and sank back in his chair. He scowled into the dying flames.

Chapter Three
THE PRINCE OF THIEVES

It was that truly cosmic time in the universe, that time when, in the cosmology of *Odd Bodkins* at any rate, everything gets done: it was Tuesday After Lunch.

Fresh from a brief yet indolent Labor Day weekend, New York City settled back grudgingly into workaday routine. That the weather smiled only made matters worse. The few small white clouds idling benignly over Central Park only reminded New Yorkers of the shore's and country's pleasures interdicted by the rude demands of daily life, and sent them grumping down hundreds of rat holes, scuttling through their underground maze to the myriad ugly towering warrens wherein the pena

nce for a few days' vacation sunshine must be served. —Or so, at least, it seemed to Greg Whitbread. As a Chicagoan born and bred (and if his childhood had been off by a block or two, it made no difference), he was heir to and a committed slave of that city's traditional inferiority complex.

While this cultural phenomenon was not unique to the broad-shouldered colossus on the lake—the citizens of Tacoma and Chicago's own satellite Milwaukee might well have recognized the affect involved—in Chicago, it found its most pronounced and profound expression, and obtained the apotheosis of an official name: the Second City Complex. Part boosterism, part envy, part neurosis, part hatred pure and simple, the whole leavened liberally with sour grapes, this irritating disability poisoned its sufferers' pride in and enjoyment of their glittering city with the thought yet one other American metropolis could boast even more spectacular achievements, as, indeed, it seemed to do as loudly as possible on every conceivable occasion.

The effects on Chicagoans were contradictory. They sniffed at New York as loudly and often as decently they might. New York was dirty, disorganized, expensive, dangerous, annoyingly self-congratulatory and—that ultimate Chicago crime—*pretentious.* Chicagoans looked in vain for a New York review of any Chicago thing that exceeded faint praise, though nothing existed there which was not available in the same or better quality "right here at home." At the same time, especially where cultural merchandise was concerned, Chicagoans' assurance of the sort of quality they might allow themselves to appreciate safely often came in the form of a New York reputation. Actors, playwrights and musicians found New York credits most helpful in obtaining work, and god help the writer or artist without prior exposure in the despised Rotten Apple who tried obtaining local publication or gallery representation. Oh, it could be done. You could also climb mountains barefoot, but why would you?

To all such provincial angst, New Yorkers were supremely oblivious, naturally. The subject came up but rarely: "Chicago? It's an extremely beautiful city—I'm told," they might remark in the three seconds before their eyes glazed. Oddly, Chicagoans themselves adopted this very attitude whenever Minneapolis was mentioned, or St. Louis, or some other place yet a further order of magnitude down the scale.

The general superciliousness of New Yorkers regarding his background irritated Greg no end. At least, this was how he interpreted the attitude of his new, New York subordinates. In fact, however, their attitude bore a suspicious resemblance to that of locals everywhere toward out-of-town honchos: that the business would go better if bossman would kindly hole up in the office and talk on the phone or something while those who knew the ground best were left free to do the work; and to further the effect, some of Greg's team also suffered an ill-concealed dose of that disbelief and career anxiety everyone experiences the first time they get a boss young enough to be, if not their son or daughter (godhelpthem!), at least a *nephew*.

Greg would have none of it. He plunged vigorously into a top-to-bottom review of CRAP's procedures for the recapture of Herbie Manning's $100 bills. Some such review was plainly necessary. The three bills recently discovered in New York had turned up more or less by accident during routine sorting in a mid-town bank's cash room. A clerk had just happened to be working beneath CRAP's warning notice.

By that time, of course, the bills' previous history was largely lost. Although a latent fingerprint scan showed evidence of only one or two handlers apiece, this meant nothing. The bills had been given Herbie Manning in bundles; there was no way to tell even such a basic thing as how many hands the bills had been through before reaching the bank.

Nor did the fingerprints themselves produce much. Except for one, they were uselessly partial or smudged beyond identification, though they did have a small stroke of luck with that one. Its owner, when a small boy, had been taken on the tour of FBI headquarters in Washington, DC, and, at the fingerprint demonstration, had been thrilled to have his prints rolled just like a grownup crime suspect! Today, he worked as a clerk at Marino's Bookstore, the largest in New York. Although this seemed promising given Herbie Manning's interest in literature, the luck ended there; not only didn't he recognize Herbie's picture, he was utterly unable to tell them anything about who might have given him the bill, or, for that matter, when. Business had been good lately, the store crowded.

When Greg arrived in New York, he knew they simply had to lock onto Herbie's money earlier in the process, while they still had some chance of tracing it hand to hand. He visited all the city's major banks in person, explaining, cajoling, insinuating and outright threatening them into a watch for those bills that would allow for more immediate response.

Resistance was massive. Checking every serial number would slow down tellers. Didn't he know Time Was Money? The cooperation he received could be lackadaisical even at banks which belonged to the Consortium! His sense of CRAP's omnipotence evaporated rapidly. In desperation and after hurried consultation with Morgan Jaye back in Chicago, he decreed that, henceforth, these bills would be treated as counterfeit. He had them listed as such in all the standard databases. Federal officers would now confiscate them unreimbursed.

At once, he was speaking language the banks understood, and had the results he desired with no further delay. Notices went up at teller stations everywhere. Banks all over the city enclosed flyers in their business customers' statements notifying them of the "counterfeit" serial numbers and offering a reward for the detention of whomever might present them.

This was more like it.

Next, they tested the system to be as sure as possible no one could pass those bills undetected, and that the alarm would be sounded in sufficient time to allow the team to respond. That there were thousands of small businessmen in New York who, for fear of counterfeiters, wouldn't have touched any $100 bill, good or bad, was both a blessing and a curse; while it made finding Manning an only barely unmanageable proposition, it also threw him back on his $100,000 in smaller, untraceable bills for the daily necessities of life. The only hope was that he would use his hundreds for the bigger ticket purchases Greg felt certain he would make, sooner or later.

Greg and his lieutenants presented the already recovered bills in as many likely places as they could. Plugging gaps and whipping recalcitrant banks and merchants into line proved to be irritating, frustrating work. The natural indifference and bad temper of New Yorkers worked against them every step of the way.

Greg also paid some attention to the other half of his investigation: the attempt to trace Manning directly. Which, however, merely wasted time. Manning's few New York acquaintances all professed ignorance as to his whereabouts, and surveillance on them failed to show any different. Only one possible avenue of approach remained: Greg's notion that some digging among the city's vast population of male prostitutes might produce results.

His own ignorance and uncertainty in this regard being as great as ever, this was one job he was glad to delegate. He commandeered a couple of vice cops from the city police, especially requesting ones with extensive experience among this population, a request the Department hemmed and hawed over before admitting it could fulfill. Yet, the officers as finally delivered came with impressive credentials and seemed quite aggressively competent. They'd been showing Manning's picture around among their contacts, and had distributed it at precinct houses serving the city's more prominent blue light districts. That no results whatsoever had yet been obtained in no way tainted Greg's relief that this portion of the investigation seemed to be in good hands.

Finally, Greg was satisfied the setup was as good as it would ever get, and sat down to wait. He ordered the captive Manning bills kept busy in tests to keep his people awake.

At first, he waited vigilantly. He sat in his hotel room staring at the phone, two armed detectives at the ready. The detectives were scruffy, unshaven types, veterans of innumerable stakeouts of all kinds. They refused to be impressed. They ate junk food and played gin rummy all day. Their conversation was basically limited to, "Hey Vinny, watch it! Ya gettin' the cards all greasy!" and "Hey boss, you ain't doin' nothin'. Howzabout runnin' down an' gettin' us a pizza?"

After a few days of this, Greg began to feel as if maybe his eagerness was indeed a pure product of inexperience. He posted the detectives to a waiting station in Brooklyn Heights. He began to loosen up and relax.

Thus, Tuesday After Lunch found Greg leaning up against the wall across from his hotel on Central Park South, catching his breath after a long, leisurely jog through the park. Lazy light jazz flowed into his head from the portable player he carried in a shoulder harness.

At first, Central Park had had an oddly, almost irritatingly familiar feel. Then he understood: the lagoon, the romantic-looking ruin overlooking it and the layout of the paths through groves, meadows and gardens all reminded him strongly of his boyhood's Magellan Park, only kept up, trimmed back, and vastly larger. He had an intimidating sense that here was the original of which Magellan Park was only a pale and grossly inferior copy. Inexorably, this also reminded him of the personal subtext with which he'd begun this expedition to New York: the opportunity to do something about his new sexual status.

Now, it's a bemusing fact of human nature that, the longer people have been settled into habits of life grown familiar with daily use, the less willing to dislodge themselves they become. Thus, vacations under friendlier skies only make many people homesick for the familiar drudgery they'd longed to escape, which is the very reason some people take vacations in the first place: to make bearable the long days of routine toil justified because they enable the escape that is so ultimately unsatisfactory. This is one of the basic maintenance cycles of an unfulfilled existence.

Such prisoners of life manage their internal realms in a predictable way: when they come across a new fact which doesn't fit the schema of their preconceived ideas, they are as likely to question the fact or, if its proofs be strong, belittle or ignore altogether its effect on their personal cosmologies as they are to revamp them.

This mass mental inertia underpins our world. Without it, who would choose to clerk at a desk or toil in a factory when he might comb a beach in the tropics? Who would be satisfied to gulp his coffee on a wintry dash to the 7:06 when he might, like Gauguin, spend the rest of his life painting pretty pictures among a languorous promiscuous people, free from the prisons of backbiting coworkers and meaningless routine? —And if none stayed behind to do society's drudgery, who'd be left to care?

For his part, Greg was no Gauguin. He might have seen the newfound prospect of gay life as an opportunity to free himself forever from the stifling conformity of middle class life. He might have heaved a sigh of relief that never would he have to fill a pasteboard house in a tacky suburb with furniture of cheap Scandinavian veneer because the financial drain of his 2.3 children, 1.8 cars, 1.4 pets and .5 divorces allowed him no better; that never would he have to deny himself dinner and a show because, at the last moment, the babysitter fancied a night out herself; that never need he be drafted to involuntary military service; that, living completely outside its pale, he was saved forever from the bonds of conventional, hypocritical morality and guilt. He might have begun a new existence exempt from the responsibilities and restraints imprisoning and deadening ordinary lives. He might have seen himself as special, blessed, as elected to live his life among a lucky few.

He might have gone even a step further and wondered whether, if conventional society was wrong about the sickness and perversity of gay people and gay life, it might be equally wrong about some other of its deeply held beliefs and attitudes.

Unfortunately, Greg's solid stable intelligent yet ordinary mind did not work this way. Although the upheavals of self-revelation had pushed him off balance, as time passed, his emotional swings stilled. The pendulum gradually tended back to stability on dead center. He retreated from self-identification as homosexual; he clung tenaciously to his unsatisfactory experiences with women, and now figured he was bisexual, with an unfortunately strong slant toward the homo side of things, maybe, but bisexual none the less. His sorrow and sense of injustice at the abuse of Lamont and Willis was replaced by a renewed sense they'd only got what they'd asked for by being so blatant. His ambivalence toward Herbie Manning had disappeared; once again, he was the lawman, Manning the fugitive from justice. His interest in checking out New York's gay scene on the quiet had softened before the obvious homophobia of his colleagues. His desire for a friend with whom to explore gay life had devolved into silent yearning for a lover to share his closet, someone exactly like himself: solid, prosperous and cautious.

Rather than question the meaning and worth of the middle class values which excluded him, his goal had become to fit his new life inside them no matter how imperfect the fit. It did not occur to him that, just as he'd been lonely and unhappy in his life before, the mere addition of a mate to share it would not solve the problem, that then there only would be two of them to be isolated and unhappy together.

He did think it would be nice if, during his time in New York, he could meet someone willing to move back to Chicago with him.

In this way, he might gain his goal without exposing himself in his own city at all. However, the improbabilities of this were manifest even to him. Just as he would never have considered uprooting himself from his prospects for transplant into the unknown, why should somebody else? The sort of somebody he wanted certainly never would.

Where would he meet this someone, anyway? He had not the slightest idea how to begin. Jogging along in his green and yellow spandex one-piece running suit with the designer logo tastefully on his hip, he saw the men lazing on the grass and ambling through the bushes. Heads turning, their eyes followed his shapely bare legs flashing in the sunshine. Once, a long sensual wolf whistle hung in the air as he rounded a corner and disappeared from view. This embarrassed him somewhat. He didn't know whether he was being complimented or ridiculed. While he hoped it was the former, he was unsure what to do. He felt the weight of his ignorance as an oppressive burden. What if he went up to someone, and they only laughed or called him fag? No, he was not ready for that kind of risk. He had waited so long, it wouldn't hurt to wait a while longer until the situation was exactly right and he felt comfortable.

Gay bars were another problem. Here in New York, he had no idea where they were! There must be some, surely, if only he had the shadow of a notion how to find them, though if he had, he thought, it still wouldn't do him much good. The person he wanted wouldn't be making that kind of public show, anyway.

But when he got right down to it, so overwhelming it constantly threatened to swamp all this endlessly rehearsed self-evident good sense, the simple desire to get laid tortured his every minute. At last, he knew what he wanted, and years of pent-up desire insisted he have it, the sooner the better, immediately, if possible. He had invested such high hopes in this trip to New York, even visiting a doctor (not his own, of course) for a dose of the Pasteur Institute's new vaccine. He was sick to think it all might go as so much wasted effort. Yet there seemed nothing he could do.

His lifelong prison remained intact. The only possible way out he could see was the same one Herbie Manning had taken. True, hiring a hustler would do nothing toward finding him a lover, and might be dangerous, besides. But at least, he told himself, it would get him the experience for which he felt such a dire need, *if* he could find somebody clean, congenial, honest, sympathetic and, above all, confidential. He reflected glumly that his reading of the Attaché Arms transcripts seemed to leave small hope of that. Still, he was desperate and willing to explore. If only they might take Manning under circumstances that would give him some information about where to look and how to proceed, then later, after the investigation when nobody was looking, he would have the means to do a little cautious adventuring on his own—but so far, even that seemed a lot to ask. So far, that trail was thermometering absolute zero. When the lead on Manning finally came, if it ever did, they'd probably take him buying a stereo.

Right now, rehearsing these frustrations was poisoning the fine day there on Central Park South. He noticed the trash blowing on the grass, the sidewalk and in the gutter. Fragments of old newspaper, plastic knives and forks, paper bags, cups and outright garbage littered the street, tramped down, ground in and rotting. This crud was all-pervasive in New York, so everpresent one usually ceased to see it after a day or two. Scuttling on the breeze, it underscored his disappointment and disgust at his inability to help himself.

From amidst a small vortex of this stuff a leatherman clanked up the sidewalk, loaded down with chains and metal clutter. His frank stare held Greg frozen like a deer in headlights. As the man's approach slowed almost to a stop, Greg panicked: his head snapped aside; he jerked around to face the park. He heard, not saw, the leatherman shrug his shoulders and jangle on by.

So what was I supposed to do? Greg wondered. All that ostentatious metal trash was so intimidatingly obvious. The fellow might as well wear a neon sign! *Handcuffs were probably cheaper,* Greg sniffed. No, this was not the sort of person he was after.

Yet, the minute the man was by and beyond recall, Greg regretted his loss of nerve. Incredulous, he discovered he was trembling with stress. It had been an opportunity—a gift straight from heaven—and he'd thrown it away! Why had he done that? All at once, he was uncertain he'd done the right thing. Well, of course he had. Instinctively he'd done the *safe* thing, but still...

A large shadow flickered across the buildings on Fifth Avenue. Greg's breath caught as he glanced up. A gleaming blimp hung over Central Park, large red letters on its silver sides: "I ♥ New York" and the sportswear manufacturer's logo from Greg's hip. Floating in the sunshine against the blue sky and luminous white clouds, it was achingly beautiful, or would have been except for the annoying message.

As he watched the shifting play of light and cloudshadow on the blimp, three sharp beeps sounded over the music in his headphones, repeated a moment later. Greg's attention refocussed, reluctantly, on business. *Probably just another failed test. They want me to go yell at some department store somewhere.* Sighing, he set the unit's selector switch to engage its cell phone. He detached the microphone tube whence it clicked neatly into the headset, swung it around and pushed the button.

The CRAP switchboard man sounded excited. "Greg, someone's passing one of our hundreds at Marino's main bookstore on 54th Street. It's not a test, either. The serial number isn't one of our test bills! This could be it!"

Yes, it certainly could. That a bill had been used there before had made repetition an interesting possibility, and Greg had singled the place out for special attention. What was that funny little man's name, the Assistant Manager in charge of security? Oh yes. "Okay. I guess I'm closest. It's just a couple of blocks. I'll be there in five minutes. Mobilize me some backup. Out."

Books. It could only be Manning. At last. Greg sighed. If he couldn't be happy and sexually satisfied, at least his career would be secure. He locked down his telephone gear and flagged a taxi. From Central Park South to 54th Street was a matter of minutes, and they made all the lights. It seemed no time at all before he strode into the buzzing fluorescence of Marino's showroom. A clerk in a blazer came past, scanning the racks purposefully. Greg grabbed his arm.

The clerk shrugged him off. "Excuse me, *sir*. I'm with another cust—" He stopped talking because Greg's CRAP card was in his face.

"Take me to Mr. Arquebus. Now."

To Greg's considerable satisfaction, the man's snooty manner melted as if it never had been. "This way, sir."

Greg followed him among brightly colored heaps of books and boxed datacapsules to the back of the store. From behind a sales desk a narrow white corridor ran between lots of black doors, through one of which they went.

The clerk disappeared. A small balding potbellied man rose fussily from his desk. "That was fast! It seems only a moment ago I put in the call." He looked Greg up and down, and smiled. "If that's the latest in law enforcement wear, I'm all for it. So comfortable in this hot weather." Greg felt his face reddening. Mr. Arquebus quickly lifted a hand. "Oh, I know! You're incognito!" He nodded. "You look just like an ordinary young person. So clever. No one would ever suspect you for a federal agent."

"You have someone with one of the counterfeit $100's on our notice?"

"Yes. This is the bill." Mr. Arquebus reseated himself and extracted it from beneath a paperweight. "I can see why you're concerned. As far as I can tell, this bill is perfect. What's wrong with it?"

"If we are successful here, no one will ever know," Greg said sharply, and truthfully. He saw right away it was one of Manning's hundreds, its serial number only three above the highest numbered of the previously recovered bills. He noted with satisfaction that the bill was still pristinely, cracklingly new, marred only by having been folded into quarters at some point. At worst, it had not come through many hands. If it wasn't Manning himself who had attempted to pass it, chances of tracing it might be good. "You have the person who came in with this?"

"Yes. He's in a room usually reserved for, ah, kleptomaniacs." He sighed. "Profit margins on books are *so* low.

You'll want to, ah, interrogate him, I presume. Right this way." Mr. Arquebus bobbed up again.

"No, wait. First, I want to get a good look at him without him seeing me. Is this possible?"

"Assuredly." Mr. Arquebus nodded. "I understand. You want to decide your approach—which will probably be nothing special this time, though he's certainly well worth a look." Mr. Arquebus flashed him the prim smugness of a cat licking its chops.

Well worth a look? Greg was going to ask, but, as they went down the hall, a small tinny voice that had been burring in the background caught his attention as they approached its source.

...a once-in-a-lifetime opportunity to live in the world's most luxurious residential building, right on prestigious Fifth Avenue here in the heart of Manhattan, world-famous capital of business, entertainment, and the arts—the most exciting city in the world! These units are going fast, so call us today at...

Greg's jaw set. They entered a tiny room banked with television monitors. A uniformed guard stood up to make room for them. On the desk, a tiny portable radio chattered. Mr. Arquebus silenced it with a delicate finger, which afterwards he applied to the tip of his chin. "Now let me see." He scanned the screens, which showed the salesroom and the offices from every conceivable angle. "Oh, there he is." Mr. Arquebus indicated a screen near the bottom of the bank. Greg sat down to look.

He saw a small bare cell-like room with one occupant. For the second time in an hour, Greg's breath caught. There, seated on a chair, legs apart, the most beautiful boy in the world pouted directly into the camera. Long thick light hair framed large widely-spaced eyes, a straight nose and broad mouth. Even on the fuzzy black-and-white monitor, skin-tight white pants revealed muscular legs and the unmistakable outline of magnificent genitalia. Between broad shoulders and narrow hips, well-veined arms were crossed on a cut-off T-shirt above a midriff ridged with muscle. The figure lounged in unconcealed boredom and impatience.

This clearly was not Herbie Manning. As to whom it might be and why this person should have one of Herbie Manning's $100 bills, the answer seemed flat-out obvious to Greg. Here could be none other than one of Herbie Manning's hustlers. Greg had to admit it: Manning's taste seemed every bit as good here as in other things. He agreed with it 110%.

But what business could such a person have in a place like this?—unless... unless... could he be on an *errand* for Manning?

Mr. Arquebus broke in on Greg's ruminations. "He's been demanding an attorney and making the usual futile threats."

Greg tore his eyes from the screen. Discovering his jaw hanging open, he collected himself and tried to sound professional. "I want you to give him his bill back, apologize for the inconvenience, and let him go. Only give me a minute to get back to the front of the store."

The little man turned abruptly. "You're not going to question him? The bill is phony, isn't it?"

"Of course," Greg lied. "But this is not our main suspect. First, I want to tail him out of here and see where he goes."

Mr. Arquebus did not look happy. "What if he wants to stay and spend this phony bill?"

"I can't believe he will. He'll be getting out of here just as soon as he can, you watch. But if he does, please accept it. Call us at the number you used before, and we'll replace it with a good one."

Mr. Arquebus nodded reluctantly, his uneasiness at the thought of funny money wandering his store plainly unallayed.

A minute later, Greg scanned the salesroom anxiously. Where the hell was that backup? *Darn it!* He should have had Arquebus wait until it arrived. Too late now. He took up a position near the front door and camouflaged himself behind the first volume that came to hand, a picture book, *Glorious New York*. Above it, he saw his quarry emerge at the back of the store.

As Greg had predicted, Mr. Arquebus' fears proved groundless. The splendid body headed directly for the street, even more impressive in fluid, graceful motion than in repose. Greg saw heads turn all over the store. The noise level seemed to drop, as if conversations were dying everywhere in mid-word. As the flat waist passed in front of Greg, the mere sight of it stirred him to an incipient erection. *God, the guy looks naked even when he's dressed.* He chucked *Glorious New York* and fell in behind the firm derriere, unable to avoid noticing how deeply split it was by the cut of the white pants. They headed for the door.

The blond seemed totally oblivious. An annoyed, disgusted expression on his face, he stiff-armed the door and disappeared into the crowded street without missing a step. The door, unused to such abuse, swung back smartly on its closer and smacked Greg flat in the face. He clawed his way past a massively gravid lady loaded with packages who materialized coming through it the other way, and sought eagerly to regain a view of the bare midriff above those hypnotic buttocks. He caught it approaching the corner, where two taxis sat waiting in the avenue. The blond headed for the first of these.

Greg sprinted for the second and tumbled in. "Follow that cab!" he cried.

The driver, a large man with terminal five o'clock shadow and glasses held together with masking tape, closed his copy of the *New York Daily Pustule* unhurriedly. ALIENS SIRED MY KIDS, SAYS DI FROM BEYOND THE GRAVE, the headline shrieked. "So what is this, a game? What cab wazzat, mac?"

"That one right there! It says 'I Love New York' on the top!" As Greg pointed, the blond's cab moved uptown and crossed to the other side of the avenue. "Come on man, we're losing them!"

The driver twisted his large bulk around in his seat a degree or so. "But mac, they *all* say 'I Love New York' on top. Wuzzit an Evian Spring Water or a Roto Rooter?"

Greg was getting panicky. Where the hell was his backup? Oh, if only he'd had his mind on business and not on the blond! He pressed his CRAP card against the plexiglass shield separating him from the driver. "Look! You get this beater moving right now, or I'll have your license. MOVE!" Their quarry disappeared into a side street two blocks up.

The driver was unimpressed. "Okay, so you're a cop. Whoopee. I been on these here deals before. We run all over Manhattan after a cab with 'I Love New York' on top. When it stops, you go racing after the fare, and all I get is a nice warm feeling for doing my citizenly duty. Fuck that shit. I gotta living to earn here. Find yourself another pigeon."

Oh, so that's it, Greg thought. He swore silently. *New York!* Fumbling in agitation, he pulled out the $50 bill he carried under his ID for emergencies. He slammed it against the shield with his palm, then stuffed it into the cash slot to the front seat. "Here! Find me that cab and it's yours! But if we've lost him, I'll..."

Greg didn't get to finish. He was slammed back in his seat, then thrown over sideways as the cab screeched into violent, tire-smoking motion. They lurched into traffic and made a U-turn in the one-way avenue, then shot directly across all five lanes of moving traffic to duck into the mouth of 54th Street. Brakes screamed, horns cursed and shouts salted the air. As they sped away from the sickening chunkclunk of metal on glass in the intersection behind them, Greg struggled to regain his balance and fish his ID up off the floor.

"So why din'tya say so in the foist place, mac? That was cab 5E78, right? Hold on tight, kid, we gotta cut 'em off at the pass!"

Greg did as he was told through another burst of acceleration. They scattered pigeons and pedestrians, and bumped up onto the sidewalk to get around a delivery van.

"Hey! Getting stopped by the regular police won't help us, you know. HEY!" They jolted down off the high curb into the street. Greg scrambled back up onto the seat.

"No sweat, mac. They hafta catch me foist." They pulled up at the light. "There's your man, right?"

Sure enough, past them from uptown came an I ♥ New York taxi. (Roto Rooter, Greg noted.) Long blond hair bobbed up and down in the back. A classical profile smoked a cigarette.

Impressed in spite of himself, Greg confirmed it. "How'd you do that?" They turned into the avenue behind Blondy's cab.

"I'm clairvoyant," the driver smirked.

Oh, right. More likely, before the blond had entered the cab, he'd given his destination through his driver's open window and been overheard. Greg figured he, Greg, had just been suckered for $50.

"Hey, mac! Is this supposta be an open tail?"

An open tail was when you didn't care whether the subject saw you following him or not. Evidently, Greg's driver hadn't been lying when he'd said he'd done this before. Here was a bright spot: at least, Greg was overpaying for experience.

"No," he sighed. "Keep back a little, and drop me half a block behind him, wherever." They probably didn't need to be overly zealous if the driver already knew where they were going.

"You got it."

They proceeded down the avenue between rows of I ♥ New York lightpole banners sponsored by the brand of running shoe on Greg's feet. He strained to keep his eyes glued to the rear end of cab 5E78. The heavier, late afternoon traffic meant they could stay fairly close to their quarry and still stay lost in the crowd. So far, so good.

At last, cab 5E78 pulled over at a corner in the 20's. The blond started off down the sidewalk on foot. Greg followed.

As his driver pulled away, he shouted, "Hey kid! You're okay! Anytime you wanta tail, call the company and ask for me, Harry Kern! Go get him!"

Greg waved him off in annoyance. Luckily, Blondy hadn't turned around. The fabulous ass swaggered down the block unconcerned. Finally, its owner opened a door and disappeared.

Greg came up to the door, set into a bead-board storefront painted plain black. Tacked on letters spelled, "Cock Robin." Obviously a bar. Greg peeped cautiously through a small diamond pane in the door. Sure enough, Blondy perched precariously at the near corner of the bar, that incredible ass hanging over a tilted barstool. The bartender was pouring him a beer and chucking his chin. They laughed.

Greg backed away. *Okay,* he thought, *he's planted for a while. Now where is my goshdarn backup?*

But when he unlimbered his cellular phone and tried to make contact, all he got was static. The "Low Battery" icon flashed. Drat. He looked around. Across the way was a standard issue greasy spoon: big windows crosshatched with burglar screens, bright fluorescent lights, time-worn formica fixtures, and a payphone.

Greg crossed the street. While his running outfit did have a little pocket perfect for his ID and a few bills, he never carried coins in it. They bunched up and made an uncomfortable lump in the spandex when he ran. But when he asked the counterman for change, this worthy merely jerked a greasy thumb at the wall above his shoulder. Greg looked up. There, above the coffee machine and below a flyspecked I ♥ New York bumper sticker was taped a sheet of notebook paper whereon was scrawled the magic talisman, "NO CHANGE." Greg sighed. "I'll have a cup of foul-smelling coffee with lumpy cream, please."

The switchboard man was eager to hear from him. "So what's up? Was it Manning?"

"No, but I think it's someone who's maybe seen him fairly recently, and may well be seeing him again pretty soon. Subject is in a bar, the Cock Robin." He gave the address. "I'm in the poison palace across the street—" Greg threw a glance at the counterman, who regarded him evilly. "Who can you send me?"

"Well, Rico and Freddie were closest when you were at Marino's, but you were gone when they got there. They figured you might still need them, though. I'd say you could have them in fifteen minutes, tops."

He ignored the implied insult. Rico and Freddie were, in fact, the vice cops he'd borrowed from the city police. The very men he wanted.

"Make it ten, in case the subject moves again. I'm not dressed for this."

"They'll do their best. Sit tight."

This was unnecessary advice. Greg took his coffee to a table at the front window and stared out at the Cock Robin.

What had happened was pretty obvious, Greg figured. Manning had found Blondy irresistible—as who wouldn't. He'd run across him someplace, perhaps in that very dive across the street, and spent one or more of his hundreds on joy unrestrained. Very likely, Greg thought, he was continuing to purchase himself a somewhat closer relationship.

The more Greg thought about it, the more sanguine he became about the prospect Blondy might be on an errand for Manning even now. The impression of hustlers he'd gained from the Attaché Arms files made it seem unlikely one would voluntarily spend his hard-earned jack in a bookstore, though with looks like that, Greg thought, just about anybody, with any background, might be tempted to see what life was like on Wild Street. Stranger things had happened.

Actually, he discounted this. After assigning probabilities to potentialities, he firmly expected Manning to saunter up the sidewalk and turn in at the Cock Robin any second.

He was still imagining, in 3-D Technicolor, what Herbie might have got for his money when Rico and Freddie walked up outside the window. Greg motioned them in.

At the table, they looked like junkies. Freddie was tall, thin, black, and looked heavily strung out. Rico was a short Puerto Rican with a little chin beard that made him look about sixteen years old. They were both ragged and dirty. In this case, however, appearances deceived. Their reputations said they were the best streetmen in the city.

"Hey, man, sorry we missed you at Marino's. Got held up in traffic." This was Rico. His voice was a surprising basso, considering his diminutive stature.

"Yeah, you can'ta been there long." The soft high Michael Jackson countertenor belonged to Freddie.

"I wasn't." Greg hastened to cover his ass. "Subject was getting restless," he said officiously. "I thought I'd better let him move before he suspected anything beyond a normal commercial screwup."

"It ain't our main man?" Rico wanted to know.

"No. It's somebody else, a hustler, I think. Your turf. I bet he's seen Manning in the last couple of days, and maybe even knows where he is."

Freddie frowned. "So why let him move at all? Why not just tie him up and ask him?"

This excellent question took Greg by real surprise. He had not as much as considered the possibility. Well, why *not*? Rico and Freddie were staring at him. He attempted to spell out his instinct as confidently as possible. "No. I can't figure this one in a bookstore, somehow. I gotta hunch he might have been on an errand for Manning, and that our man'll turn up around him soon. Plus, he was real sharp in the bookstore about saying nothing and insisting on his rights. So let's leave him under his own power and see if he won't take us where we want to go. And if he doesn't in a day or two, we'll have info for an approach."

"It's your call." Rico shrugged. "Just so long you sure the Manning man ain't getting farther away all the time." He bumped his partner with his shoulder. "Freddie, my man, go check it out."

Greg filled him in. "Long blond hair, white jeans, cutoff T-shirt, at the corner of the bar when I looked."

Freddie nodded and crossed the street. He took a check through the small diamond pane, then crossed back. "My my my! Wetdream city!"

Rico rolled his eyes. "Okay man, we got him. You go off to your palace on the Park and have yourself a nice elegant dinner. We just hunker down here at Chez Roach. Send me a Steak Tartare to go."

Greg got up. "Report to me at the hotel. I think I'm going to make all you New Yorkers happy by staying out of the way on this one."

Five minutes later, he was in a cab headed uptown toward a shower, fresh clothes and good food. All in all, things were looking great. Manning would turn up soon—Greg didn't very well see how he could stay away from *that* for too long—and they'd nail him. Meanwhile, they'd find out everything worth knowing about Blondy. Here, it seemed, could be the solution to both his problems. Later, with the operation closed up and the heat off, maybe he, Greg, would go shopping for a piece of Blondy himself.

In fact, there wasn't really any maybe about it. With considerable shock, he realized the true explanation of his instinct to leave Blondy free and with no chance of discovering his own existence, at least, until he was ready—and if the team would please assume he was keeping his distance because of his distaste for homosexuals, so much the better. The intensity of his resolution surprised him and its danger unsettled him: he was going to have Blondy, and he didn't much care what it might take.

※ ※ ※ ※ ※

In the next several days, they did, in fact, learn a great deal about Blondy, among other things that his name was David Alexander and that he lived in room 413 of the old Harrington Hotel, a scant block from the Cock Robin.

The Harrington was no ordinary hustlers' flophouse like the Attaché Arms. The progress of its degeneration had been unique. It had opened as an international-class grand hotel in the later nineteenth century, when elevators were still a new-fangled invention. Although the Harrington provided itself with all the latest conveniences, it yet had to bow to the tradition of centuries wherein the best customers expected to climb the fewest stairs; its most ornate suites were on its lower floors. When, in due course, expectations reversed and the carriage trade moved on to grander, more modern hostelries where you got a view, a tenacious innovative management saw a vacant market niche. They walled its upper floors in studio glass for artists, and carved its ornate lower suites into cheap rooms for the impecunious, Italian marble fireplaces the only remaining legacy of the original grandeur.

The Harrington Hotel, like the Chelsea a few blocks away, had endured for decades as a fixture of avant garde artistic life in lower Manhattan. In its cracked marble hallways the double-H's of ornate moldings and wrought iron balustrades lived on as shapeless pentimenti beneath layers of institutional gray paint; heated argument echoed on the scent of oil paints and thinners; and violin calisthenics from one room might compete with a rock band's rehearsal several floors away. Apparently, the artistic temperament allowed concentration and production even amid the bedlam of this perpetual, 24-hour-a-day conservatory atmosphere.

Now, actual working artists taking advantage of community gestalt, managerial tolerance and reasonable rates were naturally a minority. Groupies, poseurs and other parasites commonly outnumber artists in any "artistic" community several times over. The Harrington was no exception. In addition to the usual hangers on, a large segment of the Harrington community was composed of those to whom official sanction of free expression and the artistic lifestyle provided absolutely excellent cover. Leathermen, drag queens, pop clothing salesclerks and others given to fashionable extremes in dress tinged the atmosphere with an ineffable *je ne sais quoi*. Retail dealers in a wide range of psychoactive contraband did land office business; the Harrington smelled of cannabis the way most other old hotels smell of whatever it is makes them all smell like a hotel. Moderately prosperous hustlers of all races and several assorted sexes found the Harrington a congenial headquarters. In fact, as some of its relatively less flamboyant residents, they were absolutely invisible there. All in all, the Harrington was a place where unconventionality, tolerated, had itself become conventional.

Naturally, this level of fringe activity attracted more than a little attention from the metro vice squad, with whom the management had not found it difficult to reach a mutually agreeable compromise. The vice squad had been furnished a room and invited to keep staff permanently on the premises, ostensibly as a headquarters for various sting operations both in and outside the hotel—a canny move. The detectives knew full well that, had they cleaned the place up completely, they would have destroyed the cover necessary for their own operations, and then would have found themselves on much more dangerous and infinitely less entertaining beats. This plus the unofficial cash stipend they received from the hotel management served to limit their impact to little more than that of the ordinary house dick. They did their best to have things run smoothly and conveniently for everybody without making undue pests of themselves. They returned lost pets, assisted the semi-comatose to their rooms, purged the community's more anti-social elements, and dealt with miscellaneous emergencies.

In this world, Rico and Freddie were utterly at home. Once tailing Alexander led them hither, they simply called on their erstwhile colleagues, the vice cops in residence, with a graphic of Alexander snapped on the street. A mere two pizzas, three sixpacks and a dime-bag produced his name, room number, and the information that, yes, he did seem to be a hustler, and no, he didn't seem to be a druggie. Promise of a further dime-bag to be delivered at an unspecified future date induced one of the vice cops to call down to the desk. Alexander had checked in April 3rd. Nothing more about him was known.

Next, Rico and Freddie made their formal appearance in the lobby among large, startlingly valuable paintings by a now-legendary artist (which, according to the authorized apocryphal version, had been—very reluctantly—accepted by the management in lieu of rent in days preceding the artist's success). Newly shaved and dressed in the season's most extreme fashions, they secured the room next door to 413. This lucky vacancy meant 413 could be wired for sound, video and wiretap with a minimum of bother, by means of small holes drilled inconspicuously through the baseboard scrollwork.

The result awed everyone. Alexander was indubitably a hustler, and an enormously prolific one at that. Said Rico, "Man, he go full out! He da only non-junkie I ever see cruise in da *morning*, man. And dis is every day. He like a machine, man, crazy horny all da time. I never see nothin' like it. An' when he ain't doin' 'em for pay, he doin' 'em for fun." He sighed a sigh just touched, perhaps, with reluctant envy at Alexander's capacity.

As they eavesdropped and tailed Alexander in and out of the Harrington, a pattern developed. That he cruised in the morning was a slight exaggeration. He spent most mornings on the phone taking and making calls, lining up business. However, a lunch date did usually follow, the Harrington being quite convenient to the financial district. After that came minor errands and a mid-afternoon stop at the Cock Robin. There, more often than not, he encountered his next trick, sometimes by prearrangement, sometimes by chance. He spent the evening fulfilling the rest of his advance commitments.

The way the team figured it, Alexander's income had to total more than any four of theirs put together—all in cash too, of course. To hard-working underpaid vice cops, this was unendurable. They longed to burn him.

When Alexander's workday concluded, generally around one or two in the morning, he returned to the Cock Robin for a nightcap. Sometimes another paying customer occurred. Sometimes a merely cute number begged for a freebie. Sometimes neither seemed sufficient to scratch his colossal itch; not infrequently, he walked over to the orgy bar in the next block to work out the rest of his horniness until closing, often dragging yet another number home with him after that. Then, after only three or four hours of sleep a night, the cycle began again. That this went on day after day without evidence of uppers was astounding. They had discovered Superstud.

It drove Greg insane with horniness. Officially disinterested in the more salacious datacapsule recordings of room 413 in action, he snuck them back to his hotel room and reviewed the best parts again and again in a state of progressive deliquescence. The enormous cock and perfect ass, naked and revealed in motion, were absolutely hypnotic. The lovely supple body rippled, thrust, quivered and contorted in amazing ways. It gave Greg an inexpugnable hardon and made him weak and shaky all over until at last his good right hand went irresistibly into motion. He just had to get a piece of that or die.

Unfortunately, there was but one small turd in the lubricant: the complete, utter and total absence of Herbie Manning anywhere in evidence. Without him, the investigation could not be concluded, and Greg could not be free to pursue his personal agenda unobserved. As the days went by, it became apparent his confidence that, where the beautiful hustler was, Herbie Manning could not be far away had been miscalculated. Irritation and impatience gnawed him.

So where the hell was Manning? Greg would have been ready to conclude, reluctantly, that a chance encounter had rubbed one or more of Herbie's hundreds off onto Alexander were it not for the coincidence of the dates. Manning had been seen last in Chicago on April 2nd. Alexander had checked into the Harrington on the 3rd. Greg hypothesized they were friends, that they'd come out here together, but no amount of effort would confirm or discount this.

Finding any evidence whatever of Alexander prior to April 3rd was proving unusually difficult. His fingerprints and DNA profile matched none in their databanks, which also came up blank for any "David Alexander" of his description; the name seemed, perhaps unsurprisingly for a hustler, to be an alias. The address he had given on his Harrington registration card was in Phoenix, but appeared likewise phony. Cautious inquiry among Alexander's acquaintances ("Wow, man, look at that! Where did *that* come from?") produced no one who'd known him before April 3rd, and no one who knew anything about his background, either. He'd simply never said. Greg transmitted graphics of Alexander back to Chicago to be shown around the bars and the Attaché Arms. These produced much admiration, but no recognition.

Nor did discreet use of Manning's picture around Alexander yield any more positive result. If they were such good friends, where was he? Perhaps, instead of friendship, their association had been briefer and more opportunistic. Perhaps Alexander had found Manning someplace on the night of the 2nd and stolen his money, perhaps even murdered him for it. Efforts at investigating these possibilities were afoot in several places, among them Chicago.

With no evidence of Alexander having yet been found there, and no evidence of Manning in New York, perhaps the thing had occurred in transit. They could only have traveled on the new, high-speed intercity electric trains; with petroleum products in ever-dwindling supply, jetfuel was reserved for military use; passenger air travel was a thing of the past, and an electric car could not have covered the distance in so short a time—and, in fact, the first of the Manning bills recovered had turned up at Union Station. Yet, trains and stations were lousy places to hide a body, especially on the spur of the moment. Manning's was noplace. Had Alexander killed him on the train and pushed the body out onto the tracks? Impossible; the trains were hermetically sealed in motion. Had he shipped it off someplace like a package? To anyone's knowledge, no dead Manning had turned up anywhere in the world, but, if Alexander had merely stolen his money, a living Manning would have turned up, stranded.

For that matter, why would Alexander bother to steal or kill for Manning's money, or do anything but fuck for it? He was far from spending all he made as it was, and at his current rate, he made the equivalent of Manning's entire stash in less than a year. Why, then, would he place himself needlessly in danger?

Besides, he didn't *have* Manning's money. They found a safety deposit box in his name at a local branch bank, and used CRAP's authority to inspect the contents. There was money there, yes there was—obviously the excess from his trade—and quite a lot of expensive jewelry too, but none of Manning's hundreds. They also searched his room. Their advance knowledge of his schedule allowed them to take their time and do it right. No secret stash of $100 bills turned up there, either. They backburnered the foul play explanation.

The atmosphere was rife with speculation and pauperishly short on fact. As Greg, projecting his own increasing obsession with the horny blond hustler, stubbornly clung to the notion that, where Alexander was, Manning could not be far away, pressure on him elevated. Increasingly, team opinion solidified behind Rico's hypothesis that Manning had treated himself to a one-night stand and that his spoor now got staler with every passing hour. The pressure on Greg from beneath to haul Alexander in and do whatever was necessary to extract the information they needed began to make his reluctance seem quixotic.

He simply would not do that. Under the influence of his nightly orgies alone with the datacapsules, his professional objectivity had long since evaporated. He would have David Alexander or crash and burn on the attempt. As Greg saw it, the team's resentment of Alexander's lifestyle and the living he was making ran so high that they now lived only for the day they would charge poor David (as Greg now thought of him) with something—anything at all—and jail him, which would put him out of Greg's reach for good! Rico and Freddie stuck to Alexander with the obsessed intensity of bugs buzzing a busted exitlight. Greg simply had to do something.

Before he could decide what, disaster struck. A review turned up Alexander on the general surveillance video taken in Union Station the night of April 2nd, the same video which had come up blank for Herbie Manning. There he was: buying a ticket, wandering around the concourse waiting for his train, boarding it.

The subsequent flurry of activity turned disaster to catastrophe. The team matched Alexander's fingerprints with some hitherto unidentified in Herbie's apartment. At a minimum, the two of them had had a meet there.

This was awful. If Alexander had paid for his train ticket with the $100 bills recovered from Union Station—and, as he was there while Manning was not, they now assumed he had—there was no longer any reason why Herbie Manning had to have been in New York at all. The best explanation of the evidence now suggested his contact with Alexander had taken place in Chicago, and that Alexander had come on to New York by himself.

However, all this was mere prologue. Further review of the Union Station video deepened catastrophe to cataclysm. "Hold it hold it," someone said. "Back it up! I want to look at his luggage. What's that he's carrying?"

They did. "Okay, freeze it there! So what's he got? A suitcase and a briefcase."

Freddie sat up straight. "I know that suitcase. We saw it in his room." He and Rico looked at each other. "So where's the briefcase?" they chorused.

"He's a courier, man!" Rico was jumping up and down. "He brought something to Chicago, sold it for a briefcase full of money, brought that here and passed it on. The hundreds he had were his payoff!"

"Drugs?"

"Drugs, bootleg computer chips, who knows? Could have been anything from pretty much anywhere in the world. Probably crossed the border in Florida or Texas. Or maybe New Mexico or Arizona. Phoenix!"

For the team, it all fell into place. Manning hadn't been in New York at all. He'd stolen the money to finance a move into the black market. For his part, Alexander had travelled to Chicago from a foreign point of origin with the goods (which might also explain his lack of previous history; foreign databases were nowhere as complete as their own) and onward to New York with the money, where he'd dropped it to be laundered.

Such triangular arrangements of product, customers and money were becoming increasingly common in all black market segments, and were giving enforcement organizations fits. Local forces argued over jurisdiction with each other and with national agencies, who likewise squabbled amongst themselves while struggling to integrate databases on syndicates that were becoming ever more diffuse, then tried to force the locals to endure innumerable processing delays by checking even the pettiest traffic offenders against international listings.

The couriers themselves were almost always amateurs, one-timers who would not wear grooves in the minds of Amtrak personnel with repeat trips. They were well-paid, and were invariably well-groomed, unostentatious and without criminal records.

By the way, sending such amateur help off on its own with fortunes in cash and property was quite safe for the cartels, who also employed some of the many information superhighwaymen. Along with computer fraud and hacking those systems used by the enforcement agencies (resulting in some of those self-same processing delays which so annoyed the locals, among other damage), these gentlefolk of the electronic road could check prospective couriers' backgrounds thoroughly enough to be sure they weren't undercover narcs, and track them if they went AWOL. Absconders had small hope of safety.

That Alexander had been such a courier and had used his fee to establish himself in New York deployed the hard data in quite the most efficient way. The only questions remaining concerned which product he'd delivered at what price points, his connections up and down the line, and what, if anything, he might have picked up in smalltalk about Manning's plans for after their meeting.

The next move was plain, and that was to ask him. The CRAP contingent on the team considered it urgent to nail down the Manning connection ASAP and make up for lost time. The New York locals had excited visions of using Alexander as a bargaining chip in their ongoing turf wars with the feds. That the Manning investigation was hopelessly off base was a real pity, but still, perhaps not a total loss.

Greg just didn't see things this way. It went completely against the grain of who Herbie Manning was. No matter how hard he tried, he couldn't see hard-working carefully methodical Herbie throwing his whole life away to set out into the air as an itinerant black marketeer. It wasn't *him*. Nor did Alexander fit the picture particularly well. He was much too conspicuous, not at all the nondescriptly conventional sort usually favored by cartel recruiters. Then there was that odd business of the time spread: the five months between when the first bills appeared at Union Station and the last one at Marino's. Assuming Alexander had got them all at once, why would he have doled them out piecemeal like that? Granted, this might have a number of explanations, but wasn't it most likely he'd been receiving them fresh at intervals?

No, the courier idea was merely a new line of conjecture, and Greg hated it, not least because pursuing it meant Alexander would be an object of attention forever. He clung stubbornly to his notion that, where Alexander was, Manning could not be far away.

He tried to lay out his concerns to the team, and immediately found himself talking to a room full of impatient exasperated closed faces. David was doomed, and so, if Greg's rapidly evolving estimation of David's character was correct, might be the investigation. Desperate measures were necessary, and, with the flash reflexes of a desperate man, Greg formed a desperate plan.

Yes, they certainly needed to talk to Alexander without delay, Greg said. But, he argued with all the persuasion he could muster, if they hauled him in, what was to prevent the guy from simply clamming up and staying clammed? He seemed a pretty cool character from the way he'd demanded a lawyer in the bookstore. If he did that again, the first question his lawyer—and he could afford the best—would ask would be about the charge. Really, they had nothing on him except prostitution, but if they charged him with it, he'd be out before they could finish the paperwork. Income tax evasion? They couldn't prove he'd been in business long enough to file. Receiving stolen goods? They couldn't show he had; Greg reminded the team that the $100 bills were Herbie Manning's own money. The stolen money had been all in smaller, untraceable bills. If Alexander had any of those, they didn't know it. And if they held him on any of a number of possible trumped up charges—suspicion of this or that—in hopes of making him talk, they'd still have to show cause, eventually. All Alexander would have to do was sit tight while they lost precious time. So why not try a soft approach first: tell him a tale to get him off somewhere quiet and private on his own turf where he wouldn't feel especially threatened, show him Manning's picture, and see what he said. If that didn't work... well, then a rigorous interrogation would be the logical next step.

The team chewed this over in uncomfortable silence. Greg rushed to fill it. In fact, he went on, he himself should probably be the one to make the approach.

The silence became a palpable thing. *Hit that brick wall,* Greg told himself, and rolled right on. It was obvious, he said. He'd been saving himself in case some such eventuality should become necessary. Because of the distance he'd purposely kept, he was virtually the only one of the team Alexander definitely could not have seen. He'd pretend to be a john, engage some of Alexander's time, and see what the application of a little more of the universal green might buy if an outright question didn't work.

The silence continued while terror forced itself up Greg's esophagus. *They know!* he told himself. *Somebody's noticed I've been taking the datacapsules!*

Sudden consensus suffused the atmosphere. People relaxed. "'Bout time you got out on the street," Rico growled. Several of the team smiled little smiles which might not have been altogether friendly.

Oh, Greg thought, *They're just waiting to see me fail.* He smiled back through rising waves of panic.

* * * * *

Thus, Greg found himself at the back angle of the Cock Robin's bar on a sultry September evening. Whence he sat, he faced down the long narrow establishment to the front door at its farther end. The Cock Robin was not a fancy place. The vinyl of its barstools mostly needed repair. Pinball and electronic game machines crouched under the movie posters and beer company propaganda decorating its black-painted walls. Unimaginative dance music blatted from a jukebox at mega-decibel levels though no one was dancing. Signed glossies of past celebrity customers lined the backbar. Greg didn't recognize any of the pictures except one. Larger than the others and in color, David Alexander's naked torso lolled in the place of honor over the cash register.

This was not surprising. Greg understood that, pre-Alexander, whatever popularity the Cock Robin once might have enjoyed had long been history. For some years it had been just another sleepy neighborhood gay bar with two drunks and a bartender, even on weekends. That Alexander had chosen it, evidently as a convenient, neutral place to meet certain of his prearranged dates and/or have a quiet beer once or twice a day, had changed its fortunes dramatically: such was his power of appeal that johns started hanging out there merely in hopes of running into him on days when they didn't have an appointment; this congregation of idle johns had drawn other hustlers into the place; and following the hustlers, an easy, loose crowd of regular cruisers had collected. From such chance beginnings great fortunes have been built in the bar business. Naturally, this made Alexander a genuine hero to the staff at the Cock Robin. He drank free, of course, and his word in the place was holy writ.

This was Greg's first visit to a gay bar. "No, no, no, my man," Freddie had sighed, "you do not wish to wear a $1500 suit. You'll stick out a mile."

141

"But I have to feel comfortable!" Greg protested, nervously fingering his new Italian three-piecer in the latest haute monde mode. "I've got to look like money too, remember?"

"Uh huh, but us having to rescue you from getting rolled definitely won't enhance your image in terms of what you got to do. Be cool, man. Think of it like a costume." This good advice brought Greg back to thinking about the evening in terms of business rather than as a personal debut.

At last, they compromised on a corduroy sports jacket, an open-collared pinstriped shirt above jeans and running shoes, and a flashy gold watch from the police evidence locker. Greg was glad they had. Between the johns in their rumpled business suits and the boys in their tight jeans and T-shirts, he struck a nice balance somewhere in the middle. Although he definitely looked like a lost straight, this was not necessarily a disadvantage. It set him apart, and meant everybody, with luck including his quarry, would be sure to notice him right off. That would save time, he hoped.

Compared to his expectations, the Cock Robin seemed reassuringly tame; the extravagant, evil decadence he associated with the very notion of a gay bar was largely absent. People gathered in pairs and groups, drank, leaned close to shout conversations over the music, or just checked out the scenery. Singles gazed into their drinks or posed at the siderails. The scene was, well, ordinary, really; except for the total absence of women—and the two boys making out back by the toilets—it might have been any corner bar at home in Chicago. Even the liplocked boys didn't disturb Greg too much. His effort was more to keep his eyes off them than otherwise.

Freddie ambled over from the siderail. "Nearly 11:30, boss," he shouted over the music. "Should be here soon, if he's coming." They knew from Alexander's morning phone calls that his last appointment for the day had been at eight.

Greg nodded, and took a breath. Here came the ticklish bit. "Okay. Then I guess that's it. I'll be fine. When he gets here, check his tail for Rico, and both of you can take the night off. I'll call you later if I need you."

"No backup?" Freddie raised both eyebrows. "This is not by the book, my man. You sure?"

"Yeah. It's just getting him back to his place and asking my questions. The automatic equipment will take care of the audio and video. If this doesn't work, we'll try the strong-arm stuff tomorrow. He's not dangerous, and he's not going anyplace—and you guys deserve a break." The music was a pounding roar. Greg's throat felt raw after shrieking this long speech into Freddie's ear.

"You sure you don't want us standing by just in case? Some weird dudes come through here, sometimes."

"I can take care of myself."

"It's no sweat, man. You sure you'll be okay?"

Mounting chagrin at this mother hen act set Greg's jaw. His studied casualness had backfired, had merely left him open to what could only be yet another backhand comment on his youth and supposed out-of-towner naiveté. He'd show 'em! "Go home!"

Freddie shrugged. "Okay, babe. It's your thing. Thanx. Guess I'll go see my girlfrien' after Rico gets here. Beep me if you change your mind." He disappeared toward the front of the bar.

Greg expelled breath in relief.

Then, as he watched Freddie's retreating back, the actuality of what he'd just done began to sink in. Did the guy have a point? This *wasn't* by the book. In no police organization Greg knew of was it proper procedure to head off to an undercover encounter with the investigation's prime subject without at least a partner standing by for backup, and rules had reasons. Was he merely sticking his neck out far enough to have it chopped through?

No! Up until now, he told himself, he'd done his best to foster a team approach out of respect for the superior knowledge and experience of those assigned to him. Ultimately, however, the responsibility—and consequently the authority—for this operation were his and his alone. His associates, competent though they undoubtedly were, had been blinded by hatred and envy. He was convinced his was the correct approach: that, with David Alexander, friendliness and personal consideration would get you farther than threats and intimidation, and there was nothing friendlier than what

Greg had in mind. He now had no choice but to step forward boldly and use his authority to save the day. Not only were these unorthodox tactics going to pay off, they were the only ones that would.

He sat back, took a swig of beer and considered the deception he was working on the team. He seemed to have all his bases covered. Before entering the Cock Robin, he'd stopped by the surveillance room at the Harrington and rendered the voice- and motion-activated recording equipment useless by the simple expedient of unplugging the power bar to which it was all attached. He bent the prongs back and forth until he found the place where they slipped in and out of the ancient socket with hardly any resistance at all. He left the plug hanging by the ground wire, apparently having fallen out of the wall more or less by itself.

At the other end of the bar, a patron argued with the bartender, seemingly about change. The patron pointed at a small sheaf of bills in his hand and screamed inaudibly over the music. The bartender shook his head and screamed back. At last, the bartender reached under the bar and turned the music down.

This not only allowed them to understand one another, but had the unintended side effect of stimulating conversation all over the bar. Greg felt as if an enormous weight had been lifted from atop his head. People turned to one another and struck up smalltalk conversations. The level of animation in the place increased noticeably.

As he watched, a tall lanky number, decidedly scruffy, Greg thought, in sloppy jeans and a hacked off sleeveless sweatshirt exposing bony arms, detached itself from the siderail and headed toward Greg. It draped itself on the corner of the bar next to him.

"Hi. What's your name?" the number asked.

Just as simple as that, marvelled Greg, who had been wondering how people went about meeting one another in a place like this. He glanced at the door. No Alexander, yet. He smiled weakly at the number and hoped it wasn't about to become an encumbrance. "Name's Greg. What's yours?"

"Delmar." There was an uncomfortable moment of relative silence. "So. Where're you from?"

"Chicago."

Delmar nodded. "Oh yeah, Chicago. Went through there once." He made an icky face. "Bet you were as glad to get out of there as I was to get outa Turde County, Indiana, huh? Lived here long?"

"Sorry, I'm just here on business. I *live* in Chicago."

"Oh, I'm sorry." Whether about the gaffe or about Greg's living in Chicago, Greg couldn't quite decide. Then Delmar smiled patronizingly and resolved all doubt. "But don't you wish you could live here, though? I just love it here. There's so much to do!"

Hmmm, Greg thought. How to get out of this gracefully? "Well, it certainly is an impressive place, though I'm not sure it's for me. I can't manage to do everything there is in Chicago."

Delmar's eyes widened. "Oh, *never* say you don't want to live in New York! Everybody wants to live in New York. Only people who aren't good enough to make it here say they don't!" He nodded. "I mean, New York is the capital of *everything*, isn't it? What do you do?"

Greg blinked. "You mean for a living?" Given the pure light of stupidity burning in Delmar's eyes, he thought he'd better be sure. "I'm an accountant."

"Oh, that's too bad. Isn't that pretty dull?" Delmar regarded him pityingly.

Greg began to get really annoyed. "Oh, now and again. So what do you do?"

"I'm an actor and a dancer." He did a little buck and wing in place to prove it.

"Really!" Greg was prepared to be impressed. "What shows you been in? Maybe I caught one when I was in town before."

"Oh, nothing yet, but I'm still trying. My big break is right around the corner. I can feel it."

"Sure. I mean that's great. So what do you *really* do?"

"Uh, I work for a law firm. I deliver the mail and run errands."

Greg stared. "I see!" He was being patronized by a gofer!

"Oh, it's temporary. You have to pay your dues, you know."

"I've heard that." Greg was noncommittal. "How long you been at it?"

"Only five years."

Greg tried not to sound incredulous. "Only five years—and you've been pushing a mail cart the whole time?"

"No. Before that, I had a job scraping chewing gum off roller skates at a rental place." Indeed, Delmar seemed to be chewing gum himself. It popped loudly.

"Do tell." Greg's anger and offended pride had been rising steadily. Now it was about to pour forth. He'd just opened his mouth to deliver a scathing and devastatingly well-phrased critique of New Yorkers, New York, and, with particularly minute exactitude, of precisely where they could shove it, when Delmar grabbed his wrist. "Wow! Nice watch!" Greg jerked it back and fixed him in a freezing glare.

Delmar shrugged. "'Scuze me. Gotta pee." He bucked and winged his way off to the john.

Greg shook his head. Maybe New York was of some use, after all, he thought. Serving as a magnet for creeps like that was a real gift to everyplace else.

With this annoyance, any lingering hint of novelty, excitement, tension and danger the Cock Robin's atmosphere might have carried vanished utterly. He saw the grime and felt the grit underfoot. His horniness vanished. He couldn't figure out why he'd been so eager to pop his head up for this assignment. He saw himself as stuck here for a grim evening amid the very lowest class of people. *What the hell am I doing here?* David Alexander? To hell with him! All at once, he was painfully conscious of making one bad decision after another from the first second he'd laid eyes on the guy, of allowing his personal problems to affect his conduct of the business at hand: not waiting for the backup at the bookstore, putting off arresting the jerk when it was the obvious thing to do, and now this, endangering the investigation and his own career, the most important thing in the world to him, by assigning himself a role for which he was plainly unfit, and just to buy a hustler? —My god, could that actually be the only reason he was here?— Wasn't that something he could do anywhere, anytime, if that was what he really wanted?—and for that matter, right at this moment, he wasn't any too sure it was. *This is crazy!* Panic rose.

And disappeared up its own asshole a moment later. An excited babble at the other end of the bar cut through the music. Greg looked up and forgot his doubts, his annoyance at Delmar the Dancing Hoosier, his disgust with New York, and every shred of pride in his body. David Alexander had entered and instantly become the center of a small group. Greg could not take his eyes off him. *Showtime.*

He straightened up. His hand lifted to adjust a non-existent tie.

Freddie had told him what to do. He waved his beer bottle at the bartender. "Give me another one of these, and I want to buy one of whatever for the blond at the other end of the bar." He put some bills down.

The bartender stared for an instant, blinked, nodded, and went. A minute later, Greg had a new beer, the tip jar had several dollars of Greg's money, and the bartender was looking and pointing in Greg's direction as he put a fresh bottle beside the one Alexander already had.

A small wave of attention rippled down the bar and washed over Greg, who reddened. He lowered his head and pretended to study his beer. *Damn it!* From beneath his brows he saw Alexander staring at him. He raised his head and met that gaze.

Even from thirty feet away, by barlight, the deep clear green of incredible eyes held him. Slowly, without shifting those eyes an iota, the blond raised a beer and nodded solemnly at Greg. Again, Greg felt himself panicking. *He sees me!* He tried to tear his eyes away and bolt, but could not. Slowly, he nodded back. He felt as if half the bar were watching this exchange, heads turning as at a tennis match. At last, with a herculean effort, he fixed his eyes on the ashtray in front of him and kept them there—and still felt the green gaze pinning him in a searchlight glare.

147

Then Alexander was beside him, was taking the space vacated by Delmar at the corner of the bar. Greg swivelled to face him. The green eyes never wavered. Outside their purview, the noisy bar seemed to recede, to become flat, unreal and colorless. Greg was alone, mesmerized in bottomless viridian depths. It seemed a place of power and of peace, sucking the soul right out of him. He fought it a moment, and was lost. He felt as if he could curl up and abide in that nirvana forever, nameless, unthinking, content.

The gaze shifted, released him as Alexander pulled up a vacant stool. They became merely two guys out slumming, having a drink in a suddenly crowded, rather seedy bar far below their social station.

The little drama over, Alexander disposed of, the bar's rhythms returned to normal. They were ignored. Music blared. Bartalk raged as the crowd folded itself around them.

Alexander smiled. He produced a slide-pack of Export Specials and offered it.

"N-no, thanks. I don't smoke." Greg fought down the urge to take one just to oblige the gesture. He grabbed some matches off the bar and hastened to light the one already dangling from the blond's wide, sculptured mouth.

Alexander inhaled deeply and expelled smoke through his nose. "Thanks. And thanks for the drink." He clinked his bottle against Greg's on the bar. "I'm David. I don't think I've seen you here before."

"Greg. Never been here before. I'm only in town for a couple days."

David nodded. His leg came to rest ever so lightly against Greg's. "So, what are you up to tonight, Greg?"

Greg paused. In the power of David's presence, his carefully fantasized approach went right out of his head. He didn't know what to say. "I... I want to talk a little business." In desperation, he'd fallen back onto The Program right off. *No! No! No!* Inside, he was shrieking, *It's not business! I want to know you, to be your friend! I want you forever!* He bit his lip.

David nodded again. "Yes?"

At the last minute, Greg remembered he wasn't supposed to know anything about this guy. "Uh, pardon me for asking, but what business are you in?"

The green eyes opened wide. One brow raised slightly. "I sell sex." The beautiful face left a distinct hint of amusement on the air as it modulated smoothly into unreadability.

Greg nodded, vaguely conscious of having embarrassed himself in some way. "I... I'd like to, uh, buy some."

David dragged on his cigarette. Again, Greg caught the barest hint of a private smile. "You're new at this, aren't you."

He wasn't asking. Greg reddened, and nodded slowly.

"Ever had a hustler before?"

Greg shook his head, staring at his beer.

David leaned closer and became confidential. "I thought not. Tell you what. You seem like a nice enough guy. I'm going to do you a favor. Some guys would take advantage, rip you off your first time. Lucky for you, it's me, and I'm the Prince of Thieves. Let me tell you how it works."

Greg flamed with embarrassment at the rather unaccountable hint of glee in David's face. It seemed as if it was his fate to be patronized by everyone he met in this place. At least this time maybe he deserved it. He humbled himself to listen.

"The first thing you do, you offer to pay me, clearly and explicitly—none of this stuff about asking my business. That way, I know you're not a cop."

So that was it. He'd come on to David as if this might be an entrapment. "Sorry," he mumbled. "I'm not a cop." *At least, not that kind.*

"So I figured. You were much too nervous." David smiled reassuringly. "Then, it may sound cold, but you have to treat it exactly like a downtown business deal. You tell me what you're into. I tell you whether I do that and how much it costs if I do. We reach an understanding. You follow me?"

In the face of this onslaught, Greg was helpless. Because he didn't know what else to do, he decided to let go, to tell the truth.

"Well, you see, I don't know exactly what I want. You see, I... I'm new... I... I've never...had sex...wi—"

"Oh, so that's your problem," said a voice in his ear. Greg's head jerked around. One of the bodies pushing behind him in the crowd proved to be Delmar, back from his pee. How much of this had he heard? Greg fought mortification.

"David darling! I missed you!" Delmar was draping himself over David, was wedging himself between them, his back to Greg, edging him almost off his stool. "Hey, guess who I saw doing what to who!" The jukebox swung into a new tune. "Ohwow, the Pointer Sisters! *Classic* disco!" Delmar's pelvis began a violent oscillation. Greg grabbed at the bar as his stool teetered off balance.

"That," David frowned, "is an oxymoron." Firmly and deliberately, he cleared Delmar away with the back of his forearm, and gave him a little push back out into the crowd.

"Oxy-what?" Delmar protested as he went. "Who's a moron?"

David hiked his stool closer to Greg's. "Second lesson: avoid mindless jerks like that." He smiled. The sun shone on them, alone together in their own, confidential little world.

Greg smiled back. The blond's hand descended to cover his own. Shapely, big-boned fingers rubbed his wrist. David dropped his voice and purred, "You don't mean... Is this your first time?"

Greg felt himself go scarlet. He grasped after any shard of dignity. "You see I... I've been thinking I may be... well... bisexual..."

David looked up at the ceiling and took a breath, oozing a deep satisfaction Greg found humiliating as applied to the mere circumstance of his inexperience. He was more than ready for these preliminaries to be over.

"Well, it shouldn't be too difficult to find out. I guess I could work up something for you in a gentle, caring, exploratory sort of way. You set the limits. Would you like that?"

Greg nodded again, a thirsty man offered nectar by a god.

"Two hours, four hundred. That okay?"

"I've got it." Greg's voice was low. The incongruity of paying four hundred dollars for a gentle, caring experience was not lost on him. Was David laughing at him? He did not care. He'd show him! His consuming desire became to give as great a pleasure as he hoped to receive, whatever that might entail.

David was suddenly cheerful. "Hey! You're supposed to haggle!" Greg looked up in surprise. "No, just kidding. You get better service if you don't. Come on. I've got a room a block over. Let's get it on."

Greg had a startling hardon at the very words. At last they were heading for the door. Eyes and hands followed them. David brushed off those seeking to detain him with conversation; he attended strictly to Greg, who appreciated it very much. Their arrangement concluded, he was anxious to get on to its fulfillment and out of this annoying place as quickly as possible.

The street was refreshingly cool and breezy. Greg took a deep breath as they headed toward the Harrington. He had to make an effort not to take the lead; he wasn't supposed to know where they were going. He felt fantastic: young, athletic, good-looking. He was about to lose his virginity at long last, and to the Prince of Thieves! His life would now change forever, for the better, he was sure. He abandoned his responsibilities and laughed out loud for the sheer joy of it.

David smiled at him, and whooped off down the sidewalk to do a two-handed leapfrog over a parking meter, another at the next meter, and the next. Still smiling, he waited at the corner for Greg to come trotting up.

Greg was enchanted. "Wow, great vault! I gotta try that."

"Better not." David put his arm around Greg's shoulders. "You don't want to risk losing something you'll need for your first night."

Greg slipped his arm around David's waist. Enlinked, they walked to the hotel. While he couldn't imagine behaving this way on Halsted Street, Halsted Street was 800 miles away, so who cared?

Still, the daring freedom of it made him nervous. He disengaged his arm as they entered the lobby. "Putting on the deskclerk?" David laughed, and scooped him into the elevator, where Greg automatically assumed normal elevator stance: eyes forwards, watching the floor readout. Softly, David's hand enclosed the back of his neck and drew him to meet full soft moist lips descending upon his own. A subtle, exquisitely ineffable scent enfolded him. Jasmine? No, not floral... He felt David's cock stiffen. His own responded immediately, painfully in his briefs.

Greg didn't notice the door opening at David's floor. David caught it with his foot just as it began to close again. "Ummm. We're here."

Arms about each other, they strolled down the hall to 413. The Harrington's distinctive conservatory atmosphere pulsed in the background. This was the first time Greg had heard it. He thought it sounded mysterious, artistic, cosmopolitan and exotic.

Inside the room, David separated them gently. "One last little bit of business, Greg, and then we can forget it. The money. Put it over there."

Greg looked around room 413 as David lit candles and opened windows. The tiny fisheye of their surveillance camera hadn't done it justice. Every inch of wall space was covered with writhing tumescent bodies carefully scissored from skinmags and artfully montaged. Most were men at or near the moment of orgasm, faces contorted in the extremity of desire. Milky jism spewed everywhere. In the uncertain candlelight, the images seemed alive, frozen forever in the agony of pleasure. There were whimsical touches too. The bathroom doorknob sprouted like a porcelain mushroom from the asshole of a model panting with desire.

Stacks of paperbacks banked a wall: lots of porn, Greg noted, but lots of other stuff too, Penguin classics, among other things. At the desk, he slipped eight $50 bills under the edge of a tablet computer. Both it and a small printer unit were filmed with dust, unused.

David adjusted a miniature boombox to a classical station and turned again to Greg. Placing his arms on Greg's shoulders, he drew him again into that deep liquid kiss. Greg's knees trembled.

Slowly, David stripped Greg's clothes, caressing his body with hands and tongue as he went. Greg stood and let it happen. The shock when David finally took his cock in his mouth was so great he almost spurted then and there. He controlled himself with an effort, leaned backward and moaned softly.

David shoved him gently toward the bed. As he went, Greg surreptitiously (he hoped) kicked his clothes from the center of the floor to the baseboard so they covered the fisheye lens concealed in the scrollwork—a symbolic gesture, as no one was watching. *This part,* he thought, *is my business.* David removed his clothes and joined him on the bed.

Greg wondered that David could seem so trim in his clothes and yet so enormously big and powerful moving naked on top of him. He surrendered himself to the sensation, and found himself once again on the brink of orgasm. As if in reaction to his distress, David disengaged and shifted himself around to sixty-nine position. With wide mouth and prehensile tongue, he licked Greg's cock, sucked his balls and tongued his asshole, seemingly all at once. Greg strove to give the same in return. The size of David's cock gave him trouble.

David put his hand through Greg's legs and tapped his back for attention. "No, just open your mouth as wide as it will go, and fuck your throat with my cock, like this." He demonstrated.

Greg's eyes teared. He fought down a wracking gag reflex as David's cock entered his esophagus. Once he mastered that, the big cock pulsed up and down his throat, and Greg discovered a completely unexpected joy in total phallus worship. His own cock became compelling again as he got close.

David disengaged again. "How are you feeling?"

He has to ask? "I'm bursting."

"Okay, let's blow off a little cum." David shifted around and pulled them onto his back; he opened his legs and laid them back aside his shoulders, raising his asshole against Greg's hips. He slicked Greg's cock with ropy-thick spit.

David sighed in helpless bliss as Greg entered him. His powerful legs encircled and gripped Greg around the neck. Fucking David seemed so different from the women Greg'd had. David's asshole was flexible and comfortable, an ecstatic, effortless, perfect fit; it caressed Greg's cock with silky hot liquid muscles pulsing and yearning for him on every stroke. Greg's eyes opened wide as he shot in frozen seconds that went on and on. David moaned, and splashed Greg's neck and shoulders with cum.

Then they were spent, collapsed together, arms and legs entangled, nuzzling each other softly. Greg's head spun. If only he could lie here like this forever, nothing else would ever matter.

They drew out the moment as long as they could. At last, David cantilevered his legs over the edge of the bed and sat up. Leaning over Greg, he wiped the cum off Greg's chest and rubbed it lazily into his own arms, chest and legs. He glanced at the clock and laughed. "Guess what? We've still got an hour and forty minutes left! Want a beer?"

Greg laughed too. It had seemed much longer. "Sure. Thanks." This was certainly thirsty work.

David arched over to a tiny refrigerator at the foot of the bed and fished out two bottles. The label caught Greg's attention: a tiny microbrewery, but oddly familiar. He'd seen this brand somewhere before.

"Want a glass?" David gestured at a couple of drinking glasses emblazoned with I ♥ New York and the logo of Greg's favorite soft drink. Greg grimaced and shook his head. As David dug the last Export Special out of a pack on the bedside table, Greg scrambled after the matches to light it for him.

David crushed the empty pack and tossed it across the room to land neatly in the wastebasket. He leaned back against the wall and blew smoke. "So, what's the verdict?"

"The verdict?"

"Are you bisexual or what?"

"Oh." Greg considered carefully, and decided his attempt back in the bar at saving his dignity by proclaiming his bisexuality might have been a mistake. While he didn't want to waffle, neither did he want David to get the impression that anything was going to get in the way of their burgeoning intimacy. "Well, I have had a few women..." Gosh, that sounded weak. "...well more than a few, really..." Oops, didn't want to go too far in that direction, either. "...well maybe not all *that* many." He rushed on to the main point. "But none of it was *anything* like that! That was amazing. I don't know what to think." What? Of course he knew what to think. "I mean, about being bisexual."

A pull on his beer bottle covered a sidelong glance at David to see how this dithering was going over. He had to gather it up and stop embarrassing himself. One of Herbie Manning's favorite clichés occurred to him, one he'd more than once heard Herbie mutter to himself at the next desk. *Warning: Engage brain before putting tongue in gear*—advice Greg admitted the guy had needed.

David chuckled. "Warning: Engage brain before putting tongue in gear, huh?" He put his arm around Greg and squeezed Greg's shoulder as if to show he was only kidding.

Touché, Greg thought, and drank more beer. The beer, he noted, was surprisingly delicious—sharp and vivid-tasting—far and away the best beer he'd ever had. He took another look at the label. Where *had* he seen this brand before? Of course! There'd been the best part of a sixpack in Herbie Manning's refrigerator. Interesting!

His mind turned to the official reason he was supposed to be here. The line he'd discussed with the team simply wasn't going to work. Their idea was that he naturally would not want to pose as a john a second longer than he had to. That was only for getting David off on his own. Once he'd accomplished that, Greg would flash his bankroll and his ID and attempt to enlist David's cooperation by stressing the advantages of resolving the matter quietly between the two of them. Tell what he knew and there the matter would end as far as David was concerned; he'd be out of the box, free to go about his business. He would receive a nominal cash payment on the spot and a much larger reward if the information actually led to Manning's apprehension. However—and Greg was to stress this particularly—failure to cooperate, holding back on what he knew or giving false information would very definitely lead to Consequences. The team liked this approach because, obviously, it was only a minor variation on the one they themselves hoped and fully expected to apply on the morrow with no particular stress on rewards and going about one's business, but lots and lots of stress on Consequences.

Greg had let himself get talked into this. He'd thought this approach would probably be as good as any other, *after* he'd done his real business. Now, he realized it simply wouldn't do to shift gears this way from lover to cop, not after the, for David, perfectly reasonable distrust of policemen he'd expressed back in the bar, and not after he, Greg, had already said he wasn't one. Besides, why waste time on what the team would do better and more thoroughly if this meeting didn't work out? They truly were setting him up to fail.

With growing alarm, he understood David really was going to have to deliver, for both their sakes. After the credibility Greg had expended in holding out so long and then demanding the team let him set up this meeting, it was the only way he could ever have enough clout to save David from becoming a pawn in law enforcement politics. That, at its worst, would put David beyond his reach forever. Even at a minimum—if, as Greg suspected, the courier theory was baloney—it would mean a nasty prolonged interrogation for David. But now he'd found the man he loved, there was no way he was gonna let the team sweat him, ever. *No Way!*

Greg calmed himself. They'd never get the chance. Not only was David a fine fellow, the two of them were becoming friends—rather more than friends, really. Greg felt deep ties growing between them. Of course David would help him. There was no question but that David would tell him anything he needed to know, just as soon as he decided how best to ask.

Meanwhile, the object of these reflections was blowing smoke rings at the ceiling. "Personally, I think almost everybody is bisexual."

"What?" Greg certainly did not want to seem distant or distracted, so, somewhat against his better judgment, he allowed his mind to be jolted back onto what they were supposed to be discussing. He still had plenty of time to do the business. He would wait for a proper opening.

"Sure. Think about it with me for a minute. Suppose everybody is bisexual to one degree or another, but that the degree is different for everybody. Picture this as a sort of bell curve: a small group of the exclusively straight at one end, the exclusively gay equally sparse at the other, and everybody else mounded inbetween. This would explain everything."

"It would?"

"Sure. The other essential premise is the huge amount of homophobia institutionalized in our culture. You know what I'm talking about. You get it from everywhere beginning the day you're born. It's Daddy dropping a football and a set of spikes into your crib. It's Mommy telling you how wonderful life will be after you grow up and find a nice girl, and how you'll understand what you're putting her through once you have children of your own. It's your teenaged buddies who let you know what a dweeb you are if you don't act out some kind of drooling, goggle-eyed fascination with the opposite sex. It's the very organization of society, which has all kinds of assumptions and benefits, both social and legal, for married couples, but never mentions gay couples at all unless we force it to. All this reduces gay people to invisibility, a mystery, a cipher, to nothing. When you're growing up, however much of you is gay sees no reflection there, and perhaps doesn't even realize it itself exists, if the straight side is strong enough to take up the slack."

"And if it isn't?" asked Greg, for whom this was the compelling question.

"For that there is overt homophobia, the glazy-eyed Jesus salesmen with the big hair and the shiny suits who shriek about how you'll be damned to hell, even though a close reading of the gospels suggests that Jesus himself was probably queer as a three-legged duck. Then there are the priests preaching the Church party line against everything that interferes with the maximum reproduction of Catholics, and the right-wing geeks who repeat that 'traditional family values' mantra over and over again as if endless repetition excuses them from telling us just what these 'traditional family values' *are*, anyway. Oh yeah, we know what these guys are *against*, no mystery about that. They're against working mothers, divorce, single parenting, sexual freedom, abortion, 'homosexuality,' socialism and evolution, among lots else. But what does that make them *for*? These wonderful 'traditional family values' of theirs all seem to have to do with repression and guilt, with locking people

157

into specific sex roles no matter how much talent is wasted, with imprisoning people for life in relationships that go wrong, with sexual self-denial, when that inevitably fails with forcing people to bring children no one wants into the world, with enforcing heterosexual preference by terror, with motivating people to support social structures that exploit them, and with demonizing everybody who disagrees with any of it—that is, with conformity, sexual repression, guilt, greed, ignorance and religious intolerance. Those are the things these self-styled decent people are *for*."

David took a drag on his cigarette. "Now, when I say they enforce heterosexual preference by terror, I don't mean only the terror of being ostracized, beat up or killed, though they certainly use that. Their method is to make gay emotions so evil that people will do anything to deny and suppress them, so sinful that anyone who can't will be too guilty to admit them. Not only is it *dirty*, you will be *damned to hell*! They want gay people to be ashamed, to consider themselves afflicted, because once they've convinced you you're sick, they've won. At that point, you repress yourself. Hey, if you want something done right... You go to any length to keep your *perversion* out of sight for life, unadmitted even to yourself, if you can, no matter how damaging the personal cost."

David jabbed out his cigarette. "But I'm getting off the point, which is that, considering all this social conditioning, it's no mystery why anybody who can will choose to function heterosexually. Now, this is easier for some people than for others. For those whose bisexual mix is mostly straight anyhow, it's no sweat. They may not realize they have a gay element in their makeup unless special, maybe unique circumstances bring it out, such as a very beautiful and very determined guy who simply won't take no for an answer." He smirked at Greg, who couldn't imagine anyone saying 'no' to David. "Even then, for this type of bisexual a gay flirtation can never be more than experimentation, at most, a fling. As you get closer to the middle of the spectrum, people achieve heterosexual functioning at greater cost, from simple suppression of recurrent troubling desires and fantasies to secret sex lives of increasing adventurousness, until you arrive at people whose secret life is the dominant one. From there it's a short step to those who function heterosexually poorly or not at all, and these, historically, are the majority of those who come out. The irony is that most of those who come out don't have enough of a straight component to realize it, while none of the straights will admit theirs isn't 100% pure. So, the result looks black and white—as if people are either gay or straight—when, in reality, it's all shades of gray."

"So what about those guys you hear about who live perfectly normally for the first half of their lives—wives, kids, everything—and then throw it all away and go gay for the second? If they started out okay, why can't they go on that way?"

David winced. "Leaving aside questions of what's 'normal' and 'okay,' any number of things could be going on in examples like that, which brings us to one of the more insidious straight myths, that there's something so evilly addictive about gay sex that, once you 'go gay,' as you put it, you'll never go back. There are guys so afraid of the demon within them they'll kill you merely for offering them a blowjob."

"And then whine about how it was sexual harassment so they can escape punishment."

David shot him a look. "You would know. Anyway, the reality can often be something less than the evil addiction these people imagine. The more tolerant the society, the farther along the spectrum people feel free to come out. In viciously repressive societies, the only visible gay people are those who can't pass at all—drag queens, for instance. The more accepting the society, the farther toward the middle of the spectrum do people find it worthwhile to bring their public lives into sync with their private desires, and the farther still are people willing to explore. So, in the late '60's and early '70's, when society became a lot more tolerant in a relatively short space of time and public identification as gay suddenly no longer meant inevitable personal ruin, the closet doors opened and people of all ages and conditions of life flooded out into the gay world."

David stopped for a pull on his beer. "People change their lives for other reasons too. As guys approach forty and start having intimations of mortality, some find it harder to deny and defer their fantasies. Somebody else's conditioning may be so thorough it takes him a while to figure out what's going on in his own head. Somebody else may simply get bored of his life and develop a need to explore. Somebody else may have been living a secret life all along, but in the end, can't take the pressure, or gets exposed by accident. One way or the other, once the secret is out, things change. It's very hard to live a truly bisexual life. Society expects you to be one thing or the other, and it's always simpler to follow society's expectations if you can. Gay or straight, the people around you, and particularly your partners, exert a lot of pressure to keep you the way that makes you available to them. Nor are they willing to deal with what they don't understand. Both men and women will put up with competition from their own sex a lot sooner than from the other. Most don't see how they can compete with rivals of the opposite sex, can't begin to figure out where they stand. More often than not, when Daddy comes out or is uncovered in a gay affair, Mommy's instantaneous reaction is to throw him out of the house and call her lawyer rather than try working something out. For every guy who goes gay and doesn't want to go back, there's one who can't go back."

David looked around for cigarettes, didn't find any, and rummaged through the top drawer of the bedside table after more. "But it's when we get to homophobia that the theory really comes into its own." He ripped the cellophane off a fresh pack of Export Specials and extracted one, which Greg had a match ready to light.

"Haven't you ever wondered about the origin of the Great Homophobic Lie, the one that says gay people choose to be gay? To gay people who never had a prayer of functioning constructively in the straight world, this is laughable, ridiculous nonsense. Yet it's the basis of everything bigots believe. It's why gay rights aren't civil rights, but 'special rights.' It's why gay sex is 'sinful,' because, according to them, it's part of human willful perversity, not their god's Creation. Boy, do they need this too. They need the Great Homophobic Lie right to the bottoms of their pinched little souls! The more you argue—the more expert opinion and personal testimony you produce—the more closed, intense and angry they become. Why? Because each and every one of them is aware, if only subliminally, that they have chosen to suppress the gay element in their own makeup. Now, that *is* a choice. But there's a difference between choosing to be gay and choosing not to repress what you already are. They confuse the two, and they do it from denial. They want to believe no one has a gay component. If no one has a gay component, then certainly *they* don't! Yet, the one person you can never completely convince of a lie is yourself, no matter how hard you try. That they are aware of their own nature, even if only subliminally, is what makes the Great Homophobic Lie a lie, and that they know it is a lie, but preach it anyway, makes them not merely ignorant and misled. This is what makes them bigots."

Greg turned this over. "So, there really *isn't* any choice about whether or not you're queer. The only choice is about whether or not you suppress it."

"Right. Suppressing it would even be a valid choice, if those who made it were willing to take the consequences and shut up about it." His voice took on a bitter edge. "Unfortunately, they're not, are they?" He bored in on Greg. "Are they?"

"Huh?"

"Willing to shut up about it? Because there is a level on which the bigots know others are expressing what they've repressed, they are consumed with anger and envy others don't see the need to suffer the way they do. That kind of suffering is only tolerable if everybody suffers it, just like those ugly values of theirs say everybody should." David's lip curled. "So, those who opt out have to be made to suffer as much as possible. Nobody gets out alive, right?"

At first, this diatribe had been curiously thrilling. After Greg's wonderment at how gay people could think themselves as good as straights, he was being told. He discovered he was hungry to hear scorn poured on things he had always believed, and eager to hear new truths that gave him a position of dignity in a rearranged universe. Yet, as David went on, those green eyes made him more and more uncomfortable. They seemed to peer into his very soul and prise up what was there to be seen, quite accurately too, until now, it was almost as if he was being accused. But that was nonsense; David didn't know him, had no idea who he was or what he'd done.

Speaking of which, it occurred to him this might offer an opportunity to inject Herbie Manning into the conversation. He might describe his own persecution of the hapless Herbie and, along the way, see how David reacted to the name. He stopped himself right on the point of opening his mouth. Was he nuts? After David's open contempt of homophobes, to confess the things he'd done and beg for absolution? Sure, he loved David, and David loved him back, he knew, but perhaps a better time to play True Confessions would come later, once they were more secure together.

Meanwhile, he had his end of the conversation to uphold. He made a play of clearing his throat to cover his hesitation, and took a nice long swig of beer. "Well, I'm sure you're right about people being repressed. On the conscious level, though, there's a lot of unfocussed resentment that goes into anything that will hold it, the all-queers-are-child-molesters-and-serial-murderers-so-we-wouldn't-want-them-teaching-our-kids-or-living-down-the-block kind of stuff. There's a lot of fear too, that unless weImeanthey obviously don't like queers, someone might think they're queer themselves and that, like you say, if they let queers near them, it might rub off."

Greg's unconscious air of authority seemed to give David some trouble about his face, and at Greg's slip with the pronouns, he knuckled an eye. "Right. Hell, in one sense, their terror is understandable. Given the unrelenting bullshit we're all subjected to from birth on, who *would* want to be gay?"

"I sure didn't." It just slipped out. Greg snuggled closer to David and willed him to understand.

"Me neither. For me, and for virtually every other gay man I've ever asked, 'gay' wasn't something we aspired to be. It was something we fought against as hard as we could, accepted only reluctantly, and then tried to make the best of. That the best we could make of it turned out to be good beyond our wildest dreams—in fact, even better than what the homophobes seemed to have—had nothing to do with it, because we didn't know that in advance."

"You too? You fought it too?"

David nodded solemnly.

Somehow, Greg hadn't suspected that. David's ease with himself was so great it simply hadn't occurred to Greg there might ever have been any struggle involved. Here was something real they had in common. It gave him hope he might feel that easy about it himself, someday. With David's help, he would. In fact, he was feeling an awful lot better already.

David moved the arm around Greg's neck and pinched a tit. He slipped his other hand between Greg's legs. "So I'll ask again. What's the verdict?"

Greg's cock made up his mind for him.

This time, they took it slower and made it last. They lay together, stroking, embracing, making out in intimacy undreamt by Greg. David's skin, warm and satin smooth, was an electric shock wherever he touched it. The boneshaking loneliness he'd suffered for eons of nights shivering alone in one narrow bed or another disappeared into the fire of David's touch: a day on the beach after an eternity of winter; a hot bath and safety from the terror of the ice. He pigged it in: an instinctive, semi-conscious hunger to get enough that, even if hereafter he might remember his lonely agony, never could it recapture him.

Amidst this ecstasy, unaccountably, he shivered. He opened his eyes and blinked at David arching above him. For an instant in the uncertain candlelight, those astounding green eyes seemed to glow with cold demonic intensity and shine out of the darkened shadow that was David with their own light. For a split second of awestruck disbelief, Greg froze.

The moment passed. David lowered himself and they kissed, eyes open. David's twin lamps became one, a fathomless well, the heart of the emerald flecked with smoldering fire. Greg submerged himself therein, and therein longed to remain enwombed, floating mindless, comforted and uncaring content. He smiled with mindless adoration, from the depths of the silent oneness he felt growing between them, and felt that David smiled back. Ecstasy!

He sighed through the evaporating years of frozen torment. This was it, what he had craved to feel. Love! Never had he imagined he could be made to feel this way, so complete, so vitally alive. Yet, true oneness eluded him. They were still two, where there should be only one.

He remembered his resolution back in the bar, to give however much pleasure as he might receive, and became uneasy. Could he really do *that*? Love conquered. He would, or die in the attempt. He felt that, if he could do it, it would bind them together forever. He took a deep breath.

"David," he murmured, "f... put it...in me, please?"

The other raised himself on one elbow between Greg and the candles. A trick of the light etched his outline in shifting gold fire. Once again, David was a demon, a powerful, but this time lovely demon. Idly, he rubbed Greg's chest. "You sure? I'm pretty big, and you're tight."

He doesn't want to hurt me, Greg thought. *He cares!* "Let's do it."

David shrugged and shifted to between Greg's legs in a single fluid motion. Kneeling, he greased himself. Its size exaggerated by Greg's uneasy anticipation, the shining pole looked big as the business end of a baseball bat. *How is this possible?* he wondered. *Will it hurt?*

David's first attempts at entry were unavailing. He was just too big. He took some grease and eased first one and then two fingers up Greg's hitherto virgin asshole. The shock of this made Greg squint with pain. It was strangely thrilling too, a dream fulfilled he hadn't really known he'd had. But how it burned! He was almost to the point of calling it off when the pain eased a notch. The conviction rushed over him that, if he did not go ahead, he would regret it forever after.

David looked down at him, and he nodded. This time, David effected entry, slowly, inch by jarring inch. Again, Greg almost called it off, but the need to have David, to possess him, to hold him inside and never let him go conquered. He gripped the sheets with either hand, body tense with pain.

"Here," David whispered, "breathe it." He passed a tiny brown bottle under Greg's nose.

Smelling salts? Really? He did as he was told. Instantly, he relaxed. The pain became good, needful, something possessed, hidden and treasured, an itch scratched to bleeding, compulsive, and powerfully all encompassing. He felt David's cock moving, slowly at first, then ever faster inside him. The motion sent waves of warm agony shooting through every inch of his body. Every nerve shrieked. He looked down and saw his own cock, bigger and harder than it had ever been before.

David was in total control, driving again and again, deeper and deeper. Finally, Greg felt David's body hitting him at the end of every stroke, and knew he had it all. He sighed in contentment.

David stopped and lowered himself onto Greg. Slipping one hand between them, he massaged Greg's cock, fucking him and thrusting his tongue into Greg's mouth. At last, they were one. The rhythm slowed, then stopped. He felt David's pulse beating through the cock in his asshole. David moved it slowly and gave Greg a new sensation, like something wonderful yet subtly indefinable going on down there, the itch tickled. Greg felt ready to shoot. He moaned softly.

"Not yet," David whispered, "Wait, I can make it better." He increased the stroke and backed Greg off the precipice, preoccupying him with other sensations.

The rhythm increased again. Greg felt his last inhibition ripped wide open, his innermost secret bared to the one he loved.

David knelt with Greg's body slanted up onto his lap. He bent over almost double, farther than Greg had thought a human spine could bend, and deepthroated Greg easily, all the way to the bottom, again and again, fucking him the while.

Greg moaned again. When he shot, his body felt like one gigantic sexual organ spurting ecstasy at his brain faster than it could soak it up. Monumental!

David straightened up and fucked him as hard and as fast as he could, the big cock coming almost completely out with every stroke before slamming home again. Greg felt as if he was being split up the middle with a pile driver. Finally, David groaned, the rhythm syncopated, and Greg felt the hard stream of David's cum shooting inside him, again and again and again.

Sighing, David collapsed on top of him, circled his arms beneath Greg and kissed him passionately. Greg's asshole felt warm and comfortable in a flood of hot liquid.

They lay without moving. Greg felt David's heart pounding wildly, in perfect time with his own. Greg matched up their breathing too. So this was love!

When they'd recovered a little, David withdrew, ever so slowly. Coming out, his cock felt as least a mile long, Greg thought, saucer-eyed in amazement. Wow!

At last it was done. Greg was completely blissed out in limp relief. David kissed his forehead and padded off to the bathroom. Greg lay flat, arms folded behind his head, savoring it, a shiteating grin on his face wide enough to crack it in two. He didn't want to move, lest he break the spell.

On the walls all around him, men exploded with the delicious sensations he had just experienced. Maybe, he thought, David should paper another room with men *after* they come. It would be so relaxing. David could wheel dates in there to recover.

Firehose-sized piss plashed in the bathroom. The flush came, and David reappeared. He stood in the middle of the room and stretched up, up and up. In one slow, smooth movement, he bent over backwards until his palms hit the floor. Bellyup on all fours, he pushed upwards until he had nearly doubled over backwards. He collapsed, laughing. "Oh, I love my work! How're you? How was it?"

Greg was laughing with him. "That was fantastic! You're wonderful!"

"Thanks. Yeah, I had a good time too. In fact, how'd you like to spend the night? We could cuddle up, maybe get it off again in the morning. No extra charge."

Greg was in heaven. To his knowledge, no other client had had such an offer. This was proof enough for Greg. *He likes me!*, he thought in ecstasy, *He really likes me!* "Sure, I'd..." His voice trailed off. He wanted nothing more than to curl up with David for the night, for always, in fact—and would, sooner or later, he knew that—but right now, business was in the way: the camera would be plugged in when whomever had the first shift arrived; the lens would be unblocked when he put on his clothes. "Yeah, I'd really like to, but I can't. Got a breakfast meeting tomorrow at the hotel." This was, in fact, true. The team expected a report. "I really gotta wake up in my own bed."

David nodded. "No sweat. But you are my favorite kind of client. Young. Hot. Horny." His eyebrows pumped up and down, Groucho Marx fashion. He twiddled an imaginary cigar. "There's a lot I could teach you, kid. Reasonable rates."

"Fantastic. I can't wait." Greg meant every word of it. He stumbled out of bed and made his way to the bathroom. Reality closed in on him there. He still hadn't asked David his questions. But what questions? He had to decide, and fast. He sat on the john and thought furiously.

The one thing he knew he couldn't do was simply come straight out with it. *Say, I wonder if you know a friend of mine, Herbie Manning?* From the surveillance, he knew David was carefully businesslike and confidential in all his professional dealings. More than once the datacapsules had recorded him dancing skillfully around the question of whomelse he was seeing. This was ethical behavior, and Greg respected him for it. If, as Greg wanted to believe, Herbie was one of David's regulars, there was no reason to suppose he'd reveal the fact to anyone, perhaps not even to a fast-becoming-intimate friend such as Greg. No, he really had to give David a reason to open the bag.

The big problem about what kind of story he could tell was all the conflicting evidence about the extent of David's relationship with Herbie. He did know David had been in Chicago the night of April 2nd when, presumably, Herbie had disappeared. The two of them had absolutely positively had a meet that same evening. He knew this because Herbie'd only got the money that day, and David was spending it later that night. Had they met just that once for a drug deal or something, as the team wanted to believe? Had David left his fingerprints in Herbie's apartment then? If that had been the only time they'd met, it would have had to have been. Or was their *association*—Greg decided he didn't like the word 'relationship' in this context—something more? Had it begun before that? Had it continued afterwards here in New York, and to what end?

Greg considered the evidence of the beer from the tiny microbrewery. Greg himself liked beer well enough, and knew a little bit about it. Although at one time or another he'd tried every brand commonly marketed, he'd never heard of this one. That both Herbie and David could have settled on such an obscure brand independently was outrageously unlikely as a coincidence. Therefore, it wasn't one. The four bottles—actually a sixpack with two empty spaces—they'd found in Herbie's refrigerator offered three possibilities. First, they belonged to Herbie, and David was, after all, some kind of courier as the team wanted to believe. Herbie had offered him one, which David had liked well enough to make his own brand after he got to New York. Against this were the two empty bottles. Although the inventory of trash in the apartment indicated several days' accumulation, Greg could not recall listings for the empties; this suggested neither had been consumed that evening. He eliminated this option. Second, the sixpack was David's, which he'd brought to Herbie's and left behind afterwards, minus two bottles they drank. Perhaps he had too, but if he had, he hadn't done it that night, not unless he'd also packed out the empties, and why should he do that? To remove traces of his presence there? While leaving his fingerprints all over the house? Besides, couriers did not usually bring sixpacks with them to large illegal transactions with people they did not know, especially one-timers who were likely to be nervous as hell. He smiled with satisfaction. It could only mean that...

David rapped on the door. "You all right, babe?"

"Uh, yeah. I'll be out in a minute." He guessed he really had been in here rather a while.

It could only mean they'd met oftener than just that once; they were friendly. The one-time-only, ships-passing-in-the-night scenario was bull. David and Herbie had formed their mutual taste in beer on some previous—or subsequent—occasion. Greg bet it was both. David had been to the apartment that evening, but he hadn't had a beer—and yes, he'd probably been there on business, all right, but Greg knew darn well what business it was. Herbie had treated himself to a royally good lay before disappearing from Chicago, and was continuing to treat himself at regular intervals here in New York. That explained not only the $100 bills David had used at Union Station, but the continuing dribble of such bills since! The briefcase they'd seen him carrying had some other explanation.

Greg washed his hands and splashed some water on his face. His gut feeling that where David was, Herbie couldn't be far away had been right all along. Herbie was close, close enough to smell. True, Greg still had no explanation for why he'd stolen the money in the first place, whether he was living here in New York or merely visiting at regular intervals, where David had come from, or precisely what, if anything, it meant that they'd both chosen to make major life moves at the same time. But then, you could expect only so much from a sixpack of beer.

When he returned to the main room, David was crosslegged on the bed, still naked. A fresh beer stood opened on the side table.

Greg started getting his stuff together. "Say, let me ask you something," he said with all the casualness he could muster, "...something to do with my business here in New York. It occurred to me in the john you might be able to help."

Suffused in the golden afterglow of truly great sex, he decided this felt absolutely right. He had an opportunity here to build on the relationship they'd established and enlist David's cooperation from a personal perspective, not with bribes and threats. Making it a partnership thing would be good not only for the business at hand, but for the relationship!

"Really." David lit an Export Special. "What kind of business do you mean?"

"I'm an accountant in Chicago. Investments, tax consulting, that kind of thing. One of my clients—also a personal friend—called me to New York, even booked my hotel room. But he missed the meeting we'd set up, and I heard nothing from him for days. Then, this morning, I got a message from him asking me to meet him in that bar this evening, but he didn't show again. I waited hours. The problem is that the deadline on certain financial arrangements he asked me to make is coming up—in fact, that's my breakfast meeting tomorrow—and I'm beginning to be very worried. So anyway, maybe you know him. Herbie Manning?" Greg held his breath.

David's arm froze in the act of lifting his cigarette. A muscle ticked once at the corner of his left eye. An instant later, he was back to normal. "Manning?" he said carefully, "Don't think so—but then, people don't always give me their real names. What's he look like?"

He's lying! Greg marked time. "Tall. Gangly. Skinny arms and legs. Goofy grin. Usually wears a baseball cap. Bad hair. But a great guy. We used to work together."

David appeared to be checking his memory. "No-o-o, don't think I remember one like that."

"Just a sec." With increasing agitation, Greg rummaged in his wallet. What was the matter? David should be helping him. He *had* to, or... "I think I even got a picture of him someplace." He fumbled the wallet, which fell open on the bed. Recovering it, he pulled out a wallet-sized print of Manning on the bicycle and passed it over.

David looked at it carefully, and shook his head.

Greg approached desperation. So much depended on this! "Please, if you know anything about him, please tell me. It's really important!" Talk about understatement! He heard himself begging shamelessly. "Please!—" David was spreading his hands in a gesture of helplessness. "Please let me tell you about this! There's more. Herbie disappeared from Chicago at the beginning of April, just walked out of his life without a word to anyone, and for no reason any of us, his friends, could figure. We began to think he'd been kidnapped or killed or something! When he called me to come to New York, it was out of the blue. It's all so strange! I think he must be in some kind of trouble."

David only stared at him. Greg played his last card. "Look, I don't know anything about the ethics of your business. From what you said back in the bar, maybe there isn't much, but if you're trying to protect a contact, well, I can appreciate that. I'll pay you for what I need to know, as much again as I have already." David shook his head. "Or anything you name, if I can have an hour to get it together. What do you say?"

David spread his hands, an odd look on his face. "Sorry, buddy, I wish I could help, but I simply don't know him." He cocked his head. "What makes you think I would? New York's a big place, you know."

Carefully, Greg, he told himself. This wasn't working. Time to back off and cool things down before he blew it completely. He calmed himself with an effort. "Oh, nothing, I suppose. It's just you're obviously a regular in that bar. People yell when you come in. Herbie picked that place for our meeting, so you'd think he'd been there before, and since he likes hustlers, I figured he couldn't miss you. You've got a lot in common too." He gestured at the books and the radio, still playing classical music. "You even smoke the same brand of cigarettes." He forced a laugh.

David shrugged. "Sorry. Nobody can know everyone. I'll certainly notice him next time he comes in, though. I'll tell him you were looking for him."

This was awful. Once Greg was out the door, what was to prevent David from getting Herbie on the phone first thing? He'd find out Greg had just shovelled him a whole pile of shit. That would be disaster, to reveal false pretenses to David at this stage. Later, he supposed, it might be inevitable, but by then, they'd have established their relationship and David would forgive him. Right now, he'd only look two-faced and sneaky. Greg's mind whirred. He backfilled manfully.

"No, please don't do that. If he's not really in trouble, I don't suppose he'd want me spreading his name around. It's just that I really needed him to show tonight. Without those documents he was supposed to sign, I don't know what I'm going to tell those people at breakfast." Boy, was that ever true. "But it's probably nothing. Forget it. Good chance I'm over-reacting. I only mentioned it because, well, like I said, I thought you might know him." He made an effort to be offhand. "I could easily have it wrong. Herbie's much too smart to get into any trouble he can't handle. I'm starting to feel pretty silly. He's got to turn up sooner or later. I suppose he was delayed or something. He knows where to find me. It wouldn't surprise me if I found a message waiting for me at the hotel. I'm sure I worried for nothing." He smiled. "As it happened, I'd already decided that when you showed up tonight. Frankly, I'm every bit as glad he didn't show. This was fantastic. I really like you." *Always end a big lie with a little truth,* he thought.

He sat down to put on his shoes in deepening despondency. Mechanically, he planned his next moves. He figured he'd better stop into the surveillance room next door to plug in the equipment again in case David did make some calls; he'd say he'd stopped in to check the recording and discovered it was unplugged. And if David did mention his name, he hoped it wouldn't be in any too-graphic context; he hoped he could expect the same confidentiality as David's other clients. He'd also better get Freddie down here on David's tail again, in case he moved. Glumly, Greg faced it: in case he'd spooked him. Oh, wouldn't that be rotten, if David already *knew* there was some reason why the things Greg had told him couldn't possibly be true? Why oh why had he been so specific? That business about an appointment for this very evening in the bar... if Herbie had been out of town all week and David knew it...

Or perhaps the bar itself had been the problem. Perhaps Herbie had never been there, knew nothing about it. That he had had been a hunch. The Attaché Arms transcripts had made it seem the sort of place Herbie would love.

Clearly, there had been too many hunches altogether. Greg's confidence in his intuition that, where David was, Herbie could not be far away began to seem quixotic, even egotistical. All the experts disagreed with it, and who was he to contradict them? Some punk kid far beyond his competency level. Maybe Herbie had never been in New York at all; maybe their association had ended on April 2nd. Maybe something else explained the slow pace at which David had spent Herbie's $100 bills—but why, then, should David lie about knowing him? He might be surprised to hear Herbie's name, but why should he lie? Unless there *had* been foul play and Herbie was in Hell where he belonged.

No! Greg refused to believe it, not of gentle loving David. No, Herbie was here. David was simply refusing to tell him. Or perhaps there was something to the damn courier scenario, after all. What was Greg's conviction there wasn't but another hunch? Maybe that was how they'd met; perhaps he'd only become David's client afterwards. Perhaps Herbie *was* lurking around somewhere in the black market. That might not only explain their simultaneous changes of life, but certainly would make theirs a connection David would think it prudent to protect.

If that was the case, Greg could think of nothing to say that might change David's mind. Only a prolonged hostile interrogation would do the trick, and that was definitely next on the program. From a strictly professional point of view it was even the right thing, absolutely—and he'd agreed to it! What on earth was he going to do about that? Not only did the growing warmth Greg felt for David render that unacceptable, but, with rigid horror, Greg realized an interrogation might turn up all kinds of things, including what they'd been doing together right here this evening! Being here, doing this, was crazy! Somehow, in his headlong rush to lose his virginity, he'd failed to think things through. Specifically, he simply hadn't considered the possibility of failure.

Maybe he had no choice but to drop all the disguises, admit to whom and what he was, and lay all the cards down face up: tell David how much trouble he, David, was in and promise to protect him if he cooperated, and if that failed, beg him to help for both their sakes. He didn't like it, admitting he'd been lying and pretending to be something he wasn't. David would despise him, would never trust him again—on top of which, he'd be putting himself completely in David's power. Extremely poor management! But what choice did he have? It was that or admit failure and throw everything away.

As Greg sat there on the edge of the bed in his agony of doubt, finally and completely at a loss for what to do, David leaned forward and massaged his shoulders. *At least he doesn't hate me, yet.*

I've still got that to work with. Greg slumped, surrendering to the massage.

David was silent a long moment, kneading Greg's shoulders. Then, softly, he said, "Well, he hasn't been kidnapped or killed, at least, not the last time *I* saw him, which was some time ago. He was just as ornery as ever."

The effect on Greg was electric. *Yes!!!* He spun around so fast he nearly fell off the bed. "You mean it? You know him after all?"

David refused to meet Greg's eye. "Usually, I like to keep my client contacts confidential. Good business practice. But if you're his friend and here on his business, and if he's gone missing..." He shrugged. "Anyway, he's got an appointment with me for tomorrow night. We'll see if he shows. I suppose you'll want to know if he doesn't."

Greg breathed a prayer of great thanksgiving to whatever gods might be, after which he threw himself on David and covered him with kisses. "Oh, that's the best news I could have had! Yes!" He thought rapidly. "Yes, if neither of us has heard from him by then, I suppose we ought to put our heads together again, you might say." He laughed in relief.

David had been knocked sideways. He laughed too, and recovered himself. "Okay, okay! Want me to call you? Where are you staying?"

No, thought Greg, that might be too risky until the heat had been firmly and definitely turned off. "Tell you what. I'm going to be in and out a lot. Why don't I call you the morning after, either way? I'm definitely gonna want to make another date with you regardless! I'll know my schedule by then."

"Anytime. I'll be looking forward to it. You know where to find me."

Greg was dressed and ready. David got off the bed and went to get the door. "So long, buddy," he smiled. "That was super. Hope our friend turns up."

Greg smiled back. "Oh, he will. I can feel it." He had a thought. "And oh, if—no, when—you talk to him, could you sorta...

kinda forget to mention you met me? Like you, my business with him is best kept confidential. I'm starting to be pretty embarrassed at losing my cool like that."

"Well, I will if you will." David opened the door.

"Deal."

Greg really did not want to leave. Not only had his whole life just opened up ahead of him in this room, there were a hundred questions he wanted answered urgently. How well did David know Herbie? How long had he known him? What had Herbie been doing that he'd managed to evade the search? What, if anything, did David know about the money? The courier business *was* bull, wasn't it? But to probe further now didn't fit with all this confidentiality they were both supposed to be giving Herbie, and if he turned up tomorrow, it would all be irrelevant, anyway. If he didn't—and fat chance of *that*, Greg thought grimly, with rising jealousy—increased curiosity would seem more appropriate.

So, he kissed David lightly on the lips. He stopped halfway through the door and looked at David, naked and beautiful. He reached up and touched David's cheek lightly, with obvious love, he hoped. Then he went.

Behind him, he heard the door close. A second later, he heard it lock.

For the first time in his life, he knew what it meant to walk on air. He felt absolutely fantastic. He felt warm, loose and graceful. He felt his clothes fitting perfectly. There was a swagger in his step he hadn't had earlier, a huge grin on his face and confidence at his core. He felt vibrantly alive and at peace with the universe. He was in love and manically happy. To cap it all, the business was practically concluded. He'd done it! He'd pulled it off, after all! Everything! His plan was running like a fine machine. David liked him! Everything was great.

Down in the street, he threw a kiss at an I ♥ New York lamppost banner and flagged a cab in the same gesture.

They headed uptown. Greg curled up in the corner of the cab. He couldn't believe how wonderful he felt. He'd just lost his virginity in a truly great fuck, and more even than that, he'd learned a thing or two about what he was. He wasn't a pervert, after all! David up close was not only really nice, but genuinely impressive. Greg was completely charmed. *And he's looking forward to seeing me again!*

He lay his head back on the cab's rear deck and looked up at the streetlights passing overhead. There was a luscious warm glow in his asshole and another in his throat. He hoped neither would ever go away. Being gay not only wasn't so bad, it was magnificent! In a leisurely, condescending sort of way, he found himself pitying straight men that they would never know the superior joy of sex with David Alexander. He felt pretty smugly superior himself. The secret world of gay life had opened up and delivered him its Prince of Thieves. He was getting hard again just thinking about it. His briefs pinched. He stuck his hand down inside his crotch and rearranged matters, a gesture that would have been totally alien two hours before. Then, he'd have had to wait for complete privacy. Now, who cared?

David was the nicest, most beautiful human being in the world. So what if he'd lied at first about knowing Herbie? Of course he had! Would he, Greg, have wanted him to spill *their* relationship to anybody who asked?—and especially to somebody who offered money to know? Of course not! That David had passed up the money impressed him enormously. They were so right for one another! Oh, how he loved him! Once this bullshit about Manning was finagled, they'd be together forever. He'd have everything he could ever want. It seemed amazingly too good to be true. He floated on clouds of triumph.

Up in his room, he threw up the sash and looked over the darkened park, the lights along its paths glowing through the trees. It was gorgeous. Warm soft night air flooded in over stale air conditioning. He breathed it in hungry chest-filling gulps. Night sounds filtered from below, from a great lovely city that never slept.

He was much too excited to sleep. He got a beer from the minibar and paced back and forth with it. He made a mental note to send a detective out tomorrow for some of that microbrewery beer.

The future! Oh, the future was going to be spectacular! All they had to do was keep up the regular surveillance. Herbie would appear all by himself, just as Greg had known all along he would. By this time tomorrow, he'd be busted and on his way back to Chicago for Morgan Jaye, that fearsome old buzzard, to dig his beak into. Fearsome old buzzard? Soon-to-be boss! Wonderful kindly Morgan Jaye! As far as David was concerned, he, Greg, needn't appear in that at all. Once Herbie was canned, he'd be a god! He'd be able to order what the fuck he liked, the team and the law be damned! He'd manipulate David's release from behind the scenes—hell, maybe they didn't need to arrest him at all if they could get Herbie on the way to see him. That'd be best for all kinds of reasons. David need never know how he'd been used. They'd go back to Chicago and live together. David would give up whoring, of course. Smoking too. They'd settle down cosily together and live off Greg's hefty new salary, at least at first. David would get a real job soon enough. Why, a super-intelligent good-looking guy like that—Greg bet he could get him some kind of entry-level job at Amalgamated Consolidated with no problem. Just cut that long hair and he'd be dynamite in business clothes. Why, they might end up working together too! Everything was going to be perfect. He had it all figured out.

He missed David already. The next day or so without him—and maybe longer, depending—was going to be agony. If he couldn't see him or touch him, he at least longed to hear his beloved's voice. He headed to the phone. He'd call him to say goodnight.

With a huge effort he stopped himself in the very act of lifting the phone. This was silly. Self-control, that was the thing. Besides, David was probably asleep by now, or maybe out on one of his midnight carouses—something else that would just naturally change soon enough. He shrugged. It didn't matter. He'd simply have to wait.

He felt deliciously weary. As long as he had the phone in his hand, he called the switchboard to leave a wake-up call for 6AM—and had a thought. They were all going to be yammering at him wanting confirmation he'd fallen flat and authorization to send in the arrest team. Well, screw them. They'd been *wrong.* He was in firm control now. He felt like celebrating, like lording it over the SOBs who couldn't wait for him to fail. They could go sit on themselves until he was good and ready. After nights of pulling on himself over a hot viewscreen, he was going to treat himself to a good night's sleep. He grinned, and ordered no phone calls until 8AM.

He stripped off his clothes and climbed into bed. Tired though he was, his mind still raced, turning it over and over again. He'd managed to get it all. David felt as much for him as he did for David; that was obvious. There was real love between them. They were going to have a wonderful life.

As he drifted off, it occurred to him that, after all, he'd forgotten to stop into the surveillance room to plug in the equipment again and call Freddie back onto the job. Oh well, it didn't matter. Everything was going to be great...

Greg's wakeup call came at 8:06. Not surprisingly, there were five messages—Freddie, the CRAP switchboard, Freddie, Rico, Rico—the last only fifteen minutes before. Screw them. He headed for the bathroom and treated himself to a leisurely, steamy shower. The phone rang again while he was in there. The nerve! He'd be there when he was good and ready. "I'm coming, damn you, I'll be right there!" he yelled at the hot water tap, and laughed. Images of David—playing with David naked in the shower—danced in his head. "I'm coming, oh, I'm cumming! Harder, harder, harder!" he laughed, playacting ecstacy. His anticipation at stunning the team with his spectacular success began to rise. He zipped through a shave, miraculously avoiding chopping himself to pieces, and threw on his clothes.

In some irritation, he checked for the last phone message, the one that had come in while he was in the shower. Rico, again. "'Get the f--- down here NOW! The Harrington!'" the operator read, dripping disapproval. "He didn't say 'f---,' sir. He said something else. This is not the kind of language—"

Greg cut her off with a muttered apology and hung up. Irritation blossomed into rage. What did they think they meant, get down to the Harrington now? He couldn't do that! He'd blow his

178

cover. Why, they hadn't as much as heard his story! Were they so sure he'd failed that they were giving him orders like this? He'd have their asses, the lot of them, as soon as he recounted his triumph. He called the room at the Harrington, the one next to David's. The line was busy. He called Headquarters. "They're all at the Harrington, Greg. I believe they need you there ASAP," was all he could get. The Harrington phone stayed busy.

He swore. He supposed there was nothing for it but to go there, after all. Well, it was still early. David seldom strayed out of his room before eleven. He'd zip in there and haul their butts off somewhere safe for their conference. He'd tell them all just exactly what he thought of them, and maybe make some personnel adjustments among the more openly contemptuous and least cooperative of the lot.

He headed for the cabstand. By the time he got there, his spirits had risen again. All around him, people were going about their morning routines, oblivious to him and his joy. *Hey, you jerks,* he wanted to shout, *I'm powerful, I command respect, and I'm in love! Look at me!*

This euphoria lasted all the way down to the Harrington. Out front, Freddie stood with his hands in his pockets while Rico paced up and down the sidewalk in barely controlled fury. "You blew it! You got nothing, man, did you!"

"How do you know what I got? As it happens..." He stopped himself. "Why?"

"He's gone, man, outa here!" Rico fairly spat it at him. "What the fuck you say to him, man?"

A bad feeling wrapped itself around Greg's spine. "Who's gone, Rico?" He knew, of course. He just refused to believe it.

"Blondy the Whore!" Rico did spit this time, at a planter, and missed. "Who else we talking about here?"

Greg was speechless. This had to be a mistake, a stupid mistake that would upset everything, and somebody was going to pay for it! He shouldered past them into the lobby and headed for the deskclerk in his glass cage. "House phone for 413, please." Hearing

David's voice had become the overwhelmingly important thing in the world.

The clerk reached for the switchboard, then paused. "Sorry, 413's gone."

Greg struggled to believe it. *Why? For god's sake, why?* "When was this?"

The clerk looked irritated. "Look. I'm busy here. Unless you want somebody else, or a *room...*"

Greg slammed his CRAP card against the glass cage. "When did he check out, *asshole*?" He oozed fury and nameless threat.

The clerk gulped. "I don't know, sir. The maid says he's cleared off. I'm sorry, sir. We always cooperate with the police here, sir, honest. You can go up to 258 and ask if we don't."

Greg was in no mood to be placated. He turned to Freddie and Rico.

"You betcha, bossman," Rico snarled. "Gone. No trail, man, I been checking, and we weren't on him, man, 'cause *you* took *total command* and gave us the night off!"

Greg turned back to the deskclerk, cold with fury. "The key to 413. Now!"

"Yessir." The clerk pushed it over.

Greg grabbed it and headed stiff-legged for the elevator, Rico and Freddie trotting at his heels. They didn't speak on the way up. More of the team were hanging around the fourth floor corridor, making a show of examining it for traces of the vanished Alexander. Greg did not like the expressions he saw on faces that turned away as he approached. The door to the emergency stairwell stood open, propped with a team member's toolbag. Soft laughter floated up.

The door to 413 was open already. Inside, the wall montage looked tawdry in daylight. On the desk, papers ruffled in the breeze from the open windows—scratched out, discarded drafts from the little printer of what proved to be porn. The printer itself and the tablet computer were gone. A blank space on the desk showed where they'd been. The tiny boomb2ox had gone too. The room showed all the signs of hurried and ill-organized flight. Drawers hung ajar. Piles of clothes were flung about, as if sorted hastily. Nothing else personal remained. Coat hangers were strewn across the unmade bed. The closet door hung open; totally empty, the closet revealed floorboards pried up to make a neatly briefcase-sized hole.

Greg turned to the detectives. Rico and Freddie were hanging by the room door, Rico still staring in cold accusation. Freddie looked down, kicking idly at the threshold.

Greg pointed to the empty space under the closet floor. "You searched this room. What was in there?" he asked.

Freddie looked up. "I don't know. We didn't check it."

"You didn't check it?" Greg's voice dripped poison.

Rico exploded. "Oh no bossbaby, you ain't pinning this on us. There was a ton a crap in that closet, and linoleum under it. *Glued down* linoleum, man. See?" A piece of old linoleum the size of the closet floor lay beside the bed, signs of fresh glue on its back.

"Yeah, he musta taken that up, then glued it back." Freddie. "It looked real, man, and permanent. We never thought something might be under it." He went and inspected the hole. "Yeah," he said softly, "Shit. Sorry."

Rico was still angry. "Hey, what you doing, apologizing to dis turkey? He the one scared da motha off, not us!"

"I thought you guys were supposed to be the best," Greg sneered. "A courier, huh? Big drug deals! It was all bull! If you'd done your job and found that money right here where it was all along, we *would* have arrested him first thing and saved all this trouble."

He slammed off into the bathroom, which showed similar signs of disarray. He slumped against the closed door. How had this happened? What did it mean? What the hell was he going to do? He really had overstated the case a bit. Who knew what had been in that hole? The money? And if so, would he have? Had David arrested first thing? He honestly didn't know. It sounded good, but somewhere along the way, his anger had become an act, a desperate effort to save his butt. Hey, that's what everybody else was doing. A tap came at the door. Freddie. "Hotel manager's here, man."

Greg emerged. A florid-faced man chomping a stubby unlit cigar turned circles in the middle of the room, shaking his head at the wall montage.

"Really something, isn't it? Hell, I'd keep it this way if I thought there was ever gonna be anybody else who could stand to look at it all goddam day." Inevitably, his gaze encompassed the closet. "What's this?" His hands went to his hips. "He gave me a deposit on the walls, that's okay, but who's been digging up my floor?" No one spoke. "I'm holding you responsible! Either produce Alexander so I can bill him, or pay it yourselves. I'm sick of all you guys pestering the permanent residents. We're supposed to have an arrangement!"

Greg looked around the room at the wreckage of his career, the loss of his so recently cherished, glorious future—at the desertion and betrayal by the man he loved. *The Prince of Thieves, huh?* He thought bitterly on how he'd been snookered, how, instead of spinning David a yarn, David had obviously spun him one to put him off his guard and escape. *Love at first fuck in a room full of cum! How could I have been so stupid?* Real fury filled him.

They were all looking at him. City sounds filtered up from the street. Slowly, a man in a dream, he picked up an I ♥ New York drinking glass and hurled it shattering against the wall.

Chapter Four
<u>STONE WALLS DO NOT A PRISON MAKE...</u>

he alarmclock burst into shattering jangling life.

For a long long moment, nothing happened. Then from under the muddled heap of bedclothes an arm probed forth and silenced it with enough desperation to tumble it off the nightstand, but silently nonetheless. That the alarmclock fell neatly into a small basket fitted with a cushion obviously for the purpose indicated this was not an unusual event.

Another long long moment later, the covers parted a crack. A single begummed eye took in the fact of a cold gray utterly cheerless March morning. The covers closed again. *Fuckit,* thought the owner of the eye, *maybe tomorrow will be better.* —But no, business called. There was an appointment to keep, one of some considerable interest too.

Thus, on this day about a month before his rescue of the djinn would make such quotidian annoyances a thing of the past forever, Herbie Manning padded sleepily naked and yawning, morning coffee in hand, to his desk in the living room, and flipped on the computer. Fumbling for an Export Special, he scrolled blearily through the job he'd completed the night before. The rows and columns of numbers swam on the screen. He made no attempt to concentrate; he simply checked details as they occurred to him, waiting for the job to take shape as a whole in his head. He sipped his too-hot coffee and burned his tongue. *Damn!* Yes, something was definitely strange.

Herbie frowned. It wasn't *his* fault. He'd double- and triplechecked each entry, and the computer had done the math. The figures were comprehensive, the conclusion inescapable: his client, Garrison Griffin, was up to something interesting, a decidedly dubious something interesting.

Could he be embezzling? If so, Herbie saw no clue how he was doing it. Herbie's curiosity was piqued, his cupidity too. He was alert to the possibility he might turn such knowledge to his advantage—a little gentlemanly blackmail between friends, perhaps, the old broad-hint-and-a-raised-eyebrow kind of thing. He'd need details, though, and knowing Griffin, whatever it was would be really clever. Griffin was lead consultant on all Amalgamated Consolidated's most crucial, sensitive and confidential systems, Morgan Jaye's pocket software genius. He'd have to go carefully with the man, keep his eyes and ears open for hints and ask exactly the right questions.

The house clocks began striking 10AM. Herbie shrugged and triggered the printer. Once the pages were hissing squarely into the tray, he headed for the bathroom.

An hour and a half later, Herbie's bicycle was hitched securely to a lamppost in Amalgamated Consolidated Plaza, and Herbie himself was in parabolic ascent of the bank in one of its antiseptic elevators.

He found Garrison Griffin in an airless interior office on the 70th floor barely big enough for the man himself, a desk, a chair, and a computer stand. No mere viewscreen for Griffin, a thick cable led from a powerful PC to a jack in the wall.

Griffin arose in such haste papers fluttered on the desk. "Herbie! Thought you were going to call me from the lobby!" Genuine alarm blossomed on the man's face.

Herbie had skipped this pre-arrangement, favoring the element of surprise. A man's office was his second home—sometimes his first—and snap inspections were often revealing. "Uh, sorry." He had a line ready. "There was a wait for the phone, so I thought I'd take a chance and come straight up."

"Well then come on in!" Although Griffin was not a small man, he maneuvered himself around the desk with speed amazing in such a small space. He literally yanked Herbie into the office and closed the door with a bang. Herbie saw actual sweat beading the man's forehead.

As Herbie stared, wondering at this postcard picture of paranoia, Griffin got himself under control. He seemed to become conscious of the effect he was producing, and affected a forced joviality. "Say, this is a pretty cheerless place, huh? What say we grab some lunch? I'm buying! We'll do our business after."

Herbie shrugged. "Sounds good to me." Passing up a free meal was against his value system.

Griffin opened the door just wide enough to poke his head out and scan the corridor in both directions before marching Herbie briskly to the elevators.

As one arrived, a commotion at the end of the long narrow corridor where the executive suites were announced another group heading in their direction. Herbie regarded this with interest. This was Morgan Jaye's floor.

Herbie had never laid eyes on the man, at least to know whom he was seeing. As the local CRAP chief, Jaye was an intriguing yet rather shadowy figure who seemed to lurk behind ever more of the Consortium's operations these days. Some of Herbie's associates, the less scrupulous ones particularly, regarded him with undisguised dread. It would be interesting, Herbie thought, to get a good look at him during a shared elevator ride. He made a move to hold the door. Given the elaborately furtive display he'd been treated to already, Herbie was not much surprised at the urgency with which Griffin bustled him into the elevator and jabbed the "Close Door" button.

This behavior confirmed Herbie's suspicions. *He's definitely hiding something,* Herbie thought. *Me, for starters!*

In the first part of the previous year Griffin had liquidated assets at a wholesale pace, but whither the money had gone was obscure. It had simply disappeared into the man's pocket without trace, and without deductible expenses, Griffin's taxes, the object of Herbie's exercise, after all, had been a less satisfactory business than otherwise might have been the case. Had that been all there were to it, this might betoken some underlying personal problem about which one might be properly sympathetic and discreetly silent. However, during the second half of the year, beginning at the same time Griffin's liquidation of assets had ceased, his bank statements had become very peculiar indeed.

All this made it seem not at all strange that Griffin should be paying him, Herbie Manning, to do his books instead of having the bank's accountants do it for nothing. He certainly could have availed himself of the in-house courtesy had he wanted—and so very well might not want to have it noticed that he hadn't.

True, there could be other reasons Griffin didn't want him seen besides anxiety over introducing him and raising curiosity about his presence. In his usual baseball cap and jeans, Herbie was hardly the picture of corporate chic, but then, Griffin wasn't either, and, presumably, he was there to be seen all the time. Fiftyish, paunchy and balding, he wore a shapeless 2-piece gray suit Herbie knew for a fact cost all of $125. Herbie himself had several like it left over from his own days at AmalCon. Cheap and sloppy though they were, they fit the dress code and were popular among the multitudinous lower-paid echelons of the bank's staff. Herbie, however, had worn them solely as a protest against dress codes in general. At what he'd been paid, he could have afforded better if he'd wanted.

Come to think of it, so could Griffin, at least in theory. While Herbie's sloppiness was a studied protest, a demand to be evaluated on the basis of what he could do rather than on his appearance, which he considered hopeless anyway, Griffin's seemed to be endemic. In fact, the guy was a mess. The suit looked as if he'd slept in it; he was unshaved and uncombed; his shirt flopped loosely at the belt; and the tip of his tie showed the brown stain of what Herbie hoped was coffee. He imagined Griffin dunking it as he leaned over his desk and cursing.

All this was new. Although the Garrison Griffin he'd known in years past had been no popinjay, he'd had no quarrels with The System of Herbie's sort. He'd been well-dressed and neat.

Herbie toted it all up with an accountant's precision: the odd bank statements, the paranoid behavior, the slovenly appearance. He arrived at a partial sum, a sub-total, and put himself on the qui vive for further clues.

Once safely alone with Herbie in the elevator, Griffin was jovial once more. "Say, like those Bulls this season?"

Herbie knew just enough basketball to get them out of the building.

The restaurant Griffin chose was a typical downtown Chicago lunchplace. Fake candle sconces with yellowed shades dripping dusty prisms hung slightly askew on woodgrained panelling of genuine formica. A bar ran down one side of the room. Barstools in red leatherette faced a brass barrail with most of its plating worn away in shiny gray smears, evidence of a generation of Chicago businessmen rubbing elbows as they soaked up the overpriced booze. Walking rapidly and without conversation, they'd passed half a dozen identical places on their way from the office. By this time, the speculation Griffin might be unwilling to risk someplace closer, where they'd be more likely to encounter somebody either of them knew from AmalCon, took Herbie with no surprise at all.

A greasy maitre d' in a frilly shirtfront broke off lecturing a busboy in Greek to look them up and down from Griffin's stained tie to Herbie's baseball cap and torn sneakers, and was openly unimpressed. The tables were too close together too. At theirs, Griffin grabbed the banquette, forcing Herbie to face the wall. Crud spotted the glassware and cutlery. Typical free lunch.

As the place filled up, Griffin craned around, scrutinizing their neighbors edgily. He answered Herbie's attempts to make casual conversation with distracted monosyllables when he answered them at all. He deferred any mention of their business until after they ate.

Closing the hopeless menu, Herbie ordered the most expensive thing on it, a steak and a baked potato. Griffin ordered a large Greek salad and two gin and tonics in rapid succession. After the second one, he excused himself to the men's room. While he was

187

gone, Herbie changed his own drink order to straight tonic. An advantage of this kind could not be underrated.

When Griffin returned, he'd straightened his clothes and combed his hair. His nervous, furtive manner had disappeared. He was relaxed, even bubbly. Herbie noticed a faint trace of white powder in the nosehair of Griffin's left nostril, and rejoiced. He re-entered his sub-total on the bottom line. The "why" had just been explained, and the "how" might be easier to get than he'd thought.

The conversation now expanded magically in ever-widening stream of consciousness ripples. As they ate, they talked of personalities they knew in common at AmalCon. They talked computers and the new work Griffin was doing at the bank. As he talked about his work all restraint seemed to leave the man. He babbled out complex details of AmalCon's financial position and its involvement in the mechanics of the Great Revision, all confidential stuff any journalist or financial analyst would have given a good deal more than the price of lunch to hear had any been within earshot and thought the scruffy-looking pair worthy of attention.

Herbie was an excellent listener. He knew how to stay focussed on the speaker even when his own mind was wandering. He knew how to drop exactly the right "Huh!"s and "No kidding"s and "I didn't know that"s to keep the flow going when pauses occurred. He marvelled at the bewilderingly artesian display of fact upwelling before him.

Finally, as Griffin's discussion of Herbie's old colleagues in the Securities Department segued into a detailed description of the department's precise contribution to the bank's overall situation in the current fiscal year, Herbie saw an opportunity to nudge the conversation in the direction he wanted to go.

"Uh, hold up a second, Griff." He flagged down the waiter for more drinks. "This is great stuff. I had no idea the department's doing so much business. So then, they must have a new computer system too, right?" Herbie, who also kept in occasional contact with one or two other of his erstwhile colleagues, knew perfectly well they didn't.

Griffin looked surprised.

"I mean, the old system was installed years ago, when I was still working there." That had been how they'd met in the first place. "You don't mean to say they're still giving you access?"

Griffin used the back of his hand to wipe a glistening accumulation from under his nose. "Well, no, not officially, anyway. Like most designers, I leave myself a private password back into any system I design. That way, I can check up on how it's working and maybe spot places where I can propose improvements. Got to keep myself in business, after all."

I'm sure it started that way, at least, Herbie thought. "Gosh. That must make for an awful lot of passwords." He grinned. "Or is it always the same one?"

Griffin made a face. "That stupid I'm not. My secret passwords are all mnemonic. That way, I don't have to write them down. Fr'instance, in Personal Banking, it might be the filing system I want to watch, so the password would be 'FILES?'—might be, but isn't, of course. In the Trust Department, I might be keeping an eye on the Prime Performance Simulation Model, and if I am (which I'm not), it's 'MODEL1.' Like that, see?" Griffin's paranoia was obviously returning.

"Isn't it dangerous? I hear the CRAPpers do routine surveillance on everybody's computers. They monitor you while you're working, and you never know it! What if they caught you at it?"

A crafty look fleeted over Griffin's face like the shadow of a low-flying jet on sunlit fields. "Oh, I guess I'm smart enough to get around that! Pardon me if I don't mention just how." His eyes shifted back and forth. "By the way, I'd resist any urge to go exploring on your own. You gotta have a direct terminal to do this, but if you use one, the CRAPpers'll gitcha!" He snapped his fingers under Herbie's nose.

This rather overtly hostile gesture startled them both. Herbie jerked straight up in his chair. As the surprise left Griffin's face, he muttered an apology and excused himself to the john again, rather unsteadily, Herbie thought. The guy was clearly losing it.

Herbie checked his watch: two o'clock. The place was emptying fast. He had the table bussed and ordered a refill of Griffin's glass. Griffin, he was now sure, would return with a thirst. As he did return, perky and bouncy once more, Herbie was laying out his papers.

"What ho! Business calls, does it? Just a sec." Griffin drained his glass in one long pull and waved it at the waiter for replenishment. "So, Herbie, what kind of shape am I in, anyway?" He folded his hands on the table, all polite attention.

Herbie was businesslike. "Well, basically pretty good shape. All the assets you liquidated means there's less interest and dividend income to pay tax on, and since the Consortium's finally scrapped the capital gains tax, there's none of that to worry about. There *is* one funny thing, though..."

"Oh, what's that?"

"I'll explain." The time had come. Herbie talked slowly, feeling his way. "There's something very odd about your second savings account."

"Second savings account?" Griffin appeared gently confused. "But Herbie, I don't have a second savings account."

"Of course you do." Herbie had it handy. "There's your name right at the top, 'Garrison Griffin, Account 2,' and the amount of the opening deposit and its date matches up with your last withdrawal from your brokerage account. It's yours all right."

On Griffin's face, confusion turned to alarm. Herbie had in fact questioned Griffin's judgment in including these papers in the first place. Their bearing on his tax position was tiny; he easily might have filed an adjustment to include it later. Certainly, the tipoff the account contained was obvious to anyone who looked at all closely. Could Griffin really have thought him so stupid as not to notice? Although such suspicions invariably brought out the worst in Herbie, Griffin's astonishment caused him to lay them aside. Plainly, Griffin had never intended to show him this account. He'd simply bundled it up with the rest in a moment of drug-soaked befuddlement. Herbie sat back. The human condition never failed to amaze him.

Griffin became elaborately casual. "Oh, *that.* Sorry, I didn't know what you were talking about for a minute. Yes, I use that as sort of a holding account while I'm waiting for new opportunities. Sure. What's odd about that?"

It was ludicrous, that was what. Herbie refused even to consider it. The man was improvising. New opportunities? Hah! From this account the money disappeared forever, straight up Griffin's nose. The amounts withdrawn seemed about right to cover a substantial daily habit.

"About that? Why, nothing at all." Herbie could be elaborately casual too. "It's this other business. You know, I almost didn't catch it at first. It's not the kind of thing I'd ordinarily question, a bank's math, but something did look odd about it, so I looked again, and sure enough."

He paused as new drinks arrived. Griffin was starting to look like he needed one. "The withdrawals are way out of line with the deposits, way *in excess* of the deposits, and yet the account never goes overdrawn."

"What? Let me see that!" Griffin took it and gave it an elaborate perusal. "I don't know what you're talking about! Look here, up at the summary section, Total Deposits, Total Withdrawals." He shuffled the papers. "Why, it all looks okay to me!"

"Oh, you put in the fix on that," Herbie said stonily. "If you hadn't, the system's self-auditing feature—which you rewrote, I seem to recall you telling me not an hour ago—would have spit this out in a nanosecond. No, you're quite right. In the summary section, if you take the Beginning Balance, add the 'Total Deposits' and subtract the 'Total Withdrawals,' you wind up with the Ending Balance. Looks legit. The problem is that if you look at the line items and add or subtract *them*, a different picture emerges. I did it. Here, look at this." He passed Griffin more paper. "The daily balances are a dead giveaway all by themselves. That's what tipped me to it in the first place. They pop right back up by themselves every time you make a withdrawal, to the tune of several hundred dollars a day. Neat trick, that. It's the damndest account I've ever seen—refills itself by magic. Wish I had one like it." He raised an eyebrow.

Griffin definitely got it. He looked worried. "Now see here, Herbie. That's uncalled for! Even if what you say is true, and I'd need time to go over your work to see if you haven't made some kind of mistake somewhere, *I* don't know anything about this! How long have we been friends? You've just got to believe me on that."

Herbie said nothing. This disclaimer was completely inadequate, and Griffin must know he knew it. He kept the stoniness going, obviously unyielding and unimpressed. Inside, his excitement grew apace.

A long moment passed. Then Griffin crumbled. His head dropped. He looked wildly back and forth, gulped his drink and stared at Herbie, eyes wide and vacant. His right hand fumbled with a desert fork.

This was excellent, Herbie felt. He was playing the man like a Mozart sonata, or, considering the man's naked internal disjunct, perhaps more like the Webern *Passacaglia*. Now was the time to adopt a more soothing tone. He leaned forward and touched Griffin's arm. "Come on, Griff, get a grip. I'm not going to burn you on it. It's me, remember? So why don't you tell ol' Herbie what you did? If you do, *maybe* I can help you with it. You didn't think you could keep this up forever, did you? After all, the money's got to come *from* someplace, right? People have a habit of noticing when some is missing, especially when it goes on month after month like this has. Worse, the evidence is right there on your statements. If I found it, so can somebody else." Herbie did his best to infuse his voice with subtle menace. "Better me than the CRAPpers, right?"

Griffin's paranoia let him evade the point no longer. He got himself in hand with an effort which seemed to Herbie like the last, desperate courage of a cornered man. He straightened up and gave Herbie an appraising look. "Uh huh, so that's the game, is it? You think you can make me cut you in on the action. Or maybe you'd prefer to join the ranks of my permanent creditors. You'd think that was safer, wouldn't you, than actually getting on record with a bank account?" His face changed. Incongruously, he smiled. "Well, you can think again." He chuckled a sly, rather insane chuckle that sent Herbie's eyes on an involuntary check of the exits. "It was pretty clever, if I do say so myself. I'm sure you'll think so too. It occurred to me while I was gearing us up for micro-trading."

Herbie knew what this was, of course: the Consortium's latest scheme for automating and streamlining the making of money. At long last, crowded market floors full of shouting, gesticulating traders knee-deep in paper trash were a thing of the past. The heart of the new, electronic bourse was a gigantic mainframe computer which matched sellers of stocks, bonds, commodities and securities of every kind to buyers within parameters specified by the parties. It made the deal, posted it to the accounts of both buyer and seller, transferred ownership of the stock and the funds to pay for it all in one operation. This had speeded up trading enormously. During periods of heavy activity, price quotes could change continuously, being updated once every hundredth of a second in increments as small as a thousandth of a penny—thus, micro-trading.

The idea was not new. The technology had been available for more than a decade, but floor traders, market analysts, and others whose jobs would be either eliminated or vastly complicated by the new system had pointed out at top volume the potential for runaway markets inherent in any such system where human beings were no longer present to scrutinize and control the flow—and what about unauthorized tinkering by computer hackers seeking to sabotage the process or influence it to their advantage?

When the Consortium came to power, it swept these critics aside with a broad brush. It was confident, it said, its software would prevent huge fluctuations unless these represented the true will of the marketplace. As for hackers, well, the Consortium would monitor the process every step of the way. Such persons would find no tolerance for their activities. The Consortium would crush them. Besides, it said, its security was absolute. Opportunities for unauthorized tinkering did not exist.

Evidently, Herbie thought, Griffin had found one anyway. He listened intently, eyes narrowed, barely daring to breathe lest he break the flow. After Griffin's lapse in composure, his sudden access of confidence made Herbie deeply suspicious. *So I can think again,*

193

can I? From where Herbie sat it looked as if he controlled the case completely.

Yet, as Griffin talked on, his voice gained a note of triumphant mockery Herbie found increasingly disconcerting. "It's very simple, right Herbie? When our brokers push the button, the trade is supposed to be entered right then. Well, I simply delay it *one second*. If the trade makes money in that time, I siphon off the extra to my account. Sure, I don't make very much on any one trade, a fraction of a cent on up to a coupla bucks max depending on the size of the fluctuation and the number of shares traded, but with all those trades every day, it adds up."

"Wait a minute. I don't quite get it. What do you mean, 'if the trade makes money'?"

"If it makes money for me, of course. Say a customer buys a rising stock. Amalcon's computer buys it from the central system right then, but posts it to our guy a second later. He pays the higher price, with the difference going into my account. If he buys a falling stock, there's no money in that for me, so I just pass it through. For stock sales, turn the whole thing around. If he sells a falling stock, he gets the lower price of a second later, and I get the difference."

"God! Weren't you afraid somebody would tumble to it? You're not the only one who ever looks at the computer code, you know."

"Oh, I fixed that. I've got a second computer jack in my office, this one unregistered. A subroutine accesses that jack, where a simple processor scrambles the connection through to one of my PC's at home, which runs the program."

So that was how he did it, how he defeated the need for a direct terminal to do his extra-curricular snooping through the bank's files: he had one, but it was unregistered and therefore not visible to the CRAPpers' routine surveillance.

Griffin crowed on, by this time very pleased with himself, indeed. "I fixed the summary section on my account to defeat the system's self-auditing, and made the system ignore the deposits as line items 'cause thousands of deposits of a fraction of a penny would make a pretty hefty statement. Somebody'd be sure to take a second look at it when it didn't fit the standard envelope. Guess I wasn't smart enough for *you* though, Herbie." He smiled.

So did Herbie, broadly. He had him! The whole thing was desperately illegal. Unlicensed brokering. Unauthorized computing. Theft!—and knowing the Consortium, doubtless six or seven other things as well. They'd send Griffin away forever! Then, a nagging suspicion he'd been having about how the whole scheme seemed somehow, well, *familiar* triggered a memory. He froze in consternation.

Griffin laughed. "That's right! It's *your idea*, isn't it?"

It was too, at least sort of. Herbie dimly remembered a conversation they'd had over drinks a number of years ago, an alcohol-elevated borderline-facetious cocktail hour discussion about what kind of deviltry the then-proposed micro-trading system might lend itself to. He'd been in fine form that evening, he remembered, had babbled out six or seven ideas, most of which—all of which, he'd thought—were perfectly preposterous. One very like this had been among them.

"A brilliant idea too," Griffin went on. "I certainly think so, and if I ever have to tell this story to anyone else, I intend to give credit where credit is due."

Well, so what? Herbie's shock faded rapidly. "Big deal. You can't connect me with this in any way."

"That's right, I can't. Not *now*. But if you want in, I'll drop you all the way in. Want your blackmail in cash, do you? Maybe you'll develop a bank account even you don't know about—maybe at our bank, maybe at some other. Come to think of it, you could own this one in about ten seconds." He tapped the statements of his second savings account.

He could too. Herbie gave up. He put on a shocked expression. "Blackmail! Who said anything about blackmail? I want no part of this, believe me! It's your welfare I'm concerned about!" In truth, with no payoff in sight, honest advice seemed the best approach. "The problem is the bank account, isn't it? If I could notice something funny about it, so can somebody else. So protect yourself. Close it. Pay tax on the interest you earned. It isn't a lot, considering that you withdrew as much money as went in. That's how I've fixed it up in here." He produced a datacapsule containing his draft of Griffin's tax return. "And can this scam for good! If you've got the nerve, go straight back to Morgan Jaye and tell him you've just discovered another loophole in the system that should be closed. You might even get a hefty bonus," he said bitterly. "That's part of your arrangement, right? Bonuses for heading off trouble?"

Griffin pursed his lips. "Guess you're right. This little scheme is pretty well tapped out. If you found it, others can too." He regarded Herbie uncertainly. "Well, thanks. I must be getting paranoid. For a while there, I thought you had a little larceny of your own in mind, and at my expense too, but maybe you're really a pal after all. If there's anything I can do for you, just name it."

Herbie thought of all the now wasted time he'd put into this. "Well, double my fee would be nice."

"Not such a pal." Griffin's eyes narrowed. "But okay, seeing as this is all you'll ever make off it. In another hour, my second savings account and all evidence of these transactions will disappear forever, and if you've made copies of the statements, it'll be a lot easier to show they're forgeries than anything else."

Herbie nodded glumly. He made a mental note to pitch his copies when he got back to his desk.

Pedalling home through the gray March air with Griffin's check in his hip pocket, Herbie reflected on the irrepressible duplicity of the human spirit. Ten to one Griffin would keep right on with his little scheme, with no percentage in it for Herbie anywhere. Or perhaps not. There was no telling how many more he might have on draught at the tap of an entry key.

Herbie had seen it over and over again: no sooner did technology reveal new ways to make a fast buck than some heroic soul would into-the-breach and make it. Complicated mailorder scams, computer technology multiplying the profitability of the classic pyramid scheme many times—Griffin's little adventure was only the latest in a long line of brilliant ideas making fortunes for those who could see the opportunity, everybody but himself, it sometimes seemed. Always, he arrived just as whatever scheme it might be was becoming over-extended, in time only to offer the honest advice that it was time to pack up shop and run, too late to get any of the goodies for himself.

So where was his? What was the matter with him? He'd always prided himself on being every bit as creative as the next fellow. —And so he was. That was the most galling thing: Griffin's nifty scheme had come from *his* idea, one it had never occurred to him actually might be put into practice. Why not? Okay, this time he'd lacked the means and opportunity, but in general, he supposed he lacked confidence, the ability to take himself seriously. Guts too. Risk always made him hesitant.

Not Griffin, though. Driven by drugs, he'd be desperate—and if he needed new schemes, hell, Herbie had given him five or six more himself, all equally "preposterous."

Back in his apartment, he paced the floor in frustration, too irritated to work. His chagrin enlarged and became general. He hated his business, he decided. These days, it often seemed to him like nothing but one damned petty entrepreneur after another who couldn't be bothered to show up for his appointment on time, or who, when he finally did show, wanted only to know how to get away with this irregularity or fudge up that questionable deduction. Herbie was sick of the way they presumed on his time, of the way they called him for free advice at 10PM, or at 8AM Sunday morning; he was sick of living protected behind his voicemail. Worst of all, he was desperately sick to death of the inevitable haggle over the fee.

"Five hundred dollars!" the client would gasp, clutching feebly at his heart. "Your estimate was three-fifty!"

"That was when you told me all the receipts were already separated and labeled. You neglected to mention that the way they were sorted was by size. *I had to reshuffle the whole thing from scratch. Slowed the job down a lot."*

*"But that's how I keep them! All the cash register receipts in one pile, the half sheets in another—*you *know! They get lost otherwise."*

"The IRS doesn't care about your filing system."

"Yes, but..."

Herbie wanted to puke merely from thinking about it. So what was the alternative? Go back downtown? Give up his convenient 20-foot commute from the bed to the desk? Put on the monkey suit for the daily hour and a half on the bus? Deal with the petty and bootlicking drudgery of office politics? No thank you!

But then there were the clients... Around and around he went. Life was a cheat, an endless cycle of one trap after another.

As Herbie thought he knew only too well. He'd encountered his first such trap at Amalgamated Consolidated, where he'd spent years as a hopelessly un-corporate drone condemned never to advance. Worse, his lack of upward viability had been his own fault. He'd outsmarted himself right at the start, tripped himself up over sexual politics, and just when he thought he'd been so clever about it too.

He'd been young, determined and idealistically gay. He'd had no intention of leading a double life, no matter how good the job. His plan had been elegantly simple. During his very first week at AmalCon, he took the department secretary to lunch and told this personage, strictly in confidence of course, that he was gay. He hoped this would have a double effect: first, that within 24 hours, the inevitable office gossip mill would spread it to everybody inside five hierarchal levels; and second, that as they'd all been told "strictly in confidence," they'd never be able to let on to him that they knew. He'd never have to cover up, and he'd never have to deal with it, either.

This worked swell, with one unforeseen problem. Several years passed before he realized he'd also made himself absolutely unpromotable. His career had come to a dead end before it had fairly begun. He didn't know what to do about it, either. AmalCon seemed so safe, so comfortable, so permanent, so preferable to the uncertain, demeaning hassle of jobseeking. He hung on several years more, watching the less senior and the less competent rise into the hierarchy and disappear.

In the end, his own handpicked assistant brought things to a crisis. This was a cute young thing fresh out of college with reddish blond hair, a perfect peaches-and-cream complexion on a fresh open face, an athletic build and obviously great legs. Herbie bet you could bounce quarters off his ass.

Herbie, who had a nose for these things, also smelled closet queen all over him and was fanatic about hiring him despite qualifications which weren't quite up to specs. This was the closest thing to another real live gay man AmalCon had ever produced in his vicinity. *Wouldn't it be great to have another fag here?* Herbie thought. While he certainly did consider the guy attractive, he thought he could probably control himself from putting actual moves on him. Screwing one's coworkers had a way of not working out. *Just someone to really talk to. Somebody on my side.*

Herbie pestered his boss and argued the case high and low. In the face of this onslaught, resistance eventually crumbled. "Okay okay! It's you who have to work with him," the boss shrugged.

Unfortunately, Herbie's new gay pal wasn't really very friendly, at least not after the first day or two. By then, Herbie supposed, the rumor about his own sexual preference had gotten around. Herbie's new friend suddenly seemed ready to crawl into his in-box every time Herbie spoke to him. The guy resisted all offers to be taken to lunch. He fled all conversations in which Herbie had a part. When Herbie tried to make friendly smalltalk, he would only smile vacantly and knit his brows over the paperwork more fiercely than before—with some reason, Herbie noted. He was not as quick a study as Herbie had hoped. In fact, Herbie was fast coming to suspect his new assistant was only slightly more perspicacious than the average houseplant. Well okay, maybe that was a bit hyperbolic, but still, so as to validate his judgment in hiring him to those above, Herbie ended up with huge amounts of extra work to cover for a person who treated him with barely concealed loathing. *Damn closet queen*, Herbie thought. *I got myself into this. How could I have been so stupid?*

Herbie had quickly come to loathe him in return, for his clothes among other things. *He's dressed for a fucking Young Ripofflicans meeting or something, for chrissakes! And if he straightens that damn tie one more time, I'm gonna piss in his pencil cup!* Herbie kept up the banter anyway. No sense in open hostility.

To cap it all, the one genuine ability his new assistant did display was a genius-level talent for personal maneuvering. He went around Herbie with ease at every opportunity. He became fond of cheap jokes at Herbie's expense which all seemed to enjoy. Herbie, who'd honestly thought he was well liked, found this crushing, but didn't know what to do about it. He felt boxed in and shut out. He still tried to behave normally while inside he felt betrayed. He'd gone out on a long limb to get himself a friend. Instead, he'd acquired a new, crueler-than-usual sort of oppressor.

As Herbie seethed, his assistant's maneuvering paid off. In quick succession he was made, first Herbie's equal, then his superior. On the last occasion, the bosses passed over Herbie himself to promote him. Herbie developed a new and deeply depressing appreciation of his own position. *He's kissed everybody's ass except mine. Maybe he's not so dumb after all.*

Within a month of taking over, the new boss had issued a series of sharply worded memos to the staff on dress (Herbie liked colored shirts and loud ties—these were now out), grooming (Herbie, who liked what hair he had longish, had just achieved a tiny ponytail, but hair length and facial hair were now strictly regulated), tardiness (never one to let a machine, in this case the clock, be his master, Herbie was five or ten minutes late as often as early), demeanor (personal chitchat and every sort of extraneous conversation were absolutely out), what things one should and should not keep on or even in one's desk, and exactly how these should be arranged.

Herbie was not alone in resenting these restrictions. Little Adolph, as he rapidly became known, was turning Herbie's department, once a cheerful and pleasant place, into an uptight workplace prison of the most repressive kind.

Little Adolph spent an amazingly large amount of time on the floor enforcing his new regulations. So who was doing *his* job, the department wondered? They did notice his secretary wore an increasingly harried look. Once neat and well ordered, her desk was now always awash in paperwork in defiance of the rules, and she was found sobbing more than once. No matter who was or wasn't doing the job, it was easy to see who was taking the blame.

Surreptitious complaints upstairs availed naught. He's young, they said, he'll loosen up. It's his department, they said, we don't want to interfere. Besides, they said, his regulations *were*, after all, not actually incompatible with a sober and professional image!

The department was defeated. Those who could, transferred out. The veterans, fearful for their pensions, knuckled under. The newcomers, unused to anything else, were uncomplaining.

Herbie, fearsomely good with the numbers, but naturally fond of open collars, general conversation on an immense variety of subjects when his work was caught up, and really rather slovenly about his desk, found his performance rating plummeting. Little Adolph dropped all pretense of tolerating the charade of normal relations between them Herbie had tried to keep up. Still, Herbie did his best to adjust and endure while maintaining a modicum of individuality—but by the day Little Adolph descended to deliver an official final warning to tighten his tie, have his hair cut, stop slouching, arrive on time, *and put those filthy cigarettes out for good,* Herbie had already had enough.

When at last he made the decision to do so, Herbie was amazed at the ease with which he acquired a new position. A number of his ex-supervisors now in exalted posts were delighted to say glorious things about his abilities. Before he knew it, he was the new personal assistant to the senior partner of a mid-sized but solid and long-established accounting firm—at more money too, a lot more.

"That's nice. Hope you got the offer in writing. Too bad if they backed out on you *after you resigned*." Little Adolph cut abruptly into Herbie's bubbling enthusiasm, pissing in the beer as usual. Herbie's mouth snapped shut. No, he hadn't got the offer in writing, but then, it was unmistakably genuine! "Speaking of which, just let me have a letter of resignation for my files, will you?" Adolph hadn't as much as looked up from making ticks with a sharp little pencil on the pile of payroll timesheets before him. Herbie caught the glint of a tiny smile.

"Of course," Herbie said in cold fury. "But get out your stopwatch. I'm going to the can first."

He marched straight down to the drugstore across the street and made a purchase. When he returned, Little Adolph was out, gone to his regular weekly status meeting. Herbie checked his watch and gave him at least another half hour. Perfect. He scrawled, "I quit, sweetcheeks," in lavender lipstick on the new cream paint of Adolph's office. He took his time and did it right: sloppy hearts and a large winged penis or two achieved exactly the proper artistic impression. Then he pulled down his trousers and took a hugely luxuriant and immensely satisfying crap onto the rich new leather seat of Adolph's desk chair. He found Adolph's ruler and smoothed this down. Some careful crosshatching with the ruler's edge rendered it barely noticeable at a casual glance. The color matched precisely. He wiped himself on the draft of a new memo he found on Adolph's desk and replaced this front and center, under a paperweight. That, he thought, ought to account for the smell. He chucked the befouled ruler back into Adolph's center drawer and closed it.

On the way down the row of cubicles, he passed Adolph buttlicking a Senior Executive Second Vice President and a First Assistant Associate Vice President toward his office. Adolph suspended sycophancy only long enough to give Herbie a phony smile. "That letter I wanted?"

Herbie matched him phony smile for phony smile. "In your office," he said, and strode off, head high. With interest, he noticed Adolph was wearing a lovely light blue suit that set off his hair and eyes really most effectively. *Very tasteful.*

He heard the shriek all the way out in the elevator, just as the doors were closing.

He was prepared to discover fresh paint, labor and the cost of leather cleaning deducted from his severance. When he saw the costs included dry cleaning as well, he howled with laughter. Well worth the price of admission, he decided.

Herbie's new position was a revelation. His new boss was an energetic and aggressively friendly septuagenarian. The old man was there when Herbie arrived in the morning, and was still there schmoozing on the phone when everyone else had gone. Keeping up with him made Herbie dead weary. The old man had a joke and a smile for everybody, often the same joke for a week at a time. Herbie would sit at his desk with the connecting door open and mouth along with it every time the phone rang.

Working for the old man was like working with a whirlwind. He literally threw work across his desk at Herbie. "Here! Do something about this! Don't let me hear about it again unless you need help!"

Herbie loved him passionately from Day One. He felt honored, trusted with all the responsibility he cared to take, and, more than a little to his surprise, once freed of all the rules, procedures and picayune pettifoggery he'd come to accept as facts of life at AmalCon, he found he cared a great deal—like working for your grandfather, he decided.

He threw himself into the old man's business. He stopped slouching. For the first time in his life, he bought good suits and wore them with pride, spending whatever it took on tailoring to make them fit his eccentric physique. He made a point to be the first one there in the morning, and stayed until the old man screamed at him to go home. Often he forgot the clock altogether except to wonder at how little of the day was left all of a sudden in which to finish what he wanted to do. More than once, he was so engrossed he didn't notice the time at all until phones he called rang unanswered.

He became the old man's eyes and ears, borrowing his authority and extending it into every corner of the office. The junior partners were suddenly under unaccustomed pressure to perform. Their specialty had been crisis management. They'd sit on projects with long deadlines until there was only a week or so left. Then suddenly they'd wake up. They loved to stride manfully about the halls bellowing about how "We've all got to pull together on this one! Yessir, *teamwork,* that's what we need here, teamwork! Overtime! I'll be here on Saturday. Who'll be here with me?" when, in reality, they should have been on tall stools in a corner with large conical hats on, writing "The firm buys me a calendar" until their fingers dropped off.

They'd been humbugging the old man this way for years. Herbie unmasked them, tracked their projects and reminded the old man when to ask about them. He also made sure the old man needed to talk to them just as they stumbled in drunk from lunch at 3PM. The junior partners rapidly came to hate him.

In addition, he crunched mountains of numbers and poured out oceans of reports for the old man's accounts. The old man loved it. "Oh, if I'd had you twenty years ago, the big firms would be nothing to us now," the old man sighed, and gave Herbie a raise, the first of three he got that year.

Along the way, Herbie discovered the myriad joys of assistantbananahood: as much power as you liked, but no ultimate responsibility—power not to keep but to use, just so long as your average at using it in accordance with its owner's probable intent stayed good. Herbie's turned out to be excellent. With Herbie's help, the old man attained devastatingly total control over the business.

The old man's ability to make decisions awed Herbie. You needed one? You got one, and right then too. No procrastinating, no hemming and hawing, no let-me-sleep-on-it-and-come-back-tomorrowing, which had been Little Adolph's euphemism for, "Let me cover my butt by checking upstairs before I decide what to do." With the old man, you went to the oracle, and it spoke! Wonderful! Miraculous! Herbie learned more about business and power from the year he spent sitting in the old man's office than he had in all his time at AmalCon. To his amazement, he discovered they were the same.

Before long, the business shuddered, bestirred itself as if from long sleep, and grew! Impressed by the new level of commitment and alertness, their clients found more uses for their service and began making unsolicited referrals among their own contacts. When the old man discovered this, he sprang into action. He dusted off his Rolodex and set Herbie to work pitching new business. He put Herbie in charge of identifying prospects, cold calling, making initial presentations and stoking the interest. The old man reserved himself to be the closer.

Initially diffident about his salesmanship, Herbie discovered to his extreme shock that his eccentric physical appearance was far from the disadvantage he would have thought—rather the reverse! Accountants, it turned out, weren't supposed to be charismatic. Prospects took one look at Herbie and decided that, not only did he look like an accountant, he looked like a *good* one!

As his confidence grew, his sales pitch sharpened. He began marching a steady stream of prospects into the old man's office for the old smoothie treatment, and new accounts signed on. The satisfaction was enormous. Herbie walked around pinching himself to make sure he was awake. After all the dreary years at AmalCon, it was so much fun it was almost too good to be true. —A dangerous thought. By definition, things too good to be true seldom are.

The old man knew what he was doing. He was over 70, and with the business on the rise once again, he'd never have another chance like this.

One day, after a long meeting with the junior partners from which Herbie was excluded as he always was from partnership powwows, the old man called him in. "Close the door and sit down, Herbie."

Herbie complied and sat waiting expectantly.

The old man's face was somber. "There's no way to lead up to this, so I'll just say it. I'm selling my interest to George and Ed."

Herbie's jaw fell. The junior partners? Those bumblers?

The old man put up a hand. "Now, I know." He paused. "Aw hell, Herbie. I've been doing this for more than fifty years. Before you got here, it'd been a long time since I'd had much fun at it, and my wife keeps after me to settle back and smell the roses." He sighed. "Not that I think *that's* such a swell idea. I smell too many roses as it is, mostly at funerals. My friends have been retiring right and left, in perfect health, most of them. They sit around six months, wither up and die—of boredom as much as anything else." He shook his head sadly. "Nope, when you get to be my age, you got to stay busy or you're through. My wife's kept after me, though. She wants us to go live at our place in France. She's had our European friends after me too, offering me consulting, and I admit I want to do it."

A very rare thing happened. Herbie was speechless.

"Oh, I owe you something all right. You made this interesting for me again. You helped me prove I could still do it if I only had the kind of cooperation I used to get around here. I'm not telling you anything you don't know when I say the recent success here is partly your doing. Because of that, I've been able to hold up George and Ed for a good bit more than I could of last year this time." He smiled wickedly. "Told 'em I was selling to the highest bidder. They're gonna have to get a bank loan too. No self-financing for me, not with those two. Cash on the barrel.

"So I'm grateful to you, and you'll be taken care of. Part of the deal is they have to keep you on for six months. You plug away and do for them what you did for me, and you'll be set for life."

Herbie's face spoke for him.

"Oh, I know you've been biting their butts pretty good, but they understand you did it for me, and for the business. You keep your nose clean, churn out the numbers and do what they tell you, and you'll be fine. They need you, believe me."

Herbie did believe him. He just wasn't at all sure George and Ed did. "You sure you don't need an assistant in Europe? Sounds like fun."

"You speak French or German?" The old man already knew the answer to that. "Besides, I'll only be puttering around with it, traveling, seeing my friends and keeping busy. You're a young man with a great career ahead of you! You should be doing something about it. Hell, if I'd had you twenty years ago, it'd be you I'd be selling the business to, and you'd deserve it too, not like those ingrates. Well, maybe I shouldn't say that. They weren't always like this, you know. They're smart enough fellas. Likely enough, they'll dig in now it's all their own money they'll be throwing away. You dig in too and help them, and everything'll be fine."

Six weeks later, he was gone.

As Herbie had suspected, George and Ed did not share the old man's assessment of his value. They resented what they considered his meddling in their conduct of the business, and refused to admit he was of the slightest use whatever. They kept him busy for a week or two handing off the old man's accounts to their own assistants, including the ones he'd helped land. Then they moved him to a desk in the hall next to the copy machine, and let him sit.

He tried his best to be useful. He thought up better ways of doing things, and caught things that weren't being done at all, but when he'd take it to George and Ed, they'd only look at him blandly and say, "That's very good, Herbie. Now show Debbie how to do that." Or Sam or Pete or Karen. Never, "Thanks, Herbie. You take care of that." He followed up on his unfinished business development work too, and landed yet another account, this time all by himself, only to have it assigned to one of Ed's assistants.

After a month or so of this, he gave up. The good suits went into his closet and stayed there. His jeans, sneakers and baseball cap made their appearance in a business context for the first time, and stayed. He sat slouching behind his desk next to the copy machine reading and doing crossword puzzles all day long, while people asked him if he wouldn't mind awfully if they used his desk to organize their papers. With regret Herbie came increasingly to suspect was largely feigned, they even could ask, "Oh, it's silly, I know, but would you mind very much moving over there a sec? I'm afraid this material is confidential."

At such times, he would wander the hall offering a hand to all and sundry. He'd prove himself willing to work, at least. These expeditions usually ended with George or Ed calling him in to admonish him about pestering the staff. In these meetings, they invariably wondered why someone with his obvious talents didn't resign and find himself a position where he could be of use. He didn't bother to ask why, if his talents were so obvious, they couldn't be of use right there. He felt as he knew he was meant to feel: gangly and in the way, invisible except when tripped over, ignored and demeaned, his intelligence deliberately insulted.

Meanwhile, George and Ed reverted to their old habits. They lost most of the new accounts Herbie and the old man had acquired with so much labor, and some of the old ones too. Herbie may have been excluded, but he was neither blind nor stupid. During their first quarter alone, he calculated their losses totaled more than 15% of their annual billing. He could see why they wanted him to resign. Money had to be getting tighter.

He was damned if he would. The harder they pushed, the more stubborn he got. It would serve them right if he sat there and did crossword puzzles for his salary! Hey, as long as draining the firm seemed to be the order of the day, he'd be glad to help. To hell with them! However, it was only partly stubbornness that kept him there. The truth was, getting another job was going to be a problem. He was embarrassed to ask his references at AmalCon for help again so soon. The old man was traveling in Europe, out of reach—and without references, what?

He needed a new plan, and promptly thought of one. As long as the firm was paying him to have nothing but time, he might as well use it for something. He spent the next months reviewing for the CPA exam, took it, and passed handily.

He fantasized about demanding a partnership. He expected congratulations at the very least, and something to do. Instead, George and Ed discharged him on the 6-month anniversary of the old man's departure. True to form, they didn't even have the decency to do it themselves. They were out "on client calls" the day a flunky came by with Herbie's pink slip. He crumpled it and left with a sigh of relief. He'd waited them out and bled the bastards for what he had coming. It felt like a victory, of sorts.

He figured to lay around on Unemployment Compensation for a while. He looked forward to a nice, extended vacation during which he could rest up and regain some self-respect before seeing what next the world had for him.

In practice, his vacation lasted exactly 24 hours. He was sitting around his living room missing the state-of-the-art PC he'd had in the old man's office and wondering how he could justify spending some of his now starkly finite savings on one, when it hit him: he could buy it if he could deduct it; he could deduct it if he had a business.

Well, why not? It was worth a shot.

In the next several months, he gave it one. He bought his equipment, placed his ads and made his calls, living on Unemployment the while.

He was pleasant, industrious and thorough. Slowly, he built a practice. In his first month, he made $150. In his second, $600. In his third, $1,500. Even before the Unemployment Compensation ran out, he was supporting himself distinctly in excess of the manner to which he'd been accustomed. It worked!

And continued to work for quite a while. He was his own boss, and loved it. There would be no going back on that, ever. If he didn't like a job, he didn't have to take it; if a client came onto him wrong, he easily could be "too busy" to agree to the deadline, whenever it was. He could arrange his hours to suit himself, within reason. If he wanted time off, there was no one's permission to ask. Everything was great.

The novelty took a long time to wear thin, as of course it did eventually. Once the excitement of making his own way unaided diminished, he began to notice he was doing the same kinds of jobs over and over again: taxes and statements for shopkeepers, small businessmen and property owners; conservative, tax-avoidance investment counselling; the yearly flood of 1040's in first quarter; annual audits for condominium associations; routine bookkeeping for those without the intelligence or inclination to do it themselves.

It made sense it should be so. Who else would use a small-scale service such as his, and for what else? As the challenge diminished, so did his interest. He became bored, less friendly to the clients, tougher to deal with. The business fell off a bit.

As his boredom deepened, he began paying closer attention to the less scrupulous element of his would-be clientele. Before, he'd have returned their material without comment after the initial scrutiny. This crowd had different problems, all right, problems which sometimes required very creative solutions. He gave them as much help as he could without hanging himself out too far. He developed a schedule of "acceptable risks."

This was exciting, and profitable too. As meticulous yet unparticular accountants were not exactly thick on the ground, he found his practice grew apace, and that he was able to charge higher than usual rates.

However, dealing with this element did have its downside. He was willing to accept payment in marijuana—that, he could always unload—but not in hard drugs or stolen merchandise. Herbie neither liked nor trusted the usual buyers of such commodities. Yet sometimes, this was all the clients had; if he didn't take it, he might not get paid at all. Worse, some of these new clients didn't need such an excuse to be slippery about paying him. He had to be careful.

He was definitely sick of it, familiar to boredom with his old clients' business and his new clients' nasty tricks. The frustration was clearly cumulative. Truth be told, he didn't really deal with the more artful sort of client very well, either. His adventure that afternoon with Garrison Griffin illustrated the difficulty nicely. The danger was starting to wear on him too. He longed to be rid of the whole mess.

Once again, just as at AmalCon and again with the junior partners, life had reached an impasse. He supposed he'd have to ride it out as he'd done before, waiting for inspiration to strike. What was he to do? What was left to do with a business such as his? Expand? He could do that. The old man had taught him how, and by this time he had a sizable stake tucked away to make it happen. He could get out his suits, rent an office and go back to business on the up and up. But why? He didn't really want to give up working at home and wearing old clothes. Those were the only things about his business he still liked. Hire a staff? Spend his days playing office politics? No thanks! Look what the junior partners had done to the old man! Where would he find a Herbie to help him?

Of course, if he were successful, he would make a lot more money, but he'd never be able to take a vacation to spend it. Offices had a habit of *not* running themselves while you were away. So why did he need the money? He didn't have a family to support or provide for when he was gone. He didn't need a bigger place to live; he liked his apartment fine. A lover? True, if he wanted a really sexy lover, he was probably going to have to buy one, but he'd be damned if he'd bust his butt working everyday to support some slug from the Attaché Arms who'd sit around smoking his grass, drinking his booze and screwing street tricks in his bed while he was out plugging.

Actually, this was unfair; his general opinion of the boys was rather better than that. He put a lot of time into entertaining them. He liked to feel he was sort of an uncle to them, helping them out when they needed it. He was pretty sure they appreciated it too, and even liked him as a person, most of the time. Still, they were what they were. It was a mistake to expect too much.

No, he really had all the money he needed: just enough to live moderately well, to indulge his taste in a few of life's better things, to buy himself a roll in the hay when he was horny—which *was* pretty often, come to think of it—and to treat himself to a little extravagance now and then. Basically, his current income was fine.

I guess my needs are really pretty simple. He stopped pacing, frozen. *That's bullshit,* he thought. It came over him all at once and yet slowly, as sometimes seems to happen with true insight. *That's bullshit. My needs are really very complex, and one of them is for the* solution *to be simple!*

Whether this revelation would prove to be the valuable insight it seemed or merely a facile irrelevancy, only time would tell. Meanwhile, the blaze of mental glory accompanying it took a long moment to fade. He stood lost in thought, going over it again and again, reluctant to relinquish the elevated mood.

He'd paced the afternoon away rehearsing his boredom and frustration. Now his depression was broken. He was suddenly hungry. Though it was nearly dinnertime, he definitely did not feel like cooking. He turned out his pockets: not enough cash for dinner out, just Griffin's check. Okay, he'd eradicate the proverbial pair of fowl: he'd deposit the check and get some green stuff. The automated teller station was only a block away.

His elevated mood vanished the minute he stepped outside, blown away on a blustery wind with a few chill drops of rain in it. As always in the early evening, the street was full of people. Talking, laughing, or striding along with obvious purpose, they went their ways: home from cocktail hour, on to dinner or evening engagements. That, as always, they were oblivious of Herbie brought him back down to earth and directed his native gloom into one of its more familiar channels.

As long as he could remember, he had resented his eccentric body and strange face. He knew what kind of first impression he made. Maybe he was merely insecure, hypersensitive and paranoid, but, in social situations, people seemed either palpably reluctant to meet him or excessively polite, engaging him in smiling rapid-fire smalltalk while their eyes darted, searching for rescue. Most people seemed to prefer pretending he wasn't there—particularly gay men. No supposed supersensitivity could explain or minimize his reception in that quarter. Gay men treated him like part of the furniture.

Virtually the only respect Herbie had ever received had come from people who'd been forced by circumstance to get to know him: co-workers, neighbors, close friends of friends. Virtually every friend he'd had since puberty had been made in this way. He'd had to work consciously and hard to bring them around. No wonder he was usually diffident about meeting people; for him, making friends was an effort of the will. Even then, success wasn't guaranteed. He did his best to be interesting, to share his large store of little-known facts and insights about the secret ways in which the world really worked, but no matter what he did, some people simply did not want to know.

Not for the first time, he wished he could be like the Attaché Arms boys. The bittersweet anguish of this longing swept through him and shuddered him with envy. That crowd did not have this problem. Those you might not consider actually beautiful still had enormous animal vitality. People wanted to meet them, wanted to like them and be liked in return. The same people who would discard Herbie on the slightest excuse would take the slightest excuse to forgive these guys. Their challenge was not to create liking and trust, but to keep it. Many of them took their innate gifts so much for granted they did not bother to try, merely using the people who approached them. They wrung their admirers for what they could get and discarded them, confident of an endless supply.

He'd first cultivated the society of hustlers because, with them, he didn't have to work to make friends; he had only to demonstrate his ability to pay. Rapidly he had become fascinated to watch them operate, awed by the ease with which they approached prospects, bewitched and terrified by their readiness to scorn and discard those who displeased them or whose utility was exhausted. In their company he could assume their social confidence, borrow their arrogance, act out his pretense—escapism pure and simple.

Herbie wished the two gifts could be combined, that the hustler's gift for attracting friends could be combined with his knowledge of their value, his practice at keeping them. If only he'd been born handsome!—no, if he'd been born that way, he might well have turned out every bit as callous himself. If only he could be transformed! What a warm and wonderful person he'd be then! Satellites drawn to flutter about his candle would not be burned; he'd treat them with humanity and respect. He'd be gracious and humble in the presence of persons physically less well endowed; he'd not approach them with veiled contempt, but would seek their mental and emotional gifts. He'd hang onto his sensitivity for their pain.

With an ease developed through frequent repetition, these reflections wound themselves quickly through their habitual groove to the accustomed conclusion: a desire for the company of his envy's objects. Perhaps he'd drop by the Attaché Arms later, after dinner.

For the meantime, he shook his head to dispel these familiar cobwebs. He'd spent the afternoon deciding his job was hopeless, depressing himself thoroughly; he'd be damned if he'd spend his dinner hungering to be what he never could, dwelling on how ugly and unloved he was.

The automatic teller machine was in the vestibule of his neighborhood AmalCon branch bank. Beyond it, double glass doors led to the locked and darkened lobby. A surveillance camera swung overhead. Out at him from the machine itself stared the inscrutable glass eye of another. "Open the pod bay doors please, Hal." He amused himself by talking to it inanely, timing things so the little door flipped up to reveal his money as if in response to his command, his usual ritual when alone with the machine.

213

As he collected his cash, a spectacular idea seized him. Hadn't Garrison Griffin designed this system? Of course he had! He'd been AmalCon's resident computer genius for twenty years. Was there perhaps a way into this system too? What had he said? You needed a direct terminal. Well, this was a direct terminal, at least of sorts, wasn't it? Fascinating! Intriguing!—the stuff of urban myth and legend. Could it possibly be true? He remembered that at some point years ago, in another of those borderline-facetious cocktail hour discussions, he'd actually raised the subject with Garrison Griffin, and that Griffin's reaction, forgotten until now, had been to change it.

He stared at the machine, transfixed. It beeped at him impatiently, threatening to eat his card. Quickly, he finished his transaction and headed off.

It gnawed him all during dinner. Problem: Griffin's secret passwords were all mnemonic, or so he'd said. Yet, the teller machines had no keyboard for entering instructions, only number and entry buttons. Therefore, the password had to be numerical—or did it? He chewed slowly. The buttons weren't configured like a calculator, with "1" at the bottom, but like a telephone keypad, the "1" at the top. Well, numbers on a telephone had letters attached, didn't they? Relics of an inefficient, less numerical past, they'd once identified telephone exchanges. Now, they remained only for purposes of advertising: C-A-R-P-E-T-S, L-O-A-N-N-O-W, and the like. He smiled, recalling that the escort service whose books he did used a number that spelled out E-A-S-Y-L-A-Y. They even had it on their business cards.

He stepped to the restaurant's payphone and studied the keypad. Pretty simple: three letters for each number beginning at "2" with the "Q" and the "Z" missing. Easy.

Okay, that problem was solved, at least hypothetically—but what might be the password? It had to be mnemonic for something. But what? G-E-T-C-A-S-H? G-R-A-N-D-T-H-E-F-T? It could be anything, he supposed.

The waitress cleared his dishes and poured more coffee. He lit an Export Special, stumped. Nor was that the only problem. You needed your card to get the system to notice you at all, which tied the transaction to you pretty firmly, and there were all those cameras. He supposed Griffin might have fudged his way around the system's recording the card number, but the cameras were a separate setup completely in Morgan Jaye's domain. No way around that; the cameras would always see you coming and give the system a look at who'd robbed it.

So maybe Griffin hadn't left an entry hatch after all. Maybe he'd given it up as too dangerous, but then, that didn't fit. He needed money, and here was a tempting supply constantly under his nose (*as it were*, Herbie smirked), when he withdrew his daily cash fix from that second savings account, for instance.

Herbie thought it through. If Griffin had provided for the system to be used this way, it would have to be in a situation where he didn't care if he were identified or not.

Solutions dawned on him. He scribbled two or three possibles on a napkin, threw some money on the table and headed back toward the machine.

The street was quieter now. Although later in the year it would be awash with miscellaneous street people and yuppie window shoppers at this hour, it was still too cold for much of that. Up ahead at the corner, light from the automatic teller installation smeared the sidewalk.

Inside, he approached the machine, self-consciously normal for the cameras. One never knew if one were actually being watched or merely recorded pending irregularities.

The machine's little TV screen displayed its normal message:

WELCOME TO ATM

INSERT CARD AS SHOWN

Herbie did. As always, the display changed to:

ENTER PERSONAL CODE

215

Now was the moment. He entered his first alternative: R-U-N-M-O-N-E-Y. The machine cut him off after the first four digits and displayed what he'd more or less expected, anyway:

ERROR. TRY AGAIN.

Of course, he thought in consternation, the machine was set up to accept only four digits! Quickly, he cancelled out and retrieved his card. He thought furiously.

He inserted his card and started over. He tried two simple alternatives: C-A-S-H, then L-O-O-T. The response was the same each time.

He was running out of tries. You only got three. If you didn't get in on the third, the machine ate your card. Worse, from watching other people fumble at the machine from time to time, he knew two card insertions were the limit. On the third, the machine was programmed to assume you were merely on a fishing expedition; it confiscated the card at once. He'd used up two insertions already and, here on the second, two tries. He now had only one try left. He could always come back tomorrow, he supposed. His finger moved to the Cancel button.

Instead, the day's frustrations rushed upon him and overwhelmed him. He became toweringly angry. Garrison Griffin had *done* this, goddamn him! It was *not* his imagination!—and how the bastard had crowed at him over lunch! Had mocked him! Had taken his, Herbie's, own idea and used it, then coolly, easily and arrogantly run him down and thwarted him in his attempt to profit from it! Herbie smarted under the sheer insult of it. He was at least as smart as Garrison Griffin. No, smarter! Anything Griffin could do, he, Herbie Manning, CPA, could figure out. He would *not* let that dribbling dopehead best him twice in the same day, he simply wouldn't!

Caution, reason and all other good sense left him. He had a flash of inspiration: if somebody wanted money because he was on the run, he'd be in a R-U-S-H. For a doper such as Griffin, the mnemonic qualities of this possible solution had a certain appropriateness Herbie found irresistible. In a blaze of bravado, he entered it.

This time, the machine whirred much longer while Herbie slithered down the long sinking slide into letdown. He pursed his lips and nodded. *I knew it. This was dumb.* He felt like kicking himself. Mentally, he prepared himself for the protracted series of phone calls necessary to retrieve his card from AmalCon's bureaucracy. *"All of a sudden my mind just went blank! I couldn't remember the number! I must have tried every PIN I've ever had, and then it ate..."*

What was this?

DIALING... PLEASE WAIT

A long moment later, a new display appeared:

**NO, GIGI, YOU CHANGED IT,
REMEMBER? TRY AGAIN.**

Herbie nearly fainted with excitement. Gigi was the name Garrison Griffin used when he talked to himself! Long ago, Herbie had overheard him do it in the 42nd floor john at AmalCon, and thought it highly amusing. So he was right after all! Most helpfully, Griffin had kept the old password in place in case he forgot. Herbie wondered how many little computers all over town were now linking up, conspiring to help him commit only-god-knew-how-many counts of grand larceny.

Meanwhile, he still had to find the right code. He thought again. Okay, if Griffin were leaving town, he might want the F-A-R-E.

NO, STUPID. IT BEGINS WITH H.

Christ, Herbie thought, *This is fanfuckingtastic.*

Just then, he heard the street door swish. Someone came and stood behind him, politely, conventionally, studiously avoiding any notice of what he was doing at the machine, he hoped. He had to hurry, but hard as he concentrated, he couldn't think what might begin with "H." Sweat turned the back of his neck cold. At last, when the machine started beeping at him, he gave up. It couldn't be that simple, but he entered it anyway: H-E-L-P.

There was another long pause. Then the little screen swam with print.

WELCOME TO INTERBANK.

FROM BANK #:

FROM ACCOUNT #:
   TAKE AS CASH? (Y OR N)
TO BANK #:

TO ACCOUNT #:

Success! He had entered the banks' own system for transferring cash around amongst themselves. All you needed were the easily obtainable bank access numbers and the numbers of the accounts you wished to rob. From the fact the "take as cash" business was offcenter on the screen, interpolated between two lines of the standard instructions, Herbie assumed that this was Griffin's own addition allowing you to bypass procedure and do the transaction in cash, right there at the machine.

Herbie cancelled out and retrieved his card. Ablaze with his own cleverness, he nodded vacantly at the person behind him and ambled up the street toward the Attaché Arms. It didn't solve any of his problems, true. Still, knowledge was power, and here was quite a lot of both. Who knew whether it might come in handy someday, or for what? It was extremely interesting.

Yes, just extremely.

Chapter Five
...NOR IRON BARS A CAGE

magine, if you can, the human being who does not dream, who has no needs unfulfilled, no goals unattained. Who is this person? A lord on a shining hill? A catatonic?

But who knows what tortures twist the withdrawn person rocking mute through the drone of an institutional afternoon?—and as for the lord in his hilltop castle, he has his own troubles with all the jealous lordlings, each of whom knows for a certainty how much better justice he could do the crumbling heaps of masonry above.

Imagine life with no expectations, anticipations or ambitions, no aspirations driving you along, lending purpose to everyday life. What a shabby, uninteresting existence it would be! The contradiction of total fulfillment is that, ultimately, it leaves people empty, restless and unfulfilled. Most of us manage to find fault with our lives, and must to survive and grow. We pity the self-satisfied and the complacent their lack of imagination, their failure to see their imperfections and their way to the next challenge.

Naturally, some problems carry with them more self-evident justifications than others. When the poor protest the limited, hardscrabble condition of their lives and fantasize about wealth and power, we may listen with more sympathy than when the rich bemoan the complications wealth, power and fame inevitably bring. The struggle of a poor man to put a roof over his head and stave off starvation is a more vital struggle than that of the millionaire to stave off boredom and become a billionaire. Yet, for successful resolution, both struggles may require much the same degree of attention, effort and, occasionally, desperation. This level of involvement may be itself life's true fulfillment; perhaps satisfaction is found as much in struggle and attainment as in actual possession of the putative goal.

Now, when we are being practical, we tackle our problems in a practical way. We shrug aside what can't be fixed and get on with what can. Still, even the most practical of us also spend time wishing for what we know is impossible, from the underemployed young man escaping his humdrum low-paid service job with paperback science fiction to the glamorously beautiful, clamorously famous and wealthily successful Hollywood star fantasizing wistfully about walking down a street unbesieged by pesty crowds or about having even the most trivial talk with a man minus the assurance he's thinking what an impressive notch she'd make on his bedpost.

Some lucky people have insufficient goals to hold their attention. Their problem is boredom. Others have problems so insurmountable that occasional escape becomes necessary. Fantasizing the impossible provides relief for both. If our dreams can't come true, we can savor them and never worry about the inevitable troubles we'd face if they did. This is the only true escape.

What would you do if, for instance, you actually did win the lottery and, in your search for the help you now needed to manage your good fortune, were besieged by hordes of ethically challenged but plausible-sounding lawyers, accountants and investment brokers all pitching your business and taking advantage of your inexperience?

All right, that's one most of us would risk, I think. But what if you really were suddenly transported to the magic land of swordsmen and sorcerers when, knowing neither Word One of sorcery nor more about swordplay than which end of the silly thing was the handle, you weren't in fact very fit to live there?

Or if you really did awake one morning as Superman? Would not you rapidly come to envy the world's Clark Kents without such powers, the awesome responsibility to use them correctly, the 24-hour demands on your time, the agonizing decisions between competing claims on it, and the recriminations of those you could not accommodate?

In an unexpected stroke of blinding luck as comes to few, the djinn had allowed Herbie Manning his most fantastic impossible wish. As he bounded down the stairs from his Chicago apartment, suitcase in one hand and the briefcase with the money in the other, it seemed as if his wish had come without penalty or consequences of any but the most trifling, acceptable and/or agreeable kind. He determined to make the most of it.

He'd spent years whining to himself about what sort of person he would be if only he were attractive. Well, now he was more than attractive; he was a dream precipitated into flesh. He'd start over. He'd be that person he'd always known he could be. As a thinking, self-examining person, he suspected that, in the normal course of events, our pasts prepare us for our futures, even dictate to a large degree what those futures must be. Now, it seemed he had slipped the rails of his past, that everything could be different, that he was equipped as few ever had been to be a truly superior sort of human being.

At the moment, however, the philosophical considerations were definitely secondary. He had matters of much more immediate import to think about: where would he go, what would he do when he got there, what name would he use?

Herbie was one of those individuals who, while agonizing over the minor decisions of life—what to make for dinner, where to go after the show, which book to pull off his "to read" shelf next—never had much trouble deciding the big things. When the time was right (that is, when he was thoroughly miserable and the problem could no longer be denied or postponed) they always seemed to resolve themselves without a lot of effort. So, in the relatively brief space of the cab ride downtown to Union Station, he quickly and efficiently sorted this stuff out.

Where to go was easy. As the densest population center in America, Manhattan's multifarious demography offered his best chance of exploring the many and various possibilities his transformation offered while providing the anonymity necessary to recover from his inevitable mistakes. Herbie was well aware that anonymity was going to be crucial to anyone who expected to live unaging through more than one lifetime, that the alternative was losing his freedom of action to public curiosity, scientific research, and perhaps worse. He pictured himself, a century or two down the line, pursued by some crackpot cult as its unwilling object of worship, and decided he'd be very very careful about anonymity from the start. In New York, he could lose himself in the crowd while he figured out how to live, and have as much fun as he wanted at the same time.

New York!—for eighty years and more, the world's most vital and exciting city. Amidst the staggering variety of choices available to the cognoscenti there, novelty was all, and all that was new hied itself thither to try itself out and see what mark might be made on the jaded sensibilities of those supremely well-qualified to separate the good and the fresh from the bad, the derivative, and the merely indifferent. As Herbie felt quite squeaky shiny new himself, New York was the obvious place to find this new self and explore for niches wherein he might put himself to use.

How to begin didn't seem much of a problem, either. He had plenty of money, and his education and interests had left him better befitted than most for a life of idleness. He'd always loved books, music, pictures, history, the humanities in general. He had an exciting sense of many talents bubbling below the surface. He had well-developed opinions about what separated good books from bad and art from not. He wrote well and discoursed knowledgeably on many subjects. He drew, played the piano passably and sang easily at sight, a skill from which he might have derived much pleasure had his voice quality not left choral directors wincing in pain. All these abilities his diffidence at putting his awkward self forward had left him hitherto unmotivated to explore. With this diffidence obsolete, these talents cried for expression, jostling and shoving one another, each demanding priority attention in an unexpected and thoroughly exhilarating side effect of his transformation.

Best of all, there was no rush. He had endless lifetimes in which to explore them all. For the moment, he'd enjoy himself, read books, see the shows, prowl the galleries, and cruise a great deal.

He'd see what time would turn up for him. Maybe now was the perfect opportunity to see if some of that torrent of fine-sounding words continually surging through his head couldn't be decanted onto paper. That was it; that would be his first project: if he got bored, he'd see if he couldn't turn himself into a writer.

Whatever he did, he resolved to live light and fancy free, to avoid weighing himself down with a houseful of possessions. Travel seemed definitely in his future. If he got tired of one place, he wanted to be able to pick up and move at a moment's notice. He entertained himself with the notion of living a few months at a time in all the great gay capitals of the world: New York, San Francisco, London, Paris, Rome, Amsterdam, St. Petersburg, Bangkok, Manilla... The possibilities were endless, and endlessly exciting.

What name to use, being a trifle more of a minor issue, took a little longer. His own was clearly dead. Not only did he want as few links with his past life as possible, but, unless he was very much mistaken, there'd be a pretty intensive hunt on for "Herbie Manning," and soon.

That bothered him. While he wasn't particularly worried they'd find him—how could they?—the money he'd stolen was still an unwanted and largely unnecessary tie to his past. Why had he taken it? He wasn't sure. His own savings, he supposed, would have been ample to get him started.

Stumped, he took a moment to try his usual first step in the process of self-examination; he opened his mind to associations, not really expecting much there in the taxi, but immediately suffered another pang of that regret and sense of loss he'd had in his living room a scant hour or two ago at the thought he'd soon be leaving behind the life he'd known. Again, it washed over him and nearly overwhelmed him—and that was the answer: only the unexpected temptation of realizing his wildest, most secret daydream could have blasted Herbie Manning from the civilized surroundings of his comfortable but bored and frustrated life. Even as he'd conceived the desire to act, he'd known in some instinctive way how strong the pull of his old life would be. So he'd robbed his clients. He'd *had* to;

in this way, he'd blocked that road forever, forestalled any possibility of resuming the least shadow of his old persona.

Yet, this very act of rejecting his old life had created a new tie to it. Rather than slip the rails of his past, he now realized the folly of thinking you could do that; he had merely set off down an unmarked branch line on an unexpected journey into unknown country. You could no more separate yourself from your history than you could from time itself. He would have been doomed always to have the connection behind him, but in only the most tenuous and vestigial form, if he hadn't blindly created this tangible connection as well, the one sitting right there on the jolting taxi seat beside him: the money.

What _name_, *dammit!* With the annoyance only an obvious truth can engender when it arrives too late to be of use, he accepted what could not be fixed and focused on practical reality once again. Finally, he settled on "David," for his second and most powerful unrequited love, and "Alexander," for the ancient conqueror to whose bust he fancied he now bore a—distinctly improved—resemblance. That would do as well as any.

Accordingly, as David Alexander, he bought himself a seat on the next bullet train to New York, and, after stashing his bags in a locker near the gate, embarked on a casual stroll about the station until it boarded. On this walk he received his first inkling of the changes his new life held in store.

We all get used to receiving a certain specific amount of casual attention in public. We know that, whether we're walking down a city street or standing in a crowded theatre lobby, we can expect other people's eyes to meet our own a certain percentage of the time, that, with predictable frequency, people will signify in other, sometimes virtually subliminal ways their recognition of our presence. They glance us over casually, make way as we approach, perhaps ask us the time, or merely acknowledge us with body language. The amount of such attention we receive varies from individual to individual and according to the situation, but no matter who we are, we work out quite early in life exactly how much of it we can expect, and take it for granted thereafter.

We monitor these attentions constantly, usually without noticing it. When the impact of our presence clicks with our automatic computation of how strong it should be, we feel comfortable, at home, appropriately groomed, at ease—but let the amount vary and we know instantly something has changed. If we're traveling, we may say, "Gee, what a friendly (or unfriendly) town." If we're in familiar surroundings, we may check to see if there's egg on our shirt, congratulate ourselves on that new haircut or on losing ten pounds. Or we may want to kick ourselves for wearing that strange tie our teenaged nephew gave us last Christmas.

Poor gawky old Herbie Manning had been rightly convinced he was an object of some attention and speculation behind his back. He stood out for his height and odd looks, and knew it. He met the occasional fascinated stare (or, from attractive young males in the latest gay fashions, smug sneer) just as the face bearing it snapped aside. This happened just often enough never to let him forget he was a freak. As a general rule, he was rigorously ignored. Wherever he went, both men and women signalled their intention to maintain complete obliviousness to his presence, and gave him enough space to make it unlikely he'd come into casual contact with anyone. A succession of rigidly blank faces marched past him, eyes forward.

His consciousness of this expressed itself in various ways. He slouched along in a vain attempt to disguise his height and, when it was equally convenient to go another way, tended to avoid open empty spaces where he could not help but be exposed to the gaze of many people. He did his own checking out of those around him in a resolutely covert way, head down, determined to give no one the opportunity to snub him. He was particularly careful not to meet the eyes of the most attractive males, or, when it happened anyway, to make sure his slid away first, gratuitous rejection from that quarter being the last thing he needed. At the same time, anger at the way he was ignored led him to push the boundaries with perverse behavior. He combed his hair and picked his nose in public whenever he felt like it, with never a flicker of manifest interest from anybody.

Given this background, "David Alexander" found his stroll through the busy terminus an extremely disorienting experience.

Comparison with the negative impact of Herbie Manning's presence was pretty intense, the more so as it yielded as many similarities as differences. Rather than the object of some attention and speculation, he now felt like the undisputed center of both—but rather than relegated to invisibility, he felt like the star of the show, as if a spotlight followed him everywhere. Everyone around him seemed to be looking him over with various degrees of openness limited only by the most minimal propriety due this public and impersonal setting. He had at least a corner of every eye, and considerably more than that just often enough that he still felt like a freak. He couldn't stop surreptitiously fingering the top of his zipper and glancing around to see if there might not be something of compelling general interest occurring just behind him. He fought a panicky tendency to hide in corners and behind pillars. Evidently, departure from the norm could be something of an uncomfortable experience no matter in what direction it occurred.

Female heads still snapped away, except for the teenaged ones, which stared open-mouthed, gum suspended in mid-pop. On older women's faces, instead of cool pity or the fascinated, freak show stare, he caught eyes gliding away from his with an unmistakable flush of embarrassment, sometimes even what looked very much like regret.

Male heads, in general, did *not* snap away. They held his eye, for a second or two, anyway. Their expressions were unfamiliar. Those which weren't blank and unreadable were cool and appraising. David detected a vague, generalized disapproval, even a note of challenge from the more obviously macho specimens as they shifted body weight subtly toward their female companions, marking territory and issuing warning.

All this was extremely confusing, especially the men. He was used to equating a frank stare from another man with a sexual invitation. It took a while to figure out that, from now on, his interest would lie with the male heads that *did* snap away. Just as before he'd usually avoided the eyes of really good looking guys, he had now placed most other gay men in the same position. They looked away, dazzled but without hope.

A teenaged boy with acne and hair longer than his own plucked at him and asked in awestruck tones if he were Dieter Hex—whom David hurriedly recollected to be the charismatic leader of the pop group, Blackened Burnt Babies. Choking down his initial reaction of, *"Kid, you must need glasses bad,"* he backed away in surprise and changed his vector across the floor. Behind him, he heard the boy say, "Okay Dieter, I'll be cool. I love you, man."

Dieter Hex? Upon some reflection, he decided he was actually a bit insulted. While there was a superficial resemblance, Dieter Hex's eyes were too close together, and years of drugs and indolence had left him somewhat out of shape—failings David himself did not share.

His crotch tugged at him. He remembered what the djinn had said, that this body was going to cum six times a day—every four hours—no matter what. Although it had been little more than an hour since his last experiment with masturbation, his cock was asking politely for expansion room. He had the distinct impression he ought to accommodate it before its demands became more insistent. At 200 miles an hour, the trip to New York was almost four hours by itself.

If he expected to relax on the train at all, now seemed a good time to put his new theory about cruising into practice. He abandoned his habitual slouch—forever, he resolved. Hey, this was admiration, not pity or contempt. Head up and eyes about, he struck out diagonally across the concourse, forcing himself to meet every eye that turned in his direction. He chuckled in delight at how often he could force them down and away in attitudes that seemed very very familiar.

He posted himself across from a men's room, watching for the heads that snapped away. Sure enough, before long a nice enough head on a better body turned the corner, caught David's eye and looked down so abruptly its flustered owner thumped straight into the "Out" door. Plainly embarrassed, the head scuttled around the railing and disappeared inside, all attempts at grace abandoned.

David smiled. Perfect. He sauntered into the men's room as casually as his rapidly stiffening cock would allow. He found the head at the urinals, took the one beside it and gratefully hung out his dick, which zoomed to full extension in relief.

The head stayed flustered only a second. It nudged David with its associated shoulder and jerked toward the stalls. David nodded.

They had to wait a minute for the one other occupant of the men's room to finish up and head off around the corner toward the sinks. They leapt for the corner stall. David assumed classic blowjob stance crouching on top of the stool, leaning forward against the door while the head bent forward and sucked him, so only one pair of legs showed beneath the partitions.

Just as he shot, David heard his train called. When he recovered, he gestured to the loudspeaker and made little zooming motions with his hands. The head registered disappointment, but nodded. By this time, others were using the men's room. Minutes passed. David heard his train called again—and for the last time. He still had to get his bags from the locker where he'd stashed them. While he certainly was having fun here in the terminus, he didn't particularly want to spend the night. The next train was at dawn. At last, the room cleared. David smiled at his partner and split for the gate at top speed. They had exchanged not a single word.

David made the gate the instant before it closed. As matters fell out, he needn't have worried about relieving his sexual pressure before he left. The train was underbooked; the steward took ten minutes off during a desolate stretch of Pennsylvania to prove himself most accommodating in the toilet compartment of a deserted car. The space was so small that, once again, David found himself standing on the stool.

Back at David's seat, the steward slipped him a free Lagavullin. As he sipped it, David considered the djinn's warnings about constant sexual urgency. But then, he'd had this body almost five hours now, and opportunities seemed to abound. He'd cum twice already, not counting his initial experiments in his old apartment. That was a comfortable advance on the required minimum. So okay, perpetual tumescence might require a little advance planning, but on the whole, didn't seem so onerous after all.

David yawned and lit up an Export Special. He'd play a little game, he thought. He'd see how long he could go on finding enough partners to keep from jacking off or creaming his jeans. It meant finding an awful lot of them, but hey, that was part of the attraction. He stretched and folded his arms behind his head, enjoying the sudden luxury of a new challenge and the knowledge that attaining it seemed a not impractical goal. He'd sure give it his best. Turning to the darkness howling by outside his window, he thumbed his nose at the djinn.

Afterwards, he was sorry he'd done that. For the rest of the trip, he had a tiny nagging feeling he just couldn't shake that the howling darkness had noted his gesture, and regarded him with disapproval.

* * * * *

The cab ride from the station felt to David Alexander like coming home. Manhattan's towers loomed around him, promising fulfillment and pleasure to eyes made keen with anticipation. Although he'd been to New York before, visiting friends and playing tourist, he'd never thought seriously to live there. As a heretofore sensible person, he'd believed that, unless you were very talented or very rich, life was apt to be less taxing and more rewarding almost anywhere else. Since then, however, things had changed. If he were careful, he wouldn't have to worry about money for a long while, and they'd see what talents he had. Meanwhile, he had leisure to enjoy New York's amusements and luxuriate in the rarified atmosphere of the cultural capital of the world. He was tremendously excited.

In fact, the excitement of contemplating some of the more recondite opportunities before him was turning the area between his legs into an uncomfortably solid ball inside his jeans. They'd better get to the Harrington pretty soon if he was to keep his resolution not to jack off.

The Harrington! How he looked forward to living in that legendary atmosphere! There, one famous novelist had lived and worked, and another had died under mysterious circumstances.

There, famous artists and popstars had honed the cutting edges of avant garde talents. He'd stayed there himself once or twice in his previous incarnation, and knew it had exactly the atmosphere he wanted—an easygoing air of cutrate pretense. There, he could be anything he liked, and be accepted unquestioningly.

They pulled up out front. The urging in his jeans was getting stronger by the minute. He paid the driver and gathered his bags. Rather stiffly, he strode into the lobby. *Oh hell,* he thought, *I'll just get the room for tonight and sort out the monthly rates tomorrow. That'll be faster.*

In the elevator, he considered jumping the man sent to show him his room. Although the man was really quite presentable in jeans, T-shirt and workboots, a surprising little something told David in no uncertain terms he was also straight, and would not be terribly receptive to the offer. This puzzled David. How did he know that? The insight presented itself in terms that could not be ignored; he forced himself to comply though his urgency was fast becoming unbearable.

Alone in his room at last, he threw his bags on the bed and dug out his copy of *The Address Book.* He thumbed through to New York and hurriedly scanned the columns. Yes, there seemed to be an afterhours club right close. If he hurried, he could catch the dregs of the late night crowd.

The gathering flood in his jeans was becoming more cramped and painful by the second. Although he longed to take them down and stop holding himself in just for a moment, he knew that, if he did, he'd never get them back on again. He needed his release, and soon. He stuffed his key into his pocket and headed for the door.

He stopped with his hand on the knob. The money. Was he really going to leave more than $170,000 lying on the bed? *Yes! yes! Gotta cum soon!* one part of his mind shrieked at him. He stood a moment in indecision. Reluctantly, he guessed he shouldn't do that. This was New York, after all.

Well, what could he do with it? Banks weren't open at night. Under the bed? Don't be silly. He opened the bathroom door. No place in there. He opened the closet: also bare. No hiding places.

He was about to close the closet door when something about the floor made him take a better look. The linoleum covering it twisted up at the edges, loose-looking.

He bent down and yanked it. His cock hurt like hell, all squeezed into his stiff new jeans. As the linoleum came up, the three or four nails that had held it made small hollow sounds dancing on the wooden floor beneath. David knelt. Sure enough, the floorboards were loose. *Fabulous!* Working frantically, he jiggled them up, exposing a space easily big enough for his briefcase.

Big enough empty, that is. Forty or fifty magazines lay in the dirt of decades: gay porn, but quaintly old. Some were in black and white. He picked one up. The typography was funny and old-fashioned looking to the contemporary eye. The text was in French. The cover illustration featured a guy wearing only a greasy ducktail haircut and baggy pants—not the genuinely ugly baggies of recent vogue, now thankfully ended (*a sneaky blue-nosed plot to make teenaged boys as sexless as possible,* David thought), but the more gracefully draping ones guys had worn in the '40's and '50's of the last century. It occurred to David that perhaps the hideyhole was a genuine relic of a time when such material had been strictly illegal and someone might have felt the convenience of hiding it from the hotel maid. Certainly, the fact the hideyhole's treasures were intact indicated the success of this tactic; obviously, no one had looked in here for decades.

He flipped through the magazine and was lost. The cover illustration alone sent cum threading into the base of his cock. Despite the cultural disphasia, David could see what a hot man the model had been. Helplessly, he undid his pants and, magazine open in one hand, gushed in relief. His aim was haphazard. He spurted all over the pictures.

He felt good afterwards, relaxed and relieved, but also a bit let down. His resolution not to jack off had lasted all of three hours. *Shit.*

He picked up the cum-drenched book. He tore the ruined, sticky page out—no sense wasting the whole thing—and slapped it against the wall in disgust. It stuck there nicely.

Now here was really a rather amusing conceit: a picture of two boys cumming, stuck to the wall with cum. How appropriate. He looked around the room. The paint was old, cracked and caked on thick, an institutional green ugliness. As his hands were still slippery wet, he rubbed cum on another page or two and pasted them up alongside the first. What the hell, as long as he as going to stay, he might as well brighten the place up a bit.

At length, he stashed the money, replaced the linoleum and piled his suitcase on top. The pressure was now off, but he was much too excited to sleep. Nothing would do, therefore, but that he should go out to the bar. In the taut anonymity of its back room, the rightness and joy of all his decisions that day seemed confirmed.

*   *   *   *   *

He spent the morrow arranging the necessities of life: settling the details of his residence at the Harrington and prowling the neighborhood to locate the essential amenities—restaurants, stores, laundromats, etc. On discovering the local dirtybookstore, he remembered his amusing conceit of the night before and stopped to see what was available in the way of more contemporary raw material. All along the short walk home, the images therein hung in his mind most enticingly. That he should spend the remainder of the afternoon making a real start on his plan of redecoration was inevitable.

Between bouts of creative frenzy, that is, when he was temporarily quiescent and out of cum for pasting, he took *The Address Book* in hand instead and copied out points of gay interest, listing them in order of proximity to the Harrington. As darkness fell, he wriggled back into his jeans and prepared to continue his explorations.

While number one on the list, the Cock Robin, was only a block away, that was its only virtue. Two old drunks sat in poses suggesting contemplated suicide. The bartender watched TV, clearly bored. All three of them looked up when David entered, the damned offered a mocking glimpse of paradise. Quickly, he backed out again. He shuddered—*Brrr!*—and consulted his list again.

He worked his way down to the Village and found the popular places, where what happened reminded him of the train station, but amplified many times. Here, the proprieties were different: open admiration was permitted. He was the focus of universally rapt attention when he came through the door, the cynosure literally of every eye. For a fraction of a second, conversation died. Although the music was usually too loud to hear this phenomenon, he saw mouths hanging open in awe, neighbors poked in the ribs, drinks suspended 'twixt bar and lip. Only gradually would people go back to what they'd been doing while keeping him in the corners of their eyes, all except the best and worst-looking guys in the place, who cruised him whenever he looked in their direction. He saw that in the case of the best-looking guys this was because they figured they had a legitimate chance. The worst-looking ones, the ones with nothing to lose, could be content to admire him as Art. He knew *their* mindset intimately. The rest continued to check him out obliquely; whenever he looked in a new direction, heads snapped aside in a wave that followed the turn of his own.

If he stayed in one place any time at all, a small crowd quickly collected around him, not a heedless crowd blocking his view as typically had been the case for Herbie Manning, but a crowd intensely focused on him. He felt the tension in them even when they didn't stare at him outright. When he looked at his watch, someone would ask him the time. When he took out a cigarette, a multitude of disposable lighters threatened to set him ablaze.

As in the train station, this unaccustomed attention made him extremely uncomfortable. It forced him out of one place and into another several times in rapid succession. He wanted to kick himself. Surely, a lot of this had to be only his imagination: that he could stop *every* eye in a place merely by walking in? No matter how impressive he had become, there had to be at least a few people who weren't susceptible, for whom he was the wrong type or who had agendas that wouldn't include him. Nobody was that gorgeous, were they?—but then, he was new to this kind of attention; perhaps he was just hypersensitive and paranoid, and even if he weren't, dammit, wasn't this what he'd asked for, what he had wanted more than anything else in the world? So hadn't he better get used to it and enjoy it?

He forced himself to settle into the next place he came upon, and noticed something more, something surreal. The tighter the crowd pressed in upon him, the more he developed an increasingly stifling and claustrophobic sense of people crowding not merely into his space, but into his very mind. Most disconcertingly, horny breathing began to reverberate through his head in an unbelievably literal—and literally unbelievable—way. He fought down a renewed tendency to panic and bolt. He forced himself to study the sensation, to determine where reality ended and this new paranoid delusion began.

As the crowd's attention washed over him, he began to separate it. Individual minds emerged. The sensation was akin to what had happened in the elevator at the Harrington the night before: an almost uncomfortably intimate sensation of seeing into people's innermost natures. Tiny voices echoed just beyond the edge of hearing. He focussed on the strongest ones. *"Choose me, oh choose me."* *"Oh god I know I'm not attractive enough but oh god please and I'll never ask for another thing..."*

He freaked and fled, partly because, what he'd wanted more than anything else in the world or not, of the unaccustomed depth of the emotion, but mostly because the ability to tell these things about people was a lot more than he'd asked for!

The sidewalk offered no relief from either. Every few paces, someone's eyes would lock on his. Instantly, he seemed to know things about these people that normally only could be the fruit of intimate acquaintanceship. In particular, he seemed to know exactly what they thought of him. A large variety of powerful reactions arrowed into him ranging from envy and desire, lots of that here on this major gay strip, all the way down to frustration and dislike; and once, a calm nondescript face-in-the-crowd kind of face projected at him a bloody mist of rage and violence.

That he could inspire such an emotion unsettled him even more, so that he ducked into the next bar he passed. Ignoring the stares of the clientele, he ordered Lagavullin, a double, and stared into it intently as he took stock. He hadn't asked for this gift, if gift it were, and the djinn hadn't at all seemed the sort to give what hadn't been asked for. So why? How could it be real? No one had perceptions like this! In the absence of any rationale why he should possess such skills, might not the whole thing be an illusion, some kind of trick the phraseology of his request had not forestalled? He thought of his wildcard request. He'd asked for luck—no, he'd ended up asking for something a little different, maybe. He'd asked for the universe to give him what was good for him, and the djinn had promised him a measure of its good will as fulfillment of his request. Was that what was going on here? Possibly. Maybe. It didn't really fit, but without more information, it was impossible to tell.

Still staring into his drink, he experimented, listening to the room with his mind. He saw a curious world, lightless and formless, given depth and dimension by the minds he saw there, singularities like stars in a limitless field. Each had strength and a place in this cosmos only through its awareness of him. The different emotions with which they viewed him gave each an individual character, as color distinguishes various kinds of light. Fascinated, he decided that was the only way it could be described.

At first, he was gratified and more than a little nervous to discover how many people seemed to be keeping on eye on him. Then, when he listened more intently, he discovered how cowardly and anxiety-ridden was their attention. Most looked at him longingly, but without hope. They would never meet his eye or lift a digit to meet him, considering the effort wasted before it was spent. These auras flickered weakly, a pale unhealthy unattractive greenish-drab sort of color. David dismissed them in disgust, forgetting already how many times he had watched an attractive man in this very frame of mind. It seemed so pointless and silly when seen through his new sight.

Of those who remained, he saw how many brought baggage he had no wish to carry. This one needed a spectacular conquest to reinforce a failing self-image. That one passionately desired David to show an interest in him and drive his faithless lover wild with jealousy. Still another knew how his friends would simply die with envy if only he could leave with David. Worst of all, many of them desperately wanted him on sight to be their lover, wanted to sap his strength to fill an endless variety of such voids. If once he let them latch on, they'd suck him dry in guilt-laden unequal relationships and never let him go without tears, recriminations, and accusations that had more to do with their problems than his. Just as the djinn had said, *"Everybody wants something from it."* So that was what he'd meant! All sought to use him. How uniquely unpleasant! He colored these auras a dank dark brown. Wrinkling his nose, he could almost smell the shit. They blinked out as he dismissed them.

Was that it? Was there truly no one left? Not quite. One mind remained, directly across the bar, it seemed. The aura glowed a radiant deep ultra-violet lavender shade. As he focused in on it, it seemed to scorch him with its heat, a singleminded wordless intensity concentrated entirely upon him. It willed him to look up with futile strength, an endless well of curiously impersonal passion approaching despair. Yet, its intensity was also self-sufficient. He seemed to know that, if he did not answer it, it would simply turn that purple glare on another object and then another until it got its desire.

Something within him answered. His crotch stirred forcefully. Carefully, he lifted his head. Across the bar, a very young and very beautiful Irish face stared at him from under curling black hair. He knew there was an asshole itching with passionate longing, and that anything more complicated than the most direct approach would be wasted effort. The quality and strength of desire were easily a match for his own. His crotch tugged him hard at the very thought.

The diffidence and uncertainty inculcated in him by a lifetime as Herbie Manning asserted its death throes. It had been years since he'd dared approach anyone so attractive without the lure of a fistful of bills in his pocket. He hung fire in the very act of sliding off his stool. Why, this was nothing more than an evil dream of djinns! He was being mocked! The djinn had found a loophole.

He would be led perpetually to approach the wrong people until at last frustration overwhelmed him and he gave up, thereby letting the metaphysical world off the hook. He had an instant's sinking feeling this could only be the case.

Grimly, he steeled himself to find out. He went around the bar and slipped his crotch over the muscular leg that turned to present itself.

Now he's going to feel me up, David thought. A moment later as he stared into clear blue eyes, he felt the hand between his legs. His cock stiffened the rest of the way at once, zooming down his leg against the tight denim.

The blue eyes widened. *Let's go,* they said.

Agreement thus efficiently achieved, they left without further preliminaries, whereupon ensued another highly efficient and sizzlingly agreeable sequence of events .

* * * * *

In the next weeks David continued as he had begun, prowling the bars, dirtybookstores, gay theaters and streets of lower Manhattan in search of that actinic purple glow. He found it too, with rapidly increasing ease.

He wandered the streets and parks during the day and the bars at night, casually checking the auras of all who noticed him. Although at first he might look for an hour or two before finding what he sought, his horniness increasing to near explosive intensity, he found the purple aura closer and closer to home as the days passed. At last, he hardly had to do more than descend to the sidewalk and wait for it to wander by. When he wondered about that, he decided he was becoming more closely attuned to it and seeing it in places where, before, it might have escaped his notice. That explanation did not entirely satisfy, but would do, he thought, until a better one presented itself.

With surfeit came boredom. It amazed David, who, after all, had lived under conditions of sexual deprivation and cringing self-image all his adult life, how one good body could become so like another, and so quickly too.

Yet his horniness did not diminish. In an effort to delay his increase of sexual ennui, he laid in a new supply of porn and began spending first rainy days, then, as his boredom inevitably increased, every day in his room continuing the work on his wall collage, which grew rapidly—but by the time it was three-quarters complete he was sick of it too. His wrist ached, the head of his cock became raw faster even than his superbly functioning new body could heal it, and the remaining blank spaces on his walls turned into merely an annoyingly unfinished project.

He tried resurrecting his interest in books. As long as he had nothing but time, perhaps now was the perfect opportunity to do the Russian genre, which before had seemed so daunting. He went to Marino's and stocked up on Tolstoy, Dostoevski, Turgenev, Pasternak and Solzhenitsyn. First project: *War and Peace*. He could tell, dimly, that in his former life he'd have enjoyed it very much. The story was intricately put together; the historical period was one he'd never studied; the philosophy of history definitely should have been fun to think about.

Except that he simply could not concentrate. His mind slipped relentlessly from the affairs of the Rostovs and Bolkonskis to affairs of the crotch. Despite his best efforts to apply himself, he suffered continual distracting frustration that the characters did not simply drop their pretenses and their pants, and hump one another.

Such thoughts were not conducive to enjoying a good book, but did lead to renewed activity on his wall collage. When at length it was finished and varnished, he faced the fact that serious reading was now, like so many other things, a dauntingly uphill battle. Unfinished, *War and Peace* found its way to a pile near the wall and began gathering dust.

Next, he descended to narcissism and found a temporary refuge there. For the first time in his life, he developed an interest in clothes qua clothes. Now that he had a body worth hanging them on, he prowled the shops looking for sexy duds (and underemployed salesmen). The way each new garment emphasized some different

238

aspect of his body fascinated him, and he quickly collected a closetful. That done, his interest in shopping waned.

Again time hung heavy about him. He remembered his vague intention to do some writing. He bought a tablet computer and a word-processing program, but, predictably, horniness got in the way. Everything he attempted developed strong sexual content. With one hand in his crotch as he dictated, he chugged merrily along until an ugly thought hit him. Apprehensively, he reread the first fifty pages and confirmed his worst fears. What he had envisioned as a penetrating analysis of emerging sexual mores and practices in the post-AIDS world bore less resemblance to any kind of social analysis than to the endlessly interchangeable drek available for $9.95 in any dirtybookstore. He chucked the manuscript in a drawer, and that was that.

So how was he to employ his time? Was he really incapable of any except sexual pursuits? Was he never to sit through a movie or play without the distraction of physical desire? Was he never to enjoy a leisurely dinner with friends without excusing himself for a fast self-manipulation in the can—and depending on the number of courses, possibly more than once? Was he never to relieve himself without developing an enormous hardon it took manual labor to deflate? In the idle daydreams of his former life, these possibilities had seemed agreeable, even deliciously interesting challenges. Now, upon their actualization, they seemed rather grimly inconvenient.

Worse, how was he to reconcile his body's continuing insatiable sexual demand with his growing indifference to conventional sexual pursuits? There was S&M, of course, an entire list of progressive kinkinesses. David knew well that many jaded gay men solved the problem in this very way.

Has the exotic become shopworn? Are your fantasies completely driven into the ground? Try new ones! Tired of mere sucking and fucking? Onwards into the unexplored! Perhaps you haven't lived until you're covered with welts, love the smell of shit in your hair and can stuff a Chianti bottle up your ass without bending over—and if you're bored of degradation, try domination! When you're chic in leather, know how to make whips from scratch and get

239

your rocks off forcing your boyfriend to lap piss from the doggy dish, true fulfillment may be yours.

David shook his head. He had given S&M a tentative whirl in the past weeks. This solution was simply not for him. As Herbie Manning, the perpetual victim, he'd hated and despised the real power games life had played. He wasn't tempted to engage in fantasy ones for fun. He saw nothing erotic about allowing himself to be bound and blindfolded while some asshole his new body could have beaten bloody without noticeable effort worked out his bad childhood by issuing commands in a nasty tone of voice, ordering him to do things he'd have done willingly for the fun of it. Okay, so maybe, under the right conditions, pissing was a lot like cumming, and maybe the line between pain and pleasure wasn't very clear and with practice could be blurred further yet. So why couldn't people explore these things without all the stupid playacting?

The distasteful also contained a loud note of the ridiculous. To his considerable surprise, David discovered unconventionality came complete with its own large and esoteric clutch of silly clichés which not only turned him off, but actually made him want to laugh. He discovered he was quite completely unable to utter the words, "Beat me, Daddy," without giggling. Nothing, he discovered, nonplussed and discomfited the master types as much as laughter.

S&M was plainly not for him. Besides, at his current rate the degree of jadedness it took most guys years to attain would be his in a matter of months. What then? Where was the ultimate? Screwing corpses? He shuddered, but forced himself to consider it, and shuddered again. Not only did it seem gross beyond belief, now, but the practical problems of the life it would necessitate were appalling—and what would he do when even that paled in appeal?

The problem seemed insoluble. The more he turned it over, the more depressed and panicky he became. At last he began to suspect that, as the djinn had told him, he'd made a terrible mistake.

He looked around at his room covered in cum both figural and literal, at the minimal comforts light and fancy-free living entailed, and thought back to the afternoon he'd said goodbye to his old apartment. He remembered its comforts and missed his old things with a pain as sharp as hopeless love. He wished himself back there now, back to that moment with his wish his to wish again. He closed his eyes and wished as hard as he could for deliverance from his heart's desire.

Nothing happened, of course, except that his cock stirred to life, reminding him it had been almost two full hours since last he'd cum. He measured the full extent of his foolishness.

Noticing that it had begun to rain, he decided in his misery to go for a walk. He went down to the sidewalk, eyes blazing, but did not get quite as far as the corner before the ardent purple glow enveloped him. A minute later, they were upstairs. It appeared he'd have to settle for whatever solace he could get from what he obviously did best.

He flung himself into the streets. For days he drifted and was pulled from encounter to encounter, often not stopping even to change his clothes or wash the residue of one scene from his body before seeking the next. His partners' looks quickly became a matter of indifference. He judged them by aura only, by the depth of their desire, their staying power. If this was what his body wanted, goddamit, he'd damn well do it. Wasn't this what he'd dreamed of all his life?

At the end of this binge, he sat alone in yet another bar staring into yet another scotch—not Lagavullin, or even single-malt; this wasn't the kind of place to stock either. He did not know what day it was, or, for that matter, if it were day or night. He hadn't been back to his room in ages. His clothes were dirty and smelled stale even to him. His hair hung in sticky strings. He had a three-day beard, and badly needed a shower and a good meal.

His mind was a blissful blank. No one hungered after him in this condition. He had succeeded in rendering even the djinn's powerful magnetism unattractive. He lit a cigarette—not an Export Special; he was out of those—and took a sip of scotch. His hand shook slightly. He didn't care. He felt curiously peaceful, home again in the world of the spurned and ignored.

Yet not quite alone, after all. A star had blinked on in his mental firmament, not the Dionysiac purple of unconditional desire but a coolly Apollonian blue, a color he hadn't paid much attention until now. He looked up.

A sleek well-dressed middle-aged man met his eyes. David held his gaze, searching for what might lie therein. Yes, he did find desire, but desire tempered by self-possession, a knowledge of self-limitations, and an absence of illusions. The man looked at David coolly, almost pityingly: *"What a shame, such a beautiful boy."*

This stung David, even in that state. He held the man's stare—no one, so far, had ever broken his gaze if he wished it otherwise—and willed him around the bar. He came.

"My friend," the man said softly, "you do indeed look as if you could use $50."

Yes, David considered, *I probably could.* He felt in his pocket and brought out three singles and some change. If he didn't take this fellow's kind offer, he'd have to go all the way back to the Harrington for more money. What did it matter, anyway? Sex was sex. His cock stirred restlessly at the thought.

The man was calmly piling bills on the bar. *Showing me he's got it.* Herbie Manning had been quite familiar with the drill, after all.

"Okay," he said.

The man nodded and collected his money.

Outside, it was definitely day.

The man took him in a taxi to a small but luxurious apartment in the east 80's. He collected David's clothes, gave him a razor and pushed him firmly at the bathroom.

Under the hot water, David emerged from his stupor. It all came clear to him. As Herbie Manning, he had pursued hustlers because only through them could he service his need for personal attention. He'd envied them the opportunities they'd had that he had not and had done his best to turn them into friends, yet always had been defeated by, at bottom, their basic lack of interest in him for himself, by a kind of shallow dishonesty that allowed them to tolerate him only as long as he was of use. He recognized this now fully for the first time. Of course. This was the very thing he'd struggled against, the thing that had made all his encounters with hustlers so ultimately unsatisfactory. Surely the job could be done better than that.

Clearly he was going to have to prove it. By his own wish, he had befitted himself for nothing else. Everything clicked. The rightness of this solution to his problem settled upon him. He would be a whore, and a damn good one too. This resolution he could keep.

Meanwhile, his host was fixing them breakfast in a very worried state of mind. Here was this young man he'd picked up... well, he didn't quite know why. There was just something impossible to ignore in those amazing green eyes. Already, he regretted it thoroughly. The young man was such a bum! Probably a drug addict on the way down. Probably? Definitely! Seemed almost catatonic. Oh, why hadn't he passed him by as he'd intended!—but no, all at once he'd been impulsive, something that very infrequently happened anymore because it nearly always led to disaster. Now he had the young man here, at home in his own dear apartment where there was lots to break and lots to steal. Ohdearohdearohdearohdear.

But when the young man—David? Was that his name?—emerged from the bathroom, his host was genuinely astonished. What emerged was a different person, a stunningly beautiful smoothly articulate professional. He thought of drugs again, until he remembered he'd sent him into the bathroom stark naked and empty-handed. He'd checked.

Over breakfast, they discussed the Pre-Raphaelite exhibit currently at the Met, rather intelligently too, the man noted approvingly. The young man's appetite was that of any normal, hungry young man, which was also reassuring. He approved the young man's deft table manners, and every time he looked into the young man's eyes, his reassurance grew. Then the young man took him into his Louis XVI bedroom and gave him his money's worth and more. That was the most reassuring thing of all.

David enjoyed it too. He enjoyed the talk about the exhibit. He enjoyed playing the part. He tried his best to inject a sense of caring, of genuine personal interest and warmth into his half of the bargain, and was glad to find it returned. He liked the fair dealing of giving full measure for the money. There was something engrossingly

243

seductive about turning this jism he was always spewing everywhere into currency of a more practical kind.

He would quench the horniness of the world, and not merely that part of it attractive enough to get it quenched on its own! If he had to be such a sex machine, he would at least fill a societal need: he would perform a necessary service for sexually frustrated guys everywhere—well, those that could pay, anyway. He had to cut the crowd down somehow. He laughed out loud to think he was going to make a real live actual contribution to the economy after all. Let's hear it for the GNP! This was obviously the life for him.

When his host was safely napping, David quietly put on his clothes, pocketed his $50 from on top of the bureau and left a slip with his name and phone number in its place—he really would have to get some business cards made first thing. He left with a feeling of satisfaction he hadn't felt since the very evening of his transformation. This truly was going to be a good thing.

So it was too. At last, he had a career he could really get behind, as it were. Clients were neither scarce nor reluctant. Now that he was looking for them, he found men everywhere ready to shove money at him.

Not only was he an immediate success, he was almost *too* successful. Perhaps it was just beginner's luck, or perhaps it was his status as a new face in a market perpetually starved for novelty, or perhaps it really was the superior personal qualities he now possessed; almost immediately, David had several extremely wealthy men battling for exclusive possession of him. They showered him with gifts and each other with insults.

The gifts they pressed on him were all conditional on David promising to be faithful to the giver and to the giver alone. When he refused to agree, they gave anyway, and made ever more extravagant promises—cars, condos, even adoption and heirship!—if only they might lock him away in the golden cage each professed himself ready and eager to prepare.

In the beginning, as David struggled to make his admirers understand he could be no one's exclusive possession unless that person's sexual stamina were at least a match for his own, his suitors, who quickly became aware of one another, assumed he was merely playing them off against the field, holding out for the juiciest offer, and baited him accordingly. Their promises betrayed more than a tinge of bullshit's brown aura.

You might have expected this perception of David's mercenary nature to put them off. David certainly did, and played the role to the hilt. He remembered the way he'd been treated by the Attaché Arms crowd and took perverse pleasure in amplifying it. He treated the suitors with a phony friendliness through which superficiality of interest brightly shone. He made it plain he entertained absolutely no objection to auctioning his services as widely as possible among any and all those willing to cough up the highest professional fees. He encouraged the bidding war, reporting offers back and forth, and upped the ante, both emotional and, whenever possible, pecuniary, by cruising outside numbers under their very noses—and waited, confidently expecting relief.

Instead, he began to get the impression he himself was becoming almost irrelevant. The auction metaphor struck him as more and more appropriate; the suitors came to resemble aficionados of Civil War memorabilia, Dresden dust collectors or other arcane stuff, lifelong auction-haunters vying for some object of second-rate status and doubtful provenance all want only to fill some minor gap in their collections, would-be buyers who start the bidding with practiced knowledge of how to play the game, with firm, rational limits in mind, yet become so totally carried away by the impossibility of yielding to a rival that, at last, the object is knocked down for far more than the bewildered successful bidder ever intended to pay—a successful bidder who, ten minutes later and the thrill of victory faded, can't quite remember why he wanted the damn thing in the first place.

—And that, thought David, was precisely what was wrong with the whole situation. The oldest of the suitors had been hiring hustlers for decades but swore, truthfully, David thought, never to have fallen in love with one before. The man himself was convinced he'd lost his mind, and wasn't it glorious? Another, who had been completely closetbound and paranoid all his life, was now eager to have screamingly explicit bitch fights on public sidewalks. David considered it extremely unusual in the same way as experienced bidders commonly did *not* lose possession of themselves at auctions, that wealthy and experienced men should be willing to throw their money and their dignity away quite so readily in pursuit of someone who, no matter how beautiful, seemed openly content to behave like a common whore. The depth of the obsession he inspired bewildered him. Good at his job though he undoubtedly was, he certainly was not the only pretty boy in New York!

It could be possible, he supposed, that someone might conceive a hopeless passion for him anyway. Hustlers' mythology was full of such tales, of mercenary young men rescued just on the point of becoming too old to continue their profession by wealthy men ready to set them up for life. So okay, it might happen once. Not inconceivably, his face, his personality, his presence might strike someone exactly right; everyone had their secret soft spots—but that it should happen with all his best and otherwise most valuable customers?

The bidding for David quickly reached all-or-nothing proportions. Ironically, not until actual desire for David seemed to have been superseded by personal rivalry among the suitors as the prime motive in the competition did he perceive the transparent golden glow of utter sincerity behind the extravagant promises he heard.

As his stockpile of expensive watches, rings, lighters, diamond posts and other trinkets grew (including even a solid gold cigarette case he would have died rather than carry), so did the bitterness and acrimony that seemed to surround him wherever he went. The suitors were obsessed, and as in all cases of obsession, the aching raw desire itself and the demands it made upon its victims had become more important than its object. His opinion no longer mattered; they were no longer willing to cede him the option of personal choice. In order to have him, they were quite willing to persecute and destroy him.

They began to turn up everywhere. He detected the auras of unknown, coldly impersonal watchers and followers wherever he went and knew private detectives had been hired to follow him around. If he sat in any one bar longer than a few minutes, one or another of the suitors was sure to show up and run off whomever he might be cruising. If he stayed longer still, another would turn up, setting off a royal bitch fight.

The entertainment value of this quickly palled on everyone. David's fellow hustlers, who at first had looked him over with envy and then had extended cautious offers of friendship and even partnership, now regarded him with disgust. Wherever he went, he attracted all the best trade to himself. The discord which surrounded him disrupted everybody else's business. David sensed dislike deepening to hostility among his colleagues. Bartenders and bouncers hinted how glad they'd be if he would please take his circus elsewhere. After a while, they did more than hint. He became unwelcome in all the best places, while on the street, other hustlers ran him off traditional cruising grounds with catcalls and physical threats. He began to watch his step around town.

Nor was he secure in his room. Though the desk clerk was supposed to call him and tell him when someone wanted to see him, his suitors and their agents could afford bigger bribes for free access to his hallway than he could afford to keep them away. He often sensed the presence of lurkers outside his door. The suitors began turning up at odd hours. Whenever he'd had a trick in his room, one or another of the suitors would reproach him about it, and seeing one of the suitors inevitably resulted in ugly scenes with all the rest.

Needing an outside place he could call his own, he remembered the unpopular and dying Cock Robin a block away. He began sneaking down the Harrington's service stairs, out the back door and through a narrow passage between the buildings to the street behind. Head down, he'd scuttle around the blocks and duck into the bar. The staff there was more than happy to let him make himself at home. At last, he had a place for a quiet drink by himself, and a place wherein he could rendezvous undisturbed with the new clients he'd collected when he could.

This refuge proved temporary. His new customers started to show signs of the same jealousy as his old ones. Worse, his old suitors, who, after all, could afford the finest in private investigation, soon uncovered this subterfuge and turned up in force. Although the Cock Robin's staff began as his strong allies, grateful for the new business accumulating around him, they were reluctant to intervene against these wealthy men suddenly spending fortunes in their bar. The staff began to make more on the bribes they were taking to inform on David's presence than they were on their wages. In desperation, he seduced the staff, one after the other. This proved not a good idea. It only gave them bad cases of divided loyalty and made them cynical.

Once again, the situation appeared impossible. Something had to be done, and fast. He had no idea what.

In one respect at least, things were not all bad. Financially, David's business was a smashing success. Even without his growing heap of expensive jewelry, he had in a remarkably short time made more money than he'd spent in all his time in New York. In fact, his business was on such a firm footing as to make it grossly unlikely he'd ever need to dip into the money he'd brought with him—Herbie's savings and the much larger amount stolen from Herbie's clients—ever again.

He was, by the way, really beginning to disassociate himself from Herbie Manning. The problems and concerns of life as David Alexander were so far from what they'd been that his former life no longer seemed quite his own. Herbie might have been a dear, close friend for whom he had boundless sympathy, but who was, if not quite deceased, at least permanently out of town.

At the point when he'd collected enough to make up the full amount of "Herbie's money" once again, he stored it in the briefcase under the closet floor, glued in the linoleum and nailed the edges down tight. If he could find a painless way to return the money Herbie had stolen, he thought he just might, and such family as Herbie'd had might one day appreciate the money which had been Herbie's own. Until then, it was all securely and permanently hidden where no one would look for it. That he had some secret cash at hand, "just in case," wasn't a bad thought, either.

He stowed the jewelry and remaining excess cash, his "profit," in a safety deposit box at a bank down the street where it was conveniently to hand if needed and where he could visit easily to add more when it started to pile up in his pocket. What with the competition between his suitors, he was making far more money than he could spend, given the limitations of light and fancy-free living. These limitations he was more than ever determined to observe. It began to look as if the only way to escape his suitors might be to pick up and leave for uncharted territory.

Yet, he knew that if he did so without resolving the basic situation, he would just run into the same trouble anywhere he went. Facing and solving the problem now was vital, if it could be solved at all. If it couldn't... well, it simply had to be, that was all. His financial success at and basic liking for this mode of life determined him to find a reasonable and equitable way of carrying it on, one that didn't accumulate problems for him as he went along.

None of the obvious approaches worked at all. He tried several times to break completely with his suitors. He told them to get lost, that he never wanted to see them again. The suitors replied impatiently with new, ever more expensive gifts and ever more extravagant promises. As for the surveillance, the suitors feigned non-comprehension; each blamed the others for it, their auras shit brown with the lie. He tried intimidating them physically; he threatened gross bodily damage if they continued to pester him, and as his annoyance escalated past endurance, discovered he was beginning to mean it.

David was on the brink of a rash act that would endanger his entire trip, and knew it. He wanted horny non-jealous fuckbuddies and easy-going generous yet non-possessive johns. He wished to acquire a worldwide network of such friends and spend his time visiting them all. This would be impossible if he could leave only jealousy, envy, anger and dissension behind him everywhere. He didn't want to feel he was fleeing every time he moved on. The world was large, but not infinite. When he'd been through every gay gathering place in it, what then?

249

These considerations reached critical mass on a beautiful day in mid-summer. He sensed a private dick lurking in the hallway when he wanted to leave his room at lunchtime. His impatience and irritation mounted as he waited. Finally, the aura dimmed in a way David had come to recognize as this particular PI ducking around the corner to relieve himself in the janitor's closet. David split for the service stairs. He bought a calzone as he rounded the block and thought to eat it over a quiet beer in the Cock Robin, but when he got there and took a precautionary peep through the diamond pane in the door, he spied two of his suitors glowering at one another from opposite ends of the bar. As he backed away, he discovered another PI on his tail. Swiftly, he strode to the nearest subway stop and descended the stairs three at a time. A train was loading as he hit the platform. Without caring what train it might be, he shouldered through the doors just as they were closing and headed off uptown, confident he'd ditched all pursuit, at least for the moment.

He ate his calzone amid the noise and jolting of the subway, not at all how he'd envisioned his lunch that day. With every bite, he got angrier. Who were these assholes that they pursued him so relentlessly? How dare they infringe his liberty in this way? Intolerable!

He left the train when he finished his lunch. By this time, his cock was throbbing. He stopped into the subway john intending to give himself a fast handjob and clear his head, but no need. A heavy well-dressed gentleman with lots of frizzy gray hair obligingly sucked him off. David hardly saw him through his anger, yet the man looked strangely familiar. With shock, David recognized him as a famous musician—just as he orgasmed.

The man grabbed at David's clothes and hissed something in a passionate whisper, aura swelling in adoration. *Oh great, oh super.* That was all he needed, to ruin the life of somebody famous, and become himself notorious in the process. David backed away in horror. He fled back to the platform and onto a waiting train, pursued by visions of tabloid photographers joining the PI's outside his door. Though any kind of limelight was disastrous, that kind would destroy him quickest.

He emerged into the bright sunshine of Columbus Circle shaking his head to dispel these evil phantoms. He avoided the park. Too cruisy. Calmer now he'd cum, he walked the streets of mid-town Manhattan. Turning the problem over and over in his mind, he reviewed the entire history of his troubles, beginning right after his transformation.

At first, horny, fascinated by the novelty of unrestrained promiscuity and frightened at involving himself in the multiplicity of personal problems he glimpsed in people's minds, he'd sought out only those in the mood for the most impersonal sort of sexual encounter, and at first, they'd been relatively difficult to find. He remembered how those with the intense purple aura had become steadily more numerous until at last they were omnipresent. He'd assumed this had occurred only as he became more attuned to looking for them, but was that really the case?

What had happened to all those greenish-drab and brown auras? Initially, those had been humanity's dominant colors. As the purple auras increased in number, the others had disappeared. Had he simply learned to tune them out?

Remembering, it seemed to him that some of his partners—many of them—almost all as time went on—might not have had the aura he sought at first. He'd seen them from afar, thought how enticing they were and what a pity their problems were going to stand in the way—but the closer he got, the clearer it would become they were really glowing purple so bright it blinded. Or he'd catch them with the last vestige of some darker color disappearing as he looked.

At the time, he'd put it down to the power of his own attractiveness. He'd been new to it then and hadn't really known what to expect. Yet, upon reflection, it didn't seem right it should happen that way. People didn't ordinarily shed their personal problems at the sight of an attractive man. In the same way drugs and alcohol provide no actual escape from one's troubles and are abused when employed in this way, so cruising was not really an escape mechanism. One's basic personality still was reflected.

Herbie Manning's certainly had been, for instance, no matter how horny he got. It didn't add up.

He remembered how, when he'd started hustling, rather than go for impersonal sex, he'd tried to find men who'd be steady tricks, who'd come back to him again and again. He'd wanted to please them and bind them to him with pleasant company and good sex. At just that time, he'd ceased seeing the deep purple glow altogether. Instead, he could find only jealous suitors, each annoyingly besotted with him.

In every case, the suitors' patterns of behavior had changed radically when they'd met him. One had been a latent who'd never before had gay sex! David had met him when they'd both piled into the same taxi by different doors. As it had been the only one in sight, he'd tried to smooth over the awkwardness so they could share the ride. To his considerable surprise, they'd shared much more than that even before they were out of the cab! Again, he had put it down to the powerful attraction his new person seemed to have on all and sundry. What obsession he'd inspired! He remembered how wrong it had seemed.

There were other very curious things too. He had never been much bothered by people he didn't want when he cruised. Until now, this hadn't struck him as odd. As Herbie Manning, he'd taken this as a matter of course; poor Herbie hadn't been bothered by much of anybody. For him, it was normal, but for David Alexander? Suddenly, it seemed incredible. He'd sat in bars and, after his first or second outing, no one had bothered him until he was ready. He'd sifted through auras, picked the one he wanted and nearly always got it! People had ditched friends, even lovers for him. This was incredible too. Just because their auras showed they desired him, where was it written that meant they were available? *No one* was that good! The most beautiful people he'd ever met in his old life had claimed a score record no better than 50%!

He remembered the first man to offer him money. The man had pitied and despised him. David had fixed him in his gaze and willed him around the bar, never dreaming he had the power to make it happen, considering the mess he'd been at the time. But the man had come! He remembered other incidents like that and reached the inescapable conclusion. He was not merely reading those around him. Was it possible he was *changing* them in some way? Just by looking at them and willing it, consciously or not, to happen? Unbelievably, this did add up. All the little incidents clicked into place. That had to be it.

This thought struck him so forcefully he stopped dead in the middle of the sidewalk. A bulky middle-aged man wearing an expensive three-piece suit and carrying a stitched leather briefcase banged into him and brought him out of his trance.

Quickly, the man patted himself to see if his pockets had been picked. Deciding they hadn't, he was still brusque and nasty. He cut off David's stuttered apology. "You from out of town or what? Look where you're going, will you? People oughta hafta have a license!"

David compressed his lips in irritation at this return for his apology. He decided on an experiment. He stared into the man's eyes and, although he saw the man was straight and thoroughly paranoid about it, willed him to sudden desire of himself, desire as intense as he could make it. Instantly, the man's aura changed from bloody red to vibrant glowing purple.

The man's attitude changed to match. His snarl turned to bewilderment and he stammered, "Oh. Oh! Uh, s-s-sorry I was so angry, friend. Hey, let me buy you a drink, whaddaya say?" He smiled a startled smile. His hand descended gingerly toward David's shoulder.

David turned and fled. The man called after him in distress, "Hey! Where're you going? I just want to talk to you! Hey, come back!"

David raced around the corner—and pulled up short. No, he decided, he simply couldn't keep running away from his problems like this. He had to face them squarely. He turned around and waited.

The man bounded clumsily around the corner and panted up, briefcase flapping at his knees. "Hey, bab... uh, my friend. You didn't have to go flying off like that. I'm not angry, really! Why don't we go somewhere and get to know each other, huh? Hey, I know this great little bar just a block away. Let's you and me..."

He stopped because, under David's gaze, things were happening. By the force of his will, the man's aura changed from lavender purple to blue, and finally to an ordinary, impersonal gray. David released him.

The man looked bewildered, embarrassed, and at last a bit terrified, as if he suddenly couldn't understand why he'd been saying the things he had. He backed off quickly. "Well-if-you-won't-you-won't-just-watch-where-you're-going," he babbled, though David hadn't yet said whether he would or wouldn't. The man now fled in his turn, radiating an uncertain nervous jangle of colors.

Sunuvabitch! David wandered down the sidewalk in a daze. He'd been doing it all himself! He'd willed himself purple auras until he'd choked on them. Then he'd accidentally willed devotion to himself until it endangered his liberty, all without realizing he was doing it!

Now that he did know, perhaps he could control it. He could put right the mess he'd made of other people's lives and, not incidentally, get them out of his own. He could have the tensions and frustrations of the hunt when he wanted them and instant gratification when he didn't. Most important of all, he could keep everyone uninvolved and on their own tracks unless he wanted it otherwise for some reason. It might take no more than a little practice. Incredible!

His mood turned jubilant. He'd discovered the key. *Why,* he wondered, *didn't the djinn tell me about this? The least he could have done was save me all this trouble!*

A very familiar voice snarled softly an inch behind his ear: "Because, asshole, you didn't wish for an owner's manual, did you."

It was, in fact, Herbie Manning's voice, exactly as he'd heard it speaking his voicemail's outgoing message back at him. He whirled in time to see the back of Herbie's balding head and gangly, unmistakable arms and legs disappearing around the corner.

David rushed three strides forward and zipped around. The sidewalk and the street were empty. The wall was blank stone. Impossibly, no one was there.

Adrenaline raced in him. He shivered. *The djinn!* he thought, *and in my old body too. He's watching me!*

He wandered down the sidewalk in a daze. The djinn's presence in his neighborhood—and in his head, he realized with shock—gave his situation an entirely different complexion. Although he was uncertain what that new complexion might be, he *was* certain he did not like it. He happened on a little courtyard plaza with a waterfall, a refreshment stand, tables and chairs, and sank into one. He lit an Export Special with trembling hands and took deep drags to force down the adrenaline.

As sobering events went, this was an icy shower. Irksome too; evidently, no matter what level of privacy he ultimately regained, it was destined never to be complete. —And downright worrisome! That the djinn might decide to take an active hand in his affairs was a bad thought which got worse the more he thought it—and in his old body? What kind of deviltry might that lend itself to? While he didn't know more about the metaphysical world than what the djinn had told him (and wasn't sure he'd understood all of that!) he had the distinct impression it had an agenda all its own.

Calmer now, he gulped, and came to a decision. As there seemed nothing he could do about the situation, he resolved to ignore it as long as he could and get to work immediately putting things right on his own plane of existence while still he might.

He visited all his suitors in turn. During the obligatory sexual interlude, he made some adjustments. With a little practice, he got quite good at it. He cancelled their passion for him entirely; he toned their obsession down to simple friendly camaraderie. From now on they'd be merely his very good buddies whenever they happened to meet. He also did his best to wipe out their hostility to one another, though that was more difficult as their auras chiefly reflected their attitude toward him. He did his level best to put *that* right, anyway, and hoped that, with the reason for their animosity removed, the rest would follow in time.

He visited the bars he'd been asked to leave and wiped out hostility in job lots, changing enemies into friends all around. He was shocked to discover how much of it he found.

He kept the Cock Robin as his personal bar. With all the new good will toward him in town, it became crowded and popular every night. Once again, he was a real hero to the staff, and kept their adulation with regular sexual service for everybody from the manager down to the newly hired extra bartenders and the boy who washed the glasses. The Cock Robin became the most popular place to work in town.

On an even keel at last, David's business grew by leaps and bounds. He had no trouble at all finding clients, so little that, out of courtesy to his colleagues, he left all the established hustling venues to them. When he was horny and didn't have a repeat date lined up, he stationed himself on a streetcorner in mid-town Manhattan or the financial district and waited for a likely prospect to wander by, whom he simply transfixed with an arrow from Cupid's bow and went to work.

He discovered some people were better subjects for his mental manipulations than others. For best results, each person required careful analysis and a slightly different approach. It all had to be done quickly too, before the subject moved out of range. The more he understood the process and the better he got at it, the more complex it seemed.

If things went well with a particular individual and business was transacted, David would plant the desire to call him when—not if—the subject wanted further service. If things didn't go well, or if he tired of a repeater, he simply erased their interest in him. His safety deposit box accumulated funds rapidly. He himself felt happy, satisfied, appropriately challenged, and fulfilled: on the right road at last, at last.

Even while David was working the bugs out of this system, there came a day when he lounged up Broadway from Bowling Green. Shirtless in tight jeans, a leather thong knotted around his neck for a choker, he strolled thumb out along the curb, trolling for limousines. He was in th right place. He'd reached only the corner of Wall Street when a stretch the length of a city bus tooled up out of the canyons and stopped at the corner. David stared at the expanse of black-tinted glass that represented the passenger compartment. He could see nothing with his eyes, but knew there to be one occupant in back, male. He picked up massive amounts of repressed homosexual interest. The aura was livid puce. Here was the worst sort of self-hating fag, a closet case virulently resenting David's open sensual display as an affront to decency.

His eyes gleamed. This sort of challenge had proved a totally unanticipated delight to his career choice. He'd discovered a gleeful delectation in manipulating the heads of rich and powerful secret queers, playing ninepins with the damned homophobic fuckers' lives.

Quickly, as the car turned into Broadway and pulled away, David changed the aura from puce to light pink. Through the rear window he deepened it to blue, and finally to blazing lavender. If the car stopped, he would tone it down, eventually. If the car kept going, some flintsouled New England banker type would be squirting into his charcoal pinstripes every hour on the hour for *days*. David smirked.

The car pulled over. The window came down. An arm motioned him up. David sauntered forward, taking his time.

When he reached the car, he gaped in surprise. A face shockingly familiar to all looked out at him, a face he hadn't in his wildest dreams ever expected to see in this situation, and never at all without flying squads of police and secret service. Harrison Keeler Frogmorton III, Chairman of the Consortium Council, the most powerful man in America and maybe the world, opened the door for him and said, "Get in."

Shocked speechless, David couldn't think what else to do. As the car pulled away from the curb, the Chairman put a hand on his knee and said, "Call me Froggy."

Chapter Six
THE PERSONAL DISASTER DEPARTMENT

ust as David was making the startlingly unexpected acquaintance of Harrison Keeler Frogmorton III, Greg Whitbread was arriving in New York to organize his investigation, and just as Greg was stepping off the train, Morgan Jaye's receptionist was answering a phone call which ultimately would tie all these events into a much wider scheme.

Outside Jaye's windows, a lowering sky threatened imminent storm. The big man moved about his office tending his jungle, watering can and shears in hand. At the buzz, he moved his large bulk deliberately to the desktop comm panel. "Rev. Billy Barber on line one, sir," it said. "'To remind you about the birds,' he says."

Jaye sat. He frowned. He regarded the clear glass of his viewscreen angling upwards from its ebony base. He positioned it with his thumb. He drummed his fingers on his glass slab desktop in irritation. At last, he pursed his lips and, leaning back in his chair, jabbed a button. The viewscreen colored and filled with the fleshy features of Rev. Barber.

"I distinctly remember asking you not to bring this matter into my office."

Rev. Barber registered shocked surprise. "Now, none of that! Through the Gawd-given gift of mah electronic ministry, ah have preached the glo-ry of the Consortium Council as Gawd's answer to the tribulations of these troubled times, and ah have preached it to millions here at home and in 47 furr-in countries."

Jaye sighed and settled in for what threatened to be a longish declamation. The Rev. Barber orated at him in the country accent that was native tongue to the vast majority of his viewership, except that his was slickly non-specific geographically, and boasted elaborate elocution as if even now he addressed the multitude. "And so, when in His infinite wisdom and mercy, our Blessed Lord Jesus Christ inspired one of your former associates to purify his soul by confessin' to me in the security and secrecy of mah office, and under only mi-ni-mal persuasion, that he had, at your in-sti-ga-tion, smuggled birds of rare and endangered species into this country for your puhsunal and prahvate collection, breaking in the prahcess many of the laws of our dear old U.S. of A. and several of those self-same 47 furr-in countries in which mah sacred message is heard weekly, I naturally considered it my bounden duty to help you expiate your sin, willingly or no, prahvately if possible, but publically if that should evah become a highly re-gret-ful necessity." Poised to continue, Rev. Billy paused to draw breath.

Jaye sat through this speechifying with increasing irritation. "Yes yes. By all of which you merely mean blackmail."

"Blackmail!" Metaphorical storm clouds gathered on Rev. Billy's heretofore uplifted countenance in perfect counterpoint to those outside Jaye's windows reflected on the viewscreen's surface. "You may call it what you will, suh! Ah have linked mahself and mah sacred message irretrievably to your cause. Ah have calmed the masses and prepared a way for Caesar in the hinterland! Ah have upheld his glorious golden visage. Ah will *not* have his feet of clay publically exhibited as well!—so if it must happen anyway, I will mahself lead the Gawd-fearing believers whose precious faith you have abused and drive you from the temple! Do ah make mahself cleauh?"

Jaye was unlocking a drawer in his credenza. He looked up. "Oh, perfectly. You want more money." He opened the drawer and produced a file. Fixing a pair of gold-rimmed half-glasses on his nose, he shifted his weight backward in the chair to leaf through it comfortably. "And at first glance, anyway, it's not difficult to see why. Your World Church of the Redeemable Redeemer has a cash flow perpetually verging on the negative."

259

LEARNING TO LOVE IT

He made a *tsking* sound. "There is your newspaper, *The Clarion Call*, which lost $800,000 in the first quarter of this year alone, though I note a new printing plant is now on order. Then there is WCRR Christian University, 'giving Christian educations to the victims of the economic readjustment.' The endowment fund lags far behind projections and last semester's 65% increase in tuition begat a commensurate decrease in enrollment, but, curiously, the building program seems still to be right on schedule. Shipments from Carrara continue unabated. Next, there's New Eden Park, your isolated desert housing development for the paranoid, survivalist faithful—$25 million in underground blast-proof construction so far, of which only 4% has actually sold, though construction continues on a 24-hour basis almost as if Armageddon were already a budgetary item. Oh, and here's my favorite: Rev. Billy's Christian Amusement Center. 'Take an inspirational run down the world's longest water slide past animatronic recreations of your favorite biblical scenes.' $5 million in the red last year."

"Hey, those are just the start-up costs!"

"Perhaps." Jaye turned a page. "And let's not forget your WCRR world headquarters project, the New Eden Complex: a vast church incorporating architecture of the most expensively experimental kind, and ancillary buildings including an 100-story office tower. The tower was topped off last month, though rental commitments for all that space are far behind schedule, no surprise considering this edifice is located in Necktie Gulch, Texas, not precisely a known center of corporate enterprise! At any rate, the ultimate use for the top five floors is not in question. They will be your own palatial residence. The projected cost for the headquarters project was $500 million, but overruns are pushing that heavenwards. Shall I go on?"

Rev. Billy waved a hand impatiently. "If I had the time, you could go on 'til Gabriel blows his trumpet. What's this about? None of that is any secret. When we need money for these projects, we go to the Christian community and ask for it!"

"You certainly do, which brings us to your Assets column. Unfortunately, although last year's total take from contributions to

260

your World Church of the Redeemable Redeemer was $125 million in round numbers, more than $100 million of this was earmarked by contributors for WCRR Evangelical Missions, and was duly deposited into that account. How commendable. The money *seems* to go to your 'sacred' work." Jaye dripped sarcasm. "Toward, as one of your many and various tracts has it, 'combating the scourge of animism among developing peoples throughout the world,' amidst many other things." Jaye looked up. "Animism, really! How picturesque."

Rev. Billy bristled. "That's right, and no '*seems*' about it. The money people give to the Missions goes right where they want it, straight into Gawd's *sacred* work, every cent! Cut to the point."

Jaye smiled. "Very well. The point is that, of the more than $100 million the Missions took in last year, less than $5 million was actually disbursed as the contributors intended, to your various evangelical outreach programs overseas or in this country. What happened to the rest? Evidently, WCRR Evangelical Missions is a partner in all those enterprises teetering perpetually on the brink of insolvency, because the highly confidential, well protected fact is that into said wobbly enterprises is precisely where the Missions' money went."

"Says who?"

"Oh come sir. You did keep your money in banks, after all."

"Okay, *suppose* it's true. So what? *The Clarion Call* and the University are evangelical institutions! The rest are sound business propositions approved by the Board of Deacons, hardheaded businessmen one and all, that will repay the Missions someday just like the loaves and the fishes!"

Jaye noted with satisfaction that Rev. Billy's hick accent seemed to be disappearing into the truculence of one rehearsing a fallback position for the grand jury. "It's the short term that interests me. Let's take a good look at the Golden West Construction Company, for just one very juicy example. They are the general contractors for New Eden Park and the headquarters tower. Although these 'sound business propositions' lost copiously, the Missions' money has paid them in full and absolutely on time for years. Let's see what we know about them." Jaye turned a page.

"Umm. Wholly-owned subsidiary of Golden West Land Development." He turned another page. "Golden West Land Development: private corporation—major shareholder, Eldorado Enterprises." The pages turned faster now. "Eldorado Enterprises: partnership—general partner, Needle's Eye Investment Group. Needle's Eye Investment Group: private corporation—major shareholder, Goshen, Ltd. Goshen, Ltd.: general partner, Jeremiah Enterprises." Jaye looked up over his half-glasses. "We do seem to be getting steadily more biblical as we go along, I notice." He turned one, last page. "And now for the payoff. Jeremiah Enterprises: partnership—Wilmore P. Barber, 51% partner, and WCRR Board of Deacons, 49%! How extremely incestuous! Or perhaps masturbatory would be a better word. The money comes in through the Missions, swooshes around through all these companies, and ends up in your pocket and the pockets of those hardheaded businessmen of yours!—and how extremely arrogant and hypocritical! You threaten me with public expiation of sin? If any of this is ever made public, you, sir, will have some praying to do." He closed the file.

Rev. Billy spoke softly. "Those are all private companies. Haven't you forgotten that, as of two months ago, unauthorized public disclosure—I refrain from using the word 'theft'—of private business ownership data is a crime all by itself? And even more serious, this year's Protection of Religious Freedom Act makes the same apply to poking your unauthorized nose into the financial affairs of a religious institution."

"Pah. Go bully someone else. That's just one track through all this. All the others, at least the ones with money in them, lead to you too. I particularly love the way you're always making a special plea for whichever of your missionary projects is in especially pathetic need at whatever moment it happens to be. What do you suppose your 'Gawd-fearing believers' would think if they knew about this... shall I refrain from using the word 'fraud'? It's just possible your adopted hometown, appellated, I understand, for its original settlers' preferred correctional method, would edify itself with its first necktie party in decades."

Jaye sat back and sighed with satisfaction. "It has taken me ten months to assemble this information quietly. In that time, you have bled me for one million dollars, which I want back, or comparable value, absolutely every cent I can raise. I grant that you can bring me down, but you'll be coming too, and that's a promise. It's time to find yourself another mark. How do you say in Texas? This hole's gone dry." He flipped the file onto his desk and folded his hands comfortably on his corporation.

Rev. Billy smiled. "Not quite. Oh, ah grant you, you've done your homework very nicely. Just what I should have expected from a man of your, ah, large caliber. But you missed something—not your fault, not your fault at all, I hasten to say. You had to do all this by yourself, so's not to tip me off. You could only follow the major lines. It would have taken years to get the full picture that way. Look in your file again. Look for the minor shareholders, the limited partners. Aren't there a few names that seem to bring up the bottom of the list just about everywhere? Summa Corporation, for example? Ever hearda them?"

Jaye looked up from turning pages. "So?"

Rev. Billy's country accent was definitely returning, this time with an offensive coarseness in place of the elaborate elocution. "So I didn't invent holding companies, you know. If you'd done the kind of job on Summa you did on Golden West, you'da 'rived at HKF III, Ltd. That suggest anything to you?"

Jaye was suddenly very still.

"Not only Summa, neither. Look for Wingflied, Inc. See that one anywhere? Oh, don't bother. That's Admiral Lowbrowski, overta the Joint Chiefs? And guess what. If you dared look into Frogmorton's and Lowbrowski's files, I just bet you'd find Needle's Eye, Goshen, and Jeremiah at the bottoms of all kinds of little lists. So here I am, big fella, come on and get me. Unless you think CRAP can take on not only the Righteousness Coalition, but the administration and the military all at the same time, none of that stuff is ever gonna see daylight."

Jaye said nothing.

Rev. Billy's hard smile softened. "Don't feel bad. You didn't have a chance. But you might have guessed. Just what the hell did you think the Consortium was for?"

Jaye still said nothing. He swivelled his chair slowly and stared out the window. Across the distance, the sky was looking very black indeed. A lightning bolt struck down at the lakefront to the north.

Rev. Billy was continuing. "Okay, so now you know." He appeared to decide something. "Lookit, we are aware of your considerable services to the Consortium."

"I can see that."

"So consider yourself initiated. Hell, Froggy took me for a lot more than that before I learned the ropes—whilst I was *proving* myself. Something tells me that in a year's time there'll be a Jaybird Corp. or some such on lots of little lists everywhere. CRAP has turned out more invaluable than *anybody* thought, but first there's a couple last little things you hafta do."

Jaye turned back to the viewscreen, his eyes narrowed to slits.

"First thing is, of course, the money. Your current payment of $100,000 is still outstanding. It's been budgeted, so we gotta have it, but if you'll do one other little thing for me as well, it'll be the last, I swear."

"And what's that?"

"Okay, I got to fill in the background, so hang on. I need something for the moral values campaign. The Consortium is a brand new political experiment, at least in this country. If the gap between the rich and the poor keeps getting wider as it damn well ought to—what else is the point?—we might need a distraction, a focus for the dissatisfaction, maybe even somebody to blame if it came to that, somebody people just naturally *luuuuhv* to hate anyway. But who that might be is a question of elimination. The Jews've been done to death. Can't keep pulling the same dawg's tail *all* the time. People catch on, and anyhow, they're too organized these days. So who else? The Commies have dried up and blown away, which is a shame. They were great the whole time they lasted." He shook his head sadly. "The black folk get violent real fast, the liberals'll scream bloody murder if we go after the dirty beaners, and as for the slants, they're such capitalists... hell, they're our strongest supporters in some places, been doing business our way for centuries. So who does that leave?" His voice dropped dramatically. "It leaves the ho-mo-*sex*-uals, that's who. Been working out just swell too. Taps straight into the church's tried and true social control method, all those centuries of sexual repression. When you got 'em by the balls, you got 'em. It's a natural. Our people hates 'em already! So far, we've been showing how powerful queers are, how they manipulate the entertainment and fashion industries for their propaganda, how not having children gives them more money and more than their share of economic influence in the retail marketplace—morally and economically destabilizing!—how they lurk unseen in all walks of life ready to undermine Gawd's People by corruptin' our precious children, how much Gawd hates their sin, how everything they say and do challenges His law and His intentions for the world, and how anybody who stands up for them is probably one too. It's been gangbusters! Lately, the liberals just sit right down and shut up everytime we start in, not a peep out of them, just like the old days. Not that they were ever very enthusiastic in the meanwhile, so it wasn't all that tough. We'll get them too, of course, but that's for later. Anyway, you follow me?"

Jaye nodded cautiously. "Yes. I do seem to recall... I tuned into some program about how, while decent, Godfearing plain people are raising offspring in poverty and hardship, the homosexuals are spending their money on piña coladas, boat shoes and black latex novelties. Then, just as the children are finally old enough to start work and repay their parents for all their sacrifices, lurking homosexual predators sexually abuse them into choosing their immoral lifestyle. Seemed rather confused to me, frankly."

Rev. Billy beamed. "Oh yeah. *Changeling Children.* I produced that one mahself. Tons of mail, just tons, all in favor. Why, a crowd in Oklahoma City trashed every fruit hairdresser's and florist's shop in town the night it aired, with a few extra just to make sure they got 'em all. Great stuff, if ah do say so mahself. Yeah, you got the idea. Anyhow, we've gone just about as far down that road as we want to for now. We've reversed mosta the progress ho-mo-*sex*-uals have made in the last thirty years, and it's time to pause. Hell, the wealth gap gets wider and wider, but there ain't *been* much dissatisfaction, yet. The standard time-honored stuff about the evils of taxation and government regulation is still keeping folks in line pretty well, and abortion is still almost enough to occupy them as need something to git mad about. We can't let this pot really boil over 'til if and when we need the mess. We got to hit the redemption angle for a while, Gawd's mercy and love if only they repent their evil ways, et cetera, et cetera, et cetera. This is where you come in."

Jaye raised an eyebrow. "Me? How?"

"You. We need someone to make into a example. He's got to be a unrepentant ho-mo-*sex*-ual, a major sinner, real hard core, but he's got to be attractive—good stage presence, look great on television, *and not too damn nelly.* Good singing voice too, that's essential. He'll be converted in tears on the air, make a emotional speech giving all his money to me, pledge eternal abstinence and preach the evil of his former ways at the drop of a dime in the collection bucket. The folks'll just eat it up. Ideally, it should be somebody already pretty well known, some wealthy pop star, for instance. Think you could get me somebody like that?"

Jaye furrowed his brow in distaste. "Why me? I don't move in those circles."

"Because you're CRAP, dammit! Stop stalling! You got the goods on everybody! Look what you tried to do to me just today!"

The big man frowned. "We're not geared to investigate people's morals, and in the financial area, I really can't see what inducement you offer an established artist with tax problems, by far the likeliest way such a person would come to our attention. Even if the interest and penalty were substantial, going to you wouldn't be much of an alternative, would it? You plan to take *all* his money, I gather, as some sort of public demonstration of good faith. So where's your handle?" He shook his head.

"Well, that is a thing, and I do need him poor so's I can control him every way I can." Rev. Billy shrugged. "Okay okay. I said I wanted somebody famous, but that's just the I-deal situation. It can work almost as well with a nobody, with a little readjustment. All I really need is for him to be sinful, pretty and up past his candy ass in the kind of trouble with CRAP you can't fix just by writing a check. Oh yeah, and he's *got* to be able to sing." He paused. "Maybe a nobody is actually better in one way. After all, I can offer to make him a star. That's a inducement I don't have with somebody who already is one." He nodded. "Okay. Either way will do." He pointed a finger at Jaye. "Here's the deal: a extension on your last payment and increasing cuts in on the goodies from there on out, *if* you get me a queer to save."

Jaye grimaced. "Why not go to the police? This is much more in their line than mine."

"Because we don't own the police. Not yet, anyway. We do own you. Besides, this is purely a Consortium operation, nothing to do with anybody else, and the more we can keep it that way, the better."

Jaye's frown deepened. "I can't say I see an efficient way to get you your result. Although a check on the personal lives of people who come to our attention for financial impropriety would likely require very little alteration in our methods, no one could say how long you'd have to wait for suitable candidates. But doing it in a more organized fashion by identifying people of questionable morality, then looking to see what legal liabilities they might possess would require considerable expansion and restructuring of our operation—all to compromise one person?"

"Oh no, not just one." Barber paused to let the implication penetrate. "Lookit, this is CRAP's opportunity to show us whut it can do. If you ever wanted a piece of the pie, the *real* pie, for you and your people, this is your chance."

"You're serious." Jaye regarded the viewscreen sourly. A moment passed. "And as for this *pie*, I suppose you expect me to trust you about the filling."

"My friend, I am the most trustworthy fella you know, leastways among our good buddies inside the Consortium. But don't take my word, no. Call Froggy. Ask him. I mean it! Call him! He was inquirin' after mah opinion of your loyalty just last week. Do this right and you're in fo-evah! Like to move up, would you? If CRAP develops the way we want, it'll definitely be needing a new Executive Director, not to mention a Southwest Regional Headquarters. As you know, there's new prime space for rent cheap right here in Necktie Gulch," he smirked. "But screw this up, bubba, and I promise you, you'll make the Bird Man of Alcatraz look like a overfed pigeon when we get through with you."

There was a pause while Jaye looked at Rev. Billy, stared out the window at the rapidly closing thunderstorm, and drummed his fingers on his desktop. Recorded birdcalls sang softly in his jungle as the sky darkened outside and wind shifted his windows in their grooves. "I will talk to Frogmorton," he said at last. "I'll need some assurances from both of you. Contractual assurances. If I can have that... I'll let you know."

Rev. Billy waggled a finger at him. "Don't take too long. This month's payment is late already."

Jaye roared, "Don't pressure me, you sanctimonious hypocritical humbug!" He cut the connection with a slap of his hand and sank back, drumming his fingers on the arm of his chair.

He *would* talk to Frogmorton, and right now too. He needed urgently to judge the depth of the Council's commitment to this change in CRAP's direction. Although he regarded homosexuals with distaste, he considered purely arbitrary vendettas against otherwise unoffending private citizens not merely repugnant, but ultimately counterproductive. Once set upon this path, rulers rarely could resist widening the field to include all sorts of enemies both real and imagined, and usually weakened their own regimes in the process. However, if this really and truly were to be the course of the future, it might be necessary to go with the flow, or be swept under by it.

As a further, purely practical matter, investigating people's personal lives in addition to their financial probity would definitely require more budget.

He leaned forward to the comm panel again as the storm broke against his windows with a crash.

The Personal Disaster Department

* * * * *

In Necktie Gulch, Rev. Billy regarded his clearing viewscreen with expansive satisfaction and addressed the air at large. "He's hooked. Gawd, ah just love the way all these thangs are a-coming togethah." Then, a busy executive only now devoting full attention to a subordinate arrived while he'd been on the phone, he removed his snakeskin boots from the French polish of his desktop and turned across it to the being in Herbie Manning's body. "Goddam! This is what all the trouble's about? This ugly, misshapen, con-SPIC-u-ous thang?"

"Small wonder he wanted to unload it, no?" The djinn's voice had a bitter edge. "Is this supposed to be some kind of joke, making me lug this around, not letting me change? I know You ordered it. Your asshole flunkies thought it was just hysterical, screaming their fucking heads off up there in the corner of the room when they made me grant his request. 'Not only will you do it,' that dinoturd Uriel says to me like a mincing queen, 'but you will keep the body safe, and wear it too, until further instructed.' Then they disappear into the ether, shrieking with laughter. I thought it was only a joke until the actual switch, when I found myself in the damn thing and tried to shuck it. *Ugh*, think I, but at least I can take it for a little walk to stretch its legs and see what, if anything, this particular set might be good for. Ha. Further instructions descend: 'You will observe the aspect constantly to ensure it is not lost or damaged,' as if there'd be much I could do to prevent that without being inside. Believe me, I prefer not to watch."

The djinn took an aggrieved breath. "I'm sure it's provided hours of amusement for You and those toadying little creeps of Yours, making me tag along after this bozo cooped up in this like a freak at the feast while he screws everything in sight! Look how I'm laughing! Hah. Hah. Or is this supposed to be another of Your little punishments. I swear, after my *millennia* of faithful service..."

"Aw, cut the crap. It was you took the mortal power and invoked The Bargain. Again."

"It was a holocaust! There was no time for anything else!"

269

"Balls. The Cowboy and the Captured Indian Brave, My ass! You shoulda kept a peephole outa that fantasy to watch for trouble. Standard operating procedure! But no, you had to be into it! You were too busy fucking to pay attention to business! Stupid djinns, anyway." He actually hissed.

The djinn gritted his teeth under the unfairness of this. "It was the aspect! It does that, as well You know! Anyway, I figured there'd be lots of mortals around to get me out again pretty quick. I figured... but You..."

"I did Myself a favor and put you in safe storage, that's what, swept you out with the rest of the trash and buried you in the lake. Then, when I finally get a real use for that sex-machine aspect of yours and bump you loose again..."

"Hey! How was I to know? You spend a century or two in a tin can and see if You don't sing to the first bozo that comes along!"

"Yeah yeah yeah. *Maybe.* I figgered it'd want what they all want, its neighbor's wife and a fat bank account, preferably its neighbor's too. I didn't figger..." Rev. Billy's brow furrowed in deep suspicion. "But you were a lot closer. Maybe you figgered. If you arranged this to wiggle out of My beautiful scheme here and fuck Me up, so help Me, I'll..."

"No master, I swear!" The djinn was alarmed innocence incarnate.

"It's not as if it'd be anything new. Seems like every time I trust you, you end up doing Me in the eye." Rev. Billy held the cringing djinn in a tractor beam gaze a long moment. "Uh huh, *maybe.* Anyway, the damage is done. And how! We got a mortal and a immortal creature welded together. You'll be astonished to learn this is the first time that's ever happened, that we've been forced to give a mortal one of our own immortal aspects and the powers that go with it. *Mosta* you djinns are pretty good at staying outa this kind of trouble. Turns out, this creature ain't stable no way."

Deep in the depths of the djinn's deeply cynical nature, suspicions of his own stirred. Cautiously, he straightened up. "Yeah? Then what gets me is why You let his request go through like that. So what it had never been done before? Surely You could have figured the result would be something strange. You're an Archon! Who knows how the power flows better than You? I wondered a bit myself, but You wouldn't let me as much as explore for a conventional option."

"Didn't matter if anybody could of guessed or not. In the total absence of hard data like we had, a Bargain's a Bargain."

The djinn raised an eyebrow. This was not the metaphysical world's usually meticulous way of doing business. In the elaborate and careful game he'd played with the Archon over the millennia, if it wouldn't have been the first time he'd spiked the Archon's plans, it wouldn't have been the first time he'd been set up, either.

"So then! The Bargain was satisfied, but cracks started appearing in The Balance practically from the moment it happened, and not just local, neither. You got any idea what went on?"

The djinn shook his head.

"That same night, zombies in Haiti started getting up and walking around on their own whack! Then came the capper. The honor guard in Iran heard knocking inside the old Ayatollah's tomb. They ran off to the authorities in holy terror. When the high council broke the tomb open, the old boy sat right up in his shroud, the flesh rotting off his face. He pointed a bony finger at them and told them Allah demanded all their heads on a platter, but first he wanted a drink of water! Gave them a turn, I can tell you. They cordoned off the area, stuffed him back in his coffin, shot the guards so's to leave nobody to tell the tale, and buried him twice as deep as before, all before sunrise. Fast work, thank god. But that's the kind of stuff was happening. This blurring of the line between mortal and immortal embodied in your friend was having echoes all over the place."

"Did he get his drink of water?" the djinn asked innocently.

Rev. Billy glared.

"Okay okay. Anyway, You said 'was.' You mean it's stopped?"

"Uh huh. My brother Archons couldn't figure it out, but They knew damn well the source of the disturbance was over here in My area. Soon as They hauled Me up, I knew what it was, no fooling. Fortunately, Me being the cautious type, I'd already made protecting the body your responsibility, and locked you into it to make double sure. So after the fertilizer hit the flywheel, I ordered you on top of your friend there. My theory was, the disturbance would be less the closer you were to your former aspect and he was to his former body. Close together, the field between the two of you resonates only over a small area. Since then, there's been nothing. So I'm right. Everything's back to normal, and the Others are satisfied."

Rev. Billy looked grim. "Sort of satisfied, that is. Professional courtesy keeps them from inquiring too hotly after the details, but sooner or later, I'm going to have to phony up something to tell 'em. I can do that, but I'm still nervous. Luckily, up to now the only creatures affected have been ones that at one time or another were under Our control, but if there were more incidents, it might echo and spread. What if graveyards started coming to life all over the place like a low-budget horror flick? Total, uncontrollable chaos!—and I gotta tell you, I'm just not happy about the stability of everything depending on a fuckup like you doing what he don't want to. Son, your record don't inspire confidence. I want the matter resolved permanent, and I want it soon, and so should you. The sooner it's over, the sooner the pressure goes off, you can get back into your aspect, and we got a general return to whatever it is passes for normalcy around here." He paused to let this sink in. "What're the terms again?"

"Until it decides to die, as if You don't know."

"Uh huh. Just want to be clear what we're discussing here. So I need to get you back into that aspect and the mortal off to hell ASAP."

"But The Bargain! You can't just kill it. It's not according to its deal! You have to wait. Unless the existence of one of us is at stake, and I don't see that."

"Don't teach your grandma to suck eggs! I just told you, son, if this echoed and spread, the existence of everything could be at stake. I don't know for sure and I don't want to, but I have a nasty little feeling that waiting for this whateveritis to have its fun and get bored is a sure way to find out. So," he paused dramatically, "I'm not gonna, and you're gonna help Me!"

The djinn gaped. "Hold it, hold it! You're telling me the College of Archons knows bupkiss about this!" Despite his suspicions, he had been secretly rather enjoying this tale of Rev. Billy's discomfiture among his fellow Archons and wondering how he might turn his own key position in the business to his advantage—but this was serious. Dangerous too. "Let me get this straight: we're going to shave The Bargain? Deliberately? Without approval from the full College?" His suspicions were confirmed. All his key position might be worth now was a scapegoat's duncecap. He twisted in the trap. "Why? Why not tell Them? So The Bargain's not foolproof after all! Big deal. It's served us well for 60 million years, hasn't it? So add a clause or something!—and blast this freak to photons, immortal and mortal parts both! So I lose my aspect." He drew himself up for a noble gesture. "I have others. I agree to be diminished!"

"Thank you very much. Your offer of grand sacrifice is duly noted, as if your consent would be required if that was what I needed. But it ain't. I got something else in mind for you." He shot the djinn a look so pointed it made him fidget.

"And I do NOT want to bring The Bargain up for re-examination before the Others at this time, or ever, if I can avoid it! Don't you know The Bargain is a compromise? Some of them greedy bastards still ain't satisfied with the even distribution of power We got amongst Ourselves now, even though it's been working like a charm all this time! They grumbled when We hammered it out and They been grumbling ever since, just waiting for a chance to put the whole thing back on the table! They all think what a swell deal We'd have here if only They were Supreme Master. Bah! As if I'd let any of Them rule Me!"

In the djinn's long experience, one Archon was pretty much like another. If there were domination schemes afoot among them, he figured the Archon he was facing was as likely to be as guilty as any other. He thought he knew this just about as well as he knew his own Name, and knew the Archon knew he thought it.

They eyed each other a long moment in mutual distrust. Finally, Rev. Billy growled, "The damn fools—and you too! Talk about the existence of everything being at stake! No, we're gonna fix this ourselves, or at least make a attempt. A kind of attempt. A particularly devious, careful and secret attempt. Luckily, things're stable right now, so we got time to do it right."

Although the djinn was far from convinced as to Rev. Billy's devotion to the status quo, he saw no option but to play along, at least for the moment. He cleared his throat. "So how?"

"We're not gonna do the killing, that's the main thing. Besides just giving us another debt to pay, there'd really be questions to answer then, like you said, about why our existence was at stake. You know there's a review board every time some damn djinn gets in trouble and invokes The Bargain! You ought to. I been in front of it often enough because of you."

The djinn nodded glumly. "But fortunately, at least for You, fulfillment of The Bargain is overseen only by the Archon in charge, which in this case is You. Funny thing, that. I understand why You All want to keep track of why and how mortal power gets taken, but you'd think the giving it back would come in for a look too."

"Like I said, a compromise. Us Archons never like the Others snooping too deeply in Our individual affairs, and of course, if it goes wrong, Everybody notices sooner or later, which is what happened, and what we gotta stop because, the way things are now, slapping down Anybody who looks like He might be trying a fast one is guaranteed easy. Fun too. So, we're gonna manipulate from really far back and make it seem like the deal's been kept to the letter. That'll keep the curiosity, of which there's already plenty, off the wrong questions if there's ever a full-scale inquiry. Win or lose, this business is gonna stay on the reservation. The only djinns in on it are ones I know I can trust. Unfortunately, I got to use you too, because it's your aspect!"

Rev. Billy rumbled dangerously. "I put up with your damned maverick independence this long because I had to, because, in your beginning, it was designed into you on purpose to make you original and inventive, to make you a interesting slave to many masters. Originality and independence go togethah, dammit. And because after, when your original usefulness was over, you knew so many IN-ta-mit details about Us, how each of Us was put together, how Our powers flowed, Our individual strengths and weak points, and, of course, the usual highly embarrassing gossip, that no Archon would let any other absorb you for reprocessing. The only way was to recreate you full djinn and make you strong enough to resist all challenges from other djinns. We drew lots for the job of being your protector. I lost. Oh, I admit your unique qualities have had uses since—like now, dammit!—and you've had the good sense to keep your mouth tight shut about what you know, or I'd have blown your circuits long ago. You're even amusing now and again. You sure can stick it to the mortals sometimes. But I've had it. You been walking a fine line, son, but no more. Them days is over. Because somehow, you always seem to end up doing Me in the eye. But not this time! I need a *new you* for My plans to work, and I mean to have it!" He glowered at the djinn, who sat up rigid.

"You're gonna stay on the team, do what you're told and ONLY what you're told. Play along with Me and I'll reward ya, and if the plan fails, I'll cover for you just like for everybody else, but if this leaks, if one word of this ever gits to the Others—in fact, if you don't do exackly whut I tell you—it won't be a tin can under a pier next time, it'll be a cornerstone! No, worse!"

Rev. Billy's voice dropped murderously. "The danger of you sniggering secrets is a long time over, son. Time's passed and We've changed. Your gossip's antique and your technical knowledge is out of date. Nobody gives a good goddam what you know anymore. So. If you don't keep faith with Me this time, it's the end for you. You will be subsumed." He pointed a finger of power at the djinn. Herbie's body slumped, leaving a glowing image transfixed in place. The image wavered. Trails of iridescent matter drifted out of it toward Rev. Billy's outstretched hand.

Yes, master, reverberated weakly on the ether.

"Good."

The djinn's image recollected and reincorporated itself.

"Now, we had to have this little chat, confidential and private like, but after this, you are gonna stick to him like pigeonshit on a nice clean windshield, got it? And let's just hope Lenin ain't been scratching on the glass while you been here! You are really gonna stay close, and I don't mean just hanging around the ether flipping him the bird, neither. You're gonna be best buddies, and I mean inseparable!"

Rev. Billy's demonstration had had its intended effect. The djinn was patting himself surreptitiously, making sure everything was all there and where it was supposed to be. "But... but how? I make him nervous."

"Can't blame him for that," Rev. Billy sniffed. "I got a plan. Me being Me, I started setting a trap for him even before it became clear what we had to do. That trap is gonna spring, and soon. My original scheme for using that aspect is now gonna be bigger, better and more be-YOU-ti-ful than ever, and it's gonna solve this problem too, all at the same time."

"That must be what all that was about." The djinn waved at the viewscreen a bit shakily. "That bit about somebody sinful and pretty to make into a star?"

"Uh huh."

"So what was all that about wanting somebody famous? Our boy's not famous. Rather the reverse, he's deliberately anonymous! How're You gonna get the right one?"

"That, son, was misdirection. Can't be too obvious about these things. Jaye will look, but he will not find. He told you why. Instead, he's gonna have to dig." He chuckled. "He don't like that, not one little bit. First thing he'll do is get onto Froggy and complain. Froggy will smooth his feathers, but when the time comes, Froggy will *remember*. That's the next place you come in." His face clouded. "You been doing what I told you? Our boy knows what he can do? Froggy turned up on cue, I know."

The djinn nodded. "Yes, master, earlier today. They're banging like bumper cars this very minute, though it makes me nervous. It's not exactly free will."

Rev. Billy waved this away. "You let Me worry about that. You just keep the birdy ready and make sure the cage closes tight when the time comes. Comprende?"

The djinn sighed. "So can I know a little more about this wonderful scheme of Yours for which I'm so goddam essential? Just what'll my 'sex-machine aspect' have to do when You get it, anyway?"

"Hey, what business am I supposed to be in here?" He jabbed a thumb at his clerical collar. "Without sublimated sexuality, it'd have to be some other. I need that aspect for bait, among other things. My plan works on *many* levels."

The djinn was deeply suspicious. "Sublimation is not exactly its forte," he said.

The Rev. Billy's tone turned smooth. "When it's necessary, you'll find out the rest. Seeing as it's you, I don't feel like overburdening you with detail until I have to. You know what you need to for now. So git."

"Yes, Your Beneficence." His tone was both glum and defiant. "Your wish is my command." He stood up and began twirling himself into his cyclonic exit.

"And can the goddam lip!" Rev. Billy swept across the desk in fury and scattered the whirling cloud with a swipe of his hand that sent the djinn sprawling across half a continent.

* * * * *

On a bright Tuesday midmorning, Froggy's limo dropped David at his corner. David was in no particular hurry to get anywhere. Froggy had given him an affectionate see-you-later blowjob before leaving the car at Central Park West, so his sexual pressure was over a low fire, for the moment. He lifted his bag and sauntered the half-block toward the Harrington.

He dropped it on a neighboring stoop, fished out an Export Special and sat on the steps to smoke and enjoy the golden September day, only to discover himself unsettled despite it. But why? Leaning back on his elbows, he exhaled, and watched the smoke catch on the breeze and drift away shining in the sun.

They'd had a gloriously long and leisurely Labor Day weekend at Froggy's upstate retreat—hiking, fishing, swimming, tennis and endless screwing in the magnificent countryside overlooking the

Hudson River. At night there'd been all 52 rooms of modest country hideaway for indoor play. Except for the usual Secret Service men patrolling the perimeter, the servants had had their holiday too. Froggy considered himself an egalitarian, at least at home. Such good PR, and, with David around, so prudent for his reputation.

David had also had the chance to investigate another of his new talents. Froggy turned out to be an excellent pianist. They'd spent much of the evening time together at his Steinway while David explored the, as it happened, abundant glories of his new singing voice. Froggy was considerably impressed, and had offered to arrange an audition for a talent agent. Flattered, David still declined, explaining that, in view of their relationship, it was probably better he remain as anonymous as possible. This convenient half-truth pleased Froggy even more.

Although impressing Froggy with his sacrifice was indeed the intended effect, David experienced no actual regret at passing up the chance of a singing career. He liked the life he'd created for himself just fine, and he'd already had unmistakable intimations what an annoying distraction his sexual pressure might be in any other line of work. While he hadn't ruled out further exploration of his other talents some day, they served him very well as things were, allowing him to amuse his clients in many ways.

So why had he this sense of... of impending doom? Or was that too dramatic? Might it not be merely the inevitable letdown of returning to everyday life after a palatial weekend—a particularly virulent and depressive case thereof, perhaps, but still? Above the bustling urban street scene, sunshine glinted off Mid-town towers. A long slow wolf whistle cut through traffic and recalled David's attention to groundlevel, where, across the street, a man stared at him and rubbed his crotch. David smiled ruefully at the thought that *this* could have become ordinary humdrum everyday life.

He got up, flicked the butt of his Export Special neatly into the gutter, and took his bag up to his room. He threw open the windows and flopped on the bed, hands behind his head.

Then there was Froggy himself. For a man in late middle-age, he really was in splendid shape. He swam and played tennis, worked out regularly and had steamrooms in all his residences. When David fired his libido up to full-power lavender intensity, he was a passionate lover. Yet, no matter how well preserved, it was still merely another late middle-aged body. David knew he was beginning to tire of it, and of Froggy himself, even though the man did know how to be perfectly charming, especially, again, under David's mental manipulation.

David frowned and lit another Export Special. Yes. *That's* what bothered him.

When, weeks earlier back at Broadway & Wall, he'd first recognized the person opening the car door for him as the Chairman of the Consortium Council, he'd known there were dangers involved, particularly the obvious one to intimacy with a famous person: that he might become fairly well-known himself. He'd had a murky sense of other dangers too, which was now clarifying itself alarmingly.

The obviously prudent, sensible course would have been to close the car door, cool Frogmorton's aura down to dull gray disinterest, and blend into the crowd. Instead, the shock of recognizing the Chairman of the Consortium Council had knocked him off balance, and the habit of command ingrained into Froggy's voice had compounded the effect. Almost before he'd realized what he was doing, he was indeed closing the car door, from inside.

Even then, he'd been so sure he could avoid the difficulties with his, after all, only recently discovered abilities at mind control. *Pride,* David reflected, *Stupid, foolish pride.* The man's aura, icy with disapproval as it had been at first, had offered an irresistible challenge, and the chance to make a conquest of the world's most powerful man had tickled his vanity. *I must have been completely crazy!* With a man like Frogmorton, that kind of game took a tremendous risk. Froggy turned out to have fearsome strength of will, something David now supposed he might have expected in the master of the Consortium Council.

Of late, his efforts at controlling Froggy had become worryingly difficult. Their relationship had gone on to an extent and reached an intensity David had never allowed with any other lover—entirely too far, it appeared. The manipulations he practiced on people's minds seemed not to exist in a vacuum completely under his control as he had thought. The longer these went on, the more they had resonations back and forth throughout the subject's being, resonations more in keeping with that person's true personality and thus very much more difficult to control. Froggy had developed a middle-aged last-fling passion for him of bewildering intensity; *a latter-day Hadrian and his Antinoüs* was Froggy's explicit thought. Resisting the man's desire to own him, to lock him away as a personal plaything, was becoming increasingly difficult, at least if he still wanted to keep Froggy's attraction to him alive. So did he?

He frowned. The dangers of ending it altogether also had become apparent. In common with most autocrats, Froggy had a strong streak of paranoia. David found this ever more difficult to control. The possibility had to be considered that, without the balancing force of Froggy's love for him, Froggy might begin to see his continued existence as dangerous, and, unlike ordinary suitors, the Chairman of the Consortium Council could command not merely private investigators but armies and police forces both secret and otherwise. That he might be tempted, however reluctantly, to use his power to eliminate forever the possibility of exposure was not a good thought. While David supposed his conditional immortality would render any attempt at outright murder ineffective—which would be a great thing if it both resolved Froggy's interest in him and allowed him to escape—the Chairman was also free to indulge his paranoia in ways with less positive consequences: prisons and mental hospitals were two grim but not inconceivable possibilities. Or what if Frogmorton did have him killed, and interred before he could slope off and vanish, for instance, in a trunk at the bottom of the ocean?

In short, David was becoming more than a little paranoid himself. He thought of his wildcard request, his request for luck, for events to be influenced in his direction. Would it prevent such things from happening? He hoped so, but, as he'd yet to see any identifiable indication of it working, he definitely preferred placing his trust in more active management. When they were together, he turned the fire under Froggy up to full-blown worshipping infatuation, and, before they parted, did his best at dialing him down to an insistent itch to see David again soon, cooperative, loving and unfrustrated, and the realization David needed to be utterly free for that to happen.

These adjustments had worked well enough in the beginning. Yet, as they went on, their invasive nature caused a reaction far more in tune with Froggy's character, and as his possessive and paranoid urges grew, the adjustments themselves became increasingly difficult. David sensed an ever more insistent black tinge to Froggy's aura during their otherwise idle chatter, usual among lovers, about each other's associates and the normal routines of their lives. Froggy vacillated between wanting to say more if only he could be sure David would never repeat it and wondering whether he might have said too much already. In his blackest moods, he actually worried David might have told someone of their relationship, this despite David's oft-repeated, most soothing, adjustment-laden denials!

The more David thought about it, the more paranoid he became. The day was surely coming, he thought, when Froggy no longer would be able to resist the desire to keep in constant vicarious touch with him, and, not incidentally, reconfirm David's nil potential as a security risk. The temptation to put David under surveillance was surfacing in Froggy's mind more and more frequently, usually rationalized by the equally strong desire to ensure David was protected from all possible harm. David combatted this in two ways: by playing Froggy's very paranoia off against it—if he placed David under surveillance, their relationship certainly must become common knowledge among the watchers—and by infusing Froggy with guilt at this lack of trust in his Antinoüs.

An unintended (but not precisely inconvenient) side effect of this guilt was that, every time Froggy felt it, his parting gift for David became larger. In this way, the parting gifts had become a measure of the man's paranoia, and lately they'd become worrisomely large indeed. The day approached when David would no longer be able to engineer any kind of balance. He must act, and act now. He needed Froggy to lose sexual interest in him, in fact, to lose interest in him as a person altogether, yet wish him well and have this overpower his inevitable paranoid urgings—a delicate, ticklish adjustment. David frowned. He didn't really know if he could do it. He wished he'd had a lot more practice at this sort of manipulation before applying his uncertain skill in this most crucial situation.

He sighed. Ready or not, he had to try. Reluctantly, he concluded he'd probably better disappear at the same time, just to be sure.

Damn. He'd settled into New York so beautifully. He sighed again, and eyed his wall collage regretfully. He supposed he'd have to pay for a new coat of paint, at least if he wanted to keep a welcome open for himself here at the Harrington. But he could afford that easily enough; he'd already given the hotel a deposit for it. Or perhaps he could pay a year or two's rent in advance and keep the room as a permanent New York residence. Dammit, he had no idea how long he'd be away; if he clicked into other places as well as he had here, it might be many years. He'd never intended to settle permanently. He wanted to travel. Come to think of it, he had been feeling a trifle stagnant lately. Given Herbie Manning's powerful propensity to become overly attached to mere places and things, the whole business was possibly fortunate after all. Suddenly, he felt better.

He lit another Export Special and settled back. So where would he go? London? Amsterdam? Rome? Foreign travel appealed strongly, but, if his adjustments to Froggy proved faulty and the intelligence community were put to search for him, he'd be a lot more conspicuous as a foreigner abroad. Where then? San Francisco? Los Angeles? Boston?

No, too obvious. Then he remembered how just the other day someone in a bar had been telling him what a good time was to be had in Texas, of all places, how it had a really uninhibited and horny gay scene. He'd been skeptical at the time, but now... Nobody would look for him in Houston, and even if they did, he might blend in nicely. Texas, said the same source, had lots of blonds. What the hell, if he didn't like it there, he could always move again in a month or two. He'd be old news by then, if he had ever been news at all. He paused a moment longer to turn it all over in his mind. No better idea came to him. Very well, Houston it was, at least for the moment.

As usual after one of these big decisions made itself, he felt reassured and revitalized. His brain had weighed the evidence, juggled the alternatives as best he understood them and spit out a conclusion. Yes, things were still working in his favor.

A plan formed. He'd see Froggy again in a day or two. He didn't know precisely when; as always, he would have to await the Chairman's pleasure. Whenever the call came, he'd make his adjustments and split town—and if he were leaving town, probably within the week, he had things to do, dozens of things. Prosaic things. He flashed on the heap of dirty laundry on his closet floor. Might as well start there, he supposed. He grinned. It'd been weeks since he'd cruised the laundromat.

He began tossing stuff out into the room, going through the pockets and making piles of colors, whites, jeans, etc. He was almost to the bottom of the heap when he discovered it: a crisp new $100 bill. He held the jeans whence it came at arm's length. These were the jeans he'd bought even before his transformation, the ones he'd worn when he'd first arrived in New York. They'd been just a bit *too* tight for comfort; he'd replaced them as soon as he could.

Suddenly, he didn't feel much like spending the day washing clothes. He'd take the stuff to the laundry and go shopping instead. Found money demanded it. He smiled. He loved shopping, the more so as the rigors of living light and fancy-free had constricted his opportunities dramatically. So what should he buy? What did he need—some toiletries in travel sizes, a new case to carry them, some light reading for the train—lots of things! Carefully, he made a list, decided where he'd buy each item, and headed out. Of the places he'd listed, Marino's Bookstore was farthest north. He'd start there and work his way south, so to juggle the heaviest load the shortest distance.

Thus, David stepped neatly into the trap Greg Whitbread had prepared for him. Upon presentation of his purchases for payment, the arrival of an unsmiling salesclerk at each elbow took him completely by surprise, and the subsequent forced march into a small bare room took place in a haze of shock. As he turned in outrage, the door swung to in his face with the businesslike click of a serious lock. A voice through an intercom invited him to "pray take a seat" pending the arrival of Authority.

David fought down adrenaline and annoyance, and tried to think clearly. What was going on here? Was it Froggy? This did not add up. Surveillance was the man's thought. David had had no hint Froggy would proceed immediately to arrest him, and if he had anyway, why would he choose here and now when he had his choice of opportunities to do it more privately elsewhere? For that matter, how could Froggy have known he'd come to Marino's in the first place? David himself hadn't known until an hour since. Nor had he been followed. With his recent paranoia, he'd kept his sixth sense alive for watchers and followers. So what was it?

On the theory a good offense might shake loose a useful clue, he went to the intercom grille and demanded to call a lawyer. He threatened criminal prosecution for unlawful restraint, civil litigation, damages actual and punitive, adverse publicity and everything else he could think of until he ran out of breath. The grille did not reply.

Bolts secured the room's sole chair to the floor. Scowling, David settled in to sulk. Interestingly enough, his sixth sense tingled. A bright lavender aura glowed nearby. A definitely horny somebody watched him. As it had now been some time since last he'd cum, this set his libido in motion. Now wickedly out of temper, he considered taking his cock out and waving it at the spy camera up in the corner.

Better sense ruled for once. No point aggravating this already alarming situation. He'd hold out as long as he could. If someone behind that camera liked him, chances were matters might move on their own soon enough. He turned up the lavender fire under the watcher, just to see what would happen.

Sure enough, not more than a minute or two later a fussy small man in a deep purple glow opened the door and extended his $100 bill. Stiffly, the man explained they'd identified it as counterfeit but, upon detailed examination, this proved not to be the case.

So it was all just a screwup, an unnecessary screwup over what turned out to be a perfectly legitimate $100 bill. David hated bad service from people whose whole job was taking his money, and, in point of service, this marked some sort of nadir. He had been insulted, assaulted, abducted, imprisoned. His time had been wasted and his libido engaged, a fact that would now complicate the rest of his afternoon's program. Though maybe not radically; the little man was running his eyes up and down, and seemed to be trying, unsuccessfully, to stop himself from hazarding a tentative no-harm-done? little smile. David almost backed him into the nearest vacant office, then decided not. Libido aside, the little man represented a system which treated perfectly upstanding customers like thieves until proven otherwise, and David resented it. Moreover, not merely had the bastard sparked this inconvenient horniness, he had actually had him caged! Such a person did not deserve to live, let alone have sex with *him*.

David snatched his bill and brushed past the man nose-in-air, ignoring his aching crotch as best he could. —Was this all a bit hasty and unfair? He had been in and out in record time, not enough for the advertised Authority to appear. Perhaps the man's appreciation of David's physicality had been worth some goodwill in the form of a more detailed look at the bill. Which was only another reason to get out of there: in case Authority in fact arrived and involved him in more complication. The department store that was his next stop had a famously cruisy tearoom; he figured he would make time to service his horny business there.

This plan lasted only as far as the salesroom. Approaching the door, he found the very last person he ever could have expected. There in the flesh, his old nemesis, Little Adolph, held a book upside down and ogled him from amidst a deep purple glow so blazing it nearly obscured his face. In David's current mood, angry and horny on top of it, he did not stop to ask what Adolph might be doing there. He assumed it was a wonderful, lovely coincidence, truly a gift from the god of vengeance. Adolph desired him, did he? On the fly he threw a hook deep into Adolph's mind and breezed out the door. This definitely required a change of plans. No department store john for Little Adolph, no sir! He'd take him back downtown and torture him properly. This was gonna be grand, indeed.

It all seemed to be working perfectly. He felt Adolph stumbling out the door after him and saw him grab a taxi as soon as his own pulled away. After that came a minute of touch and go before David felt the presence re-establish itself behind him. Let him scramble!

They headed downtown. Adolph was still hot on his trail as he entered the Cock Robin. Then nothing. Ten minutes passed. Twenty. Adolph did not come in! Yet David felt him somewhere nearby.

He almost went out of the bar to fetch him, but decided against it. *Fuckit. Why bother with him, stupidshit no guts closet queen! I'm through with him! He's too scared to cum in after me? No problem. He'll torture himself the rest of his life wishing he had! I can live with that, I'm sure.*

Whereupon, David settled his hook as deeply as he could in Adolph's mind and forgot him. He solaced his now painfully pressing horniness in an encounter with the bartender in the otherwise empty bar, after which, time lacked to go back uptown and resume his interrupted shopping program, at least with anything like the degree of leisurely enjoyment he'd planned. He decided to get ready for the day's dinner appointment instead, to have a bath and see how long he could sustain a hardon in all that lovely hot water and tickley foam before he cummed all over the fucking place, then maybe see if he couldn't better his mark, maybe keep trying until he did.

Little Adolph had gone when he emerged from the bar. Two other guys watched him, but with more ordinary, typical regard, the sort he was used to as an everyday matter, it appeared. With his mind on other things, David paid them small attention and promptly forgot them.

A day later, he had a new problem. The same two guys, the short Latino and the tall skinny black dude, were foremost in what was almost a small army following him around every minute of the day. He knew himself to be always in the mind of somebody or other in a coldly analytic way he recognized instantly as surveillance. One day more and the followers actually had moved in next door. The tiny glass eye of their camera appeared in his baseboard and he felt them watching him. The disaster had overtaken him even sooner than he'd expected. This time, compute it did: it really was Froggy. Who else could mobilize such an army? Exactly as he'd feared, the man's paranoia had gained the upper hand. David had waited too long.

He forced himself to consider the matter clinically. These watchers were very professional. Secret Service? But wouldn't merely employing them compromise Froggy when they got an eyeball on David's life, subtracted two from four, and arrived at the extremely large amount of extremely private time they already knew he and Froggy spent together? Froggy wouldn't dare use them. Or perhaps the Service had decided all on its own to run a background check on the Chairman's frequent visitor—but Froggy'd specifically told them not to, had told them it was completely unnecessary, that David was the son of two very old and very dear friends, that he'd known David all his life, etc. etc. etc. It didn't seem likely they'd disobey direct instructions. So, if not Service, who were these guys? After the past months, David considered himself a connoisseur of surveillance. The Latino and the black guy had seemed like street people when he first saw them, then had recreated themselves as way-out fashion gonzos, perhaps like the finest private investigators money could buy.

Another interesting question: if this surveillance were at Froggy's behest, how was he insulating himself? Who was running it for him? The only logical candidates were Froggy's butler/valet and chauffeur: they had been his private bodyguards for years, since pre-Consortium days; their loyalty was absolute; they knew the particulars of Froggy's new relationship already, the only ones who did; and just as Froggy's paranoia had become ever more difficult to suppress, so had their suspicion and jealousy of David for his growing closeness to The Boss; they would enjoy organizing this persecution.

Most important of all, what would happen when David and Froggy met? How could the identity of David's client be concealed from so organized and professional an outfit? Unless... unless Froggy had determined to put their relationship on hold while he satisfied

287

his curiosity; prudence surely would suggest this as the proper course—but without as much as a word of excuse to David? The man was testing him. That was the only possible explanation.

So how long could Froggy hold out? Upon reflection, David didn't believe it would be all that long. In the weeks he'd known him, his hold on Froggy had become too strong to be stretched very far. A few days at most, and David would have a chance to work things his own way.

Until then... that he'd never covered up to Froggy what he did for a living was his damnable vanity, again. When they'd met, Froggy had considered prostitution a scourge, a major embarrassment to the innate morality of capitalism and the capitalist state, an excrescence. Yet, under David's mental management not merely had the man been able to set that aside, he got a vicarious thrill from screwing the sleaziest of public whores. He couldn't get enough of it, and David had gloried in telling him about it in vivid detail, the while enjoying a thoroughly delicious sense of pride in manipulating such a strongwilled man, of which a certain part of the charge had been suppressing Froggy's native possessiveness and paranoia, forcing him to share his beloved with the world at large and like it. Now, however, David had a most disturbing feeling that screwing the Chairman of the Consortium Council simultaneously with every other john in town really had been pressing his luck.

So what was he to do? Not have sex? He would go insane, and Froggy definitely would know something was up if his surveillance showed David living celibate. At the very least, David would show himself a liar. Now, Froggy himself lied whenever he found it convenient—what political man didn't?—but, naturally, hated being lied to. So, as a measure of his devotion, he had resolved, most unusually, never to lie to David, to keep their relationship pure, which thus assumed for him a clean, almost holy aspect laden with commitment. David had taken the most scrupulous care always to hold up his end, not to trip Froggy's hairtrigger bullshit detector and shatter this agreeable fantasy. The man would dissolve into self-righteous outrage, besmirched and betrayed. Never again would he want to trust anything David said, and controlling that would add one more thing to the pile David already manipulated. —And that was the best case. In the worst, Froggy would see plots everywhere, his weakness suspected and exploited by enemies real and nameless who employed David as an agent. No, foregoing sex was not an option.

Days passed. He did his best to act normally, ignore the surveillance, and make sure Froggy's name never passed his lips. He abstained from having so much as a political discussion. He wanted the Chairman to see his reputation was safe no matter what David did, or, more accurately, continued to do.

On the other hand, he didn't want to be *too* normal. He supposed Froggy would be mortified if his absence weren't as much as noticed. David imagined his johns and casual partners marked for death, victims of Froggy's jealousy, and nearly lost his hardon. He avoided screwing in his room, directly under the camera's eye, but had to now and then. He began to feel caught up in a war of nerves. Who would crack first? Would Froggy break down and see him before he did something foolish?

He hit on a way to tweak Froggy's heartstrings and perhaps hurry things along without threatening the man's insulation. Because he assumed there was a tap on his own phone enabling whomever listened to get the numbers he called from the pitches of the beeps, when he tried Froggy's most private number, he did it from payphones, a different one each time. Under the circumstances, he did not expect the line to be answered, nor was it. When the answering system clicked on (no outgoing message, not even a beep; one ring and a click), David murmured simply, "I miss you," and hung up.

Whenever his own phone rang, he leapt at it, certain it must be Froggy. It never was. Three days passed, four, then five. Froggy hadn't let so much time go by between visits since they'd met. Ye gods! Considering the strength of the itch David had left in the man's mind, his self-control must be iron!

David's heart sank. Perhaps he'd misjudged. Perhaps Froggy's possessiveness had won out; perhaps he'd *hoped* David was lying about his life, merely spinning stories for his entertainment.

Perhaps he was so appalled and outraged by the reality that he had determined to renounce David without another word—and if his possessiveness had won out, why not his paranoia? Perhaps Froggy even now, right this very moment, made the reluctant, nay, agonized decision David would have to be removed forever as a potential threat. The more David thought about it, the more tempting it was to believe this only could be the case.

Although the prudent, compromise course of action would have been to continue his activities, but on a reduced scale, he couldn't stand to be alone, and *that* meant having sex. In this way, he found himself having even more than usual. No matter how awful it must look to Froggy, his terror would not let him quit. He prowled the town each night until he was ready to drop. The constant fear any passing car might screech to the curb and disgorge thugs to arrest him, or worse, was still better than waiting in his room, where, when utter exhaustion drove him there at last, dread of the traditional three predawn knocks kept him tossing and turning until past sunrise each day. He was short on sleep and sick with fear, but, in his fevered imagination, to be alone meant death.

At last, on the morning of the seventh day, he awoke from some muddled angry nightmare with tension coiling his stomach into knots. He went into the bathroom, closed the door carefully for the camera, and retched until his throat was raw, a hell of a way to start the day.

He knew he simply could not go on another minute. He went out into his room to face the camera and beg it come get him, cease this agony of suspense, kill him if that were its mission, but end the waiting no matter what. He had just taken breath to begin when the phone rang.

"Hello, Davey, it's me." Froggy at last!—sounding as if nothing whatever had happened.

Froggy's conceit, a not uncommon one among lovers and even merely good friends, was never to use his own name on the telephone, simply to assume his voice would be recognized. Very well, mindful of the surveillance and of the probable ill wisdom to overstressing the man's insulation, David would pick up his cue and not use it, either. "Hi! I missed you!"

"Me too, lover, oh so much. Sorry. It's been agony every second, but I was called out of town very suddenly. Sorry I couldn't let you know."

Oh, right. This just had to be an act. But David's sixth sense required proximity. It worked through walls, but not on the phone. He couldn't even see the man; Froggy's most private line, his bedroom phone, naturally did not have a viewscreen. He *sounded* perfectly genuine. Christ, what a performer the man was!

But then, David supposed, the travel part might be true. At least, he knew nothing to contradict it. The news had mentioned nothing of Froggy's activities in the last week, which was normal; the Consortium saw no advantage to advertising the extent of its control, a point its growing hegemony over the media allowed it to carry. —And a trip would have allowed Froggy to indulge his curiosity without a period of abstinence not already unavoidable. How convenient.

"I've managed to clear my schedule for this evening," Froggy said. "May I see you?"

"Of course!" David gushed in relief. "The usual time? About eight?"

"Yes, that's fine. Shall I send the car for you?"

David's paranoia scented a trap. The mere idea of confinement with Froggy's hard-eyed chauffeur, whom David knew must have a share in managing the surveillance, reeked of one. "Uh. Well. I was planning to have dinner up in your neighborhood, anyway. I can just walk on over." With his mind on traps, he hit on a bold stratagem. "By the way, do you think I should be using your service entrance?" he said, on the theory that, if Froggy were planning one, the maze of back passages in the Byzantine 19th-century hive containing his private and confidential city retreat would provide the perfect setting, and foreknowledge might force a rethink of the entire plan.

There was a pause. "But whatever for?"

David relaxed cautiously. Very well, if he were overplaying the trap idea, he could exit by showing he was conscious of the confidentiality issue and looking out for it himself. "It's just that I've been there a lot, lately. Your hallman might be getting curious."

"My dear boy! He's been thoroughly vetted, and is extremely well-paid to do no such thing. As always, you may use whichever of my entrances you please." The man seemed to be amusing himself. "No, actually, I would prefer not to have you negotiating the back passageway. It's narrow and rather creepy even by day, as I discover every time I try to get quietly to my car. Though your concern for our privacy is always welcome." What? Did that mean something? "Very well then. Until eight."

Froggy hung up, coincidentally having left nothing on Greg's tape to identify himself as anything other than an obviously wealthy and potentially paranoid john. Without viewscreen transmission, the watchers had no picture, and while their equipment did reveal the telephone numbers of those who called, Frogmorton's was protected. None of them tumbled to the voice, either. It may have been the last they could have expected to hear. The team only knew it wasn't Manning's, and, for the moment, that was enough.

David put down the phone. At least the waiting had ended. His plan could now move forwards. He spent the day making such preparations for his departure as he might, given the conditions of the surveillance. He did some last-minute shopping, and cruised the laundromat after all. Back in his room, he announced casually to the air that, seeing as fall was coming on, he might as well get his summer things out of the way. This allowed him to fill a suitcase with essentials. In the bathroom, out of camera-range, he packed up his toiletries.

In the interest of acting normally, he forced himself to eat and take an early evening cruise, though when it came right down to it, he was much too nervous to do more than beat off in one of his favorite tearooms. At last, the time came to leave for Froggy's. He decided to walk. The exercise, he hoped, would calm his nerves.

As he led the small parade of himself and his surveillance uptown, he supposed Froggy's lobbyman must be very well vetted and paid indeed for Froggy to have this much confidence in his discretion never to reveal which apartment would be David's destination—but then, the fellow had to be Secret Service. Rather a nice bonus for the other residents of the building, David thought. Good help was so hard to get these days.

Although the warm summer twilight soothed his nerves, his paranoia returned in the elevator. What was that look the lobbyman had just given him? Was it a trifle colder, more supercilious than usual? Would there be a goon squad waiting for him when the doors opened? He steeled himself. There wasn't. He pressed Froggy's bell and prepared for battle with the beast.

From the moment he entered the Chairman's presence, he had him fixed firmly in his sixth sense. Froggy met him in his opulent drawing room, arms outstretched, clearly awaiting the usual rush of passion when David turned him up to flaming violet. As they made love, David conducted his examination at leisure and in depth. The result surprised him thoroughly. He found no sign of duplicity in the man, at least not concerning David himself. There were, as usual, plenty of indications that, in the Chairman's ordinary relations with the world, he lied, cheated and manipulated as a matter of course, behavior ingrained to the point he seldom thought about it. Plainly enough, he would never have attained his position otherwise. However, he still seemed to regard the largely distinct area of his mind David had created to contain the authorized version of their relationship as a refuge from the subterfuges of ordinary life just as David had intended. Against all expectations, David found no indication that, in his own case, the Chairman's paranoia had moved him to action. The unmistakable conclusion was that he had nothing whatsoever to do with the surveillance.

This surprised and relieved David considerably. He was so caught up in the past week's travails and so grateful Froggy was not responsible for them, he almost abandoned his readjustment plan. Then he remembered deciding on it even before the surveillance began. Further examination revealed significant indications that, even if Froggy's jealousy and paranoia were still controllable, they might not be for long. David's private preserve in Froggy's mind, the size of which had become a continually renegotiated compromise between his will and Froggy's, was smaller than at any time since the beginning and seemed even more unstable than he remembered.

David realized the bewilderingly intense middle-aged last-fling passion he thought he had created in Froggy was, in fact, natural—at least in a way. Clearing the snakes from David's private preserve had allowed profound passion to stir Froggy for perhaps the first time. Yet, true, fulfilled love cannot last forever, or even very long. Inevitably familiarity must cool it and replace it either with common interests, experience and acquaintances; pleasant companionship and productive partnership; or, if these things be absent, with boredom and indifference—or, likeliest in the present instance, David thought, with renewed condemnation and suspicion at the turpitude of David's profession. Froggy's passion had been David's essential ally in keeping open his private preserve. As this passion dissipated, paranoia and guilt became Froggy's ruling forces. Possessive, jealous and mistrustful urges of several sorts pushed inwards from all sides and receded only under the greatest pressure ever. That he and Froggy had been separated for the longest time ever did not help—maintenance was reaching the point it soon would need to be continual—but then, travel was necessary in the Chairman's job; he would be away again, and for longer. David never would be able to count on seeing him twice a week as hitherto. Perhaps, he reflected, he had been extremely lucky already. It was all so complicated!—and the longer it went on the more complicated it became.

As they lay relaxing, wordless and spent, David proceeded to put Froggy gently to sleep, and as he slept, reduced his own preserve to zero. With this essential irritant gone—the grain of sand at the heart of the pearl—the oyster of Froggy's mind should cease to take action against it, he thought. He made himself someone the Chairman remembered dimly, permanently resolved from his life with no ill will. In fact, he left a considerable reserve of good will for himself there just in case, albeit with no firm commitment. That, he decided, would have kept his image too near the surface, an intrusion at odds with the Chairman's character which might trigger a reaction.

It all seemed to go easily and well. At last, he surveyed his handiwork and was satisfied. He locked in his changes as best he knew how, put on his clothes and left. He noted the parting gift waiting for him on the hall table was the largest yet. Even if Froggy hadn't been responsible for the surveillance, surely he, David, had acted just in time. He felt wonderful, as if an enormous burden had been lifted.

He indulged himself with this feeling all the way to the sidewalk, where, down the block, the short Latino had, apparently, just buried his head in a doorframe to light a cigarette. David hailed a cab and, with the corner of his eye, watched the Latino scramble into a waiting car.

Yes, he did still have a problem. While it wasn't the huge disaster he'd imagined, of what kind was it, exactly? Perhaps it was after all merely an improperly adjusted jilted john or a wife pursuing a divorce or custody action with unusual fervor. He'd simply confuse the watchers and split. Ditching these assholes would be no problem for one of his accomplishments. The days when he'd had to run and hide from his pesty suitors and their detectives were long over. David felt perfectly confident of his ability to have these guys tripping over each other at a moment's notice, or even see him where he wasn't and follow some stranger while he made his escape.

Still, he ought not ignore the possibility the surveillance might have some other cause, for instance, the valet and the chauffeur acting on their own. He chuckled. Endangering the Chairman's security merely for their own private vendetta? Oh, they'd be in a heap of shit if Froggy found out, as, instantly, David decided that, if they were responsible, find out he should.

Even if they weren't, it might be prudent to discover, if he could, just whom he'd led to the Chairman's lobby, even supposing they'd never get any further. He glanced at his watch. After eleven! Had he really spent that much time in Froggy's mind? He'd planned to go home for a good night's sleep; tomorrow clearly would be a long and interesting day. Yet, if he were to wrap this business up before he left, it would have to be tonight.

He rapped on the shield and gave the driver the Cock Robin's address. Yes, he'd take them there. Lately, one or another of the watchers always came into the bar with him. He'd corner whomever it was tonight and do an in-depth analysis. That seemed the obvious next step.

He changed his mind the instant he entered the bar. There in the back, Little Adolph blazed with deep purple glory. *I'll be damned,* David thought. *The chickenshit pigfucker finally got the balls to cum after me, and it only took a week. Look at him straightening his damn tie like a goof, and he's not even wearing one!*

David shrugged off the surveillance. After his tribulations of the past week, he had no intention of dealing with it when here on the hoof was prime butt to kick. If the surveillance reappeared when he got to Houston, he'd deal with it there, though now he knew Froggy wasn't involved, he was willing to bet it wouldn't. Licking his lips in anticipation, he settled into the serious business of vengeance. The very idea of having Adolph in his power made him crave retribution for all Herbie Manning's unresolved issues—the indignities Herbie had suffered from the world at large and from Adolph in particular—and the terrifying powerlessness he himself had felt in the past week. Making Adolph pay for it all, right here and now, was completely irresistible.

His barbuddies crowded around. He stared down the bar at Adolph. Yes, his hook was still there itching in Adolph's brain. He yanked it, none too gently, either. *Let the coward make the first move!*

His plan was simple. He would screw with Adolph, oh yes. So Adolph had humiliated him with lying sniggers about his supposed sexual advances? Adolph would make the advances this time, very public ones. So Adolph had never wanted him around? Now, Adolph would have him close as close got, and pay good rates for the privilege! Meanwhile, sex would give David the chance to ram his hook in as far as it would go. On the morrow, he'd disappear, leaving Adolph to carry a torch for him the rest of his life, a torch too heavy for anyone to bear and so hot Adolph could only be consumed. Thus would he be destroyed. David savored it.

Sure enough, Adolph gulped and sent him a beer, to rolled eyes and snickers from the assembled company, which David let go on a long long moment. Finally, he sauntered down the bar and got into the serious business of examining Adolph's mind. Yes, mountains of sneakiness were in there—that was Adolph all over, wasn't it?—but at the moment this was totally buried under horniness, and on his slight acquaintance with the inside of Adolph's head, he could go no deeper. It didn't matter. He controlled himself and played it straight, only patronizing Adolph a little—he couldn't resist a little.

He did notice his surveillance hadn't turned up after all, and back in his room with Adolph, for the first time in days no inquiring mind looked at him from the next room, wanting to know. Although no time existed now to stop and decide what this meant, he was vaguely disappointed. Involving Adolph in whatever trouble this was had been an attractive sidelight to the entire affair.

He relished every second of it: the sexual encounter in which he rearranged Adolph's mind, the way Adolph hung dotingly on every word of the lecture that dissected his slimy character to atoms, then split those. Only the attempt—too subtle to succeed, really—at getting Adolph to admit the homophobic things he'd done to Herbie and beg for absolution failed, but small loss. David could live without buttercream flowers on this already completely satisfactory cake. All by itself, pumping his big cock up Adolph's virgin hole was a dream come true. He'd never dared screw a virgin before; he'd been too afraid of damaging them. This time he simply did not care. He made Adolph want it, made him *ask* for it, and performed with fiendish intensity. Another fantasy fulfilled. He even offered to let him stay the night so he could do it again.

Then Little Adolph dropped his big bombshell. When finally he worked himself up to mentioning Herbie Manning, David went into shock. This was deeply weird. That Adolph should describe Herbie Manning as a personal friend was ridiculous. That he'd had an appointment with him anywhere, let alone the Cock Robin, was a flat out lie. What was going on here?

What was Adolph saying? He was describing Herbie Manning. Gangly? Goofy? Bad hair? Adolph sure didn't sound like such a friend; that much was real enough. Adolph's aura was definitely brown, but shot through with streaks of truth such as this and such as the fact Adolph certainly did seem to want something, presumably Herbie, awfully badly. Separating the truth from the bullshit was impossible.

Then, looking for Herbie's picture, Adolph fumbled his wallet. It landed on the bed, almost in David's lap. In the half second before Adolph snatched it back, a gleaming gold and white CRAP card stared David unmistakably in the face. The absence of the surveillance suddenly made chilling sense. *They don't need to be here because he is!*

Although Adolph was rambling on again, this time begging shamelessly, David was too worried to enjoy it. He'd had a terrifying thought. The djinn! Had he a part in this? Had he been around again, meddling, playing games in Herbie's body? Had he made Adolph's appointment for tonight in the bar? As knowing the truth about that seemed urgently important, David declared his intention to mention the supposed missed appointment to Herbie if he turned up.

Immediately, Adolph's aura turned the deepest brown David had ever seen, and no, Adolph certainly didn't want that. So the appointment was one of the lies. David relaxed slightly. That was something, anyway, one big and completely uncontrollable variable pushed into the background.

Then what was going on here? He needed to think! He wanted Adolph out of his space, and right then too. Seeing nothing wrong with the obvious way to achieve this, he promised rush delivery of Herbie, which, not incidentally, still wouldn't be until he himself was safely out of town. This genuinely overjoyed Adolph, the sap. His aura glowed gold with sincerity and satisfaction.

At last, Adolph was pointed at the door. David checked again to make sure the hooks were securely planted; vengeance aside, it couldn't hurt to have a mole in the enemy's burrow if worst came to worst. Adolph was such a tool.

Would the fucker *never* leave? When finally he did, David closed the door, locked it, and fell back in relief against the mirror framed on its inside.

He pulled conclusions at random out of the whirl in his head. If the surveillance team and Adolph were a CRAP unit looking for Herbie... He flashed back on Adolph's first appearance here in his new life. At Marino's! It suddenly seemed to him that Adolph's purple blaze very well might have been the same purple blaze he'd felt in the detention room. He'd thought at the time it belonged to the fussy potbellied store manager who also liked him, but he'd had no reason to think otherwise, and he'd been pissed and not paying strict attention. If that had been Adolph... CRAP specialized in financial crimes... The $100 bill...those had been his first pair of new jeans...my god the bill must have been one of Herbie's... Counterfeit? Of course not. He knew exactly where Herbie had gotten it: The Amalgamated Consolidated Confederated International Bank, no less! *Oh shit.* The surveillance had begun immediately after...

While he couldn't quite understand why that perfectly legitimate presumably untraceable $100 bill should have given him away, he put it all together accurately enough. He groaned out loud. His past life had become so remote, the possibility it might still trip him up hadn't occurred to him in months. The hot rush of identity with his former self he'd had at the chance to avenge Herbie's indignities melted away. He felt framed for someone else's crime.

So what was he to do? He certainly had found out about the surveillance after all. Cut and run wouldn't play now, not with CRAP. CRAP might not have been very well known to the general public as yet and its powers might still be largely amorphous, but Herbie had been well enough plugged in to know tracing fugitives was one of its particular specialties. He'd be one forever! Ditching the watchers would do him no good. Wherever he turned up, they'd find him. They had a lead now on the cash machine thefts, and he was it! They'd nail him for receiving stolen goods, maybe even as an accessory, unless he told what he knew of Herbie Manning, and how could he do that?

Spending years in the federal pen with a sexual obsession and a faggot label definitely did *not* appeal to him. So how could he get free? He had only one card to play, and knew it. There was but one place he could appeal for help against CRAP. In common with all hustlers since time began, when serious trouble loomed, his first thought was to run to Daddy. Only this time Daddy might not even remember who he was! He groaned again, and cursed dumb luck.

He saw no choice but to risk it. He dialed the number.

Froggy's sleepy voice came on the fifth ring. "Yes. Frogmorton. This better be good."

David gulped. "Uh, Frog... Mr. Frogmorton sir? I'm sorry to bother you at this late hour. It's David sir. David Alexander?" He held his breath.

There was a long long pause. Without a viewscreen David had to imagine the frown on the other end. "David? Oh yes, David." The sound came of Frogmorton yawning. "My, it has been a while, hasn't it?" Another pause. "Ah, just how long has it been, anyway?"

About three hours, you old fool!! To the phone, he said, "Oh, quite a little time sir I guess. As I say, I'm sorry to bother you so late."

"That's all right, I suppose. I seem to have dozed off quite early this evening." A rustle came, as of Froggy rearranging himself on his silk sheets. "So, considering the late hour, what can I do for you, ah, David?"

Nothing that requires getting out of bed, huh? David took a deep breath. Here came the tricky part. "Well sir you did once say that, if you could ever help me in any small difficulty, I should call you anytime." He heard a sigh on the other end and rushed right on. "Oh, it's nothing much, not for you sir, no. I should think about one small phone call from you would do it sir, please?"

David hated this. In desperation, he tried finding Froggy's aura, over the phone, hopeless.

"Very well, David. If I can help you without compromise, I shall. Tell me about it."

David felt humiliated. Three hours ago, Froggy would have danced naked across the George Washington Bridge for him. Now... Worse, he'd done this to himself, dammit! He gave Froggy a gymnastic version of the facts vaulting over djinns and transformations and turning other somersaults as required. He told Froggy at top speed how a one-time-only acquaintance—he thought the name had been "Manning," but after all this time couldn't be sure—had left a briefcase, a locked briefcase, in his room; how he, David, had put it away for him, but he'd never come back for it; how now there was a CRAP man from Chicago asking about Manning; how David had just cracked the briefcase open to find it chocked with money, oh thousands and thousands of dollars sir; how he'd only seen this Manning, if it was even the same person, the one time and knew nothing about his business, but how he was afraid the CRAP people would think otherwise—a boy in his position had problems with the police—and could David please arrange to give the briefcase to him, good, kind Froggy who'd been so nice to him, because poor little David didn't want to go to jail, no sir. David ran out of breath and gasped.

He swore he could *hear* the gears turning in Frogmorton's head. "From Chicago, you say."

"Yes sir."

"Thousands and thousands of dollars."

"Yes sir."

"And you haven't touched this money, have you?"

"Oh no sir."

"And you know nothing that would help find the person who left it with you?"

"Nothing at all sir."

"Well, strangely enough, I believe you. I do seem to recall you as a good honest boy, most unusual in your, ah, position. Very well. Close that briefcase up again and wait. I'll call Morgan Jaye in Chicago and see what's what. I dare say that, if you do just as I instruct, there may even be a reward in it for you. Stay where you are. I'll call you right back. Ah... what's your number?"

David rolled his eyes. The readjustment certainly had been a success. He gave Froggy the number and hung up.

He emptied the closet, ripped up the linoleum and got out the briefcase. Quickly, he broke the locks, then taped the thing back together to make it fit his story.

He lit an Export Special and sat down to wait. Five minutes passed, then ten.

He became uneasy. The extreme weakness of his story to Froggy began to prey on him. Why would anyone bring a briefcase with "thousands and thousands of dollars" in it to a casual encounter with a hustler, let alone leave it behind? Resect this as you might, it suggested a far closer connection with this Manning than he'd given the Chairman to understand—who would have doped this out already, just as soon as he'd roused himself from his sleepy stupor. He imagined Frogmorton on the phone with Morgan Jaye even now, getting the details of Manning's cash machine thefts. There'd be a goon squad at the door for him and the briefcase within minutes! Nothing he'd left in Frogmorton's mind would prevent that, not where such a serious and intriguing crime was concerned.

They'd haul him in for questioning. No matter what he said, they'd examine every facet of "David Alexander"'s past life—and find nothing! Would they let it go at that? Not a chance. His position was horrifying.

He panicked. He'd been very stupid indeed. He'd have to run for it. Yes. He'd head straight for the terminal, put the briefcase in a locker, mail the key to Froggy and get on the first train anywhither. They'd never stop him. He could make people look right through him. Meanwhile, they'd have the money back, and Froggy could take a "no harm done" line and make them forget all about him.

Would Froggy do that? Yes, he thought the reserve of good will he'd left in Froggy's mind might be just enough for that, if he himself were out of reach. While he wasn't all that sure about it, it was his only hope.

Damn! That was what he should have done in the first place. He never should have called Froggy at all! He could have been on a slow boat to Borneo before the Chairman had even gotten the key! *Shit!* What a stupid panicky bonehead he'd been!

Fortunately, he was mostly packed already. He flew about the room getting the rest of his things together. Money! Damn and double damn! He sorted through his pockets and turned up about $1,500. He'd been saving the trip to empty his safety deposit box for last thing before he split. That wouldn't work now, not at this hour. Well, what he had would get him out of town. He'd make more fast enough wherever he went, and if the surveillance did follow him—he gulped—it wouldn't matter anyhow.

At last, he was together. He was checking himself in the doorback full-length mirror and giving his hair a fast combjob before grabbing his bags when it happened. The djinn walked through the door. The thing was, it did not happen to be open at the time. David saw his reflection shimmer, change form to that of Herbie Manning and stride straight out of the mirror at him. He jumped back a foot and just caught himself giving a small shriek.

"Boy, you sure do know how to make an entrance," he said, and sank down on the bed.

He watched the djinn saunter the room. Herbie's body looked larger and more substantial than it had ever felt to wear. The djinn moved it with an air of assurance and power Herbie had never had. Herbie's height, which he himself had always tried, unsuccessfully, to render inconspicuous by stooping, was now commanding. The way the djinn used it, Herbie's body looked as if it could be almost attractive. *But then,* David thought bitterly, *it's only drag to him. He didn't have to live his life in it.*

"Love what you've done with this room," the djinn sneered. "So tasteful."

David recovered a little of his self-possession and became wary. *He's not here to discuss interior decoration,* he thought.

The djinn looked at him. "You're right," he said, "I'm not."

David stared, then remembered their encounter on the street. *Oh great,* he thought, *on top of everything else, he reads minds.*

"Don't you?" the djinn asked. "Yes, you do, at least sort of."

303

David tried to see the djinn through his extra sight, but got only a confused blur of flashing specks and the hum of power. He'd barely begun formulating the question when the djinn answered it:

"That's because I'm much more powerful than you. All you can see is my scrambler."

"Stop that! Reading my mind, I mean! People finishing my sentences is irritating enough, but if you're going to start them too, we'll *never* get anyplace. It'll drive me nuts!"

"Sorry, kiddo, just doin' what comes naturally."

"Then at least pretend! It's like rape or something. Obviously, I need a scrambler too. How do you do that?"

The djinn looked up sharply. "Forget it! And I mean right now! You are currently the weakest metaphysical—quasi-metaphysical, excuse me—being on this planet. Any one of us could smash your defenses like paper, and if you lose a duel like that, you'll get more than a Heidelberg scar."

David stared. There were several new concepts here. He took a cautious approach. "Thanks for the warning."

"It wasn't for your sake, believe me." The djinn pulled out the desk chair and sat it astraddle. "You have one of my aspects, complete with a certain amount of my essential power, in fact, most of the power that was mine in the beginning. Naturally, I have an interest in what happens to it, and when you're done with it, I'd like it back intact."

"Uh, pardon me, but I have a stupid question."

"What a shock."

David paused a second, eyes narrowed. Evidently, the djinn was going to humor him and let him ask it. "What, exactly, is an aspect?"

The djinn was already nodding with the gloomy satisfaction of one whose worst expectations have been amply realized. "That's right, *now* he asks the essential question, instead of when it would have been useful, when I all but begged him to. *Then*, he refused to be deflected from doing the wrong thing." He dripped disgust. "You really didn't know what you were asking for, did you. You fucked it after all." His face puckered in contempt. "You mortals are all hopeless. It's unbelievable how deep this mess is, and all through the usual combination of mortal ignorance, idiocy and greed."

His lip curled. "I suppose, if you're to protect yourself and my aspect, you'd really better know exactly what you've done." He sighed. "Very well then. It's not easy for us djinns to manifest ourselves in the mortal world. The bridge between is provided by the mortal and metaphysical powers, which are like two kinds of foreign currency, each convertible into the other. The quick and dirty way for us to appear in the physical world is simply to infuse some handy inanimate object with our own power and animate it. We can make pretty much any object—a rock, a cloud, a lamp—come temporarily 'alive,' can make it develop a face, eyes, ears, a voice, whatever we need to produce an interface, but because doing this is a load of intricate detail work, the modifications don't have to get very extensive before they take up our whole attention all by themselves. One way to ease this is to use an object that's already got arms, legs or a mouth if we need them—a statue, a figurine, whatever's handy. Considering the sad state of popular taste, you can imagine the amount of time most of us have spent as kitsch.

"The problem is that, while this can make the thing possible, especially on short notice, it isn't always appropriate, especially if our purpose is to communicate with mortal beings or masquerade as one to play a part. When rocks and clouds start talking, people tend to think in terms of divine visitation, and when the bricabrac leans over and taps them on the shoulder, they doubt their sanity—all well and good if that's the idea, but if it isn't... you can see there might be times when we want to appear as ordinary living mortal beings.

"This is tougher. There are several options. Naturally, we can always do the same thing to living beings we do with inanimate objects—just take one over—but if we do it to you people, there's all this pointless dithering about 'demonic possession' afterwards. We can be kind of heedless sometimes too, and damage to the being while we're inside violates The Bargain. Strictly verboten. Major pain in the ass."

He shrugged. "Another option is to take a mortal body just at the point of death, like I've done with this cast-off thing of yours, which otherwise would be an inanimate object since you're elsewhere, and which now lives, breathes and pumps its (yuk) blood only at my command. You can see the logistical nightmare in finding just the right one when you need it." He shrugged again. "Another solution is to make some more serious modifications on an inanimate object, to take that rock or whatever and make it completely resemble a living being. The way to do this is to organize the changes into presets, sort of like software for one of your computers.

"Trouble is, this takes too much power and effort to be worthwhile for one-shot effects, and if you intend to reuse the thing, you have to lug it around or store it someplace and keep track of it. Although we can draw objects into the metaphysical ether as a bubble of physical substance that can be stored indefinitely or moved from one physical place to another according to laws that have nothing to do with physics, that doesn't mean it can't be a pain.

"For about the same investment in effort and power as it takes to modify that inanimate object, we can produce a counterfeit from scratch. Technically, we use that same process to organize air into a fully functional simulacrum of a living being which afterwards can maintain itself by life's normal processes for as long as we need it. We call this an aspect. It's the most useful option. Aspects last forever, can be customized exactly to the purpose with any appearance and any set of powers and abilities we choose, can be invested without worry because all the power that operates them is our own, are reprogrammable into new ones if they become obsolete, and can be shut down completely when not in use."

David couldn't help running his hands over his body and giving the very solid-feeling flesh a cautious pinch or two. "Excuse me, are you trying to tell me that, since, apparently, I have one of your aspects, I'm made of air? That's ridiculous! The other day I cut myself and I bled—briefly, to be sure, but I bled. So what's the essential difference between me and somebody who looks, feels, sounds, bleeds, etc. like me, but is made of actual flesh while I'm not? If it looks-waddles-quacks like a duck, it's a duck!"

The djinn grinned wickedly. "Only to you ducks, which is the point."

"How many of these things are there walking around, anyway?"

"More than you think. Each aspect has its own appearance in your world and its own set of abilities and powers—attributes. Djinns like me who spend most of their time operating in the physical world inevitably collect a large closetful of aspects. Although we ourselves normally occupy any aspect in use, they also can be given separate existences as semi-autonomous beings—demidjinns. The advantage of this is that I can be in two places at once. The disadvantage is that each demidjinn is obviously much weaker than the whole, and runs a serious risk if challenged to a duel by a stronger entity. The party losing the duel is enslaved. That aspect (or what's left of it) and the power that ran it ceases to belong to its original owner. It can be controlled by or even subsumed into the winner. As you can imagine, we are very careful about subdividing ourselves into demidjinns." He frowned at David accusingly.

David's head whirled with questions. To the one, *why is he telling me this?*, an obvious and extremely unsettling answer occurred. "Uh, and you're trying to tell me some other djinn's after it?"

The djinn shook his head. "If only it were that simple, The Bargain would protect you. Unfortunately, it's much worse. You've run afoul of an Archon. Which means setting yourself up for a challenge is definitely not the way to go here. While blowing your circuits isn't necessarily in His plan, it won't bother Him if He has to. In fact, I'm not sure He wouldn't consider that a plus."

David stared.

"You just keep yourself open to any and everyone who wants a look. It may be humiliating, and you will definitely have to do what you're told, but you can't be challenged if you don't resist. What the fuck, you can just join the club, because that's how the Archons control us djinns!" He adopted an air of patient resignation as he waited for the question.

"So refresh my memory. What's an Archon, again?"

"At least you remember I mentioned them." He sighed. "The Archon's power exceeds mine by as much as mine does yours, and more. If He wants me to do something, I have to do it, no matter what. In return, my service is exclusive. I answer only to Him, and the Others can go blow Themselves. I'm protected. My only other choices are to make a deal with one of those Others to do His service instead, if He'd have me—but They're all alike, so what's the point?—or fight a duel that would last about a trillionth of a second maybe, have my circuits blown into babbling imbecility, and end up in yet another damned bottle, this time forever. Do you get we're talking bigtime now, baby?"

David did, or thought he'd better, anyway. "So what's he want with me? Just to engulp me?"

"Wrong." The djinn jumped up and began pacing. "He doesn't give a damn about you that way. Compared to Him, you're too weak to be of any value, not to mention dangerously unstable! He would much prefer you didn't exist at all. He wants that aspect for a scheme He's got cooking. He's decided that, if you don't cooperate, it will fuck Him over. Therefore, non-cooperation is not an option."

"Unstable? What do you mean, I'm unstable?"

The djinn stopped pacing and sighed. "You still don't understand *anything* yet about what we are and our place in things."

"Actually, I have wondered about that a bit."

"I'll bet." He sighed again. "What did I say we were before?"

"Something about hopes, dreams and innermost wishes?" David raised an eyebrow.

"Uh huh. A metaphor, I said—a rather selective one, anyway. I see you guessed that much." The djinn took a breath. "I'll tell you what we really are!" He struck an heroic pose. "We are Chaos! We are war! Social upheaval! Dangerous ideas! Tyrannous oppression! The mortal world itself creates and empowers us. We are the manifestation of its collective dissatisfaction, and we are eternal! You mortals have an irritatingly strong tendency to settle down, carve out cozy little niches for yourselves, teach your kids to think the same garbage you do, in short, to stagnate. But it doesn't make you happy! Only through us do you have the chance to evolve and become whatever it is you're going to become. We shake the foundations, upset people's clichéd existences, break down established orders, motivate rebellions, and in general blow people off their fat comfortable butts! We work for the glorious cause of Chaos because only from Chaos comes change!"

"Change? You mean progress, grand ideals, all that shit?" David was incredulous. The djinn as social reformer was definitely a new thought. "All right, what 'dangerous ideas' have *you* ever had?"

The djinn shrugged. "Search me. I'm in the Personal Disaster Department, myself."

David shook his head. "Okay, you're telling me that, not only is there some sort of collective consciousness, but it gets up and flies around on broomsticks?"

The djinn sat down and crossed his legs. "No need to be insulting about it. How to explain this..." His brows contracted in concentration. "Your mortal power—your lifeforce—arises directly out of your physicality. They're bound together indissolubly. All other things being equal, it ceases to exist when you die, and vice versa, but while you live, your lifeforce has sympathetic vibrations beyond physical measurement—at least, no one's invented a way to meter us yet. I don't say they never will. In something like the way musical notes have overtones you can't hear that both arise from them and determine their character, you define us and we influence you in return. We simply crystallize, reflect and reinforce your dominant characteristics."

David frowned. "Unhappiness, dissatisfaction, chaos, okay. I can see there's a lot of that around. So what about all the other universal human feelings? What about curiosity?"

The djinn was shaking his head.

"What about generosity? Mercy? Pity? Compassion? If you reflect us, aren't they part of you too?"

"Don't be disgusting," the djinn snapped. "Oh, some of those things do reach critical mass sometimes. Once in a while there's an effect you just can't explain any other way, but generally, the amount of all that stuff put together not motivated by unhappiness and the desire for change wouldn't animate even a garden gnome."

"Love! What about love? Doesn't love have some echo in your world?"

The djinn laughed. "You're kidding! In terms of unhappiness, desire for change and pure aching misery..."

"Okay, okay," David groaned. "I get it. Humanity hates the things it loves."

"And loves the things it hates. Like I said, we're eternal. When the struggle disappears, the romance is gone. Though now you mention it, of all the other things which sometimes reach critical mass, pure, unconditional Love puts in an appearance more frequently than most. *I* haven't seen Her in centuries, though, which is fine. Silly bitch screws up everything. I hope She's dead."

"I bet. So what else?" David thought. "Faith! What about faith in god? Religion. I don't believe in it, but lots of people seem to get quite a charge out of it."

The djinn sighed contemptuously. "I despair of you. Tell me what's *caused* more misery than religion! Or original thinking in opposition to it! We're very big in religion. Gods were our first and maybe our best dangerous idea. Think about it. Don't people believe in religions to alleviate various human miseries? It's a cheap fix. Faith justifies the meaninglessness of existence, and absolves them of responsibility for it. It's an anodyne for exploitation, which, then, by no coincidence, can be inflicted without limit! Hey, it's all some god or other's plan. Belief allows them to beseech that god to solve their problems for them, and saves them the necessity of doing their own thinking, which most people will beg to avoid. People are incredible. You can manipulate them, lead them by the nose absolutely anywhere and into anything, even slavery, and it's easy! You merely promise to tell them what to do here on earth, with eternal life as their reward. But wait, it gets better. You don't have to deliver on that reward until *after they're dead*! They don't even ask for proof you'll be able to! They're anxious to take your word, though the word of dead people in books is better, which might be understandable if said doornails were showing any actual signs of life themselves, but they're not, and the longer it's been since they have been heard from, the better it gets. I have never figured that out."

"No afterlife, huh?"

"Sorry, you make your own heaven and hell right here, and we're the only angels and devils you get, or deserve, the ones you make yourselves."

"Can't say I'm much surprised. Always figured it for the ultimate case of wishful thinking. So okay, let me see if I've got this straight. When people are miserable, they naturally want things to change. You and your boss, this Archon thing, you feed off this desire for change."

The djinn held up a hand. "Not 'feed off.' We are it, its resonation on a metaphysical level. That's where the hopes, dreams and innermost wishes metaphor comes in."

"Metaphor? Sounds more like hyperbole to me. If I have this right, you go around making people *more* miserable. This increases the desire for change, and by no coincidence, strengthens you at the same time!"

"It's two sides of the same coin! Unhappiness *implies* the desire to do something about it, and vice versa!" The djinn's exasperation began to show again. "You know, some ideas you claim to value were created in this service, ideas like liberty, equality, democracy, social justice. When people have always been oppressed, sometimes they can't realize it until you tell them, and even then, you have to show them too. You have to provide examples so they can see oppression working in the light of the new idea. Then they're convinced. It takes a lot to get people moving."

"So according to you, people don't know how miserable they are until you rub their faces in it? People are satisfied with their lot until you dangle something better in front of 2them?—and when they get that, you dangle something else? It's ghoulish! We struggle and yearn endlessly at your instigation, but you're the only ones who benefit! We only get to keep on struggling no matter what. We mortals strive and die to support your immortality!"

"And make yourselves a royal pain in the ass too, especially when you refuse to understand! Look, we help you do only what you yourselves want done. You fight us every step of the way, but get what you want the sooner for it, and that's the only way it will work.

Oh, sometimes we can influence the range of options, but if you don't want it, it doesn't happen. It's a cooperative system. We've been around in one form or another since the very beginnings of life on this planet. I said we arise out of your physicality, but it's every bit as easy to analyze it the other way around—to say our existence gives off sympathetic vibrations that transcend us, and that those vibrations constitute a necessary precondition for life on the physical plane. If I wanted to be chauvinistic about it—and make no mistake, more than a few metaphysical beings are—I might even say we are the primary creatures here. After all, we're permanent and you're not. But there's no way to prove that, to decide which came first, the dinosaur or the egg. Ultimately, your kind and mine are different halves of the same process. We are creating you at the same time you are creating us and both sides have veto power. If you ruin this planet for life, we'll disappear right along with you."

"Sounds like you'll be more than equally responsible too! The difference is that, while you know all about us, we know nothing about you. While we influence you collectively, you influence us individually! That makes us a good deal less than equal partners. It makes it a patronizing and manipulative system—and by the way, while I've heard an awful lot about how you can take mortal life whenever it's necessary to preserve yourselves, I haven't heard *anything* about how we might do the same to you, which presumably we can if it's an equal and cooperative system. No wonder you've kept us ignorant of your existence all this time! You guys are just a bunch of exploiters! Parasites! I despise you, and I despise your low regard for human life. I want no part of it!"

The djinn raised one of Herbie Manning's eyebrows, and clapped his hands in applause. Once. Twice. "Your scruples are noted. They are also hypocritical, considering your whole wonderful new existence here is powered by Nate Bummer's life and nothing else."

"I had a choice? You threatened me. You turned into something out of Stephen King, which I want you to know you do very well, by the way—it's *you*—and told me if I didn't choose, you'd reach

312

inside my mind and give me something whether it was what I'd choose or not. So I chose."

"Bluff. You mean you didn't see it?" The djinn smirked. "The Bargain says the mortal power must be returned by mortal choice for mortal purposes. Where'd've been the mortal choice if I'd done that? I had to make you take things seriously, and I did, to my cost, as usual, and it wasn't as if you got something you didn't really want. You wanted it, all right. A lot."

David looked at the djinn with distaste. "You tricked me."

The djinn shrugged. "Hey, I didn't have to twist your arm all that hard, you know! On the whole, you've been having a perfectly wonderful time, haven't you?—and if you let me tell you what you need to know to get through this crisis here, there's just a *slight* possibility you'll be able to go right on having it. So you might as well get used to your new set of ethics, because, in important ways, you're now one of us. Besides, this time, you've got *no* choice."

"Great. Just super all around." David looked up at the djinn. He couldn't help noticing the djinn's eyes. Herbie Manning had never had eyes like that. Large. Black. Hypnotic. With a tiny burning star in the depths of each. He tore himself away. "So, according to you, not only am I unstable and about to be totally screwed over by this Archon thing, but, to get that way, I've had to feed off the pain, misery, and oppression of the human race?"

The djinn very obviously gave up. "Animals too."

"Oh thank you very much."

"Hey, don't thank *me*!"

"Well, I didn't wish for *that*!"

The djinn waggled a finger at him. "Oh yes you did! And you'll kindly remember I advised against it too!"

"Excuse me! All I asked for was a new body!"

"No, you asked for *my* body."

Illumination dawned. David groaned again. "I would have settled for one *like* it. It didn't have to be the very same one."

"Uh huh. Obviously. But you didn't say that, you stupid sonuvabitch. You said, and I quote, 'I want a new body, and I want the one you appeared out of the cookie box in yesterday.' Your exact words. And then you wanted all that extra stuff: regeneration, conditional immortality, and very specifically, the ability to control how people *feel*! So not only did you ask for the aspect, you asked for the attributes, which confirmed it. You got 'em too, which is why you can see auras and influence mortal minds in certain very basic ways." He leered.

"I didn't mean that literally! It's been handy, I admit, but what I had in mind was just a goodlooking body lots of people would find attractive!"

The djinn rolled his eyes at the impenetrable greed and stupidity of mortals in general.

"So how was I supposed to know? This wasn't covered in your lecture! And hey, you guys read minds! Are you telling me you didn't check it out to make sure what I wanted?"

"Not allowed when The Bargain is being fulfilled. No intervention at all. Some advice about consequences, maybe, when they're definitely known, and that you got, but no contradiction and no interference. Strict adherence to the literal wording of the request. You appeared to ask for a metaphysical aspect. That'd never been done before, not in all the millions of years we've been in business, which is why it wasn't covered in the lecture. Later, after you spoke, nobody knew what consequences there'd be for sure. It might have worked out okay. So you weren't warned, and we went ahead and gave you what you *asked* for." A shadow fleeted across the djinn's face. "That's the official line, anyway. There were even two of my loving fellow djinns in the room with us to make sure your stupidity got put into effect just as you ordered it."

"My stupidity? Seems to me there was enough of that to go around!"

"Hey, I'm not real happy about it, either! My party body—my *original* aspect—in the hands of a demidjinn! The object of an Archon's greed without me being in it to defend it properly! He's got a second agenda for it too, one I definitely do not like!" He scowled. "*You* may have had a choice, but *I* didn't. Firestorms disrupt the ether right at the interface with the physical world. We get cut off, trapped and evaporated. I used up a mortal to protect myself, and you know the terms."

The djinn sighed. "Usually, when it comes time to give the power back, the recipient wants wealth, dominion over his fellow mortals, a sex object, something like that. No problem. There are established ways to use the power to give it these things. Even when it wants to employ the power itself on an as-needed basis—for instance, to turn everything it touches into gold, as one *particularly* stupid and greedy mortal had it—we just give it the power on tap to use for the purpose specified, a sort of personal bank account under the mortal's complete control. The power passes back into the physical world, nice and clean. But no. I'm always getting stuck with guys like you who have to be different. That aspect drives everybody nuts."

"So why don't you just do that?—I mean, skip the special effects, the personal appearance and the lecture. Just give mortals the power, maybe with a little card attached—"Greetings From Your Metaphysical Friends" or something—so they know what they're getting, and let them wish for what they want until it's gone. Wouldn't that solve your problem?"

"Uh huh. Until the first time one of you idiots got up on the wrong side of the bed, absentmindedly wished the leader of some country he didn't like would kindly go sit on a Stinger missile and light the fuse, and fucked up half the world by mistake. Even so, I've thought of it, believe me." From my perspective it would be a plus, but that's just not how The Bargain operates."

David was getting impatient. "Who made this stupid Bargain, anyway? And who with? Pardon me, but it doesn't seem to have been particularly well thought out if I came out unstable! I'm still waiting to hear about that, by the way, and about the consequences. Tell me! I think I have a right to know!"

The djinn's face clouded. "Don't talk to me about rights, demidjinn! If you didn't have my essential aspect, Bargain or no Bargain, I'd..." He sighed again. "Oh fuckit. The Archons made it, and I don't guess they made it with anybody but Each Other. It's just something They doped out along the way to keep Themselves in business."

He got up and started pacing again. "The Archons were here first. You might think of Them as the metaphysical aspect of evolution. Of course, you could also say evolution is just the physical aspect of ethereal development." He shrugged. "Anyway, They were pretty primitive and powerless in the beginning. In fact, in the *very* beginning, there was only One." He grinned. "Kind of funny, imagining my Archon as a kind of super-amoeba. Tyrannosaurus Rex, I can see." He sat in the chair again. "As life got more complex, the One got more sophisticated and powerful right along with it, and when things really got going, It subdivided, pretty much fell apart under Its own weight. The Archons were the result, the lot of them, and not a happy one. They fought all the time, and somebody was always grabbing power from the mortal world to gain an advantage. That didn't work out so hot. Sure, that Archon would come out on top, but it also meant gross problems in The Balance. Less mortal life led to horrendous automatic corrections. Changed the course of evolution around here more than once. In the last big battle, about 65 million years ago, there were massive extinctions, both from the Archons' borrowing and from power exploding back into the mortal world to correct The Balance. The result changed both worlds forever."

"Wait a minute. Are you talking about when the dinosaurs went extinct? Scientists say that was an asteroid impact. Big one."

The djinn nodded. "All actions in the metaphysical world have physical consequences, and vice versa. Must have been awesome to watch. I've never seen an Archon battle." His eyes flashed. "After that, the winning Archons, the ones still largely intact, decided to see if They couldn't take a hand in Their own development. Maybe They were getting smarter too. They collected the remnants of the destroyed Archons and enslaved them, apportioned them into weaker subsidiary beings—us, the djinns—and set us to doing Their dirty work. Figured we'd be too weak and too busy quarrelling amongst ourselves to threaten Them again, I suppose. That's also when They made The Bargain: no metaphysical being, Archon or djinn, can take the mortal power except to preserve his own, and then it has to be given right back before he can rejoin our world. This way, the Archons keep us djinns in our places, and both worlds evolve together in an orderly way."

"Ummm. Isn't that pretty galling for you, I mean, as totally devoted to chaos as you are and all?"

"Uh huh. It has indeed occurred to some of us djinns to band together and overthrow Them. I'm told we actually tried it once, about 10,000 years ago, but, the story goes, we only managed to cause enough trouble so that afterwards things got *adjusted*, several new Archons with fewer djinns each to look after, so everybody's under tight control." He spat on the carpet in disgust, a shocking, ugly gesture. "I don't know if it's true. I was made just after." Tiny plumes of smoke arose from the blob of spittle on the carpet. There was a sizzling noise. "But no djinn remembers anything before that. The Archons sure do, though. Those bastards are the key to everything. Or maybe it's all a lie, just a story They float to keep us from trying it. Maybe They just got bored and decided you mortals needed a civilization to play in, and this organization was better for that. I dunno. What I do know is that you can't get off as much as a decent duel these days without some high mucketymuck wanting to know what's going on." The sizzling stopped as the spittle burned itself out, leaving a burnt spot about the size of a quarter.

David raised his eyes from the carpet. He found himself trembling with stress—an unfamiliar sensation in his perfect new body. He shook out an Export Special to calm his nerves, and looked around for matches. "It's all so... so transcendental. Everybody shifting, subdividing, re-combining... You guys bear the same relation to the Archons as demidjinns bear to you. You're actually, well, demi-Archons, aren't you?"

The djinn glared at him. "Unflattering, since comparisons to the oppressor are always invidious, but basically accurate, which is surprising, considering your general level of stupidity."

"You know, I think I've had about enough of that stupidity shit." David patted his pockets after matches. "As far as I can tell, it's you guys who've screwed up. I'm *still* waiting to hear about how I'm unstable and about the consequences. So why don't you tell me about *that*, goddammit, instead of all this pissing and moaning about how stupid I am! Tell me what I need to know! That is, if you can manage to figure out what it might be!" Still in search of a light, David opened drawers in the bedside table.

"Here, let me get that for you," the djinn said. A blinding beam of light flashed from the fire in his left eye and lit the first inch of David's cigarette, which David dropped instantly. It bounced under the bed.

"Oops," the djinn said calmly.

David went down on his knees and fished it out, uncomfortably aware this pointed his upturned behind squarely at the source of the effect. He scrambled back up onto the bed.

"Comfy?" the djinn asked.

"So...?"

"Uh huh." The djinn spoke slowly and deliberately. "When I made you, I had to use the power I was obligated to return, the power of The Bargain, to weld my aspect onto your brain and the upper part of your spinal cord, to hook them into their new support system and preserve them from the normal effects of aging."

David stared.

"That's right, I cored you like an apple."

"Then... what's in there?" He gestured at Herbie Manning's head.

"Besides some bypass work on the plumbing, pretty much the same as always was. Nothing."

"Now just a goddam minute. You're telling me I've been butchered, and if only I'd made a slightly different choice of words, this wouldn't have happened?"

"Butchered?" The djinn was indignant. "Personally, I would describe it as the very finest sort of microsurgery. You were lucky to have me. The result was trouble anyway, but that's not my fault." He shrugged. "The problem was your own, unique, original mortal lifeforce. This arises from the sum total of your physicality, and affects what that physicality can be. It had to be kept intact to avoid

318

violating The Bargain. We are, remember, prohibited from diminishing your mortal power in any way, lest it upset The Balance. Also because, otherwise, your central nervous system and the aspect would assimilate one another to produce a truly hybrid creature, thus polluting both of them, warping each in the image of the other. Strictly speaking, the aspect then would no longer fulfill your request (nor would you be the you who'd made it), and eventually would be returned in damaged condition—like loaning a favorite shirt to someone you know will stretch it permanently out of shape, a little more than most people feel obligated to do, me definitely among them. All of which meant even the part of your original body you no longer wanted had to be kept alive and connected to the rest of you in some way so it would all function together to produce your mortal power intact and unaltered. Thus, just as you have something of mine, I have something of yours as you see. The technical challenge was to solve two problems, each the inverse of the other. The first was to separate one being, you, into two parts which still functioned together as one, and the second was to combine two separate creatures, you and the aspect, into one while keeping their mortal signatures separate, which could be expected to cause severe problems of communication and cooperation between them, to say the least. Both these situations are impossible in your world.

"But then, all problems have solutions. Two physically disjunct segments can produce mortal power as a unitary being if their mortal powers are connected through the metaphysical ether. Trouble is, mortal power has no existence there. We hit on the, I think, brilliantly efficient, perhaps even elegant (though also, when you think about it, it must be admitted fairly obvious) notion of a coherent beam of metaphysical energy. Think of it sort of like a laser beam which can carry information back and forth between two terminals and allow nothing to escape, a beam which cannot radiate, diffuse, or interact in any way with the metaphysical world at large. So much for problem one. Next, just as a laser beam has to originate someplace, it's generated by me on this end and the aspect on yours. The aspect, as a demidjinn, has a built-in familiarity with mortal/metaphysical transformational mechanics mortal creatures lack. This also aligned the aspect and the organic portions of you inside it into an operational cofunctionality that allows them to communicate and cooperate short of assimilating one another. Nifty. Are you following this?"

"I think so, which worries me."

"I answer his question, and he gets sarcastic. There's just one problem. Actually, it isn't you that's unstable, it's what you do to the space *between* you. This is the thing nobody anticipated. Remember those harmonics your lifeforce is supposedly resonating out into the metaphysical world at large? The coherent nature of the beam that connects your two halves exerts a sympathetic effect on the mortal portion of the system, partially polarizing the mortal resonance produced everywhere inside it, not only yours and the power of The Bargain's, but mine and the aspect's as well because, to operate in the mortal world, the aspect and I have to do so as physical beings, and physical beings produce mortal power, and because, to handle this end of the connection, I'm aligned with your body in that same operational cofunctionality which makes you so simpatico with the aspect. The result is a strong field, an ellipsoid of unresolved mortal resonance spanning the ether with you and the aspect at one focus and me and the rest of your body at the other, and, because this resonance is grossly distorted from its usual pattern, so is the effect on whatever metaphysical ether it encounters."

"Stop, wait up. I just got Error 42, Conceptual Overflow."

"Windows strikes again." The djinn shrugged. "If we're lucky, we might get a chance to discuss it in depth someday, but I warn you, it's stuff only the kind of people who can't resist taking clocks apart find interesting.* The essential thing is that the effects were exceedingly weird. You remember I said the mortal and metaphysical powers are like two different currencies, each convertible into the other? This field allows power of one kind to convert itself into the other in ways normal transformational

---

* Readers of this type are directed to the Appendix, §III.
Available at http://samainweb.org/LTLIAPP.pdf

mechanics don't. You've become a Gate. Before His Masturbatory Majesty figured out what to do about it, nightmares began coming to life all over the place. Thus, my job is to stay near you so all these elements are collected more or less in one place. That narrows the size of the field and minimizes the chance of strange phenomena, especially phenomena that'll fuck up His plans."

"Surely somebody could have figured! I don't care how complex it sounds. If you guys have been dealing with this stuff for millions of years, you'd think you'd know something about it."

"Uh huh. Why is this conversation starting to sound familiar?" The djinn scowled. "His Flatulence did figure, or figger, as He so elegantly puts it, but even He didn't know for sure." A shadow of deep dark suspicion passed over the djinn's face. "Or so He claims." He shrugged. "Makes no difference if He did or didn't. The result is the same. We crawling creatures must scuttle and obey."

"And you're stuck wearing Herbie Manning until... until I choose to die?"

The djinn grinned. "Actually, I'm getting to kind of *like* it. Wearing it has possibilities. It really bothers the fuck out of people. In fact, when this whole mess is over, if it's ever over, I'm thinking of recycling an obsolete aspect into one just like it."

David rolled his eyes. "You don't suppose we could just cancel this whole deal, do you? Go back to square one and I'll rephrase?"

"Don't I wish! But no. His Malevolence figured out a way to turn our discomfiture to His advantage almost immediately. Several ways, I think. He's good at that."

David's eyes narrowed a hair. The bitter edge creeping into the djinn's voice was far from lost on him. *Our discomfiture?* And what was that the djinn had said about the Archon having a second agenda for the aspect, one he definitely didn't like? What, exactly, was the djinn's stake in this?

If the djinn heard these thoughts, he ignored them. "So we're stuck. You're two beings rolled up and held together by the power of The Bargain. The aspect is actually a demidjinn, a nice

321

clean one with no memories of its own to interfere, whose power you get to use. Even so, it does have the potential for separate existence, a mind of its own with desires, goals and allegiances that don't have anything to do with you. Right now, its mind is superimposed on and coextensive with yours so you can use the attributes, but its will is totally subjugated." The djinn leaned forward and spoke earnestly, with deadly intensity. "*When you see the Archon*, He will attempt to reverse that, to bring the aspect's will to life and allow it to possess you in the same way we can possess any mortal being if we choose. Once that's done, He can dominate the aspect any way He pleases and still claim He's not interfering in *mortal* will. If I'm right, this is what He'll do, and you're the only one who can stop Him."

"How?"

"By getting there first and using the aspect to access your own mortal power! If you can mobilize your own lifeforce, I *think* you'll be able to stop the switch no matter what He does. The way I figure it, if you can use the aspect to touch the mortal power just as if this were some emergency in which the aspect was about to take the power to protect itself, the power should expand out of your mortal center to envelop you just as it always does before we convert it to our own uses. He'd have to smash through that before He could have His way with you."

"Oh, right. Whenever there's trouble, let's use a *mortal* lifeforce, and mine to boot. Naturally. God, you guys are stingy."

"Think! Give it a try! We don't have the metaphysical power to stop Him. He's an Archon! But if He smashes your mortal power, you'll die, which will give Him a new problem with The Bargain. That's the last thing He wants. There's a review board before a committee of Archons every time The Bargain is invoked." He grinned his wicked grin again. "So He won't dare touch you. You'll remain in control. He'll have to deal with you instead of the aspect, and with you in control, you'll never allow anything which could possibly damage or twist the aspect, because anything that would do that would twist you too. You'll be able to tell Him to go Fuck Himself." His eyes flashed.

"And what will playing with my own lifeforce do to *me*?"

322

"Since you'll still be inside it, it shouldn't do anything to you, as long as you don't transform it into a spell."

"So how do I do that, access my own lifeforce?"

The djinn spread his hands. "I don't know. It's only theoretically possible. Before this all came up, I would have said it was altogether *im*possible. The mortal power resonates directly out of your being. For you to touch it should be like a camera trying to see itself directly—impossible! But you! You're a Gate, goddamit! So *use* it for something instead of just flapping in the breeze for every passing zombie!"

Zombies? David decided he didn't want to know. "Oh thank you so much! Access my own lifeforce? 'Your freedom depends on it, not to mention my aspect, but how you do that is a mystery, so good luck'? Come on! I need instructions, at least a clue, not just 'I don't know'!"

The djinn jumped up in agitation. "How the fuck should I know? I'm not a mortal, and I'm not a Gate. You're both! Use the attributes! With the resources you've got and the experience you've had, if you can't figure it out, no one can!" He put his hands on his hips and gave David a flat stare. "Frankly, I don't think you can do it, not if this conversation is any indication, but it's our only chance, and you've got to try."

"Oh, thanks a heap!" David was outraged. "According to you, some superdevil is about to toast me on its trident and all you've got for me is a theoretical possibility you don't think I can handle if it's possible at all? If you're so incredibly worried... Hey, just what exactly is all this *we* and *our* I've been hearing all of a sudden? *Our* discomfiture? *We're* stuck? *Our* only chance? The aspect the object of the Archon's greed? Why? Just what kind of a big deal is this aspect, anyway? Why does he need it?—and why should he want to damage or twist it? If he's so powerful, why doesn't he just make another one to his own specifications?"

The djinn's bitterness was uncontained. "Because of who and what I am, that aspect is unique, just as I'm unique among djinns! Once you got the hang of how to use it, being a whore felt pretty natural, didn't it? Solved all your problems? Well, guess what?

That's what it was created to be: Cupbearer to Their Omnipotencies, The Alfuckingmighty College of Archons! Sounds distinguished, doesn't it? The College of Archons? Well, you should've seen what They got up to in the old days. I sure did, and Guess Who's been assigned to keep an eye on me and stop me from blabbing it, as if I'd ever be that stupid! But now, He's gotten greedy too."

The djinn's voice slashed out. "Man, I am trying to help you! I want you to stay in control and, as a by-product, save my aspect. With it disconnected from me and the taboos on me like it is now, there's nothing to stop Him twisting it toward Him until it's absolutely slavish—the core, the essence of my being! Then, once it's free again and He can ram me back into it, I'll be changed too, into just another tool drooling after His favor, just another of His tame djinns. I *know* this is what He intends. I know *Him*! He had the nerve to as good as tell me so! Besides, why else would He allow... this!" He waved a hand at David. "He *must* have known what would happen! He could have disallowed giving you the aspect if He'd wanted—forced you to clarify. Even *I* suspected. I think His plot was formed the instant you opened your mouth!"

He jumped up and paced the room savagely, an animal in a cage. "That sneaky bastard! My secrets forgotten? Bullshit! They've changed, have they? Hah! Moved uptown, maybe—but changed? Not so's *I've* noticed! It's pure bluff. Goddammit, I know His very Name, though I'd never be stupid enough to Speak it—but because of that, I've had to fight and scheme and connive for every second of freedom I've ever had! He'd just go ahead and *do* me if He thought He could get away with it! It's a ploy, a rotten, sneaky, opportunistic ploy to make me spill what I know so He can get a leg over the Others and neutralize me as a threat at the same time! It's prime stuff, The Compleat Archon.

"Because then, when He used His new knowledge, They'd all think I was a traitor." He looked at the floor and froze. His voice sank to a mutter. "My protection would vanish. There'd be no one to stop Him getting rid of me completely to hide forever just how it was done." He seemed to have forgotten David was even in the room. He went on almost in a whisper. "So what do I do, complain to the

Others? Without proof?—and expose all this too, when I don't know where He's going with it? Very, *very* dangerous." He sank back into the chair. The torture of his helplessness and uncertainty was palpable.

David's curiosity was piqued. "Those secrets must be pretty hot," he murmured.

It didn't work. Bleakly, the djinn refocussed on David. "Like it or not, and believe me I hate it, I need you. By saving yourself, you'll save me too. So I'm shaving my instructions by telling you these things. I was supposed to make sure you understood what the attributes could do, but I doubt that meant this, so if I'm found out, it's big trouble, but there's really no choice, and no way out." His eyes glittered with hatred and contempt. "I suppose it's all inevitable now, you being the weak sister you so obviously are."

David was becoming madder by the moment. "Well, what about this free will your precious Bargain says I'm supposed to get to employ the power for mortal purposes? Who'll be employing it with the aspect in charge? Any chance we can make something out of that?"

"He has the power, and the rules are His to play with if He dares," the djinn said gloomily. "Your free will went out the window the second He decided to have it some other way. The free will bit has no effect on The Balance directly. It's only to keep metaphysical beings from using power taken from mortals against other metaphysical beings, with mortals as pawns. He's not doing that, exactly. Oh, He's subtle. As it worked out, the power of The Bargain only holds you together and solves various problems in your construction. It won't be touched; it'll keep right on doing what it's doing either way. Voilà, your free will becomes irrelevant, and if He gets His way, no one will ever know or care. You might, of course, but you'll be suppressed and, eventually, dead. That's His plan. How you're supposed to die, I can't figure yet. I don't know much about the scheme He says He wants you for. Other djinns are handling that. He's 'way too smart to let me in on it before He's got me where He can see me."

"So I've just got to deal with it, huh?"

The djinn made no answer.

David mastered his rage with an effort. If the djinn were to be believed, each of these creatures sought to make him a tool against the other. The only thing to do was to opt out altogether, to leave.

Leave? Omigod! Utterly intent on the djinn's revelations, he'd completely forgotten his own urgent travel plans. He sprang off the bed. "Hey, babe, since you read minds, you know I have to get out of here!" He reached for his bags. "Y'know, it was great we had this chat, a real revelation." He was elaborately phony-sincere. "Fortunately, I can solve your problem for you right now. I don't say I'm the brightest bulb in the hardware aisle, but I do know bullshit when I hear it, and to claim exercising direct control over this body isn't direct control of its components is bullshit. Either I control them for my purposes or your Archon thing does for its. So give it my regards, with my regrets. I'm just not going to help you guys in *any* of your little plans to feed off the misery of the world." He let his voice sharpen. "Stupid? Ignorant? Idiotic? Greedy? Weak sister? If I have to take this kind of abuse off you, I can't imagine what dealing with it would be like. Not to mention being cored like an apple and suspended in mid-air when, if I understand you correctly, you suspected—no, you *knew* a simple recontour of my own body would have satisfied me just as well and avoided all this complication!" He started for the door. "Forget it! You girls are just gonna have to bitch it out amongst yourselves. I want all you hobgoblins out of my head and out of my destiny effective immediately, or I'll take it to the College of Archons myself! Sounds like they'd be pretty interested, with all that ancient gossip at stake."

The djinn was shaking his head in dejection. "Well, if that's your attitude, it is hopeless. You really are as dumb as this body looks. Froggy's men are getting off the elevator as we speak."

"Why you..." David gaped. "You knew it all along! That's why you evaded my questions and spun me all this stuff? To waste time and keep me here for this? Am I off to see your precious Archon now?"

The djinn nodded.

"And Froggy? Adolph? Did you manipulate all of us to create this?"

The djinn nodded again. "Me, and others. But relax, it didn't take much."

David fought speechlessness. "So why! I don't understand! If you were oh-so-concerned about your precious aspect, why did you set me up? For chrissake let's get out of here NOW!"

The djinn slumped back in defeat. "You don't get it. My destiny is now as it ever has been, to be His unhumble but obedient servant. Welcome to the Personal Disaster Department."

A leaden fist beat on the door. "David Alexander! Open in the name of the Consortium Council!"

David looked wildly at the djinn, who just shrugged.

"Open now!" A heavy thud rattled the doorback mirror.

The djinn retreated into a brown study. Frowning, he examined his fingernails.

An even louder thud shuddered the door in its frame.

David saw no choice. He opened the door. Two large men, obviously in the act of another rush, fell in on top of him and wrestled him to the floor. He recognized Frogmorton's valet and chauffeur. The chauffeur twisted David's arm behind his back and dragged him roughly to his feet. "You. Looks like the boss has wised up to you at last. You're under arrest!"

"Hey George!" The other spoke. "The boss said undamaged, remember?"

The grip on David's arm loosened an almost imperceptible fraction. "Come quiet," George said, "or I will break it!"

David had been twisted away from the djinn. In rage and pain, he saw only one, last thing he might try. "It's not me you want! It's him! That's Herbie Manning, right there! He's the one gave me the money!"

George was amused. "And who would that be, now?"

"Right there! Are you blind? In the chair!"

George swung him around. There was no one in the room but the three of them.

David panicked. "Where is he! You let him slip past you!"

George sighed. "Jesus, Frank, do you believe it?" He spoke softly to David then, in a bored voice full of menace. "Okay fag, let's go, and let's go quiet. If you make a noise, I might just lose my grip and drop you down the stairs. Now move!"

The other one, Frank, picked up the briefcase and David's luggage. As they hustled him stumbling down the back stairs, David reached toward their minds to see what damage he could do there, and found the way blocked. He cursed the djinn silently, but with all his might. Suddenly, there was a voice in his head. *Oh, can it,* it said. *Remember the mortal power!*

Chapter Seven
A COP WHEN YOU NEED ONE

bout the most obvious thing you can say about time is that it passes. Yet, beneath the cliché lies an enormity of complication.

Take two people, their desks next to one another in an office, doing the same job. For one of them, it's a new job, a promotion. She is interested and challenged. Every day there are new problems to solve, new people to meet, new procedures to learn. The day goes by swiftly. Before she's drunk half her morning coffee, it's lunchtime, and after a working lunch at her desk, she races the cruel clock to do the most she can before five o'clock, when, reluctantly, she must leave off and go home.

Although her hours fly swiftly by, the weeks of these fast-paced days may seem like months when she looks back on them. She has much to remember; the many separate incidents, the individual successes and failures invested with so much of herself, each unique novelty she remembers, when strung together, make the time seem to have been an eternity.

The other person has been at the job many years. For him, each day is an eternity. He is completely bored. Every item arriving at his desk is *"This* again." He arrives ten minutes late every morning. He sits with one eye watching the clock crawl toward noon. After his longish lunch, he can barely keep his eyes open, torpid with food. Same old stuff every day, same boring idiots to talk to, same tedious non-problems over and over again. For him, the clock is also cruel, not because it moves too quickly, but because, often, it barely seems to move at all.

Just as for the novice, the larger passage of time is a paradox for the veteran. The crawling hours gather together into weeks and months that pulse by with barely a flicker. One minute, it's Easter. Before he knows it, Thanksgiving arrives, and after a short nap, it's Christmas. The whole tedious year is gone in a flash, leaving only the prospect of another just like it ahead. With few separate incidents worth remembering at all, his stagnant present compresses itself as it passes. Before he knows it, his very life will be over, barely noticed.

For Greg Whitbread, despite the novelty of his situation, time was an agony. The next few days seemed then and would remain forever in his memory as the longest he'd ever spent. By the time on the morning of David's disappearance he collected himself sufficiently to phone Morgan Jaye and attempt some damage control, the big man seemed to be extremely well informed already, with a version of events that showed Greg's shortcomings in high relief. Probably, Greg thought with dismay, Rico had slipped off to phone him while he, Greg, was still smashing glasses in the Harrington Hotel. Clipped with rage, Jaye's voice cut off Greg's protestations virtually at word one and ordered him home pending further orders. Click.

Greg decided to take him literally. He left for Chicago on the first available train. He went straight to his apartment, locked himself in, engaged the answering system to screen his calls, and began to brood.

In the following days, he did nothing but sit in his apartment pondering his disgrace. Hermetically sealed in cool savorless air conditioned air, he sat at his high windows watching the life of the city through his telescope: the careless surewinged gulls skysculling the lakefront over acres of naked flesh turning malignant in the ozone-depleted sunlight; the boys and men in tanktops and tight jeans dancing their endless promenade on Halsted Street; the cozy dioramas of everyday life seen through thousands of far-off windows. Greg watched it all in growing alienation.

This view of life, wistfully circumscribed by the jiggling soft-focus blackness of his eyepiece, accurately reflected what he now took to be his own position vis-à-vis the world: doomed by his own hand to the perpetual shivering periphery of life. Not now would he hold a place in the magic circle of power around Morgan Jaye. Not now when he'd laid the onerous yet oh-so-rewarding burden of command aside for the day would there be a golden lover to welcome him to an evening of sensual delights.

David! Greg lived with the image of his newfound beloved every moment, even finding it in his dreams when at last he slept. The glorious golden visage stood between him and all he saw as if etched into the eyepiece of his telescope or seared permanently onto his retinas. After the silken electricity of David's skin, all else felt dull and unimmediate, as if like Achilles he'd been dipped by the heel into a vat of invulnerable armor which prevented him from truly touching anything ever again.

David's loss slammed shut the door into the whole of that rosy future he'd imagined so confidently; he felt himself locked out not only from his career goals, but from life itself. Without his beloved by his side, living could be nothing but a hollow sham, his triumphs unshared and empty, his defeats and failures forever unconsoled. The thought he might be condemned to this hopeless sort of existence depressed him utterly. Condemned! That was the only word for it: condemned for life without parole.

If only he might be saved! Finding David seemed to Greg his one wild chance at a normal, happy life, and might even unlock the door back into his career as well. Surely, with the love Greg just *knew* David had felt for him while they were together and the obvious rewards of the career Greg had been promised, rewards he was eager to share, David would forgive him and cooperate in snagging Manning, this time for real. He just had to find him. David was the key to everything!

Find him? With all this depending on him, how could Greg have allowed him to be lost in the first place? What an idiot he'd been! He tore his hair with both hands and wanted to kick himself. If only he'd stopped to recall his watchers instead of floating out of there on that fatuous flush of love and trust, oblivious to simple good sense! Or better still, much better, if only he'd levelled with David when he'd had the chance! If only he'd revealed himself as a CRAP agent and drawn David a picture of the obvious benefits for both of them in cooperating to put Manning where he rightly belonged! What could he have been thinking, beginning his relationship with the man he loved by keeping secrets and trying to trick him?

How could I have done it? This was the cruelest thing: not that David had lied to him, fobbed him off with that story about having a meeting with Manning the next day and dismissed him, but that he himself had told a series of what David must have seen as the world's clumsiest lies in the first place!

That had to have been what had happened. His story had been much too elaborate. Somewhere, he'd used a detail based on something David knew wasn't true, and likely more than once. He'd been aware of the danger, but had been unable to stop himself. He'd simply babbled on and on, desperate to get the response he wanted. Pretty clearly, David had picked up on that. All Greg had done was make himself easy to get rid of when David wanted to buy time. Probably, David had been on the phone to Manning the minute he'd been out the door.

He put himself in David's place and examined what his own reaction might have been had somebody he quite wanted to like behaved the way he had. How disappointed in him David must have been! Humbly, he admitted he might have acted much as David had done. In fact, they were two of a kind: sharp self-respecting young guys ready to squeeze the world dry who weren't going to let anyone or anything stand in their way. It only made him love David more. They were perfect for one another.

Instead of showing David the size of the stakes, how high the rewards could be if they worked together, he'd chosen to let David see him stumbling blindly about in a minefield of inept mendacity. David was more than intelligent enough to see through that and certainly had enough self-esteem to resent it. Who wouldn't? Greg hated himself. Over and over, the words he should have used poured through him in futile post-facto rehearsal, words that would have

332

revealed their kindred nature and goals instead of spurring David into contemptuous disregard, abandonment and flight Greg knew not whither.

Nor, as long as he remained cut off from CRAP's resources, could he find out. Morgan Jaye *had* to give him another chance! Not only must he salvage his career, he must find David and explain, must apologize for having seemed to underestimate him so insultingly. He must make plain his admiration and respect. He must beg forgiveness on his knees if necessary and not stop 'til he'd wiped out the smears of insincerity, uncaring manipulativeness and simple stupidity David must see on him. Surely David would forgive him when he saw his agony. He must! Greg had to find him, now!

Instead, his powerlessness tortured him into fits of caged pacing lasting through the nights until he collapsed in exhaustion. Why was he locked up here doing nothing while his life fell to pieces around him? Would Morgan Jaye *never* call? He, Greg, was surely the logical man to continue the pursuit. Didn't Jaye *see* that?

Or maybe Jaye hadn't called because David had been found already! His heart stopped every time he had this thought. He had to know! He would spring for his viewscreen, then freeze, his hand on the controls. No. Jaye had unmistakably ordered him to wait. Greg knew well enough one got nowhere disobeying the big man's instructions. Greg's eyes would close and he would tremble in agitated frustration. He would simply have to contain himself and wait.

After three miserable days of this, his release came at last on Saturday morning in the form of a condescending male voice oozing from his viewscreen. When he cut off the answering system, the voice ordered him immediately to a meeting with Jaye at Jaye's suburban home in Bummers Grove.

Back to the inside at last! At last he could get back on track toward David and make everything right. He dressed furiously, ties and jackets flying in all directions. Almost before he knew it, the expressway shimmered in 100° heat around his little car as he raced toward his beloved at maximum warp.

LEARNING TO LOVE IT

Although he was under no illusion as to the probable content of the coming interview—he was about to have his butt kicked—he burned with hope and furious determination. If only David hadn't been found! If only he, Greg, could persuade Morgan Jaye to let him head a renewed investigation, or at the very least, take part in it! All might yet be saved! He hadn't a minute to lose.

He cloverleafed recklessly up the ramp and slowed with difficulty, fighting his eagerness, as he entered the conventional, plastic opulence of Bummers Grove.

* * * * *

Bummers Grove. This place name was not an idle one. By curious coincidence, it traced itself back through circumstance and family connection to that very Nathaniel Bummer whose incontinence had landed the djinn in the cookie tin.

Concerning Mr. Bummer, a dispassionate observer might be inclined to agree with half, at least, of the djinn's assessment of him. He was certainly very greedy, if not all that stupid.

After a dissolute youth spent mainly in the Mississippi riverboat trade and in various St. Louis and New Orleans waterfront taverns at either end thereof, he had found his fortune at last in the California goldfields—not, one must add, through the tiresome labor of *pick and pan*, but with the altogether less chancy and more congenial gamble of relieving the miners of their newfound wealth at the poker tables of San Francisco, of rendering them, as old Nate liked to say, *spic and span*. He delighted in chortling out this rather elephantine rhyme to all who would listen, right up to the moment the fifth ace flopped inopportunely from his sleeve at a game in which the chairman of the Vigilance Committee was losing heavily.

Nate split for his room in a flurry of kings, queens, and large dice. All of the latter, the committeemen noted with interest, fell neatly into various combinations of seven. This possibly unintended diversion gave Nate the extra minute he needed. Before they broke down his door *et tout le tremblement*, stripped him naked and dragged him out whither the tar and feathers were held in constant readiness, he had just time to shove a truly awesome stack of $50 gold pieces up his asshole. Thus, while the committeemen thought that smile on his face as they jounced him out of town on the rail was false bravado, it might well have been some more recondite affect.

From San Francisco, Bummer came east. As a city only slightly less wide open and brawling than the one that had just bounced him, the atmosphere of 19th century Chicago proved an irresistible lure. He had learned his lesson and avoided games of chance as a career choice. Using the modest start his stash money gave him, he invested in downtown horsecar lines and local politicians. Later, his love of gambling never to be denied completely, he dealt in corn, wheat and livestock. When he won, prices rose. When he lost, they fell. Mostly, they rose. By the time of the Great Fire in 1871, he owned a fortune in downtown real estate and was one of the richest men in the city.

Of the relatively few persons actually to perish in that spectacular catastrophe, Bummer was easily the most prominent. As such, the news reports which electrified and titillated a horrified world included his name and a general description of the assets he left behind, along with the highly interesting fact no will had been found. Perhaps, the newspapers speculated, it too had gone up in flame. What to do with the property was occasioning a great deal of interested discussion.

While perusing one such account, in *The New Orleans Daily Picayune*, the name Bummer leapt off the page at Nate's estranged wife like the sounding of heaven's trumpet, or rather, with an effect more nearly akin to getting blackjacked with it in a dark alley. Nate's name sat Mrs. Amelie Bummer straight up over her morning café au lait in mingled surprise, wonder and loathing. Three hours later, she, a florid affidavit from the sacristan of the church where she'd been married, and Nate's grown son were on a train chugging up the Illinois Central Mainline toward what was left of Chicago.

Now, Bummer and his wife had been estranged for reasons his relations with the djinn would suggest. To the daughter of a genteel and highly Catholic New Orleans family, Bummer's sexual predilections very definitely came under the heading of Abomination.

335

Naturally, these had not been on view during their courtship. As the sole survivor of her family, she'd had no relatives to forbid her interest in the handsome and dashing young man. Her guardian, a doting elderly family lawyer, had not put up much resistance. Even had it been otherwise, she thought, her own strong will would have breached all obstacles. She'd wanted him despite his lack of means or antecedents and had been determined to have him.

After their marriage, his lackadaisical interest in her bedroom had worried her. His passionate wooing had led her to expect rather more. That such interest ceased altogether after the birth of their son depressed her. At his befriending a succession of distinctly goodlooking boys from the social class she was accustomed to refer to as White Trash, her depression turned to suspicion, which in due course grew to alarm as their ages diminished precipitously toward the pre-pubic, and when at last she discovered him late one night in an outbuilding with the colored boy...

At that point, an altogether new start in San Francisco had begun to seem like a viable option to Bummer. The obvious conclusion that his interest in his wife had been limited to her name and her money outraged and embarrassed her. She'd been had. She'd heard nothing of him since and had fervently hoped this would continue indefinitely. Yet it hadn't. Life played such strange tricks. As the train plugged on northwards, the image of Bummer with that boy came to her and made her shudder. Grimly, she held it in front of her and stared it down.

Now he was dead, and surprising to her with her intimate knowledge of his habits, the newspaper accounts seemed to leave no doubt of his solid position in Chicago society. Either he'd learned discretion, or Chicago society wasn't remarkably particular. Chicago society? Parvenu upstarts! That innkeeper's wife, Mrs. Whateverhernamewas—Pothole Palmer?—and her dauby art collection! Still, if Chicago society seemed distinctly dubious to one whose ancestors had arrived in America with the sieur de Bienville, that list of assets would enable a great deal of condescension on her part, she thought. She was determined to have every cent. She would repair the family fortune destroyed in the Civil War and avenge her wounded pride at the same time. He'd thought to live off her money, had he? Now she would live off his. *Touché.* It seemed like simple justice.

Long before they reached Illinois, the image of him with that boy had ceased to trouble her. In fact, she decided a memorial to her poor deceased husband would be most appropriate—a stone of some kind, a large one and as gaudy as she could find, for prominent placement in whatever cemetery Chicago aristocracy might favor. Her impression was that, in Chicago, size equalled both taste and depth of emotion. She was prepared to play Grieving Widow to the hilt.

Thus was the Bummer dynasty established.

But 64 years later, by 1935, the family fortunes were again in disrepair. Trust-busting began the decline. The Depression finished it. In his old age, Mrs. Bummer's grandson was forced to begin the selloff of the extensive acreage surrounding his country estate to such of his associates who'd had the foresight not to be invested in either stocks or land. Problem was, such persons were in understandably short supply. Prices were miserably low. By the birth of his own great-grandson, Morgan Jaye, the family fortune had been reduced to just the house and barely enough income to support it. This income it had been Jaye's lifelong struggle to augment.

As he prowled the corridors of the faux-Gothic mansion Nate's son had built atop the only hill in Bummers Grove, he looked out over the fortunes made by later speculators on the Bummer estate and reflected on his family's reversals. He would have sniffed at the "magic circle of power" of Greg's imagination.

As a younger man, even as a precocious teenager, he'd seen beyond the security of blue chips to the promise of Intel and Microsoft in their infancies. He'd begged his mother to sell the house and provide the seed money whereby the family fortune might be rebuilt. Always, she had refused. She'd seen no reason why the remnants of her grandeur should be risked on her son's entrepreneurial ambitions. Instead, parlaying the only capital he'd had, his boarding school connections, Jaye had wangled himself a position at the Amalgamated Consolidated Confederated

International Bank and, all in all, had not done too badly in keeping things together on his relatively meager salary.

Now in late middle age, he had been the sole survivor of his family for some time. The estate was his to do with as he pleased, but the fire was long gone out. Just as his mother had been, he was loathe to surrender the familiar surroundings of a lifetime. Besides, where now were the Intels and Microsofts, the growth stocks of the future? They must exist, but he could not see them, only the risks. He had outgrown this young man's game, it seemed.

Then there were The Entities, as he thought of them. He knew nothing about them: what they were, how they worked, whence they came, whom they served. They seemed simply to Be. They worked sometimes against the state and sometimes for it. They built individuals up and tore them down again according to no pattern he could divine. They were disrespectful equally to God and the Devil, though their working method seemed distinctly more reminiscent of the latter. As a conventionally religious man, this worried him somewhat because, worried or not, he needed them.

As builders and developers turned the once-virgin parkland surrounding him into a wealthy suburb fashionable among the city's new top management elite, increasing its value many times, the assessed valuation of the remaining family property grew right along with it. Throughout his lifetime the estate suffered a perpetual financial embroglio of ever-increasing severity apexing whenever property tax payments came due.

One blustery November evening years ago now when the wind swirled dead leaves through the air and naked tree branches clawed imploringly at his windows like the limbs of old men crooked in arthritic agony, The Entities had first appeared to him. As he'd sat poking the fire in a blackly bitter mood, contemplating the final dissolution of the estate his forbearers had fought and schemed and scrabbled to assemble, the crowd of gargoyles decorating the room had come impossibly alive. They'd swarmed the ornate moldings and romped on his mantelpiece, mocking and teasing him with his impotence in the face of his ever-eroding power and position.

A man of no small nerve and presence of mind, Jaye had not remained long cowering open-mouthed in his chair. In a rage, he'd demanded they either help him do something about it or cease to plague him.

And so they had. They had helped him, in pieces, a little at a time, whenever his cash flow exigencies hit crisis level. Their help took the form of instructions, and always, these instructions produced a windfall. Always too, however, was the mechanism odd: files that must disappear, money lent in certain ways to certain people, preferment granted to some or denied others equally worthy, or so it seemed to Jaye. As promised, these dealings invariably worked to Jaye's ultimate advantage, though, equally invariably, in a hair-raising way. The Entities, it appeared, had a considerable sense of humor, something Jaye himself rather conspicuously lacked. The result, therefore, inevitably made him intensely uncomfortable.

On one occasion, an AmalCon loan Jaye approved at the behest of The Entities went sour, very sour, indeed. The oil company geology reports on the basis of which land had been accepted as collateral turned out to have been faked. The borrower disappeared with the bank's money. At the last moment, just as Jaye was collecting his papers for the staff meeting where he expected to present his embarrassed final report, the phone rang. The geologist who'd determined there could be no oil on the land announced he'd discovered titanium instead, a very rich strike. As account supervisor, Jaye was entitled to, and got, a substantial bonus.

A company to which AmalCon, through Jaye, had extended an ample line of credit at The Entities' direction went bankrupt. Upon distribution of the remaining assets, AmalCon's share amounted to nothing more than a few worthless patents—worthless, that is, until three weeks later when an obscure scientist in an unrelated field at a minor university in a distant state announced a new process worth millions, and for which those patents were essential. Another bonus.

So it went for more than twenty years. Although The Entities helped Jaye with windfall after windfall, their help was never quite enough to allow him to escape his troubles entirely. Indeed, the farther upwards he worked his way in AmalCon's labyrinthine hierarchy, the more frequent his crises became, and the more power he accumulated to influence events, the more wideranging and freakishly unpredictable became The Entities' instructions.

He had not the feeblest guess what The Entities might be getting out of their arrangement. It had to be something. Nobody in this world or out of it ever did anything for no gain. That was a Law. More and more, he had the feeling he was being run, and he did not like it. He wondered whether his emergencies weren't manufactured simply to allow The Entities to use his position, with his windfalls a byproduct, a sort of tip—and once he started thinking along these lines, it occurred to him to wonder whether they weren't attempting not only to use his career, but direct its course to place him more conveniently for their own ends, whatever those might be.

The day came when Jaye fired an apparently able and efficient account executive on the sole basis of an off-hand hint from The Entities' that this would work to his advantage. In short order, a hated rival institution hired the man to command their Oil & Gas Department, which he remade into a profit center unrivalled in that institution's history—until it transpired that most of his loans were either fraudulent or laxly inept. He went to jail. The hated rival needed a federal bailout to keep its doors open in abjectly reduced circumstances. It became obvious to all, and especially to those who'd questioned Jaye's judgment in firing the man, that the fellow had been merely a crook waiting for a crime.

This eventuated in a completely unanticipated career development for Jaye. After decades of weird speculations that, somehow, always seemed to come right in the end, he had acquired a reputation as a bold maverick gambler whose luck never flagged—a reputation Nate Bummer would have envied. Trouble was, Nate's thrice-great-grandson thought of himself, against all the evidence, as an essentially conservative and prudent manager, strictly a numbers man. As such, he found his colleagues' perception of his character distinctly embarrassing.

Said colleagues were definitely looking him askance. According to their own mythology, the top executives of major financial institutions were supposed to possess vision and imagination, but were not supposed to be buccaneers setting their courses by the seats of their pants, riding the waves in search of huge windfalls at the price of colossal risks. As time went on, Jaye was seen ever more clearly as a buccaneer. His colleagues dared not get rid of him and risk him lavishing his extraordinary luck on one of their competitors—the hated rival, it was known, ached to have him. Yet, the closer he came to AmalCon's center of power, the more uncomfortable that center of power became about having him there.

When the Senior Executive VP slot in Security opened up, they rushed to offer it to him. His expertise as a judge of character had been demonstrated convincingly in the case of the Oil & Gas man, and buccaneering in protection of AmalCon's profits was okay with everybody. They offered him a free hand. The job would allow him complete range through all AmalCon's multitudinous departments and outposts, and carry more power than only a handful of the most successful upper executives ever got. It would also separate him completely from management of the actual *money*. This, they thought, would be perfect. They sweetened the pot with a healthy raise, stock options and a platinum parachute, and held their corporate breath to see if he'd take it.

He nearly didn't. Not only did he see how his colleagues were maneuvering him, which was insulting, but an alternative existed. The hated rival had made him a really most attractive offer, "to acquire your unique working method for this institution." The only problem was that, if he accepted it, his new bosses almost certainly would change their minds about his "working method" when they saw how it in fact operated, especially with federal regulators hiding close herd after the oil and gas debacle. He thought bitterly of his property taxes and his perpetually crumbling great house.

On the other hand, to a conservative and prudent manager, strictly a numbers man, the idea of the largish, dependably stable income AmalCon was offering seemed definitely preferable to The Entities' freakish windfalls. Unfortunately, he needed those windfalls; AmalCon's offer, substantial though it was, simply would not be enough. Slate roofs, for example, last a long long time, but not forever. They also cost a fortune. His was in imminent need of replacement.

By this time, Jaye's suspicions that his colleagues might not be the only ones attempting to maneuver him were bubbling to the surface. He remembered that this situation had come about purely as the result of a hint from The Entities that firing one man would work to his advantage. Yet, the career decision as presented seemed to come down with roughly equal difficulties on each side. On which did the promised advantage lay? He suspected that, once again, The Entities intended him to call upon their advice. Therefore, he refused. In the name of asserting control over his own destiny, he made the decision on its merits as best he might.

He stayed with AmalCon and took the career change with what grace he could. He hadn't been sorry, either. He'd squeaked by financially. He'd got the masonry repairs done, thank heaven, though the roof, that vast, intricately turreted and dormered expanse of fragile weatherbeaten slate, had had to wait—but then, it leaked in only a few places, as yet.

The good news? To be done with all that buccaneering, the agonizing waits under the tree to see which would fall first, the apple into his lap or the branch on his head, was a thoroughgoing relief. Moreover, the job itself interested him. He'd discovered a genuine aptitude for the work, and his abilities had been recognized most gratifyingly, especially after the Consortium came in. He'd become a considerable power quite near the top of a security apparatus with tentacles stretching ever farther beyond the confines of the bank. He liked power, and used it efficiently, even if he did think so himself. He was *good* at it. In fact, he'd been good enough at it to dispense with The Entities entirely.

Good riddance too. He'd been glad to have a job where, apparently, he did not need them. He'd resolved never to call on them again—and hadn't.

Until now.

His lifetime of scrimping and careful planning had almost gone for naught. That irritatingly crude and irreverent self-anointed reverend, Wilmore P. Barber—a fellow nobody'd ever heard of until a decade or so ago when certain perilous multilevel marketing schemes of his had caused essentially conservative and prudent numbers men everywhere to cluckcluck in anticipation of his imminent comeuppance, which, irritatingly and inexplicably, had never quite come to pass—had sapped Jaye's wherewithal to the breaking point, had sucked him dry by threatening him with his only extravagances: his collection of exotic birds smuggled from all over the world at precious expense, and the respectful reputation he'd established as an organizer and backer of serious, academically-oriented, conservation-minded ornithological expeditions to the last remaining wild corners of the planet. The former was his highest personal interest and fulfillment, the latter, the chief of all the things money had bought him. He would fight to the death to keep them both.

There in the third floor gallery of his house, he glared at a crumbling waterstained patch of plaster crown molding with the same malevolence he'd have felt had Barber himself been there poking it with a stick. Still, he'd held off summoning The Entities until the very last, until he was desperate. The result had been typical. Their instructions? Send a certain person, a mere boy, off on a mission for which he was plainly unqualified, and which, on the surface, anyway, had absolutely nothing to do with the matter at hand.

The boy had failed his assignment most miserably of course, embarrassing everybody in the process. Jaye gritted his teeth to think of it. Yet, also as usual, the matter had gone weirdly right as well. Finally he was off Barber's hook, as Chairman Frogmorton had made quite clear. That the ATM thefts had also resolved themselves as if on cue, albeit complete with yet another annoying embarrassment, all fit a familiar pattern. The mechanism, however, was even more dizzying than usual. He was far from sure he understood exactly what had happened.

All this piqued his suspicions anew. Almost casually, The Entities' latest mouthpiece had mentioned some sort of grand design or other. At the time, he'd thought the remark referred merely to the means by which Whitbread would resolve the blackmail for him.

Now, he wondered. Jaye could not help but notice that, although his release from Barber's grasp had not resulted from any of the intense efforts he himself had been making to effect it, these efforts had consequences and implications for the future which were more than disturbing. Hideous! That was the only word. He had been manipulated into acting very much against his better judgment.

It'd begun with Barber's last and most outrageous demand, that he supply a homosexual—a pretty one? Who could sing?—for Barber's scurrilous purposes. What had he, Jaye, to do with such persons? The indignity of it made him tremble with helpless fury—and beneath the fury, the barely admitted fact that his precarious circumstances had long necessitated the ruthless suppression of certain deeply troubling and very specific urges in order to maintain his childless marriage and subsequent divorced state in a manner AmalCon found respectably blameless tinged the whole subject with deep uneasiness and self-serving loathing.

On the surface level, fulfilling Barber's demand in any organized way meant reconstituting the Commission to Reduce Accounting Problems as the sort of secret police force capable of reaching deep into citizens' private lives and using what it found there to control them. Not only had Barber understood this, he had approved of it! He'd seemed to think this the appropriate direction for the future! Ultimately, it might mean networks of informers, interrogators, operators skilled in applying personal pressure of all kinds, and, presumably, gulags for the recalcitrant. Jaye found this deeply disturbing. It played directly to a contradiction in the belief system by which he'd lived his life.

As a lifelong member and fervent supporter of the ruling elite, a natural conservative, he believed implicitly that no sacrifice possibly could be too great for ordinary citizens to make in support of the established order. The poor and powerless had an absolute duty to lay down their money and even their lives to support the rich and influential, who protected society and shepherded it along the road to prosperity. Anyone who said differently was a dangerous radical who must be ruthlessly suppressed for the good of all.

Against this, the conservative ideology in which he'd been drilled relentlessly in his youth laid a certain stress on privacy and personal freedom. It taught that individuals must be absolutely free to believe what they would and conduct their lives and their businesses without government interference of any kind. Only in this way could they fulfill their destinies. Intelligent abstemious dedicated right-thinking individuals must be free to rise as far as their talent and vision could take them. According to the theory, the ideological marketplace naturally would elevate those who believed, as he did, in the capitalist system, which, since the (possibly lamentable) demise of feudalism, alone was capable of producing the kind of wealth and glory with which he preferred to associate himself. As for the weakminded and those mired in ideological stupidity or self-destructive immorality, if they would not serve society, they must be allowed to fall unhindered to the depths and be discarded so that society might be purged of them at no cost to itself. This was true conservatism, and Jaye believed in it with every fiber of his being.

Now, the Consortium was certainly the apotheosis of the ruling elite. It upheld freedom, the freedom of any man to come up and join them, if he could. As such, it deserved the support of everyone. Jaye fully understood how, were this support slow in coming, the rulers might feel a natural obligation to do whatever they could to coax it along. He even agreed with this obligation, to a certain degree.

He had no problem with propaganda, as long as no one were forced to believe it. Indeed, force seemed not to be required. On the whole, people seemed willing, even eager, to believe what they were told. Although every public library contained resources people ignorant of propaganda's nature could use to educate themselves, naturally there always would be vast numbers of those too lazy or weakminded to take proper advantage. That was their lookout. It was even right it should be so; for the shepherd's job to have any meaning, there must be a flock. Unfortunately, such a system as he'd been asked to construct lent itself all too easily to enforced belief. In his reading of history, this was counterproductive. Enforced belief seemed all by itself to produce a counter-reaction, a mindless aversion to the belief enforced no rational argument could overcome. This could only precipitate more enforcement, a vicious circle.

But then, there was also the certain danger from radical agitators with propaganda programs of their own. These Jaye saw not as they purported themselves, as the people's representatives protesting oppression and lack of opportunity, but merely as agents of competing power structures seeking only to replace the existing ruling elite with another: themselves. He saw no point to that. Not only would it dispossess those who'd worked hard and played by the rules to get where they were, but the disruption such a switch caused could go on for decades. History showed that. Thus, prudence dictated having some mechanism on hand to deal with such radicals as appeared.

The system the Consortium wanted him to create could serve that purpose admirably, and Barber's plan to ease it into being by playing on homophobic hysteria was a good one, he thought. It would probably work. But what then? Sacrificing a few homosexuals didn't bother him. His initial squeamishness conquered, he'd decided he was willing to show himself on the right side of *that* issue any time—but after homosexuals and genuine radical agitators, whom else would get swept into the net? Police states got carried away. *Show me one that hasn't,* he thought. Inevitably, they ended up paralyzing the societies they were meant to serve. Of course, that wouldn't happen as long as he was in charge, but then, he wouldn't live forever. Altogether, this was a most dangerous way to go.

As he'd promised Barber he would, he'd called Frogmorton, there from his office on the day Barber had made his outrageous demand. He'd had some trouble getting through, and when finally he had the Chairman on the line, the man seemed to be in his car. The line crackled, Jaye heard street noises quite close, and the Chairman kept breaking off to give directions to his chauffeur.

Jaye said nothing about blackmail, of course, but complained bitterly about Barber's demand for some sort of male houri on short notice, and attempted to lay out some of his concerns about reorganizing his Commission along the lines Barber seemed to think necessary.

The Chairman cut these off abruptly. ("Davey, slow down.") The change in CRAP's mission had already been debated and approved on the highest levels, the Chairman said. The Midwest Region had been chosen for initial implementation solely on the basis of Jaye's dedication to the cause and obvious organizational abilities. If all went well there, Jaye would be promoted. He would become CRAP's Executive Director as soon as might be, so that any lessons learned could be applied to the national reorganization with the greatest possible continuity. The current Director, Lester McClellan, was a good man, very sound indeed, but just not right for a job such as this.

The Chairman was more sympathetic to Jaye's concerns about Barber's demand for immediate production of a vulnerable singing homosexual. He seemed quite to understand the organizational changes necessary would take a little time. ("Roll over, Davey. Down—no, stay down.") On the other hand, as Chairman, his function was to keep all the branches coordinated and working together. The propaganda arm performed a crucial function at this stage. If Barber needed something, why, he, Jaye, ought to do his level best to produce it, and if news of some suitable person wound its way to the Chairman through any of the Council's many tentacles, he'd let Jaye know. That was it.

Perhaps Davey wasn't the chauffeur, after all. An obstreperous small dog of some kind?

There the matter lay throughout the intervening weeks while Jaye began the reorganization. This proceeded on schedule. Burdensome and tiresome though it was, it also challenged him. To take an organization run by accountants trained to ignore the personalities behind the numbers on their desks down the shortest road into something essentially rather different required great ingenuity and force of personality, and a lot of very carefully chosen new people to be fit into an organizational structure and culture that, for quickest results, simply couldn't be scrapped overnight. If it hadn't been for the small voice of his conscience, he thought he might be quite enjoying it.

Nor had his conscience been the only nag. All through it, Barber had been pressing him relentlessly from Texas, threatening him with dire consequences were his homosexual not produced on the spot. This enraged Jaye. Good lord, what did the man want? The mechanism wasn't half in place yet. Half? Not a quarter! Not an eighth! Nor would or could be for some time, short road or not. What was he supposed to be, a magician? Did the fellow have any notion what was involved? Barber did not care, but lashed him on into ever greater and more furious effort.

Predictably, no even remotely plausible candidate for Barber's propaganda campaign turned up. Jaye complained about the pestering to Frogmorton until the Chairman, in irritation, told him he had an eye out as promised, but that, ultimately, Jaye would have to solve his own problems, *if he could.* Clearly, no additional assistance could be expected from that quarter. Further complaints would only damage Jaye's hard-earned reputation as an able manager. After that, he suffered Barber's whip in growing anxiety, but in silence.

Finally, four nights ago now, the situation had broken. Lo and behold, the Chairman had kept his promise after all.

After a hard day, harder than usual, Jaye had been exhausted. He'd spent the whole of it battling the inevitable change resistance of subordinates fearful of losing their carefully built-up and protected little bailiwicks of power. Stung by his conscience, his consciousness that the whole project went against the grain of his convictions, he'd pushed back a little harder than he'd had to. Feelings had been hurt. He'd be propitiating bruised egos on the morrow. More trouble, drat it.

He'd cut his evening short and gone to bed. The ringing of the phone—the special phone with extensions only in his study and his bedroom—caught him deeply asleep. The insistent summons worked its way into his dreams so that only slowly did he realize what was happening. Sluggishly, he shifted his mountain of flesh and fumbled for the receiver.

Frogmorton's voice cut into his sleepy muddle. He tried to gather himself and understand what it told him. The Chairman had, quite by chance, acquired a person eminently suitable for Barber's purposes and would send him on directly to Texas. They even had a pretext to hold him, it appeared: this person had money which interested Jaye's Commission—one of Jaye's agents was after him—and a most improbable story about how it came into his possession. Did the name "Manning," or something like that, mean anything to Jaye?

Jaye struggled to bring himself more fully awake. Manning? He had a bad thought. This person, the one the Chairman was sending on to Barber, he wasn't a tall gangly individual was he? Scraggly hair, odd expression?

The Chairman laughed. Oh no! Barber should find him most suitable.

Jaye grunted. Well, then, who was he? What was this about Manning's money?

Somewhat stiffly, the Chairman said he'd rather hoped Jaye could tell him something about that.

Whom could the Chairman have? That Alexander person they'd been following around might fit the bill—and he had had one of Manning's hundreds, though they'd caught no hint he had any of the rest of it. Jaye's sense of discomfort growing, he sidestepped. He explained in the fewest possible words AmalCon's problem with its ATM machines and the reference to Manning, that Manning had disappeared and, as of yestereve at bedtime, his money had not been found. If Manning's money had turned up, its possessor was a crucial link. Jaye wanted him for questioning, probably intensive questioning, and fast. Barber could have him after.

That was impossible! The Chairman's tone turned very sharp, indeed.

Really? Jaye paused. *Whyever so?* He proceeded cautiously to stress the importance of the investigation in progress.

The Chairman's tone sharpened even further, if that were possible. Jaye's agents must be very clumsy indeed, he said, if he, Frogmorton, a completely uninvolved person, could learn of the money before they did. Were that the situation, the Chairman certainly hadn't anticipated any such thing. Direct interrogation of this person was going to have to be unnecessary, he said. He wished to notify Barber that the fellow would be on his way this very night. He was poised to send agents to collect him even as they spoke, which would resolve the problem of Barber's homosexual to the Chairman's complete satisfaction. Everybody could now stop pestering him about it and this important long-term plan could proceed apace. (Evidently, Jaye thought, Barber had been after him too.) Did Jaye wish to call Barber and ask him to approve a delay?

Jaye did not. He growled, then remembered whom he was talking to. He begged the Chairman to hold off the collection effort a few minutes, at least, to allow him to contact his agent. Obviously, there were very recent developments, evidently within the last several hours, of which he had yet to be informed.

The Chairman hung up on him.

He swung himself heavily out of bed. Barefoot, he padded down the hall to his study and flipped on the light. He looked up the number and rang Whitbread's cellphone. "The mobile customer you have dialed is unavailable, or has travelled outside the coverage area," a pleasant recorded voice told him, and offered to connect him with voicemail for the CRAP administrative office if only he would trouble himself to press "1." Instead, he tried Whitbread's hotel. The hotel was sorry, but Mr. Whitbread was not taking calls. Jaye demanded to be put through, but the response did not change. Angrily, he cut the connection and drummed his fingers on the desktop. He tried the surveillance room at the Harrington Hotel, which was supposed to be manned 24 hours a day, but received no answer there at all. What the devil? He moved on to CRAP's New York administrative office, where, once again, this time more or less as he expected in these pre-national reorganization days, only voicemail was available at this hour. He left an urgent message.

What the hell was Whitbread doing? Jaye cursed him from amidst an agony of ignorance. He very much wanted to believe no one could be reached because they were all busy following up on this break in the investigation, that Whitbread had things under control—but equally much feared the reverse. Whether he did or didn't, the pressure on Jaye to dispose of this other matter and get everybody off his back about it approached the insupportable. There had better be some answers in the morning! He called Frogmorton back and, fingers crossed, told him everything was fine, no problem at all.

All trace of sharpness disappeared from Frogmorton's voice. In fact, the man began to purr. As long as he had him, Jaye, on the line, the Chairman expressed his complete satisfaction with the reports he was getting on Jaye's reorganization efforts. The Council had decided to announce Jaye's appointment as CRAP's Executive Director Designate forthwith. As befitting the new importance envisioned for CRAP, this carried with it a seat on the Consortium Council!—and as befitting Jaye's new position, they had authorized a program of "financial incentives" *not* for public announcement, but which he hoped Jaye would find most satisfactory. Details on those would be reaching him by hand quite soon. Welcome to the club.

Jaye went back to bed, considerably mollified.

When Rico, as the first to arrive in the New York CRAP office the next morning, returned Jaye's call, he dispelled most unpleasantly the mystery of what Whitbread had been doing. They now had evidence which, except for Greg's instructions, Rico said, they would have had days earlier, evidence to suppose the subject they'd been watching, one David Alexander, familiar to Jaye from previous reports, had possessed Manning's money all along. He had disappeared during the night following an undercover contact Whitbread had had with him, inexplicably alone and without backup.

Of all the damned...

When Whitbread called a full hour later and reported his meeting had been unsuccessful, that he'd uncovered no more about the connection between Alexander and Manning than that there did, indeed, seem to be one, Jaye's rage was unbounded. He cut off Whitbread's protestations about how it had all seemed to be going so well and ordered him home, fully intending to let him stew while he, Jaye, took his time figuring out what to do about him.

At that point, he had learned the provenance of the person Frogmorton had forwarded to Texas, but the Manning investigation was a disaster! After months of work, they were worse off than when they'd started. Yes, AmalCon had recovered the money—a special courier had delivered it promptly the following morning—but that was insignificant. The whole thrust of the investigation, the sole object of the exercise, had been to lay hands on Manning, the one person, so far as they knew, who could tell them how the thefts had been done. Thanks to Whitbread's bumbling, their only lead, an individual who might bring them a step closer to Manning, had slipped most irritatingly beyond their reach. It took Jaye yet a further hour before he calmed down enough to call New York again and redirect whatever investigation still might be continuing onto the only remaining open trail, albeit one that heretofore had proved stubbornly futile: a renewed examination of Alexander's past to find the link with Manning.

No matter how much he needed Alexander, Jaye had not fancied asking for him back once he himself was personally safe at last. Under no circumstances would he interfere with that. Barber had his homosexual and could keep him. In Jaye's opinion, if the Chairman thought he was "suitable," it wouldn't matter much whether Barber agreed or not, though from the reports Jaye had seen about David Alexander, he certainly ought to. To sweeten the cake, Jaye emailed Barber details of the charges against Alexander: receiving stolen property, prostitution, and everything else he could think of on up to and including suspicion of the murder of Herbert Manning. In short, he made sure Barber had everything he'd need to exact compliance with any scheme he fancied. Jaye would now wash his hands of the matter. Barber's other demand, for a final $100,000, he could shove. No one squeezed a member of the Consortium Council.

In fact, he was fully prepared to do a little squeezing himself. Back in the present, he stared unseeing through a leaded oriole window at the sprawling ranch houses and swimming pools below. Where squeezing was concerned, Barber was top of his list. The man had dared threaten everything he held dear, and not only his birds and his good name. Why, he'd had to dissolve what remained of the family portfolio and even re-mortgage the house and land to make up the difference. It had kept him up nights for months. When his liabilities had begun to total more than his assets, his own staff had seen credit reports on him—Morgan Jaye!—turning up in routine lists of individuals who might warrant further scrutiny. He'd been *this far* from total ruin.

Barber deserved to know what that felt like and more. The man's arrogance was insupportable. Jaye's anger churned at the very thought of it. The fellow was going to have to watch his step. In a few months or maybe more—at any rate, once Jaye's position was absolutely secure—Barber was going down on the very first opportunity that offered, with the full force of Jaye's new secret police apparatus on top of him. Jaye smiled to think of it. He was living for the day. The thought had been a prime motivation in his setting his quibbles aside and getting to work on CRAP's expansion and reorganization plans.

While he was on the subject of his shitlist, his thoughts turned to Garrison Griffin, the computer genius with the baggy suit and the runny nose. He'd always seemed to be working odd hours, telecommuting by viewscreen and email, or ducking around corners whenever Jaye appeared. Jaye hadn't had a really good look at him in months. Until yesterday. Finally, *that* had been rectified... Jaye growled. Which readied him to deal with Whitbread in short strokes, now that the ATM business had wrapped itself up with an acceptable minimum of loose ends.

—Most intriguing ones, though. Although he'd learned the mechanics of the thefts, no hard evidence except the money connected this David Alexander person with Manning—but that point, how he obtained it, might now be moot. The engrossing question involved how the fellow had come to Frogmorton's personal attention at such an unusual hour. Why, the Chairman obviously knew the fellow's appearance! Only one theory bore much credence: they had some sort of acquaintance, and when spooked by Jaye's agent, the fool had sought help by rushing straight into the treacherous embrace of the Chairman of the Consortium Council. This David Alexander certainly posed an interesting subject for speculation.

Jaye froze, his eyes compressed to slits. David Alexander. *Davey.* Could it be? In this context, the asides Frogmorton had addressed to *someone* in the car with him made perfect sense right down to the tone of voice, which hadn't fitted either a chauffeur or a dog very well. Good lord, no wonder Frogmorton hadn't wanted CRAP to question the fellow!—and how nicely and immediately he, Jaye, had been rewarded when he complied!

Jaye opened his eyes with the conviction he'd stumbled on a key fact, one which, judiciously employed, might unlock events in almost any manner he chose, for instance, regarding his current obsession, Wilmore P. Barber. As Barber had pointed out—quite correctly, Jaye knew—Jaye could not touch him without the support of the Consortium's other branches. Any attempt to do so would result in Jaye's ruin, not Barber's. He badly needed support from within the Consortium.

Levering the Chairman onto his side would work wonders, he thought, and using the homophobic hysteria Barber himself had so ably prepared, these suspicions would be a lever tailor-made, if they could be substantiated.

A lever? A fulcrum he might use to move the world!

Jaye groped his way along the gallery. He sank heavily into the nearest chair, crushed by a sense of responsibility that pressed upon his shoulders with leaden hands. His qualms about the things the Consortium had asked him to do rushed over him once again: his conviction that a police state was a grave mistake, that it would carry within itself the seeds of its own destruction. Now, might not he have the power to do something about that?

Although he knew the Consortium was vulnerable, Barber was the only member of it currently within his grasp; his files on Barber were comprehensive and amply sufficient to discredit the man forever with the flock he had fleeced. Jaye's evidence of wider financial irregularities within the Consortium consisted only of the bare hints Barber had given him, and with the Council aware of his investigation of Barber, any further exploration plainly would be out of the question (especially after, as he'd been promised, he became implicated himself). However, with his large sense of history, Jaye knew the Consortium was not yet so well established as to defend itself from both the removal of its chief drumbeater on the religious right and the simultaneous exposure of Frogmorton, its principal front man, as hypocritical by its own moral code. With the door thus cracked, a public investigation of the Council's financial legerdemain would be possible. The Consortium would fall; a reversion to democratic government would occur. While this would deny the ruling elite some of the power it currently enjoyed under the Consortium, democracy was still the form of government under which it had evolved. Society would survive largely intact.

Jaye knew this was probably the last moment such a strategy could be effective. Once the Consortium had established a full-service secret police force, there never again would be anything one single individual could do to it, not even that force's director, who would merely sign his own death warrant if he tried. The inherent organizational inertia of all established power structures would see to that, he thought.

It was now or not at all. The man on the fulcrum, able to swing the balance one way or the other with a breath, closed his eyes and swayed in his chair. The sensation of power was vertiginous. For generations to come, schoolchildren might read how he, Morgan Jaye, had singlehandedly saved the country from totalitarianism. As an added bonus, he could remove Barber right now, or at least, after what he assumed would be only a brief investigation into Frogmorton's personal life. Whereas, if he waited, the opportunity he'd need to destroy the man might be a very long time in coming...

His eyes snapped open. Unnoticed, his finger had idled itself through the chair's threadbare brocade to root around in the stuffing. He jerked it back in disgust. The decision made itself in that instant. There was no decision, really. The Consortium wanted him and had labored long and hard to arrange matters so that he had only one choice. By playing along, he would not only salvage his own position, but by increasing the wealth and power of the agency he headed, he would increase his own immeasurably; this had been promised him in no uncertain terms. While the alternative entailed statesmanship of the noblest order and immediate personal vengeance on Barber, it also meant personal ruin. Without quick relief of the sort Froggy was promising him, his over-strained finances must necessarily crumble in confusion. Doubtless, the Consortium also would throw charges about his smuggling into the mix to make sure he accompanied them all the way to the bottom. He'd end up as deep in the mud as any of them.

He sighed heavily as streamers of historical glory dissolved about him. Whatever his scruples, he was no statesman, let alone martyr, and knew it. He accepted reality. Evidently, statesmanship was for those who could afford it.

Very well, he would wait to move on Barber, and repair his tattered fortunes in the meantime. As for society, he would look after its interests as best he could. Fatalistically, he supposed its eventual fate would have to be its own affair. He quashed his scruples finally and forever. They were clearly out of date. Frogmorton's secret, if it existed, was safe with him.

He experienced a last moment of doubt. Were that Frogmorton's secret, why would he shuffle the evidence of it off to Barber for safekeeping? Didn't he know what kind of person Barber was? He must!

—And that surely was the answer. Obviously enough, if there were a secret, Barber knew it already. He certainly seemed to have the dirt on everybody else. Jaye sighed again. Doubtless, Barber and Frogmorton had been blackmailing each other for years. What had Barber said? *Hell, Froggy took me for a lot more than that before I learned the ropes...*

He wondered exactly how deep Frogmorton's support of the rapacious reverend ran, anyhow. Perhaps, just perhaps, the Chairman might be as eager to get rid of him as he was himself if the right occasion offered, and if the right pressure could be applied to help Frogmorton make up his mind. A small highly discreet investigation of the Chairman's personal arrangements beginning with a detailed re-examination of their existing surveillance records on David Alexander might well be in order. One way or another, if blackmail were common currency among members of the Council, he'd better start accumulating stock in trade so as to ensure the level of support he'd need in the event...

Somewhere in the house, a phone rang. His reverie broken, Jaye headed downstairs. His houseman met him at the study door. "Rev. Barber is on the phone for you, sir."

Speak of the devil. Jaye nodded and closed the door. Barber's heavy features filled the viewscreen at his desk. "Good morning," Jaye said coldly.

"Howdy." The reverend was matter of fact. "Just calling to acknowledge receipt of your part of our bargain from New Yawk."

"Satisfactory?"

"Oh heavens, yes. They'll eat him up. Uh, about the money, that last hundred thou."

"Yes?" Jaye's tone was freezing.

"Well, okay." Barber pursed his lips thoughtfully, as if calculating the balance due. "Considering the fine work you been doing—everybody's talking about it—I'd say you're off the hook. So welcome to the club. Froggy says there'll be a few little deals for you in the by and by. Guess he'll want to talk to you about that hisself. But you and me is square, I figger. Say hello to the little birdies for me." With that, he flashed his oily smile, perhaps even a bit sheepishly, and was gone.

The big man grunted. Nobody'd ever said Barber wasn't sharp on the uptake. Sticking him wasn't going to be easy.

He levered himself out of his chair. The reverend's parting shot had reminded him it was feeding time in the conservatory.

This had been added in his great-grandfather's time, before the family's significant troubles began. It ran the entire length of the house, and served now also as Jaye's aviary. As his mother had been unable to afford a gardener, Jaye had tended the plants himself from boyhood. Gardening had been his first passion, and the desire to see his trees and shrubs alive with inhabitants had been his initial motivation for bird collecting as well. He picked up a pail of seeds and fruit the houseman had left for him at the wrought iron and glass entry door in what once had been the outside wall of the house. Beyond it, he moved among the carefully tended rareties noting with satisfaction an unusual variety of Dieffenbachia unfurling a spiky green flower, a Japanese plum tree heavy with ripening fruit... Hmmm, time to mulch those orchids again. He furrowed his brow at them.

"Whaddayaknow, seems a bird in the bush beats two in the hand, after all."

The voice was familiar, yet also not, as if one Jaye heard every day suddenly had said something startlingly unusual. He craned his vast corpus about to see the speaker. No one was present, no one at all.

A large blue bird sat in a tree rhododendron. Head sideways, its gold and black eye regarded him unblinkingly. Jaye approached it, eyes narrowed. "Pretty baby? Baby wants a peanut?"

"Actually, I'd prefer a belt, if you've got one handy. Barrel bourbon's a treat that doesn't exist where I come from." The bird stuck a prehensile tongue out at him, and waggled it.

"Oh. It's *you*." Jaye grunted in annoyance. "That is a rare, Hyacinth Macaw. Fewer than 100 remain in the world. It is priceless, and I do not want it damaged."

"Then you won't be taking any swings at me with the poker this time," the bird said, "Or with those." It nodded its beak at the pair of pruning shears around which Jaye's knuckles were whitening.

With an effort, Jaye relaxed his hold on the shears. "What do you want."

"Why, to be congratulated on the outcome of our little venture in New York. Everything's satisfactory, no?"

Jaye allowed himself a second to accept the Entity's habitation of his macaw, then shifted grimly into business mode. "As per contract, but congratulations are scarcely in order. Your boy Whitbread..."

"Spooked the solution to your problem straight into the arms of the Chairman of the Consortium Council, which led to its delivery to Texas via the shortest route. That was what you wanted, wasn't it." It was not a question.

"As usual, my convenience was disregarded, and this time, the cost to me in personal embarrassment was even greater than usual. How this will impact my ability to perform my duties in the future is unclear. I hereby serve notice that this has been our last association. In my position, I can no longer allow..."

The bird clacked its beak. "If you don't want our help, don't ask for it. You've always done extremely well from our little deals, and it all turned out okay this time too, didn't it?"

Jaye scowled. "I see how expendable you consider people. What happens when my turn comes, eh? I don't like it. From now on I prefer to rely on my own judgment and initiative. If misfortune is to strike me, I would prefer it to be on my own account. I would even prefer it to result from random chance rather than from my being an ill-regarded pawn in games I do not clearly understand."

"Now now, I wouldn't worry about that if I were you. Sure, the boys have had their fun with you now and then. It's just their way. Forget it. I happen to know you're very highly regarded up top. How do you think you got 'your position' in the first place? The Master's had his fingers up your asshole from the very beginning."

So it was true. The Entities had been manipulating him for years, at least since his first introduction to them and possibly even longer than that. He should have been toweringly angry. Yet, the casual way the bird dropped the information, as if acknowledging that the damage was done and there was no longer anything he could do about it, stunned him. He thought of the years of struggle and wondered how much of it he'd endured only to suit the goals of these creatures. Some of it? All of it? He took a step closer to the bird, which flapped its wings nervously, eyeing the shears. "You've been using me, using me toward ends of which I am completely ignorant. I've felt it for a long time, and now you admit it. You will tell me what the purpose is. Now."

"I've told you before. Like you, I am..."

"...ignorant of the grand design, yes yes. I no longer accept that. If, as you give me to believe, I occupy a place of importance in your schemes, I make knowing a condition of future cooperation. Tell your master that."

The bird was muttering something under its breath, something that sounded very much like, "Me and my big mouth." To

Jaye, it said, "Maybe you noticed your cooperation wasn't exactly required before."

"*I demand...*," Jaye roared, then reminded himself he wasn't in a position to demand much of anything where these creatures were concerned. He controlled himself with an effort. "Very well, then. I will make my *request* reasonable. Tell me the remaining mechanism of Whitbread's mission to New York. Surely you know, now that it's over, and surely I can be accommodated to this extent." He fixed his grimmest, normally most effective stare on the bird. "How did Alexander get Manning's money?"

The bird sighed and said nothing.

"What connects this Alexander person to the Chairman?"

"I should tell you your business? What kind of secret police chief are you? If you want to know, find out."

The bird mocked him. Jaye's grip tightened on the shears. Again, he controlled himself. "That leaves only the boy, Whitbread."

"We continue to have a strong interest in him."

"Whitbread..."

"Is zooming in on your front doorbell."

A solemn gong echoed from the front part of the house. In the pause ensuing, the bird began straightening some feathers under its left wing.

"So what am I to do with him? I was about to fire him." Jaye waited for an answer, which was not forthcoming. The bird ignored him and turned its attention to its breast plumage. Jaye cleared his throat.

The houseman appeared at the edge of the clearing. "Mr. Whitbread is here, sir." Jaye's scowl deepened. "You'll remember you asked me to phone and summon him."

"That's right. In here please, Henry."

The houseman headed off. Jaye jerked with annoyance as the bird continued preening. This, plainly, was the purpose of the Entity's visit, not pointless banter, but to monitor the upcoming interview, which, apparently, carried the potential not to be the cut and dried little affair he'd envisioned.

"Well?" he demanded.

The bird lifted its head. "Well what? *If* you'll recall, you specifically requested Whitbread back. Evidently we were able to accommodate you, because here he is. What are you to do with him? Why ask me? What did you want him for?—and if there's a problem, why not rely on your own judgment and initiative, if you're so big on it? What's your own favorite phrase? I suggest using your intellect as enlightened by experience," the bird said, and renewed explorations under its wing. Jaye's knuckles whitened on the shears.

* * * * *

Greg followed the houseman into the conservatory. After the stillness and dark of the great hall where he'd waited, the bright colors of the flowering trees and bushes and the flashing, jewel-like creatures zooming through the air dazzled him. The sound of avian chatter was deafening. His hand strayed to adjust his tie. Obeying the houseman's gesture, he followed a twisty little path to a sort of clearing, brightly colored Mexican tiles on the ground, wrought iron benches echoing the patterns leaded into the glass roof overhead, and Morgan Jaye standing mountainously before him, a pair of gardening shears in hand. Behind Jaye, a large blue bird regarded Greg with an unblinking stare. So hypnotic was the bird's eye, he could not tear his gaze from it.

The big man's voice broke the spell. "Sit down, Whitbread."

The obvious wealth and taste of the house intimidated Greg beyond belief. In the great hall and later on his short tour through to the conservatory, he hadn't been able to help noticing that not only was everything in the place obviously first-rate, but it all had that slightly shabby look of long use about it which bespoke very old money, indeed. The furniture and fittings all looked as if they'd been born in their places. You couldn't buy this atmosphere at any price.

He backed up slowly until one of the wrought iron benches touched the backs of his knees. He perched the smallest possible portion of his behind on the edge of it and cleared his throat. "Wonderful, sir." He gestured vaguely around at the conservatory and the birds. "Is all this your collection, sir?" Greg bit his lip. Whom else's might it be? He was being inane.

The blue bird spoke. "Not entirely."

Both Greg and Jaye stared at it. The same thought occurred to both of them. Would the bird take part in their conversation?

Fantastic, thought Greg.

Damned unsettling nuisance, thought Jaye, *if this is on my initiative, let me handle it!*

Jaye noted with relief that the bird seemed to respond to his thought. It screeched and whistled insanely, then went back to rooting around under its wing. "Pardon me," it said. "I've got fleas."

The effort to keep from sputtering with laughter turned Greg red in the face. Here was a most unexpected side of Morgan Jaye. You really had to hand it to a guy with the balls to teach his bird to say a thing like that.

Jaye himself went white-lipped with fury. He swung back to Greg and made an effort to forget the damned bird was there. He focused in on Greg. "I've called you here to discuss the consequences of your mission."

"Yes sir," Greg broke in. "I wanted to talk to you about that. We had no idea he had the money, sir. Rico and Freddie screwed up bigtime. They..."

The big man aimed a finger. "Rico and Freddie were not to blame. They followed your instructions. You ordered their search of Alexander's room be surreptitious. They were to leave no traces of themselves, and they didn't. Moreover, you know perfectly well you should have had them as backup when you went to interview the man." Greg looked down at the tiles. "However, as it happens, your mission, while badly botched, was not a total loss. Although you spooked Alexander, you would seem to have spooked him into conspicuously bad judgment. Within hours of your interview, he ran himself afoul of the Council's personal security forces. Both Alexander and the money were recovered."

Greg sat bolt upright. David's whereabouts were known? He struggled to contain himself. "W-where is... where is Alexander now, sir?"

Jaye looked at him squarely. "That is no longer your concern."

"But sir! Surely, he must be questioned. I'd like to do that, sir, to redeem myself."

"The matter is out of our hands."

"But *sir!*"

"It's over." The big man's voice took on an edge that defied contradiction.

Greg stared at him bugeyed. He felt like a drowning man struggling up through the water whose vision of the surface has just revealed a solid sheet of ice. He half rose, and made small motions flailing the air with his hands. Jaye *knew* where David was and must tell him! Quickly, he recovered himself. He must know what was going on here!

He forced himself to meet Jaye's eyes. "But sir, the investigation! I know I botched it, sir, but I've learned from it! Surely you can imagine that I have! I'm overwhelmed to find out my mistakes weren't fatal. Please give me a chance to redeem myself, to prove your confidence in me wasn't misplaced! So we have Alexander and the money. That's wonderful! But we don't have Manning! He's the key to the problem, isn't he, sir? The problem with the ATM thefts, sir? Please let me speak to Alexander again, sir. I can get what you want, sir, please let me." He realized he was begging shamelessly, and subsided. He stared at Jaye wide-eyed in supplication.

"The investigation is closed. You yourself spooked Alexander into the clutches of the Council's security forces. He is no longer available to us." Greg bowed his head. "Even if he were, I would not trust you with him. You say you've learned from botching it? Explain to me, please, how Alexander knew you were an agent of the Commission?" As, of course, he had. He'd told Frogmorton a CRAP agent was after him.

Greg gaped. This was the first he'd heard of that.

"Some undercover agent! As for the ATM thefts, there have been some recent developments."

Quite recent. Purely as a matter of routine, Jaye had put everyone who'd programmed on the ATM system under surveillance from shortly after the thefts occurred, including Garrison Griffin. Although this surveillance revealed no obvious connections to the ATM thefts, it did show Griffin to be very far from the paragon of prudence and probity they'd thought. His troubles with drugs and alcohol were apparent from the start and the amounts of money he spent on them were astonishingly beyond his means, but the origin of this money could not be pinned down. It seemed simply to appear in his accounts.

Because of Griffin's intimate involvement in all of AmalCon's most sensitive systems, this was extremely disturbing, and triggered an entirely new, priority investigation to discover how and whence, precisely, he obtained his funds. Aware Griffin could have software in place to erase all evidence of illegal transactions at the touch of a button, or perhaps automatically if he did *not* reconfirm them periodically, they considered it imperative not to arouse his suspicions. For five solid frustrating months they confined themselves to following him around and monitoring his computer traffic, discovering nothing untoward.

The break had come purely as a matter of unrelated routine, as the kind of accident which had The Entities' signature written all over it as clearly as if they'd sent cherubs blowing trumpets to announce it in AmalCon's mainfloor teller lobby. During a makework audit of a now disused bookkeeping program, Watkins in Software Security had stumbled on a line of programming code which did not appear in the master copy. This line of code led to a likewise uncharted subroutine which derailed the master program through to a computer jack unlisted in any inventory of such they had.

Rather than shrug it off or shove the matter upstairs to some middle manager who'd dither for days deciding what course of action most likely would advance his career, Watkins, bright boy that he was, had taken the initiative in the form of a cab to the office of the electrical engineering firm that had designed and installed the system. There, he looked up the offending jack on the master schematic. It turned out to be in Griffin's office, which led to an obvious suspicion why it did not appear in the inventories: with Griffin's knowledge of and complete access to their system, it would have been no trouble for him to remove it.

In short order, surveillance of traffic through this jack had resolved their investigation of Garrison Griffin. Under interrogation, the man had crumbled immediately. He was relieved to be caught; he needed help badly, and begged for it. He threw himself on the interrogator's mercy and copped not only to his current schemes, but to dozens of others all evidence of which had been removed from the system long since, including the ATM access program. In fact, the man's confessional urge seemed limited only by his memory, which improved hourly. As his list of past perfidies lengthened, that such chicanery could go on immediately under Jaye's nose for so many years was proving an ever-elongating embarrassment. Jaye was more than ready to let some attorney begin insisting on the man's Fifth Amendment right to shut up.

"After a lengthy investigation," Jaye continued, "Garrison Griffin, our most trusted *consultant*—" The big man's face twisted into an ugly grimace. "—confessed to a whole series of unauthorized manipulations run by the PC's in his office and home, including the ATM access protocol. How Manning learned of it, Griffin claims not to know. Considering how cooperative he seems to be in every other respect, I suppose we must believe him. However, he and Manning were associated. I suppose Manning may have had opportunity to find it out. Griffin probably babbled it. He will enter rehabilitation for substance abuse." Jaye sniffed. "If he survives, I expect he'll end up teaching BASIC in some prison education program—but our compelling interest in Manning is terminated. The access subroutines have been eliminated and provision is being made to protect our systems from any such schemes in the future. We no longer need him. He's purely a police matter now."

Jaye dismissed Manning with a wave of his hand and looked at Greg. The young man was staring at the floor, the very picture of dejection and hurt. Jaye softened. Plainly, he thought, the boy felt his failure keenly. Why wouldn't he? He wasn't at fault; he'd been given a task far beyond his experience and ability, and now would be asked to pay the price.

Jaye felt himself moved by the injustice of it, and the waste. The boy was bright, loyal as they came, and pathetically eager to please. Jaye discovered himself warming to Greg. Once this obligatory dutch uncle treatment was over, he could still retain Greg in CRAP's service. Stifled fatherly feelings arose. If he'd ever had a son, this was just the kind of attractive, intelligent and tractable young man he'd have wanted that son to be. Given professional progress and discretion in his personal life, the boy could yet attain the place he'd been promised on Jaye's personal staff, and might even come to be his protégé.

Then he remembered the Entity inhabiting his macaw. The fatherly feelings collapsed. The Entities were as far beyond his control as they were his comprehension. They were completely unrevealing and annoyingly insolent. His involvement with them had become infused with futile anger. Their now open admission they'd been manipulating his life made it plain he should not be mixed up with them any more than he had to be, no matter the cost, if he wanted any control at all over his own destiny.

He regarded Greg. The Entities weren't through with him yet. They had a *strong interest* in Whitbread. The bird had used those very words. No, if he really wanted a protégé—and just now he wasn't very sure he did, after all—he had plenty of suitable candidates: for instance, Watkins, also bright, loyal and tractable (if not markedly attractive; he rather reminded Jaye of a hedgehog with a skin condition). Watkins had demonstrated the ability to take initiative *properly*. Good family too. He'd make an excellent protégé, that is, if The Entities didn't have a finger up his asshole as well.

The shocking impropriety of the Entity's image, coming upon him unexpectedly this way, turned Jaye red in the face. *Protégés, bah.* His inclination to cut himself loose from Greg solidified into definitely the prudent thing to do. Very well.

"As for you," he continued, "although your mission turned out well in the end, the damage was considerable none the less. The

Commission to Reduce Accounting Problems is a young service struggling to establish itself among the powers that be. I cannot afford to forgive this kind of stumbling about."

Jaye steeled himself to the dirty deed. "It has been impossible to contain knowledge of your role in the disgrace of our service. Shall I tell you how it appears to your colleagues? You struggled for weeks with three dozen men, and as a result of your bumbling, what you could not do was done in half an hour by a couple of muscleheads from a rival service. Shameful! The Chairman himself called you clumsy." He had too, if not by name as Jaye made it seem. The memory of the unprofitable fancy dancing Whitbread's clumsiness had occasioned stiffened Jaye still further.

"Surely you must see your position is untenable. Looking your colleagues in the face would be difficult, to say the least. Your chances of promotion would be small and indefinitely delayed. Nor will news of this stay confined to the Commission. People whisper, no matter what you do to stop them. This will follow you anywhere you go in the security field. Your best choice is to develop a new career altogether. With your obvious talents, you'll certainly do better almost anyplace else."

He paused. The boy was plainly crestfallen. In fact, he looked dazed, hopeless, and ready to cry. Jaye unbent a little. Was he going too far? He really had overstated the case rather baldly.

He hastened to soften the blow. "Now, I understand I'm partly responsible. You were too young and inexperienced to head up an assignment of this complexity. I'm sorry. Your severance will be *substantial*." If he were throwing the boy to the mercy of The Entities, at least he wouldn't leave him destitute. "That, in addition to the separation pay you have coming from Catchem Billem & Stickem should allow you as much time as you need to rest up and decide what you'd like to do next."

Drat it, the boy really was crying. This display of emotion embarrassed Jaye deeply. He proffered his pocket handkerchief. "I'm sorry, really..." But Greg had turned and fled.

Jaye wheeled on the bird. "I did not enjoy that," he snapped, "and did it only to keep your *strong interest* in him from contaminating me as well. Now get out. I'm through with the lot of you."

The bird shrugged. "You've got aphids too."

Jaye forgot himself completely. He bellowed in helpless rage and jerked upwards with the shears.

The bird squawked in completely birdlike confusion at the sudden movement and flapped off to a higher perch. Jaye was alone with his collections once more.

* * * * *

Outside, the relentless heat and sun were a poisonous shock. Greg fumbled in agitation with the door to his car, tears still streaming down his face. He jabbed the key at the lock furiously. He felt he couldn't afford a single second to recover lest Jaye come down the steps after him still waving that ridiculous pocket handkerchief. That he'd cried had surprised and shocked him. His tears weren't tears of embarrassment at being discharged as Jaye clearly had thought, but tears of frustration and towering rage Jaye would not—or could not, it hardly mattered—tell him where David was. He'd fled lest he do something else equally bizarre, such as attack the man and destroy what little future he seemed to have left.

By the time he reached the expressway the tears had stopped flowing. His driving had steadied up a bit, but his mood was more hopeless than ever. The enormity of what had happened overwhelmed him. He'd lost his job. The last toehold into his once so glowingly imagined future had disintegrated beneath him. How would he find David now with no resources at all? And what if he did? David had known he was a CRAP agent? He puzzled at that. He could not imagine how it had happened. Oh, why had he not levelled with David when he'd had the chance? How deep his perfidy must seem to his beloved now! David's golden image glowed reproachfully through the windshield at him, and resolved into a throbbing ache. Most likely, that was all he'd have of David ever again, a dull everpresent ache. It was too much to bear.

As he approached city limits, depression overwhelmed him to the extent that, once again, he had difficulty concentrating on the road. He thought it might be a good idea to pull over for a while. He turned up the next exit ramp and found himself on the boulevard where Magellan Park bordered the expressway.

Magellan Park! Even though he had never entered it again after the murder of Jimmy Snyder so many years ago, it still occupied an important corner in his heart. As the scene of so many of his happiest and most interesting childhood exploits, he was confident he knew every inch of it, every path and every bush even yet. Especially since his recent self-revelations, the mere fact of its existence, permanent and unchanging amidst the shifting substance of life, had provided a thread connecting his present with the hard reality of his past. Now, with nothing to do and no place to go, with his dreams for the future and all his hopes for happiness, the whole structure of his life once so firmly within his grasp shown for the mirage it had been, the thought of touching base with the real and tangible memories of his childhood drew him powerfully. This was just the place for a little quiet soul searching, just the place to help him decide who he was by getting some concrete reminder of whom he once had been. As for the Puerto Ricans, well, let them kill him as they'd threatened. Just now, he didn't much care. Eagerly, he parked the car in a bus stop and wandered into the park.

To his great wonder, he barely recognized the place. The tangles of undergrowth he remembered were gone, cut down long ago, he guessed, to eliminate the cover necessary to the murderous gang for their predations on the neighborhood citizenry. Instead, wide green lawns studded with large trees spread before him. Other changes were apparent too. The new residents of the surrounding neighborhood had settled in and prospered, and their park with them. The grass was smooth and freshly cut. Inky black walks exuded the chthonic aroma of fresh asphalt. The lagoon had been cleaned of its weeds and green scum and shimmered blue in the heat. The artificial ruin overlooking it shone with fresh tuckpointing and looked not nearly so ruinous as in former days.

The rock garden, when, by accident more than memory, Greg finally found it, had shared in this prosperity. The dark tangle of dead and stunted trees overhead had been cleared away, as had the ferns, weeds, and scabrous roots overgrowing its limestone terracing. Sunlight streamed down on cleaned and relaid stones along the steep banks. Pansies, petunias, snapdragons and geraniums grew in the terraces. Brightly colored garden statuettes of the Twelve Apostles occupied niches furnished with floodlights which, Greg supposed, must provide a brilliant light to deter adventurers in the night. For the first time ever, Greg saw the little stream. Guarded by the Blessed Virgin, it burbled clear from a rocky cleft at one end of the canyon. Dazed, Greg followed it to a small pool at the other, where Mary Magdalene stared pensively into crystal depths at a shiny steel drain.

He stumbled back along the little path through a haze of pain and loss. In one day, he had lost not only all his future, but his past as well, his childhood. He felt completely bereft and adrift. Why was this fair?

Behind him, Mary Magdalene lifted her head from contemplation of the drain and gave a hard look at his retreating back.

David's image diffused before him for the first time in days. In its place, a sad undirected anger bubbled up inside him. Some retaliation against the sheer perversity of fate was necessary. He shrugged in impotence. What could he do against Morgan Jaye or Harrison Keeler Frogmorton III? If he so much as brought himself to their notice again, they'd squash him like a loathsome yet soon forgotten slug. As for the wanton destruction of this, the only even vaguely romantic locale of his childhood and its replacement by the cheerful hopeless vulgarity he saw around him, how could he strike back at a whole city neighborhood? His essentially conventional and law abiding soul forbade any remotely adequate plan to occur to him.

He shivered in rage and frustration. At least he could make a gesture, a small and private, if futile, gesture that yet would express his contempt at this desecration of his childhood's holy of holies.

A suitably defiant and completely appropriate act occurred to him. From the depths of the rock garden he stared around, a hand straying to straighten the knot of his tie. He was alone by the fake brook. The heat was a silent oven. An Apostle posed in sober saintliness..

He unzipped his pants and took matters in hand. He urinated into the little stream, watching the yellow liquid blend gradually with the water as they ran off together around the bend whither Mary Magdalene awaited, the yellow stridently apparent against the white stones below. Good. The, to him, daringly unconventional nature of the act began the rebuilding of his confidence. Perhaps he could struggle against fate and win, after all.

A voice broke the silence on the bank behind him. "Hey you down there! Holster that!"

Greg's whole body clenched. The stream of urine choked off at once, leaving a small dribble of wet down the otherwise immaculate crease of one trouserleg. Hurriedly, he stuffed himself back into his underwear and zipped up. Turning around, he cursed fate yet again. A young policeman stood, hands on hips, glaring ferociously down at him. The sun glinted off the shiny star of his badge.

The policeman descended the bank rapidly, leaping from limestone crag to flowered terrace in a recklessly agile way that seemed somehow oddly familiar. He landed on the path a bit unsteadily, which was also familiar, and proved to be a well-made athletic-looking fellow a few years younger than Greg. He was shortish for a policeman, Greg noted, with a handsome-ugly, innately cheerful Irish face and a no-nonsense air. "Look, pal, the public facilities are down by the lagoon. Citizens 'round here don't want no pre-verts. Whadaya suppose'd happen if some nice Rican lady walked her poodle down here for a drink, huh? You could scare the poor pooch to death, that's what, and where would we be then?" He smiled, but a hand strayed toward his nightstick.

Greg stared at him intently. The impression of familiarity had grown stronger with every word and gesture. His eyes dropped to the policeman's nametag.

371

"Mulligan! Tommy Mulligan? I'm right, aren't I? It's me, Greg! Greg Whitbread! Don't you remember me?"

The policeman gaped at him, then grinned widely. "Greg! Sonovabitch!" He came forward fast and grabbed Greg by both biceps hard enough to hurt. "Nice to catch up with you, man! Whaderyou doing here?" He laughed. "No, I can see what you're doing, relivin' old times, that's what! Scene of my finest triumph, huh?" He laughed again, punched Greg playfully in the chest and backed off a step, laughing even harder. "So okay! No bust for public urination today! Bring on those poodles! Just don't let Johnson catch you. He's my partner. Old fart, okay for a black guy, havin' his lunchtime snooze right now up by the castle. Shit! This place's so peaceful now, they only assign old bulls and rookies. That's me, Rookie Mulligan! First beat outa the Academy, but you just watch me! I'll be plainclothes in a year, you bet I will!"

Swept up in this typically Mulligan outpouring of words and physical enthusiasm, Greg's anger and frustration melted away. Almost against his will, he felt the one emotion he'd have been sure he would not feel today. He was charmed. "That's great, Tommy. I'm in law enforcement myself. Got a job in bank security chasing embezzlers, counterfeiters and computer thieves." He shrugged. "Or had, anyway, until this morning."

Tommy seemed not to hear this last bit. "Wow! Really? That's fanfuckingtastic! I'd really like to talk to you about that sometime!"

Greg changed the subject. "Not much like it used to be around here, is it?"

Tommy smiled sadly. "No, not much. The Ricans're on the up and up, these days. Citizens 'round here are very particular somebody might notice they're the same guys chasing us and beating us up when we were kids—least, the ones left after they finishing putting holes in each other and doping themselves to death—all oh-so respectable now. You gotta laugh."

They quickly lost themselves in mutual nostalgia. "Hey, do kids still climb the castle?" "You remember the old ladies with their binoculars?" "What ever happened to Frankie?" "And Whitey!

Remember Whitey?" In this way, they babbled happily on, their bond magically re-established just as it had been the last time they'd seen one another, best buddies, until their reminiscing brought Greg to the awesome, solemn and terrible thing that had happened in the park, and the bit of ground associated with it. "Hey, Tommy, you remember our clearing, our little private place, where they found Jimmy Snyder? I looked for it on the way in, and couldn't find it. Where was that?"

Tommy looked at him fixedly. "Yeah, I remember. Over there." He waved vaguely in the direction of the boulevard.

Keenly aware that Jimmy Snyder wasn't the only thing that had ever happened there, Greg remembered the carefree abandon of their little boys' naughty play. Vividly. Oh, if only they could do that again; if only they could recapture those days, just for an hour! Adrift in his friendless world, he badly needed to find the trust they'd once had in one another, to re-establish with this newfound old friend the willingness they'd once had to go anywhere, do anything, and share everything.

Everything.

He knew for a fact those old days had stayed with him. Queer he'd been and queer he was. Had they stayed with Tommy too? A policeman? Dare he try to find out?

The man he loved had fled, hopelessly beyond reach or comprehension. His life was shattered. So what if it went wrong? What did anything matter now? What could Tommy do to him? Hit him? Bust him as a public nuisance? What difference did it make?

He gathered the crumbs of his shattered courage and looked into Tommy's eyes. These weren't the hypnotically compelling eyes of David Alexander, but were nice enough normal human eyes. Brown. With good cheer and kindness, reckless courage and confidence in them—enough, more than enough of all those things for two. Suddenly, he wanted Tommy badly, and knew he would act. "I remember too," he said softly. "I... I was thinking about those days not too long ago," Damn, it sounded flat! How *did* one do this? "I mean... I've been thinking about it—I mean them—quite a lot." He trailed off.

Tommy held his eye a long moment. "Jeez, it's tough to be a cop."

What the hell did that mean? Greg backpedalled hastily. "But I guess they beat all that out of us, anyway. Me in high school, and you in military academy, probably." His voice broke on the last word. The way it came out was as much question as statement.

"Yeah, they beat it out of us, all right." Tommy came forward a step and put his arms around Greg's neck. "But they never should have. You think?"

Greg trembled. "No, they never should have," he murmured, just as Tommy kissed him.

Chapter Eight
A MIGHTY FORTRESS IS OUR DJINN

e each of us have our personal mental landscape, that unique set of assumptions, values and subjective impressions which comprise our view of the world. Where we stand determines what we see, and this is the matrix which forms our opinions. It establishes not only our reactions, but whom our friends will be, our life goals, how we approach them, our place in the community—and vice versa: where we live, what we want, what we do and whom we see shape our landscape in return. For most people, both halves of the process arise together into a coherent, self-reinforcing way of life.

The longer and more successfully we live in our landscape, the more it becomes part of our identity and the more self-evidently right it seems, until, ultimately, self-evidence can become smug self-satisfaction. From a well broken-in, conveniently arranged landscape come comfortably automatic responses to the most difficult issues of the day. This saves the labor of protracted thought most people find so disagreeable and so potentially destabilizing.

We seek to render needless the difficult and uncomfortable process of challenging our assumptions and striking thence to uncharted territory. We're most at ease among more-or-less likeminded individuals who share, and thus reinforce, our view. We're strongly tempted to dismiss opinions (and often the people who bear them) that differ in any significant way from our own. We tend to make much of information that fits in our landscape regardless of how ill it may be established as fact, and belittle or ignore even the best established facts that don't. So successful are we at this that many of us develop our mental landscapes in youth and reside in them throughout our lives.

When we are young, all territory is uncharted and the exploration equally difficult no matter its direction—so difficult that some will always opt not to do it at all, assuming unaltered the convictions of their forbearers. Others, however, move relentlessly outwards and set new standards for us all.

When we are old, the painful process often seems unnecessary. At great personal expense, we have already settled the shape of our universe. Unless someone or something comes along to jolt us out of it, therein do we dwell.

If only the world would stand still for us! While we remain largely the same, new youth tread upon our heels. They revise our opinions and alter our view, only to be superseded themselves when their youth has passed. In this way youthfully idealistic liberals become kneejerk reactionaries in old age.

Of course, jolts do come. Wars, social upheavals and other basic threats to our settled way of life can force reappraisal. In sections of society where these occur or where independent thinking is a basic value, intelligent and courageous persons of all ages break with the past and change with the times. In places where such threats are less frequent, or where powerful vested interests maintain the settled order successfully, independent thinking is usually seen as either unnecessary or actually dangerous. "Traditional values" reign and progress moves at a slower pace. Some places where life has gone smoothly, placidly, conventionally onwards for decades wind up generations behind.

In such a place the Rev. Billy Barber had his headquarters. Before his arrival, Necktie Gulch had been merely another small Texas town. The last great revolution in its thinking had come when its original settlers exchanged the sureties of their roots for the challenges of life in the untried frontier. Their values—independence, willingness to learn the state-of-the-art trades of the place and time, and trust in a strong benevolent god, values which made their journey and the town itself possible—had, in their descendants, long since ossified into prideful rejection of outside ideas, refusal to change what once had served their forbearers well, and religious intolerance.

Their town reflected this preoccupation with better times long gone. The beauty salon offered the last word in hairstyles twenty years out of date. The café eked out a marginal breakfast and lunch business by advertising periodic specials at "1995 Prices." Except for a certain progressive loss of paint, the old-fashioned false fronts on the courthouse square remained just as they had been, frozen in time when the Wal-Mart opened outside town and caused them to be boarded up. —And after the Wal-Mart itself closed to be replaced by a megastore across the county line, grass literally grew in the streets.

In the center of the square, beds of petunias banked the war memorial cannon as they'd done a hundred years and more beneath Sam Houston's finger uplifted as if in warning toward the wide and barren sky, a gesture apt for reasons possibly unintended by the sculptor. This sky was the dominant physical feature of the place, a vast blue bowl stretching from horizon to wide horizon. A trick of the light made it appear almost solid, as if one might scale the nearest church steeple and touch it.

But because solid it was not, a fact that seemed never more than just on the edge of obvious no matter how long one stared, terror lurked unseen in insane depths. The town huddled prostrate to the earth, the natural adversary of such a sky, in supplication for protection. Such a palpable presence was this sky that building in the proud and permanent medium of stone must have seemed provocatively imprudent. Few had chosen to do so, even among those who could afford to. Most of the town was wooden, as if, by interposing the least possible inconvenience should this sky will it be blown to smithereens, it might pose as merely temporary and, perhaps, escape notice altogether. The three exceptions each seemed conscious of its offense. The brownstone courthouse sat like a medieval fortress on its little rise, protected against assault by tiers of crenelation. The long-shut up bank building, a Louis Sullivan architectural bijou in once-white limestone, anchored itself firmly to the ground with wide arches. The WPA post office dared defiance;

the art deco workers in its cement relief grasped their tools and glared upwards in iron determination and suspiciously socialist solidarity. Surrounding these impertinences, a mile or two of period wooden houses baked in the sun, froze in the rain or swirled in dust, depending on the season, the direction of the wind, and the will of that all-impending sky.

Rev. Barber's arrival had stirred up this changeless place as never before. Oh, they knew who he was, all right. Who didn't? The Reverend Wilmore "Billy" Barber was a famous figure in all such places. A voice crying in the wilderness against the sinfulness of these degenerate times, he had appeared from nowhere about twenty years before and almost singlehandedly revived an evangelical movement reeling rudderless from the scandals of the last century. His fiery uplifting oratory could doubtproof the shakiest rural believer, at least until next week. He told them in the most forceful terms exactly what they wanted to hear: that their immemorial lot of stoop labor, grinding debt and hopeless subjection to the rich and powerful was the highest and most honorable estate of all—that the men of wealth and pride would be laid low before the awful judgment seat of Gawdalmighty, but those who had kept up their payments and borne their humble lot with patience, humility, loyalty and joy would rejoice on the right hand of Jesus and see their oppressors crushed in the fiery pit of Hell for eternity. Further, in an apparent contradiction that bothered no one, he taught that faith worked miracles right here on this damned and ephemeral mortal coil; that faith was, in fact, redeemable not only for a secure place in the afterlife, but for health and wealth, even great wealth, in this life too. His famous admonition, "Redeem Thy Redeemer!" became his catchword.

As proof that faith could make you rich, he instituted a vast computerized pyramid scheme to gain converts to his church. Under this plan, you received a percent of everything contributed by those you brought to see truth in the same light you and Rev. Barber saw it, a percent of all contributed by those they converted, by those they converted, and so on. When the pyramid's shares sold out, the occupants of its upper tiers were paid off and encouraged to reinvest their earnings in the bottom ranks of new pyramids capstoned by those who formerly had made up the lower tiers of their own. In this way, faith demonstrably produced riches—and if your returns were poor, why, brother, it could only be because *someone's* faith was weak: either yours, in which case you must redouble your efforts; or that of those you had converted, who must be exhorted to greater attention to the word and example of Rev. Barber, to redoubled fieldwork and, what was most important of all, to ever greater "investments" in the World Church of the Redeemable Redeemer as proof and reinforcement of their faith. "You must believe, my friends! Every dime you invest in Jesus' work will return to you a hundredfold, a thousandfold, as it has to tens of thousands of true believers already! Isn't that so, my friends?" In the enthusiastic "Amen" which rolled back at the Reverend from the reinvested faithful, many a shy and wavering believer doubtless found inspiration. Meanwhile, Rev. Barber's following (and his cashflow) grew, literally at an exponential rate.

Were there still any question of the awesome power of faith, Rev. Barber had a yet more convincing and genuinely awe-inspiring demonstration to make. He was a powerful faithhealer. Indeed, his amazing skill at healing the sick had been the earliest foundation of his fame.

In this he truly exceeded the common run. Not only had he dominion over the usual run of migraines, colorblindness, arthritic aches and pains, internal cancers and other invisible ills which were the stock in trade of most of this divine art's practitioners, but, under Rev. Barber's blessed healing hands, shattered joints magically reassembled, cataracts cleared from the eyes of the blind faithful, and hemorrhoids shrank without surgery.

Although you might suppose a talent of these dimensions would absolutely guarantee its possessor a great deal of attention from the world at large, this proved somewhat less than the case. No matter how prodigious the medical miracles Rev. Barber produced, the scientific community dismissed reports of such as either overblown or indicating clever charlatanry. They refused even to come and look, suspecting their mere presence would be used to imply endorsement of a mountebank—and, in truth, without their validation of Rev. Barber's gift, his fame and influence never were what clearly he expected.

One who did come and look was Harold Smithson, Professor of Orthopedic Medicine at Harvard Medical School, who turned himself into a persistent, and frustrating, interlocutor. Intrigued by the beneficial changes wrought on the frame of a patient he'd pronounced beyond help, he came to see for himself again and again. Each time, he had free reign to examine subjects before and after Rev. Barber's divine ministrations, but never quite managed to believe what he saw. At last one day, annoyance overwhelmed him in unfortunate proximity to an open microphone. An entire hallful of people heard him mutter, "I simply cannot find the trick!"

As the crowd held its breath, Rev. Barber's patience ran out at last. He turned a baleful eye on the unfortunate professor. "The trick? The *trick*, sir? That does not surprise me, sir, for you come here not with an open mind, but as a debunker! There is no trickery here.   Faith alone cures these people—mine, and that of all assembled in this room. This is not something *I* do, sir. *Anyone* with faith can do it. Why, even"—and here he named two or three of his best known rivals—"can do it, after a fashion." He paused as the crowd tittered in appreciation of his wit, then cut them off with a roar. "I say you are GODLESS, sir, and as you have no faith, you see only what you wish to see, which is tricks—or rather the puzzling absence of them, which amounts to the same! Your faithlessness now hinders the process and makes it impossible for us to continue. So begone, sir!   Back to your operating room!   Go practice your unnecessary tortures upon your fellow Godless, who doubtless deserve them."

The professor felt his will crack under the loud approval of the crowd. With scarcely a glance at the Rev. Barber's uplifted gaze, he shrugged his shoulders and left. The reverend then proceeded to heal three broken limbs, fix a deviated septum and a cleft palate, and restore consciousness to a woman who'd lain in a coma for 23 years.

It seemed recognition of the power of faith must be forever limited to the sort of people scientists and intellectuals considered notoriously gullible. Even so, as Rev. Barber's fame spread amongst these, there were compensations. The rate of donations increased steadily. He looked upon his work, and lo, it was not so bad.

Years passed, and he seemed to prove what he said about faith. He himself retired from the faithhealing operation. He delegated these responsibilities to his pastors, all quick young men with a clipped way of speaking and hypnotic, fiery black eyes. And behold, their cures were as miraculous as his. Donations doubled.

The announcement that Rev. Barber had chosen Necktie Gulch as the site of his New Eden sent a stir of excitement through the town. This could not fail to put it on the map! The local Chamber of Commerce, all twelve post-Wal-Mart members of it (including a spouse or two), met to discuss the implications in the Café de Paree, the back room of which, panelled in elegant old-fashioned formica, served as their council chamber.

They figured the advent of the famous Reverend could have only a positive effect on the local economy. First and most obvious were all those pilgrims who'd be coming to get healed. They guessed they'd better spruce up the place a bit for visitors—and what about all those vacant storefronts? Who owned all that property these days, anyway?

This brought them via the shortest distance to the very exciting question of land. The Reverend would have to have a church someplace, wouldn't he? Would he want one of their vacant ones, or would he be building new? Not a one of them but owned an empty lot or a falling down old house or two in what each thought was probably a prime location. They turned to the local real estate agent, currently daylighting as their waiter. What did he think?

He set down the coffee pot and reckoned they'd have to wait and see. He'd been doing a little investigating, he said. Seemed there'd been this big Dallas outfit, Golden West Land Development, quietly buying up everything in sight for years, a piece at a time, mostly, through several surrogates. Owned most of the town square at this point, plus miles and miles of the semi-arid rangeland outside city limits. Had bought most of the latter from those here assembled, in fact, for not-very-much an acre. Didn't they remember what a swell deal they'd thought it at the time? He figured the Reverend would probably be dealing with these Golden West folks, whoever they were. Still, the locals might not be quite shit out of luck. If things did heat up some, why, their small parcels of land in town might be worth a little something.

The reality surpassed anyone's wildest expectation. Plans were announced for an enormous amusement park with an Old West theme which was to tie into the town as well. The Reverend, it appeared, believed in the latest theories of urban commercial development and had fancy consultants from Boston to help him with them. The ultimate result, they gathered, would resemble a cross between Disney World and Colonial Williamsburg with giant waterslides. The locals were offered first chance at all the new jobs, plus reasonable commercial rents and low interest business startup loans to turn the courthouse square into a tourist center. The Reverend would assume the cost of all capital improvements himself. For instance, he intended to remove the pavement around the square and restore the original cobblestones and gas street lighting.

Cobblestones? There warn't no cobblestones down there, just dirt! And no gaslamps, neither.

Why then, he'd put 'em in new.

There was also to be a horse-drawn stagecoach taxi service to bring visitors from the high speed railroad depot to the hotel.

Hotel?

Railroad?

Necktie Gulch boomed. A splendid new tabernacle seating thousands, all stainless steel and rose-colored glass, arose outside town in an orgy of solid geometry: spires, turrets and intersecting solids. New people poured in, floods of them, the employees of the World Church of the Redeemable Redeemer and its related enterprises, and church members, people who wanted nothing more than to be members of a big well organized church that would control and coddle every aspect of their lives from the cradle to the grave and, presumedly, beyond. Property values skyrocketed. The real estate agent quit his day job. All those empty houses and vacant lots sold at once. The locals scratched their sunburnt foreheads, asked twice what they thought the properties were worth, and, like as not, were paid cash on the spot. When those were gone, plans were announced for new subdivisions surrounding the town.

Where would all those people work? Besides all the new businesses, the greatest wonder was yet to come. The Reverend broke ground for the tallest building in Texas to be his headquarters. An enormous tower in steel and rose-colored glass rose beside the new tabernacle like a campanile. The natives hugged themselves in delight. If it all hadn't been so obviously true, they'd have sworn it was just too good to be.

* * * * *

Toward this little bit of Heaven David now winged his way, though he knew it not.

Air travel was a luxury available to few these days and he himself had not been on a plane since childhood, but the flight from New York aboard Froggy's private jet held other novelties to preoccupy him. Tied immobile to a chair, he replayed endlessly in his mind his last conversation with the djinn. The helplessness of his situation, the perfidy of the metaphysical world and, most specifically, the djinn's insults and patronizing attitude lashed him to fury—and puzzled him. If, as the djinn claimed, he was utterly dependent on David's strength and resourcefulness for his own salvation, why had he striven so relentlessly to undermine his savior's self-image and grind him down? Reverse psychology? Although that was often a dangerous tactic, the djinn had had the opportunity to plumb David's mind to its depths. On the basis of what he'd found there, perhaps he'd decided that was the best way to spur his champion on to maximum effort. Grimly, David admitted the possibility, also the fact it was working. He felt really and truly stung. Weak sister? He'd show that spineless craven what a mortal could do! He simply would not allow himself to give up.

In a pool of light at the other end of the cabin, the butler and the chauffeur played gin, clearly bored. They took frequent breaks to help themselves from Froggy's private stocks of liqueurs and cigars, and stretched their legs by wandering back whither David sat glowering in darkness. Once, idly, the butler poked at him with a finger, exactly like a caged tiger might be stirred up by the sort of cretin whose pusillanimous egotrip is to provoke it without actual danger to himself.

David's rage flared. *This won't do at all!* When they returned to their game, he focused them in his extra sight. To his considerable gratification, the blocks on their minds gave at a touch. Immediately, he reached out toward the unseen pilot. A block there held firm. Obviously, the djinn, if it were he controlling this journey, could allow no manipulation that might affect their destination.

At least, David thought, he could ensure he'd be left alone. He deepened his captors' concentration on their game to maniacal intensity. Their brows furrowed, conversation ceased, the slap of cards grew louder and angrier, money appeared on the table, their cigars burned out forgotten. When he'd satisfied himself he'd no longer be disturbed, he closed his eyes and began the search for the mortal power. He did something it had never before occurred to him to do: he turned his extra sense inwards, on himself.

The result was impressive. Unsuspected inner eyes opened on a wide panorama. A point of awareness floating bodiless above a parapet, he looked down, out and across a darkened formless landscape, as if from a great height. Turning in wonder to see what else might be here, he discovered the parapet edged a broad terrace, across which lay a thing of brilliant flashing color, the aspect, his metaphysical center. Its tightly logical organization seemed to betray conscious creation by a power greater than itself. He stared, fascinated by the exciting sense that, if only he studied it long enough, he would be able to see exactly how it had been made. Tantalized with the lure of apocalyptic knowledge, he willed himself forward, into its glowing maze, and lost himself immediately in hypnotic complexity. The answers he sought—as the questions began to escape him—seemed forever only a turn or two deeper on. It lured him endlessly, but revealed little of what it promised.

He did discover the ports through which other metaphysical beings could enter his mind, and how to close them. He discovered the switches that would allow him to sense when such probing was being carried on, jammed firmly into the OFF position. He pried them loose and turned them ON, then went looking for other handy things. In total absorption, he lost his purpose and buried himself timelessly in the magic labyrinth.

The pop in his ears as the cabin pressure changed jerked him back to himself. They were descending and he'd done nothing about finding the mortal power, the one thing he knew would help! Angrily, he re-entered his inner landscape. With a wrenching effort, he turned his back on the aspect's seductive network and faced the formless darkened landscape of his first vision. From the parapet a single track led down into whatever he had left of Herbie Manning, of *himself*, through a labyrinth of a different kind. The track crossed back on itself through a maze of intersecting canyons and lost itself in deadend side trails dimly seen through a pervading murk of heavy mist. The shallow, ambiguous, easily obliterated trail markers alarmed him acutely. If something should happen to them, climbing back up to reclaim his ascendancy might not be so easy. Just as the djinn had indicated, his position was precarious.

Below, he could make out nothing clearly, and the farther he descended, the heavier the obfuscating murk became. Only when he emerged at the bottom did certain details begin to resolve. Dimly glimpsed through the brume, nameless terrors shifted uneasily over a blasted heath. Bottomless pools glimmered in dark hollows, their still surfaces filmed with the sickly rotten glow of primordial intuitions. Primal desires twisted wraithlike through the mist, pleading in unquenchable need and clutching with clammy grasp at all that moved. The murk itself was a sort of evolutionary angst, covering and smothering all.

David recoiled. Was this what the metaphysical world saw when it looked at mortal life? No wonder they viewed it with repugnance. Yet, David knew he must go on, that what he sought lay somewhere at the heart of this mist.

Then a new force broke over the landscape. A chill wind stirred. A sense of impending doom arose and loomed. David's eyes flew open. The seat belt sign glowed at the front of the cabin. They angled in on final approach. No one had told him to what place he might be going, and now they were arriving, no one told him where he was. No one needed to. This location occupied a capital position on a very special map having nothing whatsoever to do with standard geography. He had the disturbing, destabilizing sense of a power center somewhere quite close, pulling everything off balance toward it. The djinn had said he'd be on his way to meet the Archon. The truth of this now had become viscerally apparent.

Moments later, the plane bumped onto the ground. Reluctantly, he released Froggy's butler and chauffeur, still intent on their game.

Further confirmation of this place's unusual nature, were any required, arrived the moment Froggy's men handed him off to his new escorts, two cleancut young men in baggy slacks and plain white shirts with pocket inserts full of pens and pencils. Their fiery black eyes and scrambled auras were instantly familiar. Djinns! Without a word, they bundled him into a white-on-white limousine, which sped off. On the short drive, the sense of a power center expanded into a whirling vortex drawing him ever closer, threatening to swamp him altogether. He closed his eyes and struggled to maintain his identity. The djinns glanced at each other in knowing contempt.

Desperation gripped him. He risked two swift sideways glances. His escorts stared straight ahead, immobile on either side of him, idling automata. He closed his eyes, retreated into his mind and found himself alone there. The djinns were not attempting to read him. That was good. Evidently, at least in the absence of overt provocation, a Bargain was still a Bargain. He engaged his defenses in an effort to shut out the ever-increasing interference from the power center.

Despite this, his inner landscape endured a howling gale. His metaphysical self seemed oddly contracted, its many flashing colors muted. With shock, he realized it was terrified. The feeling clutched at him.

He turned to face the darkness of his mortal being. Beyond the parapet, the interference was a deafening wail, a blinding veil through which he saw nothing. Yet, though the interference masked what lay behind, it also revealed; by obscuring details, it allowed the larger form to become evident. Behind the blackness of the storm, he felt the presence of what he sought, the mortal power. He had a bare instant's intimation of something large and warm pulsing behind the blinding veil, the source, behind and below the terrors, desires and intuitions, that powered them and made them go.

Then the howling gale closed around him, and it had teeth. Like carpet tacks driven on a rising gale, it stung him randomly, with ever-increasing frequency. Yet there *was* something out there! With his last strength, he lunged forth at the large warm thing he'd felt beyond the circling winds. He groped frantically in the shrieking void, but again and again touched nothing at all.

A vortex of howling knives tossed him about, tearing him mercilessly, flaying him apart. He knew he had no choice; he must drop his defenses or be destroyed.

He surrendered, and was overwhelmed; the vortex swept him up and swallowed him. At its bottom, the power center was huge, impending and immediate. It permeated him; he swam through it like a jellyfish through unsteady waves. The car rolled to a halt; wherever they'd been going, they had arrived. He opened his eyes.

He allowed himself to be led limply out of the car, through an underground garage, into an elevator, down a hall, through a series of antechambers, and at last into the Presence. As if outside himself, he noted his own surprise at recognizing the jowly features of Rev. Billy Barber, a face he'd seen hitherto only in network news pieces on the resurgent power of fundamentalist religion. Something no television broadcast could show, the eyes were icy black holes to noplace. At the very sight of them, the aspect left his control. It whimpered the single word, "Master," and flung itself carpetwards in a ritual prostration sufficiently self-abasing to propitiate an Oriental potentate. That part of him which had been Herbie Manning breathed rug dust with surprise and shame at this apparent cowardly grovelling upon the floor.

He felt a probe touch his mind, at which the aspect curled itself into the fetal position and refused to budge. The Archon looked at him with distaste. Humiliatingly enough, the Herbie

Manning part of him felt itself brushed aside, as of no value whatsoever.

"'The clapped out power elite,' huh?" The Archon touched him again, a sharp word of command. There was a horrifying upwelling at the core of his being. David felt his head fill at lightning speed with visions, plans, data, explanations and instructions.

It lasted only seconds. The djinns reappeared and took him to a small white room with a cot and a sink. They closed the door and locked him in.

He sank onto the cot, grateful to be alone. After the terrifying night and day culminating in this extraordinary experience, his head was whirling. How many people was he now, he wondered? The answer wasn't clear. He needed time to mull it all over and straighten things out, to *reboot*.

But first things first. His crotch, painfully denied for hours, rose in swift rebellion. He beat it off fast. Cum spattered the walls. He fell back depressed and exhausted, and sank through vague and terrifying dreams toward an awful, inexorable oblivion.

Somehow, he had company. A small voice in his mind carried on bravely against the tumult like a promise. He grabbed at it and tried to listen. It was... It was... At last, he had it; in the moment before noise overwhelmed it, he decided it was his own voice—singing. Backed by a large choir and orchestra in splendid, soaring harmonies, it sang words and a tune that were vaguely familiar. Was it? Yes, it was, one of his oldest favorites, it seemed: *A Mighty Fortress is Our Djinn.*

* * * * *

"My Lord, I gave myself to thee.
Thou cam'st to me across the sea.
And Lord, thou'st made me a man.
I do, Lord, just what a man can."

David rasped out the words in a voice choked and raw with emotion. Under the leopardskin vest, his bare chest glistened with sweat. He sank onto his knees in an attitude of prayerful supplication as guitars and synthesizer wailed passionately to their climax.

The music ended. Screaming whistling pounding adoration rocked the hall. All fluid motion, David rose to his feet and led the band in a bow. Everything was going really well, he thought, far better than he'd dared hope. The band, *Rood Boys*, was a success, their first album a smash hit with the Christian rock crowd, and now this! As the ovation thundered on and on, he smiled up at Heaven, at God who had made it all possible, and led the band in another bow. The tour had been going on for weeks, or was it months? He didn't care. The important thing was that it too was a success: sold out houses in city after city. Where were they, anyhow? Pittsburgh? Philadelphia? Someplace in Pennsylvania, he was pretty sure.

The exact place wasn't important. What mattered was that The Lord had turned his life around from drugs, degradation, disease and despair to this thrice-weekly megadose of love and adoration. He was so incredibly grateful. And now, of course, he must tell them so. His testimony came next.

That was the format: two songs, then testimony. Scott Jacobs, the drummer, had already told them about his glorious conversion from the primitive blind superstition of Judaism. The keyboard man, Al Michaels, had talked about how his parents beat him almost to death before Jesus brought the whole family into His radiant light to live happily together ever after. The bass player, Bobbie Beaman, had told about his childhood leukemia and how Rev. Barber had healed him when he was about to die. Gerry Axehammer, the lead guitarist, had recounted his long and losing battle with drugs and thanked The Lord on his knees for his salvation.

David never ceased thanking Him for Gerry's salvation, either. Quick, funny, loyal, caring and eager to please, Gerry was definitely his best friend, and maybe the only real and true friend he had ever had. They were inseparable.

After himself, Gerry was definitely the mainstay of the band. On the street, you would never take the guy for a rock star. His long skinny arms and legs, odd features and scraggly thinning hair didn't fit the classic job profile at all. He became a different person on stage. Magic—no other word described it. Often, as David watched Gerry stride up and down, his face intense with passion and commitment, David thought his energy alone could be enough to carry the whole band. He was a great performer, and showed it nowhere better than in his testimony. The climax, when Gerry bared his arms in a dramatic gesture and cried, "Look Jesus! No tracks on me!" was always an electric moment. David cried every time. The Lord was so powerful, and so good!

Despite this, you could tell life had scarred Gerry. Every now and then, his laughter would fail, there'd be a hint of something secret in his flashing black eyes, and he'd become biting and unapproachable until the mood passed.

David's heart went out to him at such times. At first, he'd tried his best to do what he could to help, which hadn't been much. They'd gone down on their knees together while David exhorted him to put his faith in Jesus and in the Rev. Barber, who'd done such a lot for them both.

He himself got much comfort from the thought of Rev. Barber. Whenever he was troubled or in doubt, which was far more often than he liked to admit, he made himself quiet and did his best to call up an image of Rev. Barber to see if he couldn't discover what the great man would want him to feel and do. The image usually came very easily to him and always resolved into concrete resolutions about how to proceed. He got a feeling of great peace and security from knowing his idol would always be with him to guide him through life's pitfalls. It gave him real comfort.

But whenever he attempted to explain this to Gerry and urge him to try it himself, this exhortation had the opposite of the healing effect David intended. Once, Gerry actually began to cry. In the end, David decided, reluctantly, there was nothing to do except let his friend be alone and try to protect him from interruptions for as long as the mood lasted.

Which never was very long. This made David glad; it concerned him to see his friend so obviously hurting, and relieved and overjoyed him when Gerry came back to his old merry self. David truly loved him, as a friend, of course. All physical desire was gone from him now. Jesus was his only lover. He loved Gerry as one true Christian should love another. (Truth be told, Gerry wasn't the kind of person he would have lusted after, even in the bad old days of his obsessive carnality.)

He looked around at the band now, basking in the warm applause. Lord, how he loved them all! They were his friends and his companions in arms, wounded souls all, and all saved by the mighty and bottomless mercy of their Lord Jesus Christ, whom they adored.

Now his turn had arrived. His story always came last, in the chief place, because it was the best, and wove together themes from the stories of his friends like the recapitulation of a symphony.

The lights dimmed. The rest of the band put down their instruments and left the stage. The soft golden spotlight played on David's yellow mane like a halo as he stepped to the microphone.

"Thank you." The crowd settled down. "Thank you so very much. I can't tell you what this means to me, no way, but I have to try." He closed his eyes and clasped his hands a long moment as if openly praying for strength—and pray he did. His past was so hazy sometimes. His life often seemed to have begun only recently. Curiously enough, he could date this beginning exactly. There'd been a glorious September morning well over a year ago now, when he'd awoke in a small white sleeping cell in the Church headquarters complex, Rev. Barber beaming beatifically down on him. His real, vivid life had begun at that moment. His memories of the time before were curiously insubstantial, like a story he'd read, or a daydream on a lazy afternoon, someone else's story altogether.

—But that was ridiculous. Some of the details were every bit as vivid as they should be. They were his memories, after all. Whom else's could they be? There were good reasons some of them should seem a little vague, he supposed, sunk in drugs and sickness as he had been. Daydream? More like a nightmare, as he remembered it now. His life certainly had changed dramatically of late with the most startling and wonderful changes. As those culminating in this intoxicating public celebrity dated from that very trip to Necktie Gulch, it all made a kind of sense, he supposed.

He had been called to headquarters when, after some initial hesitance, Rev. Barber at last agreed a Christian rock band might be a good way to reach out to young people in the cities, where the Church was weakest, and especially to those sunk deep in the despair of drugs and the sinful depravity of sexual degradation. David had a special interest in ministering to people like that, and had been pushing the idea for some time, he seemed to recall.

Once Barber got behind a project, things happened! He wanted to see the songs David had written. He had some guys he wanted David to meet—Scott, Al, Bobby and Gerry, as it turned out!—and was willing to put up the money to get things rolling. Rockin' and rollin'! From that trip, from his first morning in New Eden, David's life had taken on a new vividness, immediacy and purpose as compared to what had gone before.

The crowd waited, silent, their respect palpable. He prayed The Lord would help him overcome his memory problems and tell his story well, that others might be saved and strengthened in their faith.

At last, at what he judged the dramatically right moment, he opened his eyes and began. "I grew up in a big city, one a lot like this. I was raised by my mother, an honest, Godfearing, hard working person. She had to work hard, because we had practically nothing. My father worked in a factory. He died in an accident at work not too long after I was born. My mother did her best for me. She worked hard, oh-so hard as a waitress in an all-night café. She left for work about the time I got home from school, and got home again around midnight. I guess you can tell I didn't get to see too much of her. Her sister lived with us until I was ten. She had a day job and looked after me while Mom was away. Then she died too.

"After that, what with school and Mom's work, I was on my own most of the time. There was no one to control me, no one to keep me home at night doing my studies. There were neighbors in our building to go to if there was trouble, but no one else. I know there are people who would blame Mom for leaving me home alone so much of the time, but they shouldn't. Waitressing was all she could do, the money was better in the evenings, and we needed it.

She had to do what she had to do, and she had to trust me to be a good boy.

"I let her down. I ignored my schoolwork and the Word of The Lord she taught me to run in the streets with the friends I found there. There's no denying we were pretty wild. We were rowdy in school, when we bothered to go at all. And at night? There's plenty of trouble to find in a big city neighborhood, and I guess we found it all. We little kids stood lookout while the bigger ones robbed stores. We ran guns and drugs around, 'cause who'd stop a little kid? We learned to hate the kids from four blocks away as if they were Satan himself, and we learned to fight dirty.

"It was exciting. We liked the cars, the lights and the action. I smoked my first cigarette when I was ten and my first weed soon after. I was an alcoholic by age twelve and started selling crack on street corners that same year.

"I remember how callous we were, how hard. When my best friend Freddie got shot in a drive-by and died, I didn't cry at all. Hey, those were the breaks! Happened all the time. Live fast, the older guys said, stay loyal, and never look back!

"Now, I do look back. I cry now for Freddie, that he lived his short life and died never knowing the power of Jesus' name to ennoble your soul and change your life."

The crowd rumbled "Amen" up at him. Shouts of "That's right!" and "Tell it!" came at him from the darkness.

"I see now we were animals in a jungle, that deep dark jungle where Jesus' sweet light never reaches. But not knowing how ignorant and miserable we were, we thought it was swell. It was all we knew.

"And when I was thirteen,"—he paused for effect—"I was stolen.

"People say there's no such thing as slavery any more, but they're wrong. One minute, I was on a streetcorner while, inside, the leaders collected money somebody owed somebody. Then a man was shoving me into the back of a car and jabbing a needle into my arm.

"I woke up locked in a small room. The window opened, but it was many floors above the ground in a tall old building. No escape that way. And the walls were thick. Nobody seemed to hear me when I yelled.

"He kept me prisoner in that room for three solid months. He brought me food on a tray and let me out only to go to the bathroom, which I did with him there watching me, I suppose to make sure I didn't smash a bottle and go for him with it. I sure thought about that, because right from the start, he abused me sexually every day."

The audience groaned. They hissed and booed the evil man.

"At first I fought him. But then, after a while, I gave that up. On the whole, it started to seem like not such a bad deal. No worries, no school, there was a TV in the room for company when he wasn't around, and he kept me well supplied with crack and booze. Pretty sweet deal after all, I thought. And in the way kids do, I started to trust him, if only because I needed to trust somebody and he was the only one around. I suppose he counted on that."

David paused. "It would have been a lot easier if not for my mother. In the beginning, I felt really guilty. I was all she had left. I knew she'd miss me, be searching for me. I wanted to get out of that rotten little room and let her know I was okay—so much that, after a while, it began to hurt to think about her. I was being held against my will and forced to do things I didn't much want to do. I was ashamed at the thought of seeing her and what I'd have to say when she asked, 'what did he do to you?' So, because I didn't much like feeling guilty and ashamed, I stopped thinking about the things that made me feel that way. Instead, I had drugs to make me feel better, and gradually, I forgot about her.

"You probably think I was pretty low, and you're right. I traded my family for drugs." He spread his hands. "But then, I was only a thirteen year-old kid and pretty easily manipulated. The man knew what he was doing. In a way, the fact I felt ashamed at all was a sign I hadn't hit bottom. I got much lower, later. Because eventually, once he was sure of me, he let me out of that room.

"I was his prisoner for three months. I stayed in his house voluntarily for three years. When I got out of the room, I found I wasn't even in my own town. I was in New York City! He must have driven all night and all the next day with me unconscious in the back seat. I'd like to think it wasn't the trunk. So there was no question of running away to my old neighborhood, and even if I'd stolen enough money to get home, what would I have done with it? When you're thirteen and never booked a long-distance trip, you don't know how, and when you've been taught to hate cops, you don't go tug on the nearest one's jacket. So I stayed. At first, the neighbors, the people we met in the elevator, were curious about me, but he made me call him 'Dad,' and explained I was his son and he'd only just got custody of me. After that, their curiosity fell off. People in New York don't pay much attention to their neighbors, anyway.

"I liked calling him 'Dad.' I'd never known my own father, and I was right at the age when a guy starts to want an adult male to follow around and pretty much any one will do. He sure beat the fathers my friends had had. Their 'my old man' stories of drunkenness, physical abuse and non-support had always made me more or less glad mine was dead. But this guy! I watched his TV, did his drugs, drank his booze and smoked his cigarettes all day long. I never had to see the inside of a schoolroom, which hadn't ever been more than a prison to me, anyhow. From the depths of my very limited experience, I decided that, as fathers went, he was probably pretty much okay.

"There was a price to pay, of course. I had to have sex with him whenever he wanted—and all the time he was doing it to me, he'd tell me how much I liked it and how much I needed it. He'd make me call him 'Daddy' and beg for it. He really seemed to get off on that. Eventually, I actually began to believe I did need it. Somewhere inside of me, I knew it was the only thing I had he wanted, the thing that kept the attention and the drugs flowing. I was learning, the hard way, how homosexuals reproduce themselves.

"I hadn't been out of the little room very long before he started bringing other guys around for me to have sex with. I didn't much want to, but he gave me no choice. Once he brought me a bald old man with sour breath, and I did refuse. He told me he was cutting off my drugs until I agreed. After only a little while, I was a mess you wouldn't believe. I thought of running away, but decided it was easier to give in and do what he wanted. I begged him to forgive me and bring back the old man. By then, I was strung out and didn't care what happened to me so long as I got fixed.

"I was so stupid. It took years before I figured out the other men were *paying* him to have sex with me! He was pimping me all over town!—and when I found out how *much* he was getting, it took no genius to figure he was *making a profit on me*! I'd been earning him enough to pay for his drug habit and mine, with pocket money left over! I was sixteen when I found this out. I felt betrayed and angry. Part of the reason I'd stayed with him was because I'd felt, only The Lord knows why, now, that he cared for me at least a little. Maybe I felt that way because he didn't beat me, because he kept me in far better style than I'd ever had before, and because he gave me pretty much everything I wanted, which was drugs. But after I figured out his game, it seemed to me I wasn't a person to him at all, just an investment.

"So I lit out of there. I took all the drugs, his loose cash, his jewelry, and split.

"Not for home and my mother, like I should have. I know I thought about that. So why didn't I go? I wish I could pretend it was because I was still ashamed—ashamed to face her with my drug habit, ashamed to answer questions about where I'd been and what I'd been doing those three years, and ashamed to look at her when she asked the inevitable questions, 'Why didn't you call me? How could you do this to me?' Certainly, I wouldn't have wanted to face her about any of those things, but when I level with myself, I have to say the real reason I didn't go to her was because I'd come to *like* the life I was living, the drugs and the men, some of them rich and established, who flattered me and were ready to prove their regard by forking over bundles of cash merely to touch me. I wasn't ready to give all that up, as I knew I'd have to if I went home, and right when I was ready to go out on my own and explore my freedom all the way. Forget it! Hey, the real adventure was only beginning, I thought.

"So I bought myself a ticket to Seattle, and disappeared. Why Seattle? Well, Seattle was where the music I liked then came from, and I thought the people there must be cool, and it was on the

West Coast, which meant I'd be getting about as far from New York and 'Daddy' as I could, and it would be nice and warm, I thought. My geography was pretty bad. All those West Coast places were like Southern California, weren't they, where the sun shown all the time?

"I got there in June. I got myself a cheap furnished room and went into business for myself, hustling on the streets. By the time I found out my mistake about the weather, it didn't matter anymore, because I was a success.

"It was easy. I was popular and made lots of money, all of which went for drugs. The street skills I'd learned with my friends at home came in real handy, and what I didn't know, I learned fast. I went where I liked and did what I wanted with nobody to tell me no. I slept with any man who'd pay my price, and there were lots. Along the way, I never failed to mock the Christian missionaries in the streets. Jesus was for saps, I thought. I didn't see why I shouldn't go on forever. Who needed them?

"But then, as someone has said, the road up is the same as the road down, and I began to slip and slide. With 'Daddy,' the drugs had been in generous supply, but there was still a daily ration. Out on my own, there weren't any limits. My habit grew and grew. On top of that, I hadn't realized a big part of the reason 'Daddy' was able to get so much for me was because I was so very young. As I got older, I became just one of hundreds all plying the same trade. My price dropped steadily, and after the drugs began to ravage my body, soon enough I got nothing. I hit bottom hard.

"By the time I was nineteen, I had become an animal: homeless, uneducated and strung out. I lived in doorways, dumpsters, alleys, in the gutter when there was noplace else. I begged and stole.

"—And that's how it would have been for me for the rest of a very short life, except there was a miracle. I got AIDS."

All at once, the crowd got *very* quiet, as it always did when he got to this point in the story.

"I was so ignorant, I didn't know what I'd got or how I'd got it until they explained it to me later, in the hospital. 'Daddy,' of course, had never bothered having me vaccinated. I suppose he

397

didn't much fancy explaining to a doctor why a thirteen year-old boy needed an AIDS vaccine—and then, he didn't really care, did he? So I got sick. Really sick. I got weaker and weaker. My eyesight dimmed, I was covered with sores, and my weight dropped to 85 pounds. And that should have been the end of me because, while we've had one AIDS vaccine or another for years now, there's still no cure, especially for someone as far gone as that! I lay on a steam grate off Occidental Square for two days, too tired to move, before one of the other bums took pity on me and told an aide worker. Or maybe he only wanted the steam grate. I wound up in Harborview, Seattle's public hospital, where, from my face and the state of my internal organs, the doctors thought I was at least 65! When I told them I was 19, they figured I was delirious—and once they decided I was out of my mind, they got careless about letting me overhear them discuss my case. I heard them give me 24 hours to live. Then they put me on a gurney in the hall, where I was forgotten.

"By the mercy of Jesus Christ, whose message comes sooner or later to all who yet breathe, there was a TV set in that hall, tuned to Rev. Barber's *Eternal Hour.* I may have been weak and half blind, but I wasn't deaf. Jesus let me keep my ears to hear his glorious message. When I heard Rev. Barber explain how Jesus loves us all, no matter how sinful and degraded we have become, and that his mercy is freely given to all who repent their evil ways and sincerely ask for it, something inside me changed. I prayed to Jesus then for the first time in my life, with all my might—and He answered me! I saw His glorious face and felt His healing touch. He told me He forgave me, and that I could choose. I could come with Him then, if I wanted, and I told Him yes, yes, yes. He frowned then, just a little frown, a sad and beautiful frown. He asked me if there wasn't someone I'd forgotten, and He showed me my mother weeping in my old room, sitting there among my old things, clutching a sweater I used to wear and crying out for me. She told me later this was a true image, that it had actually happened at exactly the time Jesus showed it to me! Anyway, I changed my mind. I asked Jesus to heal me instead, so I could go to her. He smiled at me then, and touched my face.

"When I woke up again, I wasn't in the hall, anymore. I was in a bed in a ward, and I felt a little better!"

The crowd started to cheer, knowing now the end of the story.

David held up his hand. "I confounded the doctors. Or rather, My Sweet Lord Jesus did. I got stronger and stronger. My eyes and my chest cleared up. I was hungry and gained weight. When the doctors examined me in their willful, sinful ignorance of The Good Lord Jesus and His works, they were amazed. They found no trace of the AIDS virus or even its antibodies in my blood, and my internal organs were starting to behave like those of a nineteen year-old again. Jesus healed me completely: my AIDS, my drug dependency, my homosexuality, everything! Suddenly, those things might never have been! The doctors were dumbfounded. Had they screwed up the initial test results? They doublechecked. No sir, there was no mixup. I'd had AIDS. I'd had 24 hours to live, if that, and now I was well. I'd been a homosexual drug addict strung out off a huge habit. Now my head felt clear and I couldn't figure what I'd ever seen in either thing!

"It was a message. Jesus sent me my AIDS as a final warning, the same as He did to all homosexuals before the Godless scientists subverted His will with those vaccines. The Lord Himself tells us so in Romans 1:26-27: 'God gave them up to dishonorable passions. Their women exchanged natural relations for unnatural, and the men likewise gave up natural relations with women and were consumed with passions for one another, men committing shameless acts with men and receiving in their own persons the due penalty for their error.'

"There it is, right in the Bible. 'Receiving in their own persons the due penalty for their error.' You can't get any clearer than that. You can't argue with the Bible, and you can't pick and choose what you want in the Word of The Lord! It all comes from the same place. Either it's all true or none of it is, even when it hits pretty close to home. The Lord meant it to, to give everybody a chance to prove they're worthy of His love.

"Because the good news I bring you is that The Lord isn't only penalties and punishments. I'm living proof of His mercy. No matter how sinful or degraded you are, you can be saved. AIDS is proof of Jesus' love. It's a warning. He hates the sin of homosexuality so much and wants those who choose it to repent and come to Him so badly, He'll do even that to them to make them see the truth—and I hope any homosexuals within the sound of my voice don't think they're off the hook because vaccines have been found. The virus keeps mutating. Each time a mutation is countered, a new one appears: HIV_1, $-_2$ and $-_3$, so far. Each was the warning for its time. There'll certainly be more. Jesus values and is grateful for the soul of every homosexual He can save, though I'm sure He's pained at what they make Him do to them to save them. I'm sure He'd be even more grateful if they repented first and saved Him the trouble of sending those warnings.

"Oh, how I wish they'd simply open themselves to the radiant joyful truth of The Lord! All those who died of AIDS could have been healed. Think of all that money criminally wasted on AIDS research and treatment, the resources diverted from cancer and children's diseases, when the cure was as close as their TV sets! Think of all that heartbreak and grief to their poor afflicted families, who many times were decent, upright Christian people and, right to the end, reluctantly but resolutely refused to have anything to do with them in their sin! Those families were the real victims of AIDS. What agony they must have suffered! All this because the Word of The Lord was available to these homosexuals, but they refused to hear it! None of this needed to be, through the boundless pity of Jesus Christ! It's truly hard to feel sorry for all the homosexuals who are in hell today and forever because they ignored it!"

The applause was thunderous. People yelled and praised The Lord with open-eyed wonder and gladness at His mercy.

With difficulty, David quieted them down and continued. "Now, I know you all want to hear some more music, so I'll get to the end of the story."

A few isolated cheers sounded, quickly shushed.

"As soon as I was strong enough, I wrote Rev. Barber to tell him my story and thank him for being the instrument of Jesus' word. I didn't write very well, having had only an eighth grade education, if that, but the nurses helped me, and we got it done. That great and good man, whose kindness and generosity, while far inferior to that of The Lord Jesus Himself as he'll be the first to tell you, are still the greatest of any man I know, read my letter, as he does all that are sent to him. Wonder of wonders, he took an interest in me! He came to see me and hear me tell my story. He moved me to the best private hospital in town and brought my mother to see me, so I could fulfill my promise to Jesus. That moment, when Rev. Barber brought her into my room and we all three fell down together and praised The Lord Jesus on our knees was the most beautiful of my life. Now, thanks to your love and support, I've been able to give her a nice house outside the city where I was born, and I see her often. She's fine, and sends you her love and thanks, on top of mine."

The hall resounded with cheers. This last bit, about seeing his mother often, was not quite the truth. What with organizing the band, cutting the album and doing the tour, he hadn't seen her in over a year. He really had bought her the house, though, and provided her with an income. —Or at least, Rev. Barber had been glad to have the Church do it, once he got up the nerve to ask. David himself was humbly pleased to own nothing. He talked to her on the phone regularly, though. He felt as close to her as if he saw her every week. She never failed to tell him how much she loved him and how she understood all about the important work he was doing for Jesus. He really would be seeing her soon too. Christmas was only three weeks away. They had plans. So, it was only a little lie he told his audiences. It was what they wanted to hear, and if it helped them in their faith, he was sure Jesus wouldn't mind.

He continued his testimony. Time to wrap it up and let them get back to their lives and use the good news he'd brought them.

"Now, I'm 21 years old. I'm studying hard and doing pretty well, though I'm having some trouble with math. But The Lord is helping me with that, and everything's fine. I don't lust after men any more. All that's like a bad dream to me now. I'm looking to get married, just as soon as I meet the right girl." Female shrieks filled the hall and went on and on.

"One more thing. I know, because I've told this story before..." He paused while people chuckled appreciatively. "...that there's one more thing you want to know. What happened to 'Daddy'? Well, Rev. Barber and I tried to find him, to convince him to repent so Jesus could heal him too, and keep him from leading any more young boys into sins they can't understand. All we found was his death certificate. He was stabbed to death on the street by a sixteen year-old he was propositioning. He was a bad man who came to a bad end in the middle of a bad act. The court let the poor kid off with a warning, I'm glad to say. Who could blame him?"

The crowd roared approval.

"Despite all the bad things he did to me, I can't hate 'Daddy.' I forgive him for what he did, for making my mother miserable, for taking my teenaged years away from me and turning me into a drug addict and a whore, crimes worse even than murder in Jesus' eyes. I don't need to punish him for those things. Jesus is doing that for me. Even as I'm talking to you, 'Daddy' roasts in hell, now and forever. I know that as surely as I'm standing here. Praise The Lord for His justice and His mercy! So, I'm free to forgive 'Daddy' and think of the wonderful things for which I have to thank him. Yes, thank him! Without 'Daddy,' I might never have seen the glory of Jesus' love and forgiveness, which are available to all, if only they know it, and without him, your love would also have been denied me, which is more precious to me than any except Jesus'!"

The hall erupted again in wild adoration. The band were back in their places. When the lights came up, they led the crowd in singing "Jesus, Sweet Jesus," their best number. At the end, there wasn't a dry eye in the house.

To see his story accepted and taken to heart this way made an intensely moving and emotional moment. That the degradation of his youth could be put to such magnificent purpose rewarded him inestimably. If Jesus were to call him home right then, he felt, almost, as if it would be enough, except for the poor souls in the next town who still hungered for his message.

In the dressing room, the band clasped arms and thanked Jesus for the stirring success of their message. Sparkling apple juice corks popped, and David wondered what greater joy Jesus could possibly have in store for him.

If there were any question about it, it could only be Rev. Barber's great Christmas spectacle, only three weeks away, in which the magnificent tabernacle of rose-colored glass would at last be consecrated and dedicated to Jesus. David had been invited to sing "Jesus, Sweet Jesus" as an anthem with the organ and give his testimony to the millions watching on television. His mother would be there too, in a seat of honor next to him on the dias. That, surely, would be his proudest moment of all.

Chapter Nine
GREEN EYES

he passing year had seen CRAP's reorganization begin to prove its effectiveness. Politics is perception, so, naturally, CRAP's first target was the media. The Consortium saw reporting which cast the slightest shadow on the legitimacy of a single nickel of profit as dangerous, radical agitation which must be suppressed ruthlessly.

Morgan Jaye found this an appropriately easy exercise to stretch his organization's new muscle. The media's owners, elite sympathizers with the Consortium one and all, were either ready and willing to cooperate or susceptible to pressure. Nor were their employees a problem. Like employees everywhere, most were happy to do as they were told. The rest were free to take their services elsewhere, wherever that might be, exactly. The few willing to make noise were easily quieted. Virtually everybody in a law-bound society has something they'd find inconvenient to have exposed, and reporters and editors—educated intelligent free thinkers, mostly—have more than their share. After decades of drug war, employees' blood could be tested routinely. The eternal struggle against crime and terrorism meant phone taps were easily arranged. Anybody could be stopped and searched when they travelled. Email had become the primary means of written communication, but using software that made email absolutely private was itself a crime. Dirt of all kinds was easy to get, and, once got, the opportunities for state blackmail, and worse, were endless. The merest whiff of illegality allowed the state to confiscate the odoriferous one's property under circumstances that made recovering it virtually impossible. Where actual evidence of a crime existed, decades of emphasis on the rights of victims had undermined the rights of the accused whether there was a victim complaining or not. Ultimately, with the media under firm control, people might disappear with no public curiosity about what had happened to them.

The Internet? This did cause some concern. Chinese model censorship did work. The more reputable sites vanished, or were susceptible to the same sorts of pressures as other media. Random bloggers might now and then come up with something worrisome; but, when the mainstream media ignored it or laughed at it, the general public was inclined to do the same. For decades the Internet had been famous for spoofs and mis- and disinformation, so this was an easy sell.

The effects showed at once. When toward the beginning of the year the Council announced the complete deregulation of the financial industry, the media voices that might have been expected to point out parallels to the savings and loan debacle of the '80's, the corporate accounting scandals and the real estate and banking implosion of the '00's were curiously muted, their cautions beset with qualifying phrases. Later, when the Council nullified anti-trust legislation, the general editorial line seemed to be that government micromanagement of business was not the 21st century way of doing things, and that large business combines were now indispensable if the North American Trading Bloc were to compete successfully with the Europeans and the Asians.

Later still, when Congress finally watered the Endangered Species Act down to mere Resolution status, sad retrospectives appeared on the many species lost forever despite decades of heroic (but economically debilitating) big government intervention. Nobody said anything about species that might have benefitted from Washington's heavy-handed interference in local affairs, or about how the absence of legal protection would affect at-risk species that remained. An impression was left on the air that most of these had already disappeared, and that the few which yet endured were all drab two-inch fish of no particular distinctiveness of lifestyle.

Even so, the press still applauded devotion to the preservation of nature. When the Department of the Interior announced extensive infrastructure improvements for the nation's best loved national parks—new roads, reasonably-priced motels, fastfood outlets, parking lots, tram lines, marinas, ski-lodges, lifts and runs, paved trails for cyclists, roller skaters and skateboarders, and other capital investments—and relaxed restrictions on all-terrain vehicles, the media hummed with praise at how much more accessible nature would be to ever-increasing millions of tourists. These accolades buried the Department's simultaneous announcement that they were issuing licenses to clear-cut the tiny remnant of the nation's ancient forests, cancelling the last regulations governing oil drilling in the Alaskan National Wildlife Refuge and off ecologically sensitive areas of the Pacific Coast and in the Gulf of Mexico, and surveying the more "underutilized" national parks for logging and mineral potential. Only the most minimal announcements of these matters appeared, under leads congratulating the government on a badly needed shot in the arm for lumber towns and on finding new supplies of rare minerals and the fossil fuels which were still so very necessary to the nation's heroic fighting men.

Many of the voices that might have lifted in sharp protest at such policies hadn't much to say on the ever-rarer occasions reporters sought them out, or were simply nowhere to be found, their owners having "Moved—No Forwarding Address." Evidently, Morgan Jaye's definition of a "genuine radical agitator" expanded by the minute.

By the end of the year, what formerly had been the nation's most liberal media outlets all quietly had instituted new editorial policies or were for sale. Congress reduced the Departments of Commerce, Energy, Labor, Education and HUD to little more than their names and demoted them from cabinet rank with barely a murmur. When OSHA, the EPA, the FTC, the SEC and the FDA were dissolved, nothing was said at all.

This left in the dark that portion of the public which might have objected to these policies. With no media coverage to substantiate its suspicions and bind it together into a political force, it remained mere isolated and powerless individuals.

The average citizen found the absence of controversy comforting. To many people, it seemed that, at long last, the nation moved forward in unanimity, finally on the right track. America heaved a collective sigh of relief and settled into grateful complacency. People turned their attention to the minutiae of daily life and hoped fervently it would last.

* * * * *

Greg and Tommy buzzed about the narrow kitchen of Greg's apartment making hamburgers and chatting happily. The time was early afternoon. They'd both soon be leaving for work. Tommy had on his uniform.

"Hey, where're the onions?"

"Right behind you. Ouch!"

Tommy, as he turned, caught Greg squarely in the right kidney with the handgrip of his police revolver.

"Will you *please* take that damn thing off? It's tight in here!"

Tommy shrugged and unbuckled his gunbelt. He turned toward the dining table, where the only available space for it was atop the towel containing Greg's Speedo. He frowned. "I still don't see why you have to have that stupid job."

Greg rolled his eyes. They weren't really going to have this conversation *again*, were they? "Out of the way! Let's eat." He brought the food to the table.

"No, seriously." Tommy grabbed a burger. "I mean, you don't *have* to do this. It pays practically nothing, an' I make plenty, enough for both of us."

The issue was Greg's by this time not-so-new job as second shift lifeguard at the YMCA.

"Gimme the relish." Greg sighed. "Aw c'mon, Tommy. What am I supposed to do while you're out working? Watch TV by myself every night? Thanks at lot! Oh, I know! Maybe I should go out to the bars!" Greg dripped sarcasm. "You'd like that even less."

"You bet I would!"

"At least this way, I get out of the house, and if I don't make much, at least it's something—and I like it. It's easy, and I like the chance to swim and stay in shape."

"Yeah, you like it, all right. You like posing in this tight little nothing for all those sleazy guys, is what you like."

"Aw Jeez, Tommy."

"No, really. I mean, at least you could wear those trunks I got you."

On the second day of Greg's job, Tommy had made him a present of a pair of super baggy swimming trunks that came down past his knees.

"Because the first time I dive in the water, they'll come *off*! How much of me will they see then?"

"So don't dive in the water."

"Tommy! I'm a *lifeguard*. What if somebody's *drowning*?"

"Hey, watch it! You're gettin' ketchup on my bullets."

"Sorry."

"I just don't like all those guys looking at you, that's all. I liked your old job better. There're no fags in law enforcement," he said seriously.

"Except for you, you mean."

"I'm no fag! I'm your lover and don't you forget it! You belong to me!"

"Yes dear," Greg sighed. Tommy's possessiveness and paranoia could drive a guy nuts. Sure, Tommy was a policeman and had to be careful, but did they really need to keep all the drapes permanently closed in case some cop might just happen to be busting somebody in a nearby tower and might just happen to amuse himself by looking through a telescope the perp just might happen to have, focus on their windows among the thousands of others, and see them eating or something?

Tommy tensed up and glowered. "You don't sound much like you mean it."

"I mean it, I mean it! But do I have to say it *every* day?"

"I'm not sure. I wasn't going to mention this, but while we're on the subject, you were late getting home last night. Your shift ends at eleven. You got home at twelve-seventeen. So where were you?"

"Uh huh, I knew you were smoldering about something, pretending to be asleep. I went out for breakfast with Irv and Jack, the locker room guys."

"Why?"

"I don't believe this." Greg stared. "Why do you think? I was hungry! And they asked me!"

"Why can't you eat at home?"

"Because you're not usually back by then, and who likes to eat alone?"

"So where did you go?"

"Mister G's, okay?"

"What did you eat?"

"Ham and eggs. Scrambled!"

"How long were you there?"

"Twelve-ten, more or less."

"How'd you get home?"

"Irv gave me a lift."

"What kind of car does he drive?"

"An old one."

"That's not an answer. What make?"

"Enough, enough, enough! You are making me crazy!"

"Answer the question!"

"Why? I'm a liar either way, right? If I didn't notice what kind of car he has, then I wasn't there, and if I did, you'll think I had sex with him in it!"

"Did you?"

"I'm not such a fool! Besides, Irv weighs 330 pounds. To Irv, a 'ham sandwich' is a 5-pound ham and a loaf of generic white bread washed down with a gallon of milk! —And besides *that*, he only likes Latin boys, straight ones from out on North Avenue! He overwhelms them with gifts."

"I don't think I like this Irv much."

"Well, I do! He's clever and fun to talk to, and he does his job. Besides, him and Jack are absolutely the only friends I've got besides you. I will *not* have them persecuted!"

"Oh, so now they're friends."

Greg rolled his eyes heavenwards.

"Well, okay, but if I find out you've been lying about any of this, I'll kill them both!"

Greg stared at him in misery. While he didn't think Tommy would actually commit murder, he knew Tommy could and would make a worldclass pest of himself. He was already calling the locker room two and three times a shift on the flimsiest excuses. When there were swimmers in the pool and Greg couldn't come to the phone, he badgered Irv and Jack to make sure Greg was really there, sometimes pretty aggressively. Irv and Jack kidded Greg mercilessly about his jealous lover.

Now this. Greg knew for an obnoxious certainty that Tommy would be calling the locker room today to grill one or both of his co-workers with a lot of hostile questions about last night. Greg didn't know how much more of this he could take. For sure, he'd have to get onto Irv and Jack before the shift started, warn them, and make sure they covered for him so Tommy wouldn't find out it was actually Jack who'd driven him home. That would be disaster. Jack was big and blond and butch, like an only-slightly-over-the-hill baseball player. Pretty sexy, Greg admitted. In fact, Greg probably wouldn't have minded fooling around with him a little, except that Jack was only interested in toned-up black guys with athletic preferences and oversized workout equipment.

When it came to cruising, both Irv and Jack were the narrowest of narrow specialists. Things were absolutely innocent between the three of them and would forever so remain—but so what? If Tommy found out one of Greg's new friends was actually attractive and that Greg had been alone with him even for ten minutes, let alone lied to cover it up, life would suck.

Greg sighed once again. He was doing a lot of sighing, lately. They finished their burgers in silence. He looked over the table at

Tommy still glowering with suspicion, and saw a man who'd taken over his life.

Sure, he had to admit there were unmistakable benefits to the relationship. For the very first time ever, he had a regular, dependable sex life. He was genuinely grateful for this, and did not want to lose it. That Tommy was wildly, gloriously passionate had changed Greg's life. He was a lot happier because of it—less depressed, lonely and weepy, more at peace with the world and himself. Also, Tommy was brave and fiercely loyal, they had tastes and interests in common, similar family backgrounds, a shared childhood and compatible outlooks on life.

Tommy really would have made him a good lover, he thought, if only the relationship wasn't so damn claustrophobic! Tommy mistrusted everybody; he'd driven off Greg's few old friends and now was starting in on his new ones. Greg did not like Tommy's turning his apartment into a prison, and he didn't like it they couldn't be seen together in public, not even to go to the store or a show, lest the beat cops see them together and start asking questions.

At first, the benefits of the relationship had seemed to outweigh the drawbacks. Greg wasn't exactly into becoming a "known homosexual" himself, and had been willing to go along with Tommy's restrictions. He hadn't minded having no friends too much. He was used to it; he hadn't had many to begin with, and certainly no close ones. Tommy's eccentricity about the curtains was merely that, an eccentricity, and besides, he could fudge on it when Tommy wasn't there. Even never being able to go out together hadn't been too bad. They downloaded lots of movies.

This gay purdah had long since begun to chafe. Greg wanted more. His new job had forced all his hidden resentments out into the open. Tommy thought it nothing but trouble. Greg wondered if he knew how right he was.

The ignominy of Greg's dismissal by Morgan Jaye had sent him into a kind of career shock. He'd worked so long, so hard and, all things considered, so well, it felt tough to end up on the street without even a reference. He balked at starting over, at taking an entry-level position in a new field and beginning again from the bottom. This left him at loose ends which got looser as time passed. Although having him safely at home thrilled Tommy, you could do only so much shopping and housecleaning, watch only so much television and take only so many long solitary walks before you went loopy with boredom. He needed something to fill his time, something meaningless and fun, until he found a job he really wanted to do. He amused himself answering Help Wanteds for various interesting-sounding things, and eventually found one that clicked.

He waited until the very last minute to tell Tommy what he'd done, until he was getting stuff together for his first day at work. Predictably, Tommy didn't like it a bit. He announced that that particular YMCA had been a known homosexual hangout practically since the descent of man, and demanded Greg stay clear of the place. Secretly, this revelation took Greg somewhat aback; he felt uneasy, and almost complied. In the end, though, he refused. He was sick of taking orders from Tommy. He'd been pretending to be straight all his life. He didn't see why he couldn't keep it up there too. Tommy was just going to have to be rational about this because he, Greg, refused to be browbeaten. He'd gone to all the trouble of getting this job and was going to give it a shot, no matter what.

Even so, Irv and Jack appalled him at first. Overt homosexuals *were* intimidating! The easy way they let their sexual predilections drop awed Greg and scared him silly. Although he tried to keep to himself and avoid them, as the gym's only three regular duty employees on the evening shift, they were necessarily much together. These two particular overt homosexuals weren't stupid, either. The sharp edge of attention in their eyes as they joked with him about how many "girlfriends" he must have made Greg very nervous. Too, the several phone calls from Tommy per shift—relatively hesitant and unrevealing though these were at first—caused eyebrows to elevate ever higher.

If Greg was intimidated, he was also covertly fascinated. As he watched Irv's and Jack's easy friendships with everyone in the place, his eyes opened. Swirling about him was that same lazy gay life that had angered him so on Halsted Street during his closet days. Here were people who actually seemed to be making this gay thing work for them, and not only florists and hairdressers, but people with upstanding careers: journalists, doctors, a lawyer or two, even a banker! How did they do that? The contrast between how they lived and the bunker life he and Tommy had created for themselves grew clearer and more painful every day.

At length, he could stand it no longer. Late one evening when he was alone in the place with Irv and Jack, he simply let go. The words poured out of him: his long isolation in the closet, his loneliness, his restrictive relationship with his boyhood friend turned jealous lover, his boredom and frustration, everything—everything, that is, except the exact nature of his jealous lover's job. He had the sense to change the subject when they got to that (and was ready prepared to lie when, not if, it came up again).

This unburdening gave him glorious relief, and not only for its own sake. Miraculously, he now had two people from whom he did not have to hide. Irv and Jack swept him right up. Their tales of strange cruising adventures, wild sexual exploits, and their gossip about the peccadillos of some of the more familiar habitués of their gym thrilled Greg in a vicarious sort of way. He couldn't get enough of it. While he was far from sure he wanted to go out and do those things himself, these tales gave him a new sense of the manifold opportunities the larger gay world had to offer, a sense that life there was not only possible, but that undreamt freedom existed among those he'd always considered society's dregs. A desire grew in him to open the bunker door a crack and see how the gay world looked a bit closer up.

But when he wondered if repeating a few of Irv and Jack's most amusing stories to Tommy might produce a similar effect, Tommy reacted predictably, with a hostile interrogation inexorably forcing Greg to admit he had revealed himself to his co-workers. After Greg had insisted endlessly that he'd said nothing, nothing, *nothing* about Tommy's job, Tommy's second thought was that Greg was getting it off with everyone in the place, and his third (perhaps better justified) was that if Irv and Jack were willing to talk that way about other people to him, they were also talking about him to everybody else. Greg thought they were more honorable than that;

he'd begged them not to—and even if they were blabbing all over the place, maybe he didn't care anymore, so there!

That had been the closest they'd ever come to blows, which scared them both. They'd backed off immediately, but tension between them remained tight. They danced around the subject endlessly—*just like we're doing now,* Greg thought, staring at Tommy across the breakfast table—himself resentful and increasingly frustrated, Tommy jealous and paranoid.

Tommy's jealousy had more than a faint odor of hypocrisy to it too. While Greg was supposed to see no one—was taking shit for a lousy ham and eggs breakfast—Tommy, in the name of allaying suspicion, had a drink with his cop pals most nights after work, and at least once a month went off with them on a more extended binge. They went out with women and, Greg strongly suspected, had sex with them too. On one particular occasion, he knew it for a fact—that is, if the lipstick stained crotch on Tommy's jeans he discovered one laundry day could be considered any kind of giveaway. Tommy's story about how it was just some drunk chick who'd fallen off her platforms in the bar...

"You mean she landed lips first in your lap."

"Hey, it happened!"

...was definitely hard to swallow, as it were, but one of Tommy's more reassuring and even endearing qualities was that he was a rotten liar, and visibly hated doing it. Tommy always preferred to come at you full force and straight ahead.

Where would it all end? Greg didn't know. Once the sexual ardor of their relationship cooled, if it ever did, would Tommy begin to think maybe he ought to make himself completely safe, and, not incidentally, make his pals and his family happy by marrying one of these bimbos while keeping Greg on the side for weekend hunting trips and a fast boff whenever he could squeeze it in? Greg almost wished he would, except he strongly suspected even that wouldn't set him free. He suspected the depth of Tommy's possessiveness was such nothing might end his need to control and restrict Greg's existence. He might wind up with next to nothing in his life, or, at worst, a dangerous stalker. Tommy was capable of anything.

As Greg contemplated his unhappiness, he began to slip down the well-worn groove into his usual reverie about David Alexander reappearing and rescuing him from all this. At once, the golden smiling visage swam before him, deep green eyes sparkling with affection, as it still did several times a day, every day, even after more than a year. Surely, David wouldn't have been so jealous and paranoid possessive. Completely inconceivable!

So where the hell was he? When Greg finally had started to make some inquiries on his own, very cautiously and circumspectly because of Tommy, the trail was not merely cold: there was no trail. Before the Manning case, Greg had not thought that possible. Although Jaye had told him David had been detained, it hadn't been in any lockup Greg could find, which made a certain sense as he had not been indicted, arraigned or tried by any Federal, state, or municipal court in the land. Nor was that all; among other negatives Greg collected, even a year later David was not licensed to do anything anywhere, even drive a car. Nor had he a passport. He owed nothing and owned nothing: no real estate, vehicles, credit cards or bank accounts. Or, for that matter, ever had. He had no Social Security number. He had never been born. At least he had not died.

Greg's beloved had ceased to exist, had stepped back into the same void whence he'd come at Herbie Manning's disappearance. Obviously, he had become someone else; the Council had either prosecuted him under an old identity, or set him up in a yet another new one—but what identity, and why? Cut off from CRAP's database, Greg might never know.

He allowed himself a moment of wordless longing for his lost love, but only a moment. It didn't feel safe to do this in front of Tommy. He had already seen what the mention of David's name could do there. Tommy's very first jealous fit had burst over Greg one day shortly after they'd met. Tommy had come over and was standing by the desk toying with Herbie's fox-headed brass letter opener, turning it over from hand to hand, when his eye caught on Greg's scratchpad covered with doodles: "♥ David ♥ Alexander ♥" Tommy had trembled all over. "Who's that?" he'd demanded. Foolishly, Greg had told him, more or less. The result had been cataclysmic. After Tommy made highly emotional love to him interspersed with frenzied ejaculations of need and eternal devotion, he'd announced he was moving in—and did on his very next day off.

In the instant Tommy had first seen David's name, he seemed to change from the guy who'd cared so little what others thought he'd kissed Greg in a public park—and in uniform too!—into the paranoid demon Greg now saw before him. His usual demeanor of easy-going cheerfulness had changed into suspicion and distrust. Or was it a change? After all, Greg hadn't known him since they were kids. Greg took no chances, and made sure he never left David's name where Tommy might find it again.

Tommy had overwhelmed him completely. Nobody had ever needed him like that. Perhaps Tommy hadn't realized it himself until he came up against the first shadow of competition for Greg's affections. Perhaps, realizing the constraints his job placed on their relationship, Tommy merely felt insecure and desperate lest Greg wander off in search of something better. Greg didn't know how to deal with these fears, or even if he should. Maybe they were justified.

They finished eating. Although Greg banished David's emerald-eyed image and got his stuff together for work, the image came back to him on the El and haunted him all the way downtown, all the way into the locker room, where he found Jack putting out clean towels.

"So how's the green-eyed lover today? Another fit?"

Greg froze for a beat. Green eyes? Who the hell was he talking about? Oh yeah, jealousy. He unfroze. "You won't believe it," he moaned. "Where's Irv?"

* * * * *

Christmastime. Greg was in his Aunt Ida's house. Evidently, Aunt Ida had been having some work done. The hall stairs were ripped out, leaving gashed paintwork and bare lathing in the stairwell. Greg wondered how she got back and forth between floors. The house seemed awfully quiet.

"That's because the power's out," Aunt Ida said.

Aunt Ida's small suburban house seemed somehow different: much larger and decidedly institutional. When he headed for the basement to see about the power, the way led down a series of sloping cinderblock corridors with green pipe handrails on the walls. At last, he climbed over Aunt Ida's ripped out stairs and came out on the loading dock.

"That's got it," Wiley Catchem said, rubbing greasy hands with satisfaction. He wore custodian's overalls. Over the pocket, a patch said "Wiley" in red stitching. Behind him in the basement, thousands of tiny colored lights blinked in mazelike patterns on the walls. Clearly, the power was on again.

Greg returned the way he had come. His teammates ran and jumped on the fieldhouse track stretching away from Aunt Ida's living room. Lamont Alcock put down the pile of towels he carried, picked up a doll party teatray loaded with dishes and headed toward Greg's relatives gathered by the Christmas tree. There sure were a lot of them, many he didn't recognize. He knew they were all related, though.

Greg's cousin was there, the one he'd been closer to than any of his relatives when he was a little boy, but who lived in Mississippi now and never called or wrote. Greg knew him instantly, though he saw only a man's back. His cousin's wife was there too. She made faces openly whenever Greg suggested they might come visit him. She made one at him now.

He wandered around the tree whither a group of grotesquely made up hookers sat smoking cigarettes. They greeted Greg with easy camaraderie. He thought of David Alexander and wished he could see him. The hookers understood. He appreciated their friendliness.

He sat with them among desks and typewriters. Mrs. Wilson, who managed the Harrington Hotel, came out from around her high desk and gave him a cup of coffee. "Oh, Greg. Nice of you to stop by. So how do you like living here after three weeks? Might as well give you the tour. Come on."

They walked along the street chatting amiably. They ran into David Alexander heading the same way in the company of two or three other guys.

"Hi Greg! Living at the Harrington now, huh? Come on—might as well give you the tour."

Greg followed him eagerly up three or four steps to the Harrington's front door. Inside, the lobby was a disco with the cashier's cage the DJ booth. A thick crowd of men danced to loud banging music. As David led the way up curving marble stairs to the second floor, Greg lost him somewhere in the crowd. The doors at the top said "Fire Escape." He pushed the bar and entered a stairwell of the same tan-colored marble as the lobby. David's voice floated up from below. "C'mon Greg, hurry up."

Greg circled down five or six flights and came out on a gallery overlooking a large indoor swimming pool barely in time to see the door at its other end swing closed. He hurried toward it through an overpowering smell of chlorine, and entered an identical stairwell.

David's voice arose from just out of sight. "Greg! I'm here! Come on!"

Greg pushed on after the voice, descending five or six more flights of marble stairs. At the bottom, he emerged into a weight room, a tangle of shiny metal machinery. He couldn't see David. He tried to search through the machines to the other end of the room, but something held back his legs. The room itself was getting a little hazy.

Someone behind him grabbed his hand. He felt the sharp impress of a fingernail into his palm.

"Hi Greg! How you been?"

He turned. Herbie Manning held his hand, wearing his foolish grin. Oh, super. Just what he needed when he was looking for David.

He looked down. In his other hand, Herbie's brass foxheaded letter opener stared up at him with fiery red living eyes. It snarled at him, lifting a forest of sharp fangs from the blade.

Greg's eyes sprang open in terror. His heart pounded. He lay in his own bed, pumped with adrenaline and drenched in sweat; the sheets were slimy with it. The bedside clock glowed 3:12.

It *was* December—that much checked out. With the heat turned down for sleeping, the room was cold, doubly so considering he was soaking wet.

Is that what cold sweat's supposed to be? *What a vivid dream!* He flapped the covers to get in some air and dry things up. Tommy shifted in his sleep beside him.

Thought you weren't supposed to feel things when you dream. He untensed his muscles. *Was probably Tommy who grabbed my hand.*

He still felt not quite awake; although his mind raced, he felt suspended between waking and sleep, as if he could live in either world at will. He slipped out of bed, moving slowly so as not to disturb Tommy. Tommy rolled after him as if to embrace him, and whimpered softly when his arms closed on nothing.

Naked, Greg padded out to the kitchen and had a long soothing drink of water. Amazingly, he not only remembered his dream, but recalled fresh details when he thought back on them. Most peculiar.

In particular, he recalled the chill horror of Herbie Manning's letter opener coming alive in his hand and snarling at him. He went to his little desk and picked up the letter opener—cold dead brass, of course. Thoughtfully, he dug its blunt point into his palm. Yes, that was it, that was exactly what he'd felt.

The half-dreaming mood persisted, an ethereal feeling of heightened consciousness. He wandered the living room in eerie suspension, as if he was the only person in the universe, lost amidst an elaborate illusion of stage sets constructed and manipulated solely for his benefit. Eerie, yes, and melancholic, but beautiful too, in a way.

He went to the windows and pulled back all the drapes. The neighboring towers appeared lifeless: silent solids. He had a hard time believing people actually lived inside their darkened façades, their few glowing windows more like the tiny lamps inside an architect's model. Around them, the lush carpet of city lights spread out to the horizon. He imagined himself rising high above them, watching them flatten and recede—a special effects city in an expensively produced Hollywood space opera.

Greg sat down in his easy chair, and discovered the viewscreen remote under his hand. Though he knew the impulse was silly, he experienced a growing urge to make some contact with the outside world and reassure himself of its continued presence.

He tapped on the viewscreen and selected the cable TV band, thumbing off the sound so as not to disturb Tommy. The first stations he came to were indeed off the air. Their shifting fields of snow and static did rather increase his feeling of isolation in the universe, a feeling which by now had become almost pleasurable. He made a conscious grasp at reality. Naturally, some stations were off the air at 3AM.

Many others weren't. He surfed through the channels. Under the restorative influence of old movies, zillionth reruns of *I Love Lucy* and high-pressure infomercials for psychic advisers and junky plastic kitchen gadgets, the mood dissipated and vanished. The familiar lulling white noise of Chicago at night pulsed up from below—funny he hadn't noticed it before—a susurrus of traffic noises and building ventilation units underlying the melancholy wail of distant sirens. Greg loved the sirens. Odd, wasn't it, how this marker of someone else's far away pain could be so restful and reassuring?

He yawned. He was becoming bored and sleepy. The idea of snuggling up against Tommy's warm naked body and drifting off to sleep again enfolded in strong arms became more attractive by the second.

Idly, merely from the sense of a task begun but not completed, he flipped through the rest of the channels—and saw something which brought him bolt upright, mouth open and staring. The remote slipped off the chair onto the end table with a small clatter. Unheeded, because there on the screen, in brilliant high definition color 35 inches from corner to corner, David Alexander stared out at him and smiled.

Green Eyes

Against a background of shifting colored lights, David wore loose white trousers and a baggy white shirt of some heavy silken material spangled with rhinestones. He had a microphone in his hand and seemed to be, well, singing. What channel *was* this, anyway?

Greg fumbled after the remote and displayed the channel ID. The *religious* station? David? This was simply too bizarre to be true. Greg wondered if maybe he was still dreaming. Cautiously, so as not to wake Tommy, he pushed up the sound barely loud enough to hear. What he heard spun his world.

* * * * *

Something's wrong, Tommy thought as he came awake. *Greg! Where's Greg?* Greg wasn't in bed with him, where he was supposed to be. Why not?

He lay still and listened. Yes, someone was moving around softly in the kitchen. He relaxed a little. He heard the muffled click of a cabinet door opening, a glass chinking against its fellows, water running.

Tommy waited, wide awake. No matter how tired he might be, he knew he wouldn't sleep again until he could be absolutely sure Greg wasn't sneaking off someplace, until he had Greg safely back in his arms where he could hold him close and know he was his, all his and only his.

These feelings of paranoia and possessiveness terrified him. He knew they were strangling his relationship, yet he struggled against them in vain. This puzzled him sorely. He'd simply never had to deal with this before.

Being queer wasn't new to him. He'd always known what he wanted. He'd had guys before, lots and lots of them, all the way back to military school, though he'd always had to be careful about it. In military school they expelled you for fooling around. His old man would have gone ballistic, then called in a priest; Tommy hadn't even wanted to think about it. —But then, all the guys had had pretty much the same problem; they were all really really careful. After

421

military school, during his stint at the local junior college, he'd been back with his folks, where the problem was unchanged. He simply didn't want to take the risk of making friends he couldn't explain or introduce at home. He knew what a rotten liar he was, and preferred to keep what lying he had to do simple. He did his cruising anonymously: in dirtybookstore booths, in those men's rooms traditionally used by queers for sex—every college had one, and his was no exception—and, weather permitting, outdoors on established cruising grounds at night. He went out with women too, and even screwed a few. Having something to say when his old man asked about his sex life really smoothed things along at home. Sgt. Mulligan was pleased and proud his son seemed to be playing the field this way.

The anonymous, casual queer sex suited him. He liked it fine, and didn't see why he should have any trouble getting as much of it as he wanted. The supply seemed endless; he was young and strong, and guys went for him; he got his rocks off pretty much whenever he felt like it with no involvement and no problems to follow. Even the danger was kind of exciting. It increased the thrill.

Paroxysms of jealousy simply didn't occur in this life. Unfortunately, academics of any kind really weren't his line. When, after a year or so of hard plugging, it became apparent his junior college career was going noplace, his career options narrowed to two: the military, but after a full course of military academy education both primary and secondary he figured he'd already had a lifetime dose of that; and the city police academy, where his old man was ready and eager to pull a few strings and get a few rules bent. Sgt. Mulligan's suburban police department hired only experienced Chicago officers, offering them better money, benefits, working conditions, and an improved class of criminal, the kind more likely to think twice about pulling the trigger on a police officer. Thus, Sgt. Mulligan was himself an academy alumnus and long-time Chicago Police Department veteran. He had friends and drinking buddies throughout the Department going back twenty and thirty years. Tommy's acceptance was a sure thing.

Green Eyes

Trouble was, Tommy knew being a policeman would have a pretty severe impact on his sex life. Queers were not tolerated in the police department, except for a few high-profile tokens who led tense, isolated professional lives. Tommy was perfectly sure he did not wish to join them. The toilets, dirtybookstores and outdoor stuff would have to go from Day One in any case; no way was this behavior acceptable in a law enforcement officer, and Tommy was pretty certain there'd be plainclothesmen hanging around checking things out, a suspicion he confirmed later.

So what would he do for sex? Only after another year or two of deadend part-time and temporary jobs and of kicking around the house being ragged by his old man did Tommy accept the inevitable challenge to find out. He had nothing else to do—if the choice was the police department or the military, it was better to be a jailor than in jail—and when he finally let himself get talked into going for the Academy, his old man swelled with pride until Tommy thought he might bust.

As it turned out, being a policeman had other compensations too. It fit his personality really well. He liked the instant deference and respect walking down the street in his uniform got him, and the way citizens looked over their shoulders at him and made sure all their actions were perfectly ordinary and legal the whole time he was in view. He liked being able to use his strength of will and body toward a respectable, socially acceptable goal: public order. Against this, the loss of some occasional sexual titillation hadn't really seemed all that important, at least for a while.

Meeting Greg made him rethink. Grabbing Greg like that, on duty, in public, he in his uniform and all, was pretty crazy, but Greg was so heartbreakingly beautiful there, fumbling painfully with the words to ask him if he still liked guys, he just had to take the quickest, most direct route to showing Greg that, yeah, he sure did still like guys, and everything was going to be swell.

At first, he envisioned Greg as a casual kind of thing. The long long stretch of no guys and the continued fooling around with women he'd done to allay any possible suspicion among his buddies on the force had convinced him he could use something of the kind.

Greg might be perfect. Tommy already knew him, liked him and thought he was hot. Even better, Greg's own law enforcement background gave Tommy every reason to believe he could be discreet. It seemed worth a shot—and what the hell: if some sort of limited fuckbuddy arrangement didn't work out with Greg, maybe it would last long enough for something better to come along.

But in the instant it became apparent Greg might conceivably want to think about him in the same way—that he himself might be a mere stopgap, that a preferred specific somebody else might be in a position to threaten his own instant access—something inside him snapped. He knew then he loved Greg and wasn't ever going to let him go. The feeling came on with a strength and suddenness that amazed him, scared him, and, in a curious way, exalted him too. He would be everything to Greg: friend, lover, provider, protector. They simply wouldn't need anybody else.

In the past year, he'd tried mightily to make this go, to have both Greg and his job. He'd thought maybe he could if he kept them in strictly separate pockets.

It wasn't really working. Those two asshole faggots at Greg's stupid job were giving him ideas, between bouts of drooling all over him. From the depths of Tommy's besottedness he didn't see how they could resist pawing him, no matter what Greg said. He'd tried hard to trust Greg. Hell, he was still trying, but even if, by some miracle, this Irv and Jack could keep their hands and their eyes where they belonged, that particular YMCA was famously infested with jerks who wouldn't. He wished he'd come down harder about the job right at the beginning. He'd tried, but Greg had brought up the stupid trust thing and made it an issue. Now, the damage was done. Greg was starting to go nuts with all the restrictions, to get bitter and want to break the rules.

Meanwhile on the other side of the problem, the guys down at the station were starting to ask questions and wonder why they'd never been asked over to drink beer and watch football. So what could he do? Was it strictly necessary to be so hard-assed about the whole thing? After all, Greg was every bit as straight acting and appearing as you could want. Tommy's folks already knew they were "roommates," of course, and that was okay. They remembered Greg from before. They'd liked him then, and were ready prepared to like him now. That made one voice, his old man's, already inside the police community to vouch for Greg as strictly okay. Combine that with Greg's background in CRAP and bank fraud investigations, and the guys at the station would probably like him and accept him as Tommy's friend right off without ever suspecting the relationship went any deeper. Maybe they could even have some gay friends too, as long as they didn't all go screaming around Halsted Street together. Greg wanted that, and the idea had obvious advantages: the more of Greg's friends he knew, the more he could keep tabs on what was really going on. So why not?

Because there was no guarantee of keeping these cats in separate bags, that was why not, and if they got out together, the row would be awful. What if one of the gay friends had been rousted for something revealing? Public indecency, maybe. There might be no arrest record he could check out; he might never know, but if some cop who did saw them all together, he'd sure hear about that in a hurry. Or what if they had one set of friends over to the house, and the other dropped by unexpectedly? What would happen then?

Worse, he sure wouldn't be able to lie to the gay friends about what he did for a living, not after he got to know them pretty well. So what if one of them got busted for something and started shooting off his mouth to the arresting officers about how he knew a gay cop? Tommy shuddered to think. Not only that, but if they were going to have cops up to the house, they'd need a bigger place for sure, one with two bedrooms. The problem there was the real estate market. He remembered Greg mentioning how he wasn't sure they could sell the little condo for anything like the mortgage price right now. Could they rent it out for enough to cover the payments and the dues? Tommy wasn't sure about anything except they couldn't pay more than they were already and stay within their income.

Something was gonna have to give. It sure as hell wasn't going to be his relationship with Greg. He was keeping that, definitely. His job then? Gosh, he hated to think of giving that up. And the money. Where else could a young guy with no college degree and no skills except shooting a gun, wrestling people to the pavement, and an encyclopaedic knowledge of the petty criminal code make money like that?

Then, staring at the ceiling, he had a little idea. Why couldn't they go into business for themselves? They could be private detectives just like on TV and have their own little security agency. With Greg to be the brains and him to do the legwork and strongarm stuff, they'd cover all the bases.

So where would the clients come from? The TV shows never made that real clear. They'd have to advertise, he supposed. "Whitbread & Mulligan, Private Investigators to the Gay Community." Sounded as if there might be an open business niche there. While that was getting established, maybe they could get some pickup work from Greg's old boss whatwashisname?, Wiley Catchem, and maybe even from Morgan Jaye himself. Greg always said his getting laid off in CRAP's reorganization had been strictly a question of seniority. Hell, the man had put Greg in charge of a major investigation. He must have thought something of his abilities. As far as living went, they both had savings to get them through while they established the business—and hey, they'd be together all the time!

Tommy succeeded in firing himself up to fever pitch on the idea and couldn't wait to run it by Greg. Hell, this could solve all their problems! Greg was clearly awake, though Tommy hadn't heard any noise from the other room in a while. He figured he'd at least get up and see what was going on.

He slipped out of bed. Soundless on bare feet, he went to the door and pulled it ajar. Greg sat in his favorite chair watching TV with the sound off, and shit!—all the curtains were open! Tommy figured he'd better fix that before the sun came up. They weren't in business yet. Tommy was about to pull the door open and make his presence known when, all of a sudden, Greg jerked bolt upright, knocking the remote off the arm of the chair with a little clatter. Greg's mouth fell open in astonishment as he stared at the screen, and Tommy heard the single whispered word, *Yes!* He looked at the screen, and recoiled.

David Alexander. *That* David Alexander? It couldn't be! Greg's David Alexander was some kind of cheap New York slut. Tommy'd known about *this* David Alexander for a while now. Coscznicki, his new partner, had two teenaged daughters in love with the guy! He and Tommy had stopped by a record store so Coscznicki could get 'em a poster. The name had struck Tommy, and he'd informed himself to the point it clearly had to be a coincidence. *This* David Alexander was some kind of queerbaiting fundamentalist in love with his mother! As a conventionally educated Irish Catholic, Tommy wasn't sure he should approve of the guy's religion, but still had to admit he seemed aggressively upright and law-abiding.

Wait a minute, now that he thought about it, now that it might be important, wasn't Alexander also supposed to be some kind of reformed street kid?

Naw, it couldn't be!

Or maybe it *could*. Holy shit, the guy was incredibly gorgeous. How would he ever compete with *that*? In mute frozen horror, Tommy watched as Greg fumbled for the remote and thumbed the sound up low. Alexander crooned some sappy ballad, eyes raised to heaven. The voice of an announcer oozed over it:

> Don't miss the spiritual event of the century! Be present at the creation and share the joy on Christmas Day when Rev. Billy Barber's *Eternal Hour* comes to you live from the New Eden Complex in Necktie Gulch, Texas, to celebrate the consecration of the Rose Cathedral, the World Church of the Redeemable Redeemer's great new spiritual center, featuring the music of Christian superstar David Alexander. Broadcast live on this

station at 5PM Eastern. Feel the
divine electricity of The Lord!

Tommy watched not daring to breathe as the television
began to talk of other things. Greg switched it off, but remained bolt
upright in the chair staring into space, plainly struck silly by what
he'd seen.

When at last Greg moved, Tommy scurried back to bed and
pretended to be asleep. A moment later, Greg joined him. Though
Tommy sidled over and attempted to wrap him in his arms, Greg
gently disengaged himself. Still pretending to be asleep, Tommy
watched through slitted eyelids as Greg stared at the ceiling.

Tommy turned and buried his face in the pillow to hide tears
of rage and frustration. So Greg had finally discovered his precious
David Alexander, had he? Just what did he think he was going to do
about it? A guy who went around making a big deal of how much he
hated queers! How could Greg imagine *this* David Alexander would
ever have anything to do with him again? Even if he would, surely the
guy would have to hide his hypocrisy pretty deep. Did Greg really
think his life would be any better than it was right now? He couldn't!

Or maybe he did.

Tommy's hands balled into hard fists. They wouldn't get
away with it! He would smash everything before he'd see that
happen!

Neither of them slept again for hours, Greg lost in a private
struggle a million miles away, Tommy watching steadily for the
slightest indication Greg might be developing an action plan. At
last, toward dawn, they both fell into uneasy slumber.

They woke late. Tommy tried several times while they
showered, dressed and ate to engage Greg in normal, non-
threatening conversation. Each time, Greg remained withdrawn and
uncommunicative. Tommy's suspicion and distress grew with each
attempt.

At last, the time came for Tommy to leave for the station.
Down in the garage, he used the payphone to call in sick. He got in
his car and parked in the busstop at the end of the block. He opened

the trunk and took off his policeman's leather jacket. He put on an old overcoat he kept in the trunk and buttoned it up to the neck to cover the rest of his uniform. He stepped inside the busstop shelter, whence he had a good view of both the building's main entrance and garage, and waited.

Tommy's agitation grew as two o'clock went by, then 2:15, 2:30, and 2:45. Greg's shift began at 3:00. If he was going, he should have been gone already.

At last, Greg appeared on foot and headed west up Irving Park Road toward the El, just as he would if he was going downtown to work. As Tommy crossed the street to follow him, he swore softly at the sight of the small suitcase Greg carried, but controlled himself. Maybe Greg was only taking stuff with him for his locker. Tommy knew Greg liked to keep a change of clothes there. Tommy'd always mistrusted that. Who the hell was he changing clothes for? Greg insisted he just liked fresh clothes once in a while, and true enough, he did seem to be changing clothes all the time even at home, so maybe.

On the El-station platform, Tommy hung back in the stairwell until well after the train arrived. He jumped into the car behind Greg's just as the doors closed, and found a place at the front of the car where he could spy through the windows into the car ahead. He located Greg, who, thankfully, sat facing away from him.

"Newop Bemmon," the intercom sang, "Chain furry Rabenuh."

When Greg stood up at the next stop, Belmont, Tommy was prepared. With his collar up around his ears, he scrambled to get off the train ahead of Greg and behind an advertising poster. If Greg had stayed on the train all the way to the Chicago Avenue stop, which was right in front of the Y, Tommy would have been satisfied. He'd have found a phone to see if they couldn't use him at work today, after all. Instead, Greg obviously intended to change for the Ravenswood train, which headed downtown around the Loop.

When the Ravenswood pulled up, Tommy reversed his maneuver. Downtown, they got off at Wells & Madison and walked west on Madison, then turned south on Franklin. On this late-

December weekday afternoon, the streets overflowed not only with the usual office workers and businesspeople, but with dense crowds of Christmas shoppers. Tommy had to stay worrisomely close—though there didn't seem to be much chance of being discovered. Greg walked like a robot, eyes straight ahead, with no glances around at his surroundings at all.

Tommy still had hope. *Maybe he's only doing errands,* he told himself. Tommy knew he had an account at a bank in the Sears Tower, and they headed straight for it—but when they got there, they didn't go in. Greg turned west again on Adams and walked right past it. They headed across the river, straight for Union Station! Tommy knew then he'd been betrayed.

"The sonuvabitch is gonna do it!" he exploded, and recovered himself with an effort as heads twitched around him.

At the station, Tommy stepped behind a pillar and watched as Greg waited in line, bought a ticket, and disappeared toward the platforms.

Tommy opened his overcoat to expose his uniform, extracted the photograph of Greg he carried in his wallet and pushed through the crowd to the ticket agent. "This man just bought a ticket," he said, and displayed the picture. "Where is he going?"

The ticket agent eyed the uniform and became very businesslike. "Yes, he was just here. Whitbread, isn't it?" Tommy nodded. "Booked himself through to Necktie Gulch, Texas, with a connection at Dallas. The train leaves in fifteen minutes. Platform 10. Just a second and I'll get you his seat assignment." She consulted her computer.

Tommy stopped her. "No, that's all I needed. Thanks." He had a thought. "Uh, how often do the trains run to Dallas?"

"Every 90 minutes until midnight." The ticket agent did raise an eyebrow at that. "It's a six-hour trip," she added, but Tommy was already disappearing toward the doors.

Outside in the exit tunnel, he jumped the taxi line and commandeered the first one that pulled up. He gave his home address and ordered the driver to hurry. Every time traffic slowed, he restrained himself only with extreme effort from climbing through the partition and pushing the man aside to do the driving himself.

Back at the building, he strode through the rooms kicking and slamming his way through doors. With mounting anger, he noted closets tumbled open, drawers hanging at angles, and scattered articles of clothing giving every indication of hasty and ill-organized flight.

Tommy mastered his rage and forced himself into a methodical survey to see what was missing. Besides the clothes on Greg's back, he seemed to have taken only a suit, two shirts, a spare pair of trousers, accessories, toiletries and a fistful of ties. Tommy found Greg's financial papers and other valuables intact, also his passport. Unless he planned to abandon his former life entirely upon short notice, it appeared he'd be returning, by and by.

Tommy did not mean to wait. Sitting around idly while events moved themselves in his direction was definitely not his style. The plan he'd decided upon when the ticket agent confirmed Greg's destination still seemed the only one worth pursuing. While his snap impulse had been to follow Greg to the platform and have it out there and then, he'd managed to see the futility of that. Oh sure, they could easily have had a mammoth public scene. Probably, he could even have prevented Greg from leaving simply by pretending to arrest him and hustling him out of the station. That wouldn't have solved the problem, though, not unless he was prepared to keep Greg really a prisoner forever and never let him out of his sight for an instant. Greg knew where his precious David was, now, didn't he?

No, Tommy would follow him to Necktie Gulch and see for himself exactly what was what. Maybe he couldn't prevent the guilty pair from meeting, but he knew for sure exactly when he'd find them both in the same place. On Christmas Day at 5PM EST—4PM in Texas—he knew Alexander would be appearing at that dedication ceremony for this Rose Cathedral or whatever it was. If Alexander was there, Greg would be too. Tommy figured he'd just join the party and take any action that suggested itself.

Christmas was only three days off, and Tommy got moving. Quickly, he stripped off his uniform and prepared a little overnight bag of his own. When he came to his gun, he hesitated. He stared at it a long moment, then slowly and deliberately laid it in the suitcase with his other things. He also slipped the fox-headed letter opener into his pocket, he wasn't sure why. For luck, he told himself, and because it belonged to Greg. He wanted something with him that reminded him of Greg, of why he was doing this.

At last, he was ready. He snapped the suitcase shut and headed for the door. Somewhere in his mind, he was aware of the possibility, maybe the probability, he'd never see this place again. Even so, he reached the door and locked it firmly behind him without looking back even once.

Chapter Ten
<u>THE GATE</u>

avid stood in the robing room of the Rose Cathedral, the World Church of the Redeemable Redeemer's new World Headquarters and Spiritual Center, breathing in the odors of newly planed and varnished walnut panelling. Overhead, the ceiling slanted sharply to follow the rake of the choir loft directly above. A door, closed as yet, in the middle of the long wall led up onto the dias via two steps. From beyond came a gathering murmur as the hall filled for the Christmas Day consecration ceremony.

David had already changed into his performance outfit, cream satin shirt and matching pocketless trousers, and, as always, was trying to decide what to do with his hands. Choir members swirled around him, donning their robes and organizing their music. Rev. Barber sat on a low chair growling into a telephone. "I don't care *whut* Froggy says, or that bastard Jaye in Chicago neither! They're gonna have to fend for themselves. You go right ahead and cash in all my shares of Tricontinental when the market opens tomorrow, first thing!..." It disturbed and rather embarrassed David to hear Rev. Barber, that great and saintly man who'd saved his life and been so kind to him ever since, dealing so roughly with others, and using such unbecoming language too.

A sense of unease had been growing on David steadily, an uneasiness which had to do with more than merely Rev. Barber's language or what he should do with his hands. There was his mother for one thing, in fact, the main thing.

His memories of her were so hazy and indistinct! After his kidnapping, he'd spent all those years away from her during his life as a dissolute teenager and more time since on the road with the band, and though Rev. Barber had brought her to see him while he was recovering in the hospital only a little more than a year ago, even his memories of her from that visit were fuzzy and incomplete: an effect of his illness, he'd thought. He'd certainly expected to recognize her when he saw her again, and to feel a surge of rightness and wellbeing as the tender feelings he had for her clicked into place and merged with their object. Instead, their reunion earlier that day, Rev. Barber's eagerly awaited Christmas present, had been like meeting a stranger, a stranger one has long known and admired by repute, perhaps, but a stranger nonetheless. David found it most unexpectedly awkward. He barely recognized her—on the street, he might have passed her by with hardly a second glance—and the overwhelming rush of emotion he'd expected had failed completely to materialize. This disappointed him considerably, seeing how much he loved her.

Even now, as she sat knitting on a bench against the wall, all frilly in pink and gray, why, she might have been anybody! True, the bones of her face did resemble his; this strong family resemblance made his lack of recognition of her even more puzzling. She looked up and caught his eye. She was certainly a handsome sweet old lady, and, when young, must have been very beautiful. She smiled sweetly at him, busy fingers never ceasing their activity with the needles and wool. Underneath the neat gray hair, her black eyes flashed at him through her bifocals. Most especially, he couldn't quite get used to her eyes. They more closely resembled the eyes of Rev. Barber and his sharply efficient young pastors than they did his own.

Above their heads, the organ struck up the prelude with a thunderous rumbling boom. Rev. Barber gave the phone a final snarl, slammed it down and arose, suddenly mountainous in his black velvet-trimmed robe. Various deacons and other dignitaries appeared and took their places for the procession onto the dias. David's mother became a small winningly disorganized whirlwind of activity unto herself: arranging her knitting into a capacious handbag, fishing out a compact to check her hair and makeup, and a handkerchief to give her glasses a final polish. She seemed to juggle all these things at once while struggling to her feet. Dutifully, David moved to assist her.

Rev. Barber sailed toward them in stately majesty, beaming geniality. "Well now, how are my stars? All ready for the great moment?" The change from his abrupt manner on the telephone was total.

"Oh Rev. Barber," twittered David's mother, "can I leave my bag here? It will be safe, won't it?"

"Why of course, dear lady! You've lived too long in one of our lawless and sinful great cities. Everyone here is entirely faithful to all Our Lord's commandments. If they weren't, I'd just waive my magic wand and change them into toads!" He chuckled expansively at his own joke.

"Oh, yes." She was all contrition. "Of course no one here would take it. I'm sorry, it's just that I've been knitting a sweater for my dear boy here. It must get so cold and lonely during all that traveling he does. It's nearly finished and I did so want to give it to him before we part again. That's why I worried about losing it."

Rev. Barber's attention had wandered somewhat during this exposition. He patted her arm. "Think nothing of it. We'll station someone here to watch everybody's things. Time to line up now for our entrance. You know where to go? Ah, David knows of course. Just mind your step on the stairs." With a final pat on her arm, he sailed off toward his own place at the end of the line.

It never failed to amaze David how many changes of tone, accent and grammar the man had, depending on whom he addressed and what he had to say: on the phone, he'd been a redneck businessman giving orders to a subordinate completely in his power; with them, an old-line churchman comforting a nervous parishioner, exactly the tack David supposed would have the most soothing effect on a lady such as his mother; and out at the microphone, as he told the faithful what to think and when to think it, David knew his manner would be a subtle combination of the most effective aspects of both. The man was a chameleon. David supposed this was part of the secret of his success, only one of the myriad great and miraculous powers The Lord had given him to do His work.

At last, David's mother had her things arranged to her satisfaction. David gave her his arm; they took their place in line. As they waited for the door to open, he eyed her sideways with renewed concern, unable to shake off the enigma of her appearance, speech and manner all seeming so totally unfamiliar. The more he looked at her, the more he hoped to find something he recognized. Instead, he was rapidly becoming convinced he'd never ever laid eyes on her before! How could this be? The underpinnings of his world trembled and shook: troubling pre-quake disturbances on his Richter scale that lingered and threatened to build.

He shook his head to clear this rubbish. He was merely nervous as always before a performance, that was all, perhaps more nervous than usual because of the importance of this occasion,. He'd lacked his usual opportunity for a minute of silent prayer, the chance to take a deep breath, empty his mind and seek tranquillity and guidance in meditation on the Rev. Barber.

Here, however, he had something better: the man himself. He glanced around at his idol—

—And turned straight into the most frightening, malevolent glare he had ever seen on a human face. The man's expression was unbelievably cold and hard. The eyes flashed deadly freezing power that skewered him through and through.

David went into shock. His head snapped front again as if on a spring just as the door opened. They marched up into music and light.

* * * * *

Out in the main hall, Tommy sat very still at the extreme, leftmost end of the front row. On top of a single-story stone structure containing the foyers, corridors, kitchens, meeting rooms and other accoutrements of a large community church, the hall soared around him in fantastic planes, curves and angles of rose-colored glass. Immediately in front of him, a splurge of red, white and green poinsettias banked three broad steps separating the congregation from the dias. A choir loft ascended behind the dias, topped by a towering organ case. From the latter's acme the edifice's front wall soared in a sheer expanse of rose-colored glass. The panes of this wall, set in a swirling, interlocking circular pattern, carried the eye irresistibly aloft and into the open mouth of a triangular glass spire. Because of its position at the foremost front of the edifice, no one beyond the first few rows could see far up into its interior, but the spire was yet visible through the rose panes of the roof. The distorting effect of the glass caused its outline to waiver and become indistinct as the eye traveled upwards until at last its tip merged indistinguishably into the lavender clouds and deeply cerulean heavens above.

The effect was most impressive, the more so as the vast weight of the walls, ceiling and spire was suspended from piers at each corner of the structure by a lattice of stainless metal cables. The suspension cables surmounted the building like a gleaming spiky crown, throwing intricate shadows into the interior and letting the entire structure seem to float effortlessly, unsupported in a sea of shifting light.

Impressive though it was, the effect was mostly lost on Tommy. He was too busy being inconspicuous to gawp. There, not thirty feet away from him, dead center along the gentle curve of the front row, was Greg.

Greg hadn't seen him, he knew, and wouldn't, he was pretty sure. Tommy was wearing a cheap gray suit he'd picked up in town yesterday, clothes of a cut and color Greg had never seen on him. In addition, he had his hair slicked back in a way he did not usually wear it. This produced an effect enough unlike his usual appearance that he felt sure Greg would never pick him out of all these thousands of people at a casual glance, the more so as Greg did not expect him to be here. That surveillance training at the Police Academy had been good for something, after all.

Also, fortunately, Tommy's neighbor in the front row was a very large and rather damp lady in a loud floral print dress who kept fanning herself with the bulletin. Her bulk shielded him from everyone to his right. Tommy hunkered as far back as he could, keeping her between himself and his quarry. He could lean forward for a glimpse at Greg whenever he liked. He did so now, cautiously lest Greg be looking in his direction—but Greg wasn't looking at anything. He was staring down into the poinsettias.

Tommy's gun in its shoulder holster rubbed against his arm as he relaxed back into his seat. Why had he brought it? He wasn't sure. His work had made it such a part of his persona, he felt naked without it in unfamiliar situations. Having it was an automatic reflex. He could barely remember packing it.

Taking it with him on the train, though, had been stupid. Because of the security you had to get through to get onto the platform, it had had to travel with his checked baggage, which went through a whole array of sensors scanning for explosives and other contraband. A holdover from the days when terrorist threats to airline travel had been a problem, all these security measures had long since ceased to be controversial. They had become simply an ordinary part of long distance travel, only one means among many of social control. A technology and an industry had grown up around them which justified their continued existence on the basis of jobs, control of the drug trade, and the potential terrorist threat to the trains themselves, though no sabotage of a train from inside had ever taken place, which, all by itself, the Consortium considered sufficient justification of the industry's effectiveness and of their right to exercise surveillance over the travelling public.

If the explosives in his bullets had set off an alarm and his gun had been discovered, he'd have had to answer questions, show his badge and fill out forms. Pretty dumb. He should have left the damn gun at home and picked one up here if he'd still wanted one. This was Texas, after all. You saw guns everywhere. His made him feel right at home. People here went about armed quite openly and routinely. In the gunshop on the square where he'd bought the shoulder holster, which was not standard issue for uniformed police, a sign on the cash register read, under Rev. Barber's picture, "This store supports your Constitutional right to bear arms. We ask no questions." Was that really the law down here? Whether it was or wasn't, he'd been getting a nice feeling that, in Rev. Barber's town at least, people could protect themselves without too much busybodying interference. Tommy approved: basic American values.

Once here, he'd had no trouble picking up Greg's trail. He'd simply called around the motels from the train station to see if Greg was registered, and found him at the third one. The dope was using his right name. Either he thought he'd given Tommy the slip in Chicago, which meant he thought Tommy was dumb, or, much worse, Greg wasn't thinking about him at all. This hurt bad. After all his devotion, how could Greg simply dismiss him like that? Could Greg really think he cared so little, he wouldn't try to find out what his lover was up to? One way or another, Tommy would show him how much he cared, and that he was smart enough to be cared for in return!

He'd checked into a motel across the street from Greg's and hung out in the coffeeshop keeping watch, sleeping only an hour or two a night to make sure Greg couldn't slip off without him. Even dopey from lack of sleep, following Greg around this tacky tourist trap town had been a simple job. Greg wasn't watching his back at all!—and this was a guy who was supposed to know something about surveillance! Greg really wasn't thinking about him. Again, this hurt.

He had watched Greg turned away at the door of Rev. Barber's headquarters on six separate occasions. That seemed promising; it meant Alexander wasn't seeing him, and wasn't talking to him on the phone, either—at least, so Tommy hoped from the fact Greg kept trying to see him so unsuccessfully. Maybe he, Tommy, didn't have much to worry about, after all. Maybe Alexander would just keep stiffing him. Greg would go home and cry for a while, then it would be over. Tommy would make an effort to be more understanding and give him some space. Maybe, if he played his cards right, Greg wouldn't have to know he'd made this trip at all. He'd try to manage it. It was good, then, he'd been so cautious.

As the days went by, the lack of sleep had caught up with him more and more. By this morning, he'd really felt it. When, bright and early at 6AM, Greg joined the crowd lined up for seats in front of the building, Tommy figured he was securely planted, and went off to try and wake up a little. He had a quad of espresso and some sugar doughnuts, changed into his disguise, and spent the day strolling around, hitting the doughnut shop several times more. This Billy Barber was quite a guy, kind of a law unto himself in this town, it appeared. Right there in the main square, across from the gunshop, Barber pointed his finger out at you from an enormous billboard: "RU-486 IS MURDER. GET YOUR LIST OF PRESCRIBERS NOW!"

He came back around the church later and gained entry through a side door. How this happened was kind of odd. He knew the guard had seen him; he caught the glint of flashing black eyes on him, perfectly expressionless; then the guy simply turned and walked away. Tommy slipped in and watched him saunter down the hall and through a door marked MEN. He guessed they must just be pretty trusting around here. Tommy walked past the guard desk like he owned the joint—but as he didn't, a broom closet provided a convenient hiding place. He closed his eyes and zoned for an hour, half awake from the coffee, until the murmur of the crowd gathering in the main hall above brought him to his feet again.

He chose his moment and slipped into a narrow stairwell rising up into the main hall beside the dias. Carefully lifting his eyes above the dias floor, he spotted Greg right away, there in the center of the first row, partially screened by the poinsettias. When Greg turned to look the other direction, he scuttled up the stairs and into the place next to the fat lady. Real slick.

He thanked fortune for lucking him into what seemed the perfect seat. Although his view of the action was almost entirely side on, it was also unobstructed; he could see Greg's profile if he wanted to, and get a close-up view of everybody on the dias. He peeked around at Greg again: no change. The shoulder holster pinched him when he sat back.

As he waited for things to get underway, the effects of accumulated stress descended upon him in a rush. The organ had been roaring huge masses of noise at him for minutes now, which didn't help his self-possession one little bit. Gaga from lack of sleep and jangling with caffeine and sugar, he seethed in emotional

turmoil. His palms were cold and damp. Just what *did* he think he
was going to do? One thing he knew for sure: he wasn't going to sit
here and watch this David Alexander take his lover away from him.
After all the sweat and blood he'd put into making the relationship
possible, the risks he'd taken, the enormous emotional investment,
he would not be shrugged aside. That was not gonna happen, no way.

Ah, they were coming in now. First, some sour-looking old
guys in suits, then, yeah, there he was: David Alexander in cream-
colored satin looking like an angel flown down to earth. God, he was
beautiful! Alexander had a gray-haired lady on his arm, whom he
steered to a seat and took the next one along himself: two in a row
of kind-of thrones against the back wall under the choir loft, like the
priests used in a real church. Who did this guy think he was, anyway?
Tommy watched his eyes rake the first few rows briefly and saw him
flash a small smile at someone. Who? Why? At Greg? Alexander
must have seen him. At somebody else? At the television camera on
its tripod in the middle of the tenth row? He had to know.

He eased himself forward and peeked around the fat lady.
There was Greg, 'way far out on the edge of his seat, staring at
Alexander with a look of intense adoration Tommy had never seen on
his face before, a look that seared through Tommy, red-hot. He
moaned softly. The fat lady didn't notice. She was moaning too,
either because of the heat—it didn't feel warm, but she was slick with
sweat—or because she was warming up for religious ecstasy. Lord,
what he wouldn't give to see Greg look at him like that! He'd kill for
it. Yes, he would. His hands clenched. Love, hurt and hate swirled
through him one after the other until they became an
indistinguishable mass possessing him completely.

* * * * *

Since his arrival in Necktie Gulch, Greg had learned a lot
about David Alexander. David's picture was everywhere! There were
billboards, and posters on kiosks and in shops promoting his
appearance at Rev. Barber's Christmas Day consecration

extravaganza. David was famous, it seemed, a very big deal in a world which had existed invisible, at least to him.

It irritated Greg no end David could have been so famous, adored and well-publicized all the time he, Greg, had been searching for him down one blind alley after another. He wanted to kick himself all the way to Chicago and back again. There was no mystery, he supposed, about how this had happened. He simply wasn't too interested in music. Oh, he knew the Top 40 stuff radio stations were always blasting at you, and he knew the famous artists celebrated in the mainstream media, where the so-called "Christian Rock" people never appeared. Mainstream artists were pretty much inescapable. If David had appeared as one of them, Greg would have been onto him like a bum after his next slug of fortified hooch.

But he hadn't. Instead, David had surfaced in this weird world of religious fanaticism, and had gotten there direct from the equally weird world of New York street hustlers.

What bothered Greg was the connection. How had he gotten from one to the other?—and why this world in particular? Had David found God?

Because it was the only source of background information at hand, Greg had hit the bookstore on the square. Between runs at the headquarters building door, he holed up in his room and tried to get David on the phone. However, like the guards at the door, the telephone operators seemed utterly unable to understand that he was not merely some silly fan, but a genuine friend of David's, somebody who actually *knew him personally* and had crucially important personal business to discuss! In mounting frustration, he left message after message with David's ever more openly impatient guardians. While he waited for David to return them, he boned up on the World Church of the Redeemable Redeemer, and in particular, on David's official, as-told-to biography, which, as Greg more or less expected, seemed to be mostly lies. At the time when, as the book described in the most pathetic and moving terms, David was supposed to have been lying ill, dying of AIDS in Seattle's Harborview Hospital and having his grand epiphany of Our Blessed Lord Jesus Christ via the televised beneficence of Rev. Barber, Greg knew from his own meticulous investigation that David had been in New York City joyously screwing everything that moved. So much for David's supposed religious conversion.

Speaking of which, David's homophobia in this new incarnation, as revealed by the book, bothered Greg for its hypocrisy—not because of the homophobia itself, precisely, and not for the reason you might expect; Greg understood the value of keeping one's head down, no one better, and that badmouthing gay people was a really effective means of going about it. Still, if there'd ever been anybody with no need to keep his head down, that person was the David Alexander he'd met in New York. Now that Greg himself had obtained a small measure of personal freedom through the release from his law enforcement career, he was ready and eager for more. He had a hard time imagining anyone voluntarily giving up that kind of freedom for a life of sneaking and hiding: surely what David was doing. How David had enjoyed that sex they'd had! David doing without did not compute, somehow. How was he getting it off now?—and with whom? Sudden jealousy gnawed Greg.

As for the Church, the books he read were most suggestive. Now, Greg was no atheist. He and Tommy didn't go to church and probably wouldn't have picked the same one if they had, but they figured there had to be a god. Everybody said so, after all. But this! To Greg, who'd lived oblivious to everything about this subculture except the bare fact of its existence, the last days had been a revelation. Why, Rev. Barber's church was all miracles and checkbooks! The man claimed to have cured every known disease. Even shattered bones were supposed to have reknit under the reverend's magic fingers—which, despite the lack of opportunity to see and judge for himself, Greg's basic common sense permitted him to doubt. What he did not doubt was that a prayer for donations followed the "miracle." The whole thing was plainly a scam.

That David could be involved in it opened hitherto unseen vistas into the cynical nature of his character. David was not merely the smooth professional Greg had seen working in New York. He was clearly an adventurer of an highly advanced type. The Prince of Thieves, was right! He'd gotten bored with what he'd had going in

New York, and an opportunity had arisen to do this instead. Sooner or later—and probably sooner, if Greg's estimation of his sex drive was correct—he'd get bored of this and switch to something else. Wow! What a life he must be having!—one lived on principles quite different from Greg's careful propriety and punctilious attention to society's rules and regulations. The freedom of it took his breath away; its insecurities made him hesitate on the verge of this uncharted territory. He just knew David would invite him into his life with open arms the minute he knew Greg was here. Was he, Greg Whitbread, really ready for this? He took the plunge and said yes, yes, YES! David would never let any harm come to him. With the Prince of Thieves to take the lead and show him the ropes, he'd try anything! David could be his tourguide any day and every day! Hey, with his insider knowledge of CRAP and investigatory procedure in general, he himself might have a real contribution to offer toward keeping them out of trouble! Greg was wilder than ever to get to David and let him know he was ready for whatever they did!

But that was the problem: getting to him past this heavy rockstar security Barber had set up. That David couldn't have been getting his messages was the only explanation. Greg's one chance seemed to be to get close enough in the hall to establish eye contact. If he could do that, David would send somebody around to escort him off to bliss eternal on the spot.

Or perhaps another thing explained David's silence: that annoying business of Greg having been a CRAP agent in New York. Surely a small matter! David loved him and would forgive him—probably had already. Given the genuineness and depth of the communication he had felt between them, surely David understood how the enormity of Greg's love had wiped out everything else. —But what if this wasn't quite as intuitive as he thought? What if David did still resent all those lies he'd told in New York? Greg's impotence in the face of this possibility gnawed at him and drove to crisis level the urgency of making contact with David, of, somehow, making clear his penitence and everlasting respect.

He'd showed up before dawn, prepared to wait all day for the best seat possible. His heart sank when he saw the long line of what could only be David's fans already in place. If he'd but known, he'd have got there the night before. He'd never get a good seat now. How would David pick him out amidst all these other young people after they all rushed for the best seats in the house?

A sterner strategy obviously would be required. Sneak in a side door? Unlikely. From previous visits he knew all doors were attended. Maybe he'd be able to catch an attendant off guard and slip through—but also maybe not, in which case he'd lose his place in line. No, a better plan was to go through and take a seat in the hall, slip off toward the men's room and see if he couldn't duck under a rope somewhere to find David backstage. In a return of his old nervous gesture, his hand strayed up to straighten his tie. He guessed that would be his best shot. The only alternative was returning home empty-handed, with nothing to compensate for the major fit Tommy would have when he got there, then deluging David with long self-justifying pleading letters until finally he got an answer.

The need for these plans evaporated completely and his dejection with it when, just inside the door, an usher plucked him from the crowd.

"Mr. Whitbread?"

Greg turned, startled by the unexpected use of his name, the hand on his sleeve and the shiny onyx marbles of the man's eyes. "Yes?"

"Please come with me, sir. You're on the list for reserved seating."

Greg attached himself to the man's retreating backside, trotting air. *Yes!* The hangup had been with the messages, just as he'd thought. They'd gotten through, but only at the last minute, or David would have called him. As it was, he'd clearly just had time to arrange this. Probably, he'd had to point Greg out on a security monitor, or from an upper gallery. Greg couldn't resist whirling around to see if David might be on view this very minute. He wasn't. Greg waved and smiled at the next security camera he saw, just in case.

This sign of David's favor sent him into delirium. David did care! He'd taken the trouble to scan the crowd for Greg and have him singled out. It was all coming true. After the show, his new life would begin!

Greg followed the usher eagerly down an aisle. The front third of the center section was roped off.

"Please take any seat in the reserved section, and God bless you." The usher turned to go.

"Just a minute!" Greg had a thought. "Uh, he didn't say anything about what I was to do after the showImeantheservice, did he?"

The usher smiled a slow, rather snaky little smile that sent chills of sudden embarrassment down Greg's spine. *I've been treated like a groupie, and now I'm starting to act like one,* he thought.

"Not to me," the usher said. "I'm sorry, sir. If He's left instructions for you, I'm sure something will find you later."

In Greg's embarrassment, the unusual use of the word 'something' didn't register at all; nor did it occur to him they might be talking about two completely different "he"s. Undoubtedly, David expected him to make his way backstage after the service. He would, whereupon his favored status would become apparent to everybody. "Uh, thank you. And bless you too."

The usher disappeared back up the aisle. None of the seats in the reserved section were taken as yet, so Greg picked the best one, absolutely dead center in the very first row. If the position of the microphone, immediately beyond a phalanx of poinsettias, was any indication, that would put him closer than anyone else in the house to David's crotch, a position he intended to maintain forever and ever, glory hallelujah, amen.

Greg thought back to the day he'd first seen David, over the security monitor in Marino's New York bookstore: sulky and sexy, a gushing mirage in the desert of Greg's repressed existence. His life had changed from that moment. Had it really been only a year ago last summer? It felt like a lifetime.

It seemed he'd known even at that moment his destiny would be forever linked to David. Now, destiny had arrived. For the ten-thousandth time, he replayed his sexual encounter with David in his mind, this time with the absolute certainty he'd be replaying it for real before this day was out and every day to come as well.

An incipient erection brought him back to reality. Perhaps this wasn't quite the place. He squirmed in an uncomfortable effort to get properly arranged in his underwear without actually putting his hand down there and straightening things out.

To distract himself, he sent his eyes up and around, admiring the spectacular building and inspecting the crowd. He had company in the reserved section now. He looked these people over, curious about what sort of person besides himself Rev. Barber's god thought merited a front row seat.

They weren't really very interesting, he decided, mostly middle-aged couples of the mink-stole-and-diamond-pinky-ring set. The men had piggy, self-satisfied expressions on their florid faces and well-tailored suits on their well-fed bodies. They held low, rumbling conversations over the backs of seats while the women, resplendent in too much makeup and rather over-elaborate hairdos that looked passé to Greg's citified sensibilities, flashed their teeth and waved their rings at one another.

There were only a few exceptions to this norm here in the reserved section. A few places to his right in the front row sat three very interesting-looking young men. While their quiet suits fit right in, their hair was much too long for this crowd, they wore patent leather shoes of the latest mod pattern, and they had exceptionally pretty faces of the sort most young Christians took great pains to camouflage with moustaches or military-style haircuts. In this crowd, they stood out like rock musicians at a Mormon picnic. Greg guessed them, correctly, to be members of David's band.

Then a fourth turned in from the aisle. *My god!* Greg whipped back in his place as Herbie Manning took a seat with the band. *What the hell?*

Gingerly, Greg eased forward again for another look. No doubt about it! What on earth was he doing here? Manning didn't believe in religion! He was an atheist! Back at AmalCon, he'd always been going on about how God was a sham, a myth perpetuated by ruling elites to keep stupid and ignorant people in line, "part myth, part propaganda, part wishful thinking, and," as Greg remembered it, "for some people, part wiring flaw. Just look them in their glazy eyes and you know they're defective." His presence here was grossly wrong somehow.

Or was it? The connection, when finally it hit him, came accompanied by the sort of sinking feeling that usually accompanies an annoyingly obvious truth one would prefer to overlook. David. Of course they were connected. Following Manning's trail had led to David in the first place! In the heat of his hopeless passion, this fact had escaped him for months. He'd forgotten Herbie completely.

Frantically, he juggled the pieces of many puzzles in an effort to make a coherent whole. Okay, if Manning had known David in New York and was here now, maybe, in some way, he was the connection. He was certainly a proven conman himself. He fit right in, there.

Herbie'd had connections in many businesses, Greg remembered. Hadn't there been a recording studio on his client list? Yes: Apex Recording on Southport in Chicago, the kind of place that was a clearinghouse for struggling free-lance performers and lower-level music business people of all sorts. Interesting! So he did have an intro of some kind into the music business.

It seemed awfully tenuous. Could you really get from there to the World Church of the Redeemable Redeemer? How did a couple of sex subculture types like David and Herbie get mixed up with a lot of holy rollers? Even holy rock and rollers? Unless this Church was even more of a con than he'd thought.

The organ crashed into life with a thunderous boom. Things were getting under way. No, the puzzle pieces didn't all fit the way they should. He looked at it again in increasing frustration. Manning! Damn and doubledamn! Could this change things? He needed more information!

Greg pushed as far back out of Herbie's view as he could and fixed his eyes on the flowerpots before him. The last thing he wanted was for Herbie to spot him before he'd figured out what was going on and how to deal with it. What on earth was Herbie's relationship to David? Were they partners of some kind? Maybe even... lovers? Could that be how David was getting it off? Somehow, he couldn't quite picture that. David and Herbie? Ridiculous! Still and all, he forced himself to admit the possibility Herbie had helped himself to David's bod at some time or another, in the course of David's former profession as hustler, if no way else. Which meant something of the kind still could be going on now. The mere thought filled Greg with sudden rage.

One thing he knew for sure about the Herbie/David relationship: whatever it was, it was bygod gonna change. Herbie Manning! God damn him to hell! Regardless of the exact particulars, here was Greg's old enemy, the despised, contemptible Herbie Manning, all wrapped up with the man he, Greg, loved and could not—would not!—do without. Plainly, there was going to be a confrontation of some kind. Well, he thought grimly, Herbie had a surprise coming. The day he couldn't cut Herbie Manning out of anything he wanted (one anonymous phone call to CRAP's 1-800 rat line might do the trick, supposing Manning was still an open file) was a day that never would dawn—and this day, David had marked him with special favor. Obviously, he had some cards to play. It wouldn't be too long before he found out what they were.

He abandoned speculation. Things were happening. The door at the back of the dias opened and people appeared. Yes, there he was—David!—not twenty feet away! From his vantage point Greg could see David seemed dazed and little confused. He blinked in the light. He had an old woman on his arm whom he dislodged into a chair, and sat. His eyes slid straight over Greg; he smiled a weak little smile at a point a few places off to his right, at—Greg peeked to make sure—Herbie Manning! No doubt about it. Herbie was smiling broadly back at him and giving him a little thumbs up.

Greg couldn't believe it. Sweat flushed on his scalp and the back of his neck at this inexplicable snub. He sat straight up and leaned forward, *willing* David to look at him and acknowledge him too.

This did not happen. David seemed to sink into himself completely and become oblivious. Greg struggled with his composure. This was not the time for a scene, he reminded himself. He must wait and watch for any clues which might come his way.

LEARNING TO LOVE IT

❋ ❋ ❋ ❋ ❋

The service droned on interminably. They stood. They sang. They sat. They bowed their heads and put them up again. Through it all, David's confusion and dismay grew steadily. Rev. Barber was clearly very angry with him about something, but what, he could not imagine. This was awful. The man had saved his life! He would never knowingly do anything the slightest bit out of accord with Rev. Barber's wishes. The very thought distressed him profoundly. What could he have done so to infuriate his idol?

He stole glance after glance at Barber, who ignored him completely. In desperation, he tried to re-establish their mental link, but instead of the clear connection from which he'd drawn such strength, the image warped queasily in and out of shape. It snarled at him in a deep slow growling language he did not understand. Each word enmeshed him in strand upon strand of sticky foulness. The effect had all the weight and feeling of an incantation—more than, worse than that, of a... no, it couldn't be...

It's a curse!, he thought, and tore himself loose in horror and disbelief. He simply could not accept this. Something was deeply wrong with this vision, and with the world into which he reemerged.

When he opened his eyes, everything looked wrong, especially the people; nobody seemed *alive*. Although he'd been at least introduced to everybody on the dias, he didn't recognize any of them, or any of the many friends he knew he had out in the congregation. All the thousands of people gathered there might have been mere robots made of meat and animated solely to give him the cues he needed to go through the motions expected of him.

With one exception. Gerry Axehammer, his best friend in this world, sat right there in the front row, minus the baseball cap for once. Gerry truly seemed to be the only living being in the hall, as if a pure white spotlight picked him out and made him real, bright and vibrant. David felt more powerfully than ever that he and Gerry were connected by some invisible bond stronger than life and stronger than death. Gerry was his rock. If this were love, then he loved Gerry at that moment more than anybody or anything else in the universe.

He was going to need a rock, and very shortly too. The moment approached. Rev. Barber even now wound himself into the passionate peroration of the pastoral prayer.

"...Dear Lord, with all our hearts. We implore Thy Mercy on our miserable, sinful selves, for we are striving, *striving* with every thought, word, deed and breath we take to obey Your Commandments and to build Your Church on earth as You have Yourself built it in Heaven. We thank You, Lord, for the wonderful sign of Your divine favor You have given us in allowing the erection of this magnificent edifice, this inspiring testament to Your Word made tangible to all the peoples of the world in glass and steel and stone. We beg it may stand forever as a visible manifestation of Your Truth and of the divinity of Your Son, whose coming among us we celebrate this day, and whose Divine Compassion and Mercy are available without stint to all who truly believe in You and who commit themselves to the observance of Your Commandments. We commit ourselves, earnestly and seriously, to the propagation of Your Revelation, and to the wider spread and observance of those Commandments, until at last, we may gather all the peoples of the world under the single, unifying roof of Your Word, of which this roof which shelters us today is but a symbol. We dedicate ourselves without reservation to this, the highest and noblest end to which man may aspire: the literal creation of Heaven on earth. We can do it, Lord, oh yes we can do it! Our movement rolls ever forward, in-ex-OR-able with the force of Your Truth behind it, and with Your loving aid. For we are weak, Lord, oh! we are weak! We are nothing without You, Lord, nothing! Lend us your strength! STRIKE DOWN the forces of Hell! Smite them, Oh Lord! The blasphemers! The atheists! The agnostics and apostates! The unnatural, homosexual degenerates who mock Thee and afflict Thy faithful here gathered. STRIKE THEM DOWN before all the world, we pray, so the world may see their folly and despise them! Uplift and strengthen the righteous, and bless us in this, our endeavor! Straighten the path before us, and set our feet firm and resolute upon it! Give Your people new courage to seize the wicked, sinful world which everywhere sets its bigotry against us, and force it to heel! Ennoble us in the face of those who revile us, and bless our quest! With Your aid, there are no worlds we may not conquer for You! Bless us! Bless us! Bless us! This we pray, Amen."

The congregation's responsive AMEN washed over the dias like the murmuring of Heaven's assent—followed by the usual coughing, harrumphing and creaking of many seats as the congregation recovered and made itself easy after the long interval of devotional concentration. With a wary eye on the television cameras, Rev. Barber ignored this and plunged right on.

"Dear friends, this is a very special and very joyous day for us. Today we celebrate the coming among us of our Dear Lord Jesus Christ, in whose name we are here gathered. What better, more appropriate day could there be to celebrate the many years of dedication from each and every one of you which now bear fruit in the consecration of the Rose Cathedral, our glorious new World Headquarters and Spiritual Center. Let's take a moment to admire it, shall we? Isn't it beautiful?"

The cameras panned the building and superimposed a montage of images of it from every possible angle. In a distant corner, the architect, whose triumph of design and engineering it truly was, patted his hair into place and prepared to rise and receive the adulation of the multitude.

"Yes, it is wonderful, isn't it? Just look what The Lord has built! But, while the credit for this glorious structure belongs to Him, He did not do it alone. The power of His message inspired thousands and thousands of you to shoulder the burden, often, I know, at considerable sacrifice to yourselves. But He has felt your pain and borne your grief. Just as the rainbow was His sign and His promise to Noah, so this building is His sign to you that He smiles upon your labors and receives your offering and it is pleasing to Him. Forever may it stand, an enduring monument to the inspiring, creative power of The Lord! All of you who sacrificed by your donations can take pride in having brought yourselves to His particular notice and favor thereby. However, while this work is completed and we can all take pride in the result, The Lord's business is not ended. Oh no! We must not rest. He calls us onwards and upwards to ever greater labors—and ever greater rewards—in His name."

As Rev. Barber segued to his next topic, the architect sat back again, struggling manfully to master his *coitus interruptus* of bursting pride.

"I am sorry to tell you today that His missions among the heathen in Asia and Africa are undersubscribed, and must shortly be cut back unless we redouble our efforts. Our outreach program to bring the glorious Word of Jesus to the young people who wander homeless and thirsting for knowledge in the hostile, arid deserts of our lawless great cities also cries out for your support! It is heartbreaking, heartbreaking! to think of the shame and degradation these young people endure in their immoral lifestyles when, but for the lack of a few pennies, they might be saved for the glory of The Lord! Our young friend David Alexander will shortly tell you a tale of their condition so heartrending and so beautiful as to melt the coldest heart. I weep with compassion for these young people every time I hear it, and praise The Lord for the miracle He wrought for David. His tale is proof! These young people long for Jesus without knowing it. Let the message be opened before them, and they will grab it with a grip of iron! We must help them open their hearts so He may enter and save them, just as He has saved all of us heregathered. Must I say it? On this of all days, when we gather to rejoice at the birth of a babe, such a donation is *particularly* appropriate!

"Of the rewards He brings us in return for our devotion, I need not speak. They are joy, health, prosperity and the mighty, eternal fellowship of The Lord! How can we deny these blessings to those who need them so desperately? As proof of our commitment, I make you a special promise. The Board of Deacons of the World Church of the Redeemable Redeemer met today and made this extraordinary decision: every penny, yes, *every penny* of the donations you make today will go directly to these works! Let the greedy shylocks of New York and Chicago, Tokyo, London and Berlin wait a

453

week for the pound of flesh due them on the bonds for our hotels, universities and other good works. We will pay them, yes we will, but first, the plight of the poor, ignorant heathens of the world and the benighted children of our own blessed country call out to us. We will minister to them first. So dig deep, my friends. I know many of you here have come with your tithe already prepared. I beg you, please take that checkbook out of your other pocket and write an additional amount for these worthy labors. Those of you at home, dig out your Mastercard, your Visa, your Discover and American Express! Call that number flashing across the bottom of your screen.

"Take a moment to decide how much more you can afford. Think about the amount right now." He paused a moment, eyes closed, obviously concentrating. "Have you got it? Is that really the most you can give to spread salvation through Jesus Christ among those who so desperately need it? Good. Now—hold your breath—I ask you to double it! This is not a donation, my friends, but an investment—an investment in the future of our world, and in your own futures as well. For The Lord sees you. He's watching you right now. He will not let your sacrifice go unnoticed, either in this world or the next. He will reward you, as He has rewarded so many firm believers already."

The cameras panned through the hall, paying particular attention to the gold and diamond jewelry adorning many in the congregation and focusing in on those digging into pockets or writing on checkbooks. "Oh, that's wonderful! Look, your brethren here in the hall are responding with the Christian charity that ensures our movement can never fail! How can you at home not do likewise? The world is holding its breath, depending on you! I thank you! Praise be to the glory of The Lord, whose inspiration to do His Work never fails! For those of you in the hall, pastors of the World Church of the Redeemable Redeemer will now pass among you to receive your offerings and bless you for your generosity to our cause. To further inspire you, the Offertory Anthem will today be rendered by that young man who in the last year has become such a pillar of our ministry to the young, David Alexander. So dig deep, my friends!

Call that number flashing on your screen. Pastors are waiting to take your calls and transmit my personal blessing! Thank you."

The moment had arrived. The microphone stood empty and beckoning. A touch on David's arm startled him. The meat robot that was his mother smiled at him and urged him up with a small movement of its head. He rose and headed forwards.

The organ began the intro to "Jesus, Sweet Jesus." The vast noise traveled down the length of the hall, crashed off the back wall and came back at him, mingling with fresh notes going the other way in warring cacophony. David literally *saw* it: a jangling electric-looking haze, into which the winter sun on the horizon poured laterally through the rose-colored glass and drenched the congregation in blood. Bloody shadows smeared everything—noses, chins and jewelry—and pooled in the aisles: a rising tide that soon would drown them all.

Struck with the horror of the vision, David let his cue come and go unheeded. The organist circled through an awkward impromptu modulation and began the intro again. Suddenly mindful of the situation, David struggled to pull himself together. He glanced at Gerry.

The connection between them was as strong as ever, perhaps even stronger. In the midst of his surreal vision of the hall, Gerry stood out in strong relief. Yet, instead of the strength and will to continue he hoped to find there, David saw the last expression he expected to see on his friend's beloved face: pursed-lipped contempt. He gawked. First Rev. Barber, now Gerry? What could he possibly have done? With this last prop knocked from beneath him, David sought desperately among the blood-soaked robots for reassurance from a human face.

He turned once more into Rev. Barber's baleful glare, twin beams of darkness that froze his soul, and felt a queasy lurching upwelling at the core of his being. His mind careened: he grovelled on the floor of Rev. Barber's office smelling carpet cleaner and rug dust as the same sickness filled him once again; yet, he could not seem to remember that actually having happened! Or could he?

From the depths of illness and confusion, his eye caught on an otherwise insignificant detail: a young man dead in front of him in the first row, a young man with sandy hair and a peaches-and-cream complexion leaning far forward in an attitude of shameless begging, mouthing his name: *David! I'm sorry!* He didn't know this person. Or did he?

From the edge of his being, something big hurtled toward him with the in-ex-OR-able force of a freight train running blind in the night.

Omigod it's Little Adolph!

Sights, sounds, smells, memories drowned him. He was Herbie Manning. He was David Alexander, no, two different David Alexanders—the devout rock singer, and a David Alexander with very different opinions and attitudes—who definitely were looking each other askance. For a moment, he teetered back and forth between these three personas.

As he struggled to integrate them, his cue came and went, again unheeded. The organist, desperate this time and without instructions, broke off entirely. The organ went silent with a squawk.

Coincident with this sudden silence, David's three personas merged into uneasy coherence. His vision cleared along with his mind. He was alone, nakedly exposed on the dias before thousands of people staring expectantly at him and starting to murmur and twist uncomfortably in their seats. The hard glass eye of the television camera on its stand bore down on him, exposing him to uncounted millions more.

Desperate to find something to hang onto that was still as it had seemed, he looked again for Gerry, his friend, his rock—and found only the djinn in Herbie Manning drag, slumped back in his seat: a study in deep black dejection.

His mother? Another djinn, of course. She regarded him coolly, as one watches a bug in a jar to see what it will do and how long it will take to die. His real mother—Herbie Manning's mother—and his father too, were far away, alone and disregarded. A sudden pang of remorse struck him.

The Gate

Wildly, he cast around for Rev. Barber. The Archon! This being of fathomless terror sat his throne, an expressionless motionless bejowled buddha. David wanted to run, to run and never stop running. He tried to move his feet, but could not. The power of those eyes pinned him literally and quite pitilessly to the spot to face who and what he was.

People in the hall were murmuring loudly now, wondering what was the matter and why didn't somebody do something. In a flash, the full impact of where he was and what was expected of him hit him squarely. My god, he'd been all over the country... preaching sacred truth? ...spewing hatred-bullshit-lies! to wildly receptive audiences. Sick revulsion filled him.

He saw his new friends, the band. Except for the djinn, who stared at the floor in hopeless gloom, the others perched on the edges of their seats, deep concern etched on their faces. Yes, they were as they had been, but how could he be true to them still? Their message was crap, he knew that now—again. His very nature betrayed them.

As if to underscore the point, his crotch, suppressed and inactive for months, came explosively to life. The pain of his sudden hardon in tight briefs might have doubled him over had not horror kept him upright, the horror of knowing nothing whatever could prevent what would happen next. In a slow, rising, agonizing, cresting wave he cummed his shorts, copiously, voluminously, fulsomely. There on the dias of the World Headquarters and Spiritual Center of the World Church of the Redeemable Redeemer, in front of a crowd of thousands and a world audience, he poured out cups, pints, quarts, it seemed, of pent up jism. Hot and gummy, it drenched his briefs, oozed through the leg holes, and slid down his legs.

Although his trousers were loose, their satin heavy and finely woven, nothing could prevent them soaking through. Soon his humiliation would be complete. In rising panic, he tried again to turn and leave the dias, but could not move his feet. The Archon's power rooted him mercilessly to the spot. —And Christ, did he want a cigarette!

Each second was an agony of embarrassment. It seemed he'd been pinned here endless minutes in the expectant and increasingly puzzled stare of this vast multitude, when in reality it had been only moments. Why had the Archon brought him here and glued him down? What did he want?

A desperate thought struck him, borne upwards through the still coalescing mass of his three personas. When the Archon submerged him, he'd been trying to do something—what had it been?—something that, according to the djinn, was supposed to help in some way. Searching for the mortal power, that was it, though precisely what magic that would work was beyond his grasp at the moment. Still, he'd try anything to shut out what was happening here. Part of him remembered how. He closed his eyes, canceled the rising murmur in the hall, and descended into his mental landscape.

Again, he stood upon the parapet that separated his metaphysical self from the gulf containing his mortal being. His metaphysical self, a glowing, pulsing labyrinth no longer, lay bound in ugliness. Girders, walkways, walls and scaffolding overbuilt it and connected it to a new feature in this landscape: a fortress of power and immeasurable strength—the Archon! Its towers and walls dominated all before them. No wonder the djinn was dejected: his aspect was in grave danger of becoming a mere annex.

He shifted focus down from the parapet, onto the darkened formless landscape of shifting terror and desire wherein lay the mortal power. The fortress detected him. Static slashed outwards to envelop him. He stared out into what was suddenly howling nothingness, and, as once before, he caught an instant's hint of something large and warm pulsing beyond the blinding veil: the thing he wanted, the mortal power. Then it was gone and the static began to flay him apart. David knew he had one and only one chance left to touch that thing he'd sensed. With a desperate effort of will, he abandoned his moorings and flung himself at it, out into the nothingness.

He fell and fell, and as he fell, he felt the static storm consume him. He struggled, a meteor blazing through a hostile hurricane, to find what he wanted while there might still be something of him left.

The maelstrom claimed him, and stripped him of all he was.

I am falling through pain...

I am falling...

I am pain...

I am...

I...

A bare essence smashed through the landscape and submerged itself in the big warm core pulsing beneath.

Memory returned. His consciousness expanded in all directions at once. Above the surface, he saw the fortress crash in ruin. Tower crumbled upon tower and wall upon wall, and disappeared, taking the webwork binding him to the Archon with it. His metaphysical self stretched and began to regain its old dimensions.

A cork bobbing upwards, he broke the surface and emerged back into the Rose Cathedral. The djinn sat bolt upright and staring, black eyes wide with amazement shading into... something else—a very familiar expression on that face: sneering mockery. The mockery, however, was directed at the Archon, not at him.

He did not understand it. He cared nothing about their disputes. He'd slipped the Archon's control; he felt it. He turned to flee—but still could not! His feet remained as firmly planted to the spot as before!

The djinn was staring at him now. That voice like the exhalation of a tomb echoed in his mind. *Free you are of Him, but not of Me, for We are One.*

Then help me! David begged.

Why? Where is it you wish to go?

The djinn filled David's head with visions then:

...of two women assaulted, raped and murdered, "Romans 1:26-27" smeared onto the wall above them in blood;

...of a tragically confused teenaged boy coming home from one of David's concerts to put his father's gun into his mouth;

...of smashed glass and gay men humiliated, robbed and beaten: an evening's bloody trail through a gay neighborhood, at the end of the trail a gang of skinhead thugs on a gleeful spree, David's own face smiling rapturously from several smeary T-shirts;

...of gay men shabby and bewildered, pathetic suitcases in their hands, herded together before a building marked "Prayer Will Make You Free," a building that looked very much like once it might have been a prison.

On and on it went: visions of riot, ignorance, prejudice, discrimination and vicious oppression both past and to come erected on foundations he'd built or reinforced, and all in the name of a superstition he repudiated.

How would he ever again show his face anywhere he possibly could want to be? Even if whatever part of the gay world he hadn't destroyed would have him back—which he doubted—his conscience convulsed at the thought.

Worse, as David Alexander, he was famous! When, as he knew he must, he recanted the vicious nonsense he'd been preaching and renounced his role as Christian pied piper, a role he now could not fulfill if he wanted to, the Born Again crowd would have to destroy him. They would revile him not only as queer, but as an apostate, and hunt him down no matter where he went.

He'd be a pariah in all camps: alone, isolated and tormented, forever. All possibility of love, joy, even of simple companionship had gone. There was only one person of whom he was worthy now: Little Adolph, whom he had enslaved, still yearning with sickening adoration in the very front row. David's gorge rose. He'd rather die.

The djinn posed him a very small, careful question: *Really?*

So that was it. Death. Only his death would solve the metaphysical's world's problems. And why not? All the djinn's contempt finally had been justified. At last, he had earned it.

The uneasy muttering in the hall had reached the stage of action. People were standing, gesticulating at those on the dias, demanding something be done. Several were in the aisles near the dias, signaling at him and asking if he were all right.

A shocking titter of nervous laughter cut through. David glanced down. Damp stains had appeared over his crotch and were spreading downwards, outwards, upwards. He glanced out at the television cameraman—who tried hurriedly to compose his face. Obviously, David's humiliation had been seen everywhere and recorded for all time. The last shreds of his will crumbled. He knew now what the metaphysical world wanted, why he'd been brought here and shamed. He gave it to them.

Okay, you win. His life was over. He renounced it. *You wanted your stupid aspect back? Take it and be quick about it.*

As if in response to his thought, he caught a movement on the dias to his right.

* * * * *

Tommy could stand it no longer. Through his own haze of pain, all he saw was Greg and this Alexander staring at each other, oblivious to everything. It twisted him again and again, harder and harder until he thought the pain of it would tear him apart from inside. He closed his eyes a long moment, willing them to quit, but when he looked again, they were still at it. The organ had stopped. Through a very long moment that seemed to go on forever, people started to talk and wonder what was happening. At last, they started laughing! It seared him, how Greg and this asshole Alexander could be so wrapped up in each other. All his wrongs came back to him: how he'd struggled and schemed so that he and Greg could be together, how he'd evaded his buddies' questions and put up with Greg's lack of cooperation, how he'd lived with the constant danger of discovery, and all for this, that this Alexander could steal his lover and humiliate him in front of all these people? No way was he going to get away with it, the bastard!

All self-possession left him. In a flash he was on the dias, his gun leveled at David in the two-handed marksman's crouch.

David saw him. He didn't know who this was, the young man with the wiry wrestler's build, or what reason he had to kill. David didn't care. It took no genius to figure that, the moment he made everybody happy by wishing to die, a means to it would appear. The young man was welcome, whoever he was. David turned to face him on feet that were suddenly free, and drew himself up tall to present the broadest possible target. He closed his eyes. A broad band of power seemed to enclose the three of them—himself, the djinn and the assassin—drawing them ever closer together in surprising intimacy. David rejected this too. As his final act, he silently and passionately told the djinn, the Archon, and the whole motherfucking metaphysical world to go screw itself.

Then, everything seemed to happen at once.

Greg's gaze followed David's as he turned. His eyes widened in horror as his worst nightmare came alive in front of him. "NO TOMMY NO!" he screamed. In a single bound, his track-trained muscles carried him over the poinsettias to the dias. He rushed to shield David with his body.

Tommy saw him coming and didn't care. Greg would betray him too? Use him and slough him like a used rubber? Treat him and his love like he was worthless? Sacrifice himself for some asshole he barely knew? Fine! Screw them both. Assholes! If he couldn't have Greg, no one would. He'd shoot and keep on shooting until they were both dead or he ran out of bullets. He was *not* worthless!

The deacons on their thrones stared at him, stern, yet frozen by the inexorable momentum which seemed to govern the event. Tommy steadied his shaking hands. There was no turning back. Now he was here, he had to make this count.

His finger moved on the trigger.

The gun went off with a noise like a tiny firecracker in the vast hall, but the bullet never reached its target. Instead, to Greg's amazement, Herbie Manning's fox-headed letter opener bounced harmlessly off his chest and fell to the carpet. Wondering, he bent down and picked it up.

Tommy was bewildered too. The gun had disappeared straight out of his hands the instant he fired. How? Had he dropped it? He looked around to see.

The hall exploded in uproar. People jammed the dias and came at them from all sides. Rev. Barber and the djinn were shouting, extricating them from the crowd, rounding them up and bundling them toward the door at the back of the dias.

As the djinn shoved David toward it, he saw nothing on its other side. Instead of the robing room he had left in what seemed a different life, the space beyond was dead black.

"Mind the step," the djinn hissed from behind his ear and stiffarmed him through, straight into nowhere at all.

* * * * *

David tumbled out onto the gray carpet of an unfamiliar room. Glass walls rose from floor to ceiling on two sides. From the floor where he lay he could see little more than dull orange sky outside them, the night glow of some great city. Inside were a desk and chairs, and a veritable forest of potted plants. Before he could discover more, Greg and the would-be assassin appeared from what on this side appeared to be a cobalt-edged rectangle suspended in the air, and likewise tumbled to the floor. The Archon and the djinn followed, managing their entrances with more practiced grace. As the rectangle shrank from two dimensions to one, then to none and blinked out, the tumult in the hall behind it died as if dialed down on a switch, leaving a sudden quiet.

David picked himself up. "Wh- what happened? Where are we?"

Greg got to his feet and looked around. "Morgan Jaye's office! AmalCon! Chicago! What the...?"

"I gotta make a deposit." The Archon was calm. He walked around the desk, unzipping himself from his velvet-trimmed reverend's robe. He dropped this across the back of Morgan Jaye's oversized chair, then sat and snapped on the halogen desklamp.

Here on the other edge of the time zone, the sun had already set. Outside the circle of lamplight, the orange sky and the glowing windows of many towers around and below them filled the room with amber radiance. The forest of plants slept in silence, the recorded birdies turned off and sleeping too.

The djinn paced in controlled fury through a small track beside the desk. David moved to one of the chairs in front of it. His wet trousers felt cold as the air brushed them. He sank into the chair and fixed his eyes firmly on the carpet. Tommy alone failed to move from where he'd fallen into the room. He drew his knees up to his chest and laid his head on them. He moaned softly.

Greg took the chair next to David's. "David? Are you all right?" He put a hand on David's knee. "Why, you're all wet!"

David ignored him, except to brush off the hand.

No one spoke. Greg looked around in bewilderment. The Archon regarded him steadily. "I'm sorry, sir. I don't understand... I thought Tommy fired a gun at us, but this fell down instead." He put the fox-headed letter opener on the desk. "Then all of a sudden we were here." He shook his head slowly. "I'm confused. What happened?"

The djinn boiled over in wrath. "Love!" He came around the desk, swivelled David to face him and pulled his head up by the hair. "That stupid cow Love! *She's* what happened. Of all the damn things! You remember what I told you back in New York? That sometimes other forces besides mortal misery could produce an effect?"

The pain brought David up from his inner misery. He disengaged the djinn's hand.

"Well, this was one of those times. Apparently, the Gate we create between us allows mortal emotions to take shape and act at 'way below normal critical mass! There's more too. Remember your last wish? Your afterthought? You asked for luck! Well, me being the stupid soft-hearted idiot that I am, I didn't know how to prescribe that, so, trying to protect my aspect and kill two buzzards with one ballista, I gave you the good will of the metaphysical world. I marked you with a secret sign and ensured that any stray metaphysical entity in your neighborhood would act in your favor. What a lunkhead I was!" He slapped his forehead with the palm of his hand. "You were supposed to die, you sonuvabitch, so I could have my aspect back and seal the Gate. But *nooooooooo*! Your buddy here is so goddam stuck on you, he breaks straight through the field Master put around us

464

and stands in front of the gun. *She* must have been acting even then! After that, the program really takes on a life of its own! *His* buddy loves him so much, he tries to kill the both of you, but can't, 'cause with all that love floating around, She comes straight through the Gate and fucks the whole thing up! She was *always* a rotten bitch. I thought She was dead.

"Love!" His voice dripped acid. "Congratulations! Thanks to bad taste, you're still here, and we're *all* fucked!"

This kicked Greg to fury. "Same old Herbie! You never quit, do you? As full of crap as ever! Except the part about wanting David dead! Somehow, that I believe. And what's all this bull about a metaphysical world? That doesn't sound like you at all! Lunkhead is right! It's the lamest scam I ever heard! Or have you gone nuts on top of stupid?"

The djinn grabbed handfuls of his—of Herbie Manning's—scraggly thinning hair in rage. His eyes welled deadly fire.

The Archon exploded into life. The crack of his palm on the glass deskslab slammed their ears and left a spiderweb of cracks in its 2-inch thickness. "ENOUGH!" The wind of his roar ruffled their hair and rustled leaves throughout the room, a gale in the forest. "That's *enough*! Now we'll sort this out. You." He focused on Greg. "You don't understand a helluva lot of what's been going on here, so shut your trap. I'm sending you back, and your buddy over there with you."

There was a moment of silence. Tommy raised his head off his knees. "Back where?" he croaked, and cleared his throat.

"C'mere, son."

Slowly, Tommy got to his feet and entered the circle of light.

"All I got to tell you is that the both of you've been cogs in a big big machine with lots at stake. I'm not gonna apologize for it, because if it'd worked out, it'd've been worth it no matter what happened to you. I'm not gonna explain it neither, because when I'm done with you, you're not gonna remember nothing, anyway. As for where you're going..." He raised his eyes to heaven. "Wouldn't life be simple if only I could *kill* people! But I can't, so I'm sending the both of you back in time to the day you hustled off to Texas. Next thing you know, you'll both be on your way to work three days ago, with all your baggage intact."

He frowned. "'Cept the gun. That's not in my jurisdiction anymore. Truth be told, I don't know where that is." He glowered off at the middle distance. "I can't see it anywhere, so I can't send it back. Damitall. It'll be a problem if it turns up, because no matter where I send you, I can't change what's already happened. You'll still be there in Texas too, doing what you did, and it's your damn gun, issued and traceable to you. I gotta cut all connection to that, and to us, somehow."

He turned his frown on Greg. "I'll start by cancelling the spell our boy here put on you in New York. You won't give a rat's ass about him anymore," he scowled, "no more fixation tearing you up and spoiling your fun." He glanced at David. "Damn shame, though. You got talent." David bit his lip.

Something happened inside Greg's head like when you swallow in an elevator and clear the pressure from your ears. Suddenly, he couldn't understand why he'd made all that fuss over David. My god, the fellow had messed his pants, probably pissed himself when Tommy pointed the gun at him. Disgusting. Where was Tommy, anyway? Why, right here, standing beside him. Unobtrusively, he slipped his hand into Tommy's, which closed tight around it.

"And you, son..." The Archon rocked the chair back on its springs and looked up at Tommy. "I've had one of my djinns hiding in that letter opener driving you nuts with jealousy for more than a year. At least, I did until about ten minutes ago, when he seems t'been evicted. You both might be a little schizy for a while. Get therapy. Anyhow, from here on out, you're on your own. By this time on your new track..." He closed his eyes a second. "Yup. You're just sitting down for a nice family Christmas dinner at his aunt's house." He jabbed a thumb at Greg. "Which, I guess I don't need to tell ya, gives you both a swell alibi for this whole sorry abortion today that *is* gonna come in handy since you been seen taking part in it on worldwide TV. That, plus the fact you're not gonna remember anything about it anyhow, is the most I can do."

His scowl deepened thunderously. "Least, that's how it's all gonna be if I can manage just one lousy little thing today without a lotta goddam interference. Anybody got any strong emotions swirling around here, right this minute, might contradict that? Good. You ready?"

Tommy looked like a man in the desert offered a swimming pool. No more jealousy? Greg's fixation on Alexander cancelled? A way out of the mess today? He didn't get any of it, but he nodded, afraid to look this gift horse in its proverbial bridgework.

Greg, however, had questions. "Wait a minute. I'd still like to understand—"

"Too bad. Beam 'em up, Scotty." The Archon pointed his finger at them. They disappeared in a perfect counterfeit of the Starship Enterprise's special effects department.

The Archon sighed with satisfaction. "That's better. Now, you lot." He frowned at David and the djinn. "Oh, it was all supposed to be swell. Went swell too, right up to the crucial moment. The sumbitch with the gun was supposed to kill you right then when you asked for it, without any hedge-jumping interference. Horror and wailing in the hall! I had Dr. Harold Smithson, a Harvard professor who'd previously expressed an interest in exposing Me as a phony, planted in the third row by extra special invitation. He comes up and pronounces you dead. Shot through the heart. Big mess. No doubt about it. Then I step in. I lay on the hands and mutter my mumbojumbo, the whole routine. And praise The Lord! You arise! Only it's not you, it's him." He jerked a thumb at the djinn. "The ugly suit turns to a heap of dust in the parking lot, but nobody notices, and nobody misses it much, either. Never did, right? Not even the band, who're all jealous of his closeness to you. Meanwhile, wonder and rejoicing in the hall! Hosannahs and hallelujahs! Your wound is gone. Closeup of Dr. Smithson, openmouth-flabbergasted. Minutes later, when calm has been restored, we get the organ started again and 'David Alexander' does your number to an enormous emotional outpouring unmatched since V.J. Day. He's been to

Heaven. He tells them so and reports back. He's an international sensation. I am the most powerful member of the Consortium Council, with the power literally to raise the dead." He spread his hands and raised his eyes heavenward at this apotheosis.

"Instead of that, what'd we get? Fiasco! My star alive with cum pouring out his jeans—I figgered the blood would cover that up. An attempted murder by letter opener and disappearing gun? Ridiculous! My star discredited and me shortly to follow when he deserts the reservation, recants his story, claims kidnapping and maybe goes some distance to proving it, and starts screwing donuts and keyholes in frustrated horniness? Disaster! Worse, I can't do a damn thing to stop him. He's figgered out how to use his mortal power to break my hold, something that hasn't happened since I can't remember!" He glowered at the djinn. "Debacle! Bungled bollixed botchjob! Not to mention that the *original* problem of the unstable aspect is still unsolved! Nice day! Merry Christmas!"

He growled savagely at David. "Ah don't suppose your deathwish's still kicking, is it? Maybe we could still help if we were sly and worked fast. How's about something in an open elevator shaft? Or you could throw yourself under a bus."

David shook his head. "Thanks, but the moment has passed."

"Umph. Kinda thought it might've." He turned to the djinn. His face clouded. "Well slave, guess you know what's next, don't you."

"Oh sure! Naturally! But WHY?" To David's astonishment, the djinn was madder than David had ever seen him. He came forward and planted both fists on the desk. "WHY? Why did you send *them* back? Why didn't you send *us* back as far as you needed to? If you were unhappy with what happened, why couldn't *we* have gone back and played it some other way? WHY NOT?"

"OUTA MY FACE!" the Archon roared, blowing the djinn back to the windows where he clutched at the frames for support.

"Shuddup and learn something! You djinns don't know *nothing* about Time! Which is why We don't let you play with it! Christ, what a mess that'd be! Okay, suppose we'd gone back. What do you think I could've done about the three of us already there? So then there'd've been six of us running around tripping over one another! *One* of you is already more than I can take! No thanks! Besides, did it happen that way? Not so's *I* noticed! So it *couldn't*, 'cause it *didn't!*"

The Archon's voice dropped dangerously. "And besides that, you don't really want it that way, do you." It was not a question. "You think I don't know what you been up to? *Some*body had to clue our friend here into the value of the mortal power. You want to tell me who else that might've been, even besides the expression on your ugly mug when he used it? You been doing me in the eye again, son. Ah warned you about that." He gave the djinn a flat and ugly stare.

The djinn's face was a study in silent desperation. All at once, David felt for him. He joined him by the windows and touched his arm. "I'm sorry it didn't work out better for you. If somebody had just *told* me when I made my wish that this might happen, I'd have picked something else, or modified my wish so we could all stay out of trouble." He turned back to the Archon. "I know you've got to give mortals whatever they want without talking them out of it when you take the mortal power. But maybe, after this, you could advise the poor unsuspecting schlemiel what's going to happen if he doesn't change his mind. Surely you could do that, couldn't you?"

The Archon nodded. "I'll do more than that, son, that's a promise." The Archon's grim face left no doubt that whatever he did would be effective.

David glanced at the djinn again and gulped. "And now, from the expression on my friend's face here, I guess something pretty bad is going to happen to us, right? Let's get it over with. What is it?"

"This," the Archon said.

Another cobalt-edged rectangle opened, this one beneath their feet. They plummeted into nothingness; as they fell and kept on falling, the light from Morgan Jaye's office overhead became ever smaller, dimmer and farther away. At last, David saw it snuffed out as the opening closed.

The Archon pondered the place on the carpet where it had been. He reminded himself that, after all, he was a Being of considerable experience and sophistication, and, as such, should be prepared to be philosophical. He leaned back and put out his hand to the air, which gave him a lit cigar. He puffed at it, and rich Havana aroma filled the room. He wondered how bad things were, really. His plot had failed in the end, so no fiddling with The Bargain had, in fact, taken place, and now, with those two mavericks out of the way, the possibility news of the attempt might surface while Anybody still cared was nil. Let them file complaints from *there*. Free will? Too bad! The Archon grunted in satisfaction.

Now, as to matters here on this damned ephemeral mortal coil...

He glanced at the time. Just gone five o'clock. He swivelled to Jaye's viewscreen and snapped on the news. He wasn't looking forward to this. That he'd picked a sure-fire slow news day wasn't mere bad luck; he'd done that deliberately to ensure maximum press coverage for his miracle.

> *"...THE Five O'Clock News. Our top story tonight comes to us from Necktie Gulch, Texas: a mystery involving a possible attempted murder and the disappearance of a well-known televangelist and dozens of his senior staff in events some are already calling supernatural. Rev. Wilmore Barber consecrated his new headquarters church this afternoon in Necktie Gulch. During the ceremony just a few minutes ago, an attempted murder apparently took place. I say "apparently" because all concerned left the stage and have not been seen since, leaving the congregation in the church and a worldwide television audience in the dark as to the meaning of the event. Investigators are currently trying to establish the whereabouts of Rev. Barber, Christian rock singer David Alexander, a member of his band, and two members of the congregation as yet unidentified. Witnesses speculate that one or more of these persons may be injured."*

The scene shifted to the interior of the Rose Cathedral, where the drama played itself out as the TV cameras had seen it.

"First, the apparent attempted murder. Singer Alexander is center stage. An unidentified man with a gun appears to the left on your screen. Alexander turns to face him. Another man comes out of the congregation as if to shield Alexander from the gun. There!—the shot! The stage fills with people. Rev. Barber and another man, identified as a member of Alexander's band, hustle the three others through a door at the rear.

Now the strangest aspects. Witnesses near the gunman all swear the gun disappeared straight out of his hands the moment he fired, and replaying that bit of the video enlarged and in slow motion appears to confirm this! He fires, and yes, it disappears, seemingly into thin air! He's holding it with both hands, so can he have pocketed it? It doesn't fall on the floor. He himself looks around as if wondering where it's gone.

Next, as you see, they clearly go through the door, yet, unbelievably, witnesses in the room beyond are claiming Rev. Barber and his party never entered it, that, in fact, the door never opened! An elaborate hoax? Sleight of hand? Digitally manipulated video? Or something purely supernatural? Apparently, we must await Rev. Barber's reappearance to find out. The search for him has been complicated by the fact that none of his assistants, the so-called pastors who undertook much of the actual ministry in Rev. Barber's vast flock, can be located at this hour. Witnesses claim many of them simply vanished into thin air. Mass hypnosis? If these reports are true, that would

*make more than 50 people missing, with the count
expected to rise!*

The anchorman looked down at his desk.

*This just in: a motive has surfaced for Rev.
Barber's disappearance, if not for the little stage
play, if that's what it was. Morgan Jaye, respected
local banker and recently confirmed Executive
Director of the Commission to Reduce Accounting
Problems, is making allegations of gross financial
impropriety against Rev. Barber and his church.
Jaye alleges..."*

The Archon slapped the viewscreen into blankness. He
needed to hear no more. Things were exactly as he'd feared.

That sonuvabitch Jaye. He'd used and manipulated the man,
blackmailed him with his right hand merely to dictate the means of
the blackmail's relief with his left; thus, he'd set Whitbread and
Mulligan in place. Constructing these Byzantine plots amused him
vastly. Then he'd lashed Jaye on to get the best out of him for
CRAP's reorganization. He'd earned Jaye's hatred in full confidence
there'd never be anything the man could do about it.

But now, in the new context, Jaye plainly intended to make
his disappearance look like flight and send him a strong message to
stay flown. The fat bastard had wasted no time, doubtless with
Froggy's approval. Probably, he'd tweaked the both of them once too
often. The goddam Tricontinental deal... The Consortium had
decided Wilmore P. Barber was dispensable. Without question,
whatever evidence Jaye supplied would be carefully edited to remove
all reference to corruption by other of its members.

The Archon closed his eyes. Jaye was even now roaring in on
the expressway, talking to the media by cellphone and marshalling an
army of subordinates to work through the night. The Archon
afflicted him with a three-day case of indigestion from his interrupted
Christmas dinner.

Well, that was that. He rolled his cigar ash off into Jaye's paperclip dispenser. His plans were smashed up good. He could see no point to going back to his role as "Rev. Billy Barber." His decades of patient effort would result only in yet another perpetual rerun on *Unsolved Mysteries*. The Others would be annoyed at him about that—when They finished laughing.

Even so, it wasn't a total waste. Think of all the misery there'd be among the pathetic true believers when he, their rudder, sails, oars and steersman all in one was exposed as a cynical manipulator, and think of the additional misery when they discovered the precious shares in his pyramid schemes and building projects on which their wealth was based were worthless. The pyramid schemes were far over-extended, and the building projects were all mortgaged up to their cornices. With the money from the new converts his miracle would have brought in, he'd have been able to keep it all working until he was so powerful it wouldn't have mattered any longer—but now...

He grinned. Well, folks, easy come, easy go. He guessed there'd be enough mortal misery out of this to keep the metaphysical world rolling for quite a while.

That life was full of surprises, even after all this time, kept him going—and truth be told, these grand schemes for world domination he and his Brother Archons were always hatching never did seem to come out right. He'd done his own share of laughing in his time—and still, somehow, when all was said and done, They always managed to wind up in the plus column.

He stood up. He guessed it was time to go. A nice vacation, that's what he needed. Maybe a trip to visit Brother Ayatollah. Brother A. had grand schemes afoot, and the Archon was interested. Or Brother Samedi down in Haiti. Business there wasn't so good anymore, he heard. It might be fun to light a fire under Him and see if He'd get mad.

Time to go somewhere, anyhow. Jaye would be here in a minute. He snapped off the halogen desklight and stood. He picked up his reverend's velvet-trimmed robe and regarded it at arm's length. Whom did he feel like tonight? A little social reassurance might not be a bad thing. He changed the robe into a tweedy country jacket with leather patches on the elbows. He put it on, and his figure changed. His shoulders broadened. He got taller. His cigar became a straight-grain briar pipe. Cavendish tinged the Havana-scented air.

The citylight caught a gold glint on the desk: the fox-headed letter opener. He picked it up. Poor Uriel had spent a year and a half in one brass implement or another, plus assorted birds, and was now whoknewwhere. What the hell, he probably deserved a vacation too—and something cushy and interesting to do next time. If only he weren't such a complete tool. It was the really independent ones like that insufferable hobgoblin the Archon had just pitched down the hole who could be truly useful, if you could control them. In a magnanimous gesture, he opened a wormway to hell and sent a bolt of power down it after David and the djinn. Poor kids might as well be comfortable. Who knew? There might be another use for them, someday. He doubted it, but he hadn't gotten where he was today by wasting resources.

He puzzled the enigma of the letter opener. Probably, all that time Uriel had spent there had energized it and made it a fit receptacle for Love to enter and take form. Love! Of all the damn things. He hadn't seen Love in ages. His eyes narrowed.

He concentrated hard.

He whistled, a whistle that went up in pitch beyond what the human ear could perceive. The letter opener wavered, grew, and took on the luminous form of a beautiful cream-colored collie dog, which gazed up at him adoringly. It held a smoking gun in its mouth.

The Archon held out his hand. "Here, girl. Give it here, girl."

Love put Her head down and Her butt in the air, and held onto the gun very firmly, never taking Her eyes off him.

"Want to play, huh? That explains something, maybe." A stick appeared in his hand, which he flung. It morphed through the window and sailed out over the city. Love looked at him, looked at the stick, looked at him again, then dropped the gun and bounded away after the stick.

He pocketed the gun and strolled after Her, out into the night. They wavered and lost themselves amidst the twinkling city lights.

Chapter Eleven
<u>BANKRUPTCY</u>

lackness.

Ka-shtink.

David squinted in the sudden light, which was much brighter than the dim, city-lit radiance of Morgan Jaye's office. Miracles were a dime a dozen today, it seemed. The djinn let go the chainpull on a gleaming brass chandelier with cut crystal globes. The chandelier hung from the ceiling of... a black box. Fighting the squint, David looked around. The box was three or four times as wide as high, and seemed to go back a long way. From the end where they stood the other was lost beyond the reach of the light.

As David's eyes adjusted, he opened them and saw the box wasn't really black. He touched a wall, then rapped it lightly with his knuckles. It seemed to be metal, enameled in gray. The floor and ceiling were the same, soldered at the joins. A thing like a piano hinge ran across the ceiling from wall to wall just where the light from the chandelier merged into darkness. "So where are we now?"

The djinn twisted his face and opened his mouth for one of his usual snarling replies, but evidently thought better of it. He closed his mouth and looked down at the floor. He stubbed it lightly with his toe and shrugged. "Welcome to my bottle."

"Your bottle?"

"Yeah. Don't you remember? You started all this when you let the genie out of the bottle. Well, I was the genie and this was the bottle. Not this very one, of course, but then, they're all pretty much alike." His voice took on a bitter edge. "I should know. I've spent the best part of the last 10,000 years in one damned bottle or another." He looked at David, and shrugged again. "At least, this time I've got company."

It began to sink in. "You mean...?"

"Isn't it obvious?" The djinn's manner was gentle, almost pleading. "You and I create instabilities in the metaphysical world wherever we go. Ultimately, these could threaten the mortal world as well. Serious business! The result of your wishes. And because of those very instabilities (among other things), the attempt to rectify the situation failed."

"The attempt to kill me, you mean."

The djinn looked at the floor. "You did well," he said softly. "When you found the mortal power and touched it, I couldn't believe it. It made it a whole new thing for me. Try to see it my way. You have something very precious to me, the thing that makes my existence worthwhile, the thing that makes me unique and the key to what little independence I get. For a wonderful, lovely moment there, I thought I was about to come out of this unscathed, unchanged, whole and with a story to tell The Others that would make me free for the first time in a long time. What would you have done?"

"Naturally, murder would be my first thought."

The djinn scowled. "You're a pretty smart guy, as amazed as you'll be to hear me say that. You constructed your wishes well. Having you want to die was the only out you gave us. When that failed, our Archon had no more choices. He couldn't try it again. You'd be onto Him next time. He probably isn't anxious to, anyway. Diddling the powers that be is dangerous, even for one of Them. So, He's walled us up, and..." The djinn closed his eyes and concentrated very hard for a second. "...and yes, surrounded us with impenetrable barriers of His own power. He's made quite an investment. I can't see *anything* out there. That's a new one." He sighed. "Both worlds are safe from us, but we're in here, stuck in these aspects until..." He shrugged yet again. "He really means it this time."

The djinn's air of resignation was catching. David sank down against a wall and looked up at him. The metal was cold against his back. "Well, for how long do you think?"

The djinn spread his hands. "Until He figures out another way to solve the problem—but of course, we're not exactly high on His list of favorites, and now we're stowed away, The Balance is safe and The Bargain needn't be threatened at all. He won't be in any hurry to let us out of here. Out of sight, out of mind. Unless, of course, He needs us for something. I wouldn't hold my breath about that, though. Except in a couple/three very dangerous respects, we're not unique. If He wants to, He can duplicate our other skills and attributes, though not very conveniently perhaps." He cocked his head and thought about that, then shook it. "We know too much. It'd have to be a very particular and desperately needed something before He'd risk letting us loose again. It's gonna be a while, maybe a long while. Count on it." He looked at the floor again.

David took a long look into the invisible recesses of their cold dark prison. Anger rose. "Or until I decide again to die, right?" he asked bitterly. "I suppose that's now your top priority."

"No!" The djinn was surprisingly vehement. "Oh, I could play that game with you, and win it too, probably—but there's no point. There're only the two of us here. *I* couldn't kill you if you did decide to die, or provide you with the means to do it yourself. I'd get your mortal power that way, a fact which *couldn't* be covered up once I was free again. Hell, even if you did die and I got my aspect back, that doesn't mean He'd let me go. He'd pretty much had it with me *before* all this happened. Like you, I was never much good at being a willing slave." His voice changed. "So then, I'd be here alone." He looked at David, his face unreadable.

David sighed. Anger left him. The djinn was right. What was the point? Everything was futile if his fate were an eternity alone in here with this creature who'd always hated and despised him. At least, maybe now he understood why, a little bit. His wishes had spelled trouble for the djinn from the very beginning.

But now, it needed him. It was *lonely*. —And considering the trouble he himself was going to have showing his face in public again, maybe lying low for a century or two wasn't such a bad idea. He decided to make the best of it, and changed the subject. "So where exactly *is* here?"

"At least it's not a cornerstone."

"What?"

"Nevermind." The djinn ran an experienced eye around their prison. "Well, He did say He was going to make a deposit." He scowled. "Obviously, we're it. My guess is, we're in one of AmalCon's safety deposit boxes. Not one of the more expensive ones, either." He gave a bitter little laugh. "We're about an inch high." His laughter died. "I've seen worse, believe me. I spent *centuries* in a reliquary in Naples turning filth into liquid blood for the stupefaction of the masses at a time when They, in Their infinite wisdom, decided the priests ought to believe in their own miracles. *That* was hell. Dirty, and twice a year sticky and wet too. Now, of course, it's considered useful if they *don't* believe, so they get to work the 'miracle' themselves. I don't know what kind of blood they use, but knowing them, I'll bet it's pig." He shook his head in disgust. "Here, at least, we can be comfortable. He's given us more than enough power for that. He's strict, but He isn't mean, at least not always. Let's see what we've got to work with."

The djinn strode off down the long box. Three times more before he reached the end, he put up his hand. A chainpull appeared in it each time and a brass and crystal chandelier leapt into light.

David sprang to his feet as a luxuriantly soft and thick, glowingly iridescent oriental rug with an intricate, tiny pattern grew up out of the floor under him. "Silk?" he asked.

"Uh huh. Only the best for my buddy."

Fantastic tapestries of the same workmanship appeared on the walls: knights and dragons warred in tiny perfect detail; boys danced naked and intertwined in, well, very interesting ways; valleys, castles and hills appeared, towns, cities, mountains, oceans full of ships and creatures in the deep—an entire world. So intricate was the detail that David felt he could probably spend an ordinary lifetime looking at it and never see it all.

The ceiling turned midnight blue and spangled itself with silver stars. Masterfully carved, inlaid and cushioned benches and stools sprang up against the tapestries. Low tables dotted the carpet. A fountain trilled between the central chandeliers. Large soft pillows scattered themselves everywhere. An elaborate brass and crystal hookah with two hoses invited indulgence in recondite pleasures.

"What do you think?" asked the djinn.

"Uh, fabulous." David paced around it. He spotted a pack of Export Specials on a table and grabbed it. The cigarette lit itself perfectly as he withdrew it from the box and tasted better than any cigarette he'd ever had. He dragged it down greedily and began rushing with that elevation only the first cigarette in a long time can give. He picked up an ashtray carved from a single enormous sapphire and joined the djinn at the far end. "Not bad at all. Arabian Nights *manqué*—bit claustrophobic, though, don't you think?"

"Sorry. My taste is not necessarily yours." The djinn gestured the *1001 Nights* trappings into nonexistence. What appeared to be David's own furniture from Herbie Manning's apartment took their place. The walls and ceiling disappeared. A spectacular vista of forests and mountains opened up in all directions. Warm sunlight shone down on them. A deliciously cool breeze blew, fragrant with hints of many flowers and alive with birdsong and the droning of unseen insects pursuing businesses of their own. "Anything you want. Different every day if you like. We can play fabulous games, and travel. Think of it like a magic carpet: we can go anywhere, or see anything in history I've ever seen, and believe me, I've had centuries with nothing much to do but look—we just can't get off." He became solemn, desperately sincere. "Seriously, I'll do anything to keep my buddy interested and amused as long as I can. *Anything.*"

They stood at the foot of Herbie's kingsized waterbed. The djinn arched an eyebrow and leered at it, and at David where he'd messed his crotch back in the cathedral. "*Anything.* Those pants look pretty sticky and uncomfortable to me. How's about we take 'em off?" The djinn was now grinning Herbie Manning's foolish grin, which admittedly didn't look quite so foolish when the djinn did it.

"Always kinda wanted to get up against that body and find out what it was like from the other side of the skin," he said.

David stared. Absolutely the worst thing about this crude suggestion, typical of Herbie, he realized with a certain amount of shame, was that the very thought had stirred his ever-tumescent crotch into life. Evidently, he had not quite discharged his backload in the Rose Cathedral. But have sex with his old body? Herbie Manning's body? Bad hair, pipestem arms and legs, oversized flat feet and all? The gawky, misproportioned, goofy, freakish, awkward, misbegotten *thing* in which he'd been imprisoned since puberty?—the body he'd hated and despised so much that, given the chance to shuck it, he'd been willing without hesitation to give up his entire life?

His mouth fell open. The irony awed him speechless. He would make love to that body for eternity, or go without. His cock felt as hard and heavy as stone. His balls tightened and began to ache. They would demand release very soon. He couldn't! He wouldn't!

The djinn shrugged his shoulders—Herbie Manning's lean, misproportioned shoulders. "Suit yourself. But it looks like you'll hafta learn to love it after all." He left David standing by the bed, still frozen with horror, and sat down at Herbie's marble dining room table. A deck of cards appeared and arced through the air as he shuffled them hand to hand.

He turned to David, black eyes oval innocence. "Gin, then?"

Finis, tandem
19 June 2000
Seattle

www.ingramcontent.com/pod-product-compliance
Lightning Source LLC
Chambersburg PA
CBHW061326050726

47504CB00013B/347